1

## Acknowledgments

This book is only what it is because of the many people who have helped me along the way. My special thanks to Adam Bradford and Kelly Sheridan for the amazing ideas I would never have come up with on my own. Thank you for taking the time to hone and craft a fun and fascinating world! Thank you to my fellow writers and friends Cris Sheridan and Travis Rivas for their critiquing and brainstorming skills. Thank you to my amazing family for their support, and especially my mother for all her time and dedication in editing this work and my aunt and uncle for their gracious hospitality. Thank you Shelly Cowper-Smith for your support and encouragement.

Thank you to all the readers out there who have made the Fantasy genre a respected and well-loved form of fiction!

# The Banished Lands

Benjamin Mester

# Part 1

Thob
Forest

Enlath

Aridatha

Estees
Mountains

Commonwealth Pasturelands

Emri

Shag River

Echlin

Shelengol Glades

Bay of Boreol

Suriya

*Dismissing hours as they pass*
*Soft upon the windswept grass.*
*The hopes of men have come to naught.*
*Nothing fair for eyes or thought.*

*For Sheyla lies on golden plain,*
*Of Cavanah, the fairest slain;*
*Who met her last and final day*
*When all was brought to disarray.*

*Of gladful things now nevermore –*
*Now bitter wind, now salty shore.*
*The peaceful world bound to unrest*
*And darkness looming in the west.*

*The world and all its light shall fade.*
*I'll stay with her beneath the shade*
*And wait until the world's remade...*

# Suriya

The town of Suriya revived in usual fashion, with thin bands of smoke appearing one by one over the scattered chimney tops, rising to a dawn still flecked with starlight. Few were stirring this early hour, in this small town in the corner of the kingdom, at the edge of the known world. An autumn wind picked up, pulling at the gray smoke and signaling the discovery of each hidden crevice in the stone cottages with a shriek of cold.

Durian awoke to a whistle of wind, nudging him from the middle of a dream. It was one he'd had before, of a woman lying slain in a field. In the dream, he thought she was only sleeping, though hesitated to draw near. A rider approached, dismounted and took her into his arms, pressing her head against his chest in despair. Then carrying her to his horse, they rode for the horizon.

The familiarity of the dream imparted a sense of loss that he couldn't quite define. Perhaps because it reminded him of a poem he had always loved, written by a king of the First Age to his wife, Sheyla.

Sleep had almost found him when he snapped back awake. A promise to his best friend, Baron, narrowed his focus. Groaning, Durian pushed himself from bed. Baron was competing in the Sea Games this morning.

This was the worst time of year as far as Durian was concerned, with no reprieve from the roving wind that swept up from the south. With winter at least came snow, piled against the walls of a cottage like a warm blanket. But the first heavy snows hadn't yet fallen and the wind moved as it willed.

Durian ambled to his fireplace and blew slow breaths, hoping to animate a hidden life. But clouds of ash greeted him, sputtering off and away. Reaching for the waning pile beside him, he seized some kindling. But he hesitated to squander its fuel, knowing he'd soon be out of doors. Thob Forest, a two day's walk westbound, was Suriya's only source for timber. Abundant as trees were, strange things had been happening there that were keeping the woodsmen at bay.

It strained Durian more than most, for he was a carpenter. A man of twenty, Durian was born and raised in Suriya. He was unexceptional, being of average height and build, with the same hazelnut hair that was standard among his peers. His mother and father were already well along in years when he was born, and both had passed some time ago.

Durian stepped into the open air and set off down the cobblestone road, keeping near the walls of his neighbors' homes to escape the wintry wind. And though not by nature an eavesdropper, proximity to the cottages granted him muffled snippets of conversations as he passed.

Soon he intercepted the broader road and was back in the reach of the baleful cold. The sun would soon warm the plains and put an end, at least for the day, to the southern winds. Until then, a chill threatened Durian's bones and kept Baron in his thoughts. Despite the almost intolerable conditions, the Sea Games festival was hard to resist for Suriyans; one last celebration before the long winter took hold of the land.

The Sea Games were once a widely attended event. But some years back, an exceptionally early frost stomped out more than the last of the summer wildflowers. Durian recalled the baffled visitors that year. One traveler from Echlin, the next closest township, declared it most unnatural, glancing at Durian warily as though something more sinister than the weather were at work in Suriya.

Durian arrived at the edge of town, where cobbled stone reduced to a rutted cart path. But the highland route through the open plains was what he always preferred. A hill midway between the town and the coast offered the best view of Boreol Bay.

A few minute's exertion bought him the distance, and filled his sight with a far reaching blue, dotted lightly with fishing vessels and black shoals. Behind him lie the two towns of Suriya, split by the River Shay. And below, an intermittent line of villagers ambled by.

One of them he recognized. It was the shyer twin brother to Baron, Blair. Both were tall and slender, and Blair had an unmistakable saunter, nearly masked by his tuck-head cowering from the wind. Durian sprang from the hill toward him, bounding the small distance and letting out a holler just as he ran in front of Blair, nearly knocking Blair down, and himself.

"What's the matter with you?" Blair demanded and pulled his collar tight against his neck, resuming his groveling posture.

"Many things," Durian said and threw his arm around Blair's shoulder. "You're up early. Where's Baron?"

Blair extended his hand ahead of them toward the bay.

"Wherever the crowds are gathered, there the Barons will be."

Durian laughed out loud. Though the twins were identical in every physical way, they were dissimilar in others, and each took the opportunity to show it. In this case, Blair's estimation of his brother wasn't far off the mark. Baron was drawn to the limelight like, well like vultures to the smell of decay.

Though at times gloomy and cynical, Blair could never be labeled a parrot of other men's thinking. Though similar, Baron carried himself more confidently than Blair, which made it easy to tell them apart.

"It's nice of you to support your brother like this," Durian goaded.

Blair seemed repelled by the thought.

"The fact is, he left me little choice," Blair said. "He's been dodging work for weeks, training for this useless race. I've been stuck with crotchety farmers like Tobin. I'm not spending another day taking grief from agitated hay makers for Baron's sake!"

The twins were blacksmiths in the West End of Suriya. With the close of harvest each year, battered tools were laid to rest. Baron and Blair spent the whole of winter hammering, straightening, sharpening, and oiling.

Durian and Blair emerged on the white, sandy shores of Boreol Bay. A crowd fifty strong stood a hundred paces ahead, cheering at a race already underway. Gusting wind hit more powerfully here.

"Are you warm enough?" Blair asked.

"Is anyone warm enough this time of year?"

"I've a spare coat, you know."

Durian opened his mouth for a retort, but only nodded his head slowly and turned his attention back to the bay. He'd outgrown his woolen greatcoat and hadn't had the money to get it lengthened. Once the wind died down, he'd be fine.

"What race is Baron in anyway? He never told me."

"Skull Island," Blair said. Durian chuckled and shook his head. Blair smirked. Of course Baron had chosen that race. A small outcropping of black rocks in the vague shape of a skull, Skull Island stretched twenty feet or so in length, not far into the shallows of Boreol Bay. The contest consisted of swimming to the jagged stone island, climbing atop the tallest rock, where a trophy lie, retrieving it, and returning to shore, prize in hand.

The trophy was an ornately decorated ram's horn, the winner's to keep for the whole of that year until the next Sea Games. Primarily an ale horn, studded with stones and a filigreed silver rim, Skull Horn was brandished often in the taverns of Suriya.

Skull Island was the main event of the morning. Evening brought the Race of Boreol Bay, a boating race

13

through the shallows, where dark shoals of rock created an obstacle course of sorts. Though the morning races attracted merely a fraction of the town, the Race of Boreol Bay would draw the balance.

Durian and Blair arrived alongside the mass of spectators just as the previous swimmers left the chilly waters. The winner was announced and the transfer of coins ensued. The Sea Games were the only time Suriyans really gambled, at least in the public arena. Now that interest from other townships had waned, the Sea Games festival had largely degenerated into a competition between the East and West Ends.

Durian saw Baron and four other swimmers emerge from the crowd at the far end.

"Get it, Red!" a man shouted just next to Durian.

Red was a young man walking in stride with Baron. As the winner of the previous year, he had already been to Skull Island this morning to return the ram's horn.

Baron paid no mind, his eyes peering like a hawk toward the prize. After nearly begging Durian to come out and support him, Baron now seemed little concerned with who was in the crowd. That was Baron for you. Durian chuckled to himself.

The race was about to begin but a distant voice called out.

*I'm gunna net me a mermaid for me son to play with...* followed by surly laughter.

Blair and Durian laughed. The voice belonged to old Gaffney, one of the eldest fishermen in Suriya who couldn't miss an opportunity to heckle the swimmers.

The prolonged laughter of Gaffney brought a general clamor among the spectators, so much so that even Baron broke concentration and smiled, shaking his head and turning to see who had gathered on shore. Noticing Durian and Blair, he waved, but the sudden ring of a bell sent the five swimmers into blue.

At first, nothing but the churning of limbs and whitewash. But one by one the swimmers fell into line, Skull Island not more than twice a stone's throw from shore. The first swimmer arrived at the island. Baron was next, along with another. They pulled forward inch by inch, frozen hands groping ineffectually on cold rock.

Baron was more fortunate in his landing than others and made faster headway climbing the steep island. Just onshore, he was suddenly dragged backward by his leg. It was Red.

"Hey!" Blair said and jumped to his feet.

Durian smiled, then stood up alongside Blair. Though there weren't specific rules as such governing the Sea Games, certain activities were considered unsavory.

"That's right, Red!" shouted someone nearby. "Drag that horse-shoer off your island!"

Baron kicked and pulled and at last prevailed in freeing himself. All five were now on the island, each swimmer occupying part of the small outcropping of rock. Baron was just behind Red in proximity to the prize. And before Red could reach it, Baron leaped. Though too numb to grasp it, his fingers were effective in springing Skull Horn from its resting place, sending it bouncing down the dark stone until landing with a gentle splash.

The swimmers converged. Baron sprang from the jagged rock, narrowly missing the edge of Skull Island and disappeared along with the ram's horn.

Jaw clenched, Blair took a step forward. The water was a flurry of limbs and foam. Seconds passed. Baron didn't emerge. Heads bobbed up for air and dove back down below. The churning sea calmed. The struggle was now beneath the waters. More seconds passed.

And then, as though the sea itself gasped for breath, the waters broke and the swimmers appeared, Baron chief among them. In the commotion, Baron broke free of the pack, swimming furiously toward shore, Red in pursuit.

A hand grasped Baron's foot and he disappeared beneath the waters. The swimmers closed in. Seconds passed and Blair took another step forward. It was ridiculous really, to hold such an event. Though none had ever perished as a result of the Sea Games, it tempted fate.

A figure broke through the waters but the churning whitewash concealed him. Only a dozen paces from shore, the swimmers were a flurried mass of limbs. But one of them stood to his feet in the waist deep water. It was Baron. Taking slow and labored strides against the dragging sea, he sought to finish the race by foot. Red swam up and hooked Baron round the waist, threatening to pull him under, but Baron shook loose, Red too exhausted to continue.

Ram's horn in hand, Baron arrived on shore, hunching on his knees to catch his breath. Applause ensued and Baron managed to raise Skull Horn above his head. At length, Baron returned to the water. Baron helped Red to his feet and hooked him round the shoulder, to the approval of the cheering crowd. Baron was always a good sport, so much so that Durian was dubious of his motives – perhaps just a ploy to garner further favor from the already adoring spectators.

Baron and Red broke company, and Baron ascended to meet his two friends. He was handed a towel, which he jealously employed.

"Congratulations," Durian said. "You must be freezing!"

"No worse for wear though," replied Baron.

"Congratulations," offered Blair, but Baron paid no mind, busy admiring the prize in his shivering hands.

"You ought to get some warm food in you," said Durian.

Baron nodded, wedging his trophy under his arm to more fervently rub his hands together.

"Blair has a pot of venison stew simmering at home," Baron said. "It's quite good."

Blair looked skeptical that his brother would praise him, as was Durian. They watched and waited as Baron shook and battled vigorously against the cold.

"My kid brother is quite the homemaker, you know," Baron continued.

"Don't call me that."

Durian let out a laugh.

"Our mother saw early on that he favored the home life," Baron said.

Durian laughed again. The fact that Baron was born a mere half minute before Blair, yet still referred to him as 'my kid brother,' or 'little brother' was a source of constant amusement for Durian. As they lingered someone came toward them. He didn't make the usual formalities.

"Where is my plow?"

Baron seemed surprised at the question. Though Durian had never met the man, he could only guess that this was Tobin, whom Blair had lamented earlier. Tobin's plow arrived like clockwork each year, beaten and battered from use. Tobin was unrelenting in his accusations of the twins' shoddy craftsmanship, disdainful of acknowledging that he owned the rockiest plot of land in all of Suriya, and equally disdainful of every copper coin required for the subsequent restoration of his tools. Tobin had been the first patron their father had awarded Baron and Blair for completing their apprenticeship. They had been so excited at the time. Their father still smiled every time the name of Tobin was mentioned.

"It's in the shop," Baron responded.

Tobin's face went red.

"Why is my plow rusting in your shop while you're off frolicking in the sea?"

Baron opened his mouth for a retort but stumbled over the accusations. It wasn't a blacksmith's job to scrape rust from old tools – just repair the damage. But Baron didn't seem up for verbal sparring.

"Blair will have it for you straightaway," Baron replied.

Then he turned to Blair with a chiding look for taking the morning off while poor Tobin's plow rusted away in the shop. Blair clenched his jaw while Durian choked on his breath and stifled a cough, turning away to camouflage laughter. Tobin didn't find the exchange funny.

"Your father never had his head in the clouds. He was efficient. Why he moved to silver-smithing I'll never understand."

Baron shrugged his shoulders. Tobin scowled and departed.

"Well, I'm off for home," said Baron, light-hearted as ever, unwrapping his woolen towel and tossing it to Blair before Blair could refuse to take it. As he was leaving, he turned back.

"Will you be at market this afternoon?" he asked Durian.

"Yes."

Then he turned to Blair.

"Farewell little brother."

Baron departed. Durian glanced to Blair with a grin. Blair couldn't help but smile a little and folded the towel in his arms, taking it to the pile heaped on shore. Then Blair removed for the homestead also. Durian took a moment to scan the crowd, still just a bit curious to see if any visitors had come from the outlying townships.

As he had satisfied himself that Suriya was customarily alone, there, on the southernmost edge of the crowd, stood an old man that Durian had never seen

19

before. Durian moved toward him. The man stood a small distance away from the crowd and seemed to be gazing somewhere beyond, or else was lost in thought. Durian watched him for many moments. As the breeze hit the old man, he closed his eyes as though trying to sense something.

Durian didn't know what to make of it. The man was here at the Sea Games but was paying the festival little mind. Durian wanted to investigate further but had spent too much time here already. He had business to attend to.

So Durian set off through the open plains, up the shallow hillside. When he had crested the largest hill, he turned round to the bay and was surprised. A lone figure had disembarked from the group of spectators and was walking southward down the shore into the indefinable distance. Durian could barely discern his features, but a feeling struck him that it must be the old man he had been watching. What was he doing? To come all the way to Suriya for the Sea Games and then ignore them. Durian didn't know what to make of it.

# Ill Tidings

The sun was warm against his back as Durian lingered on the large hill. The form at the edge of his vision blended with the distant sands, slowly shrinking from sight. There was nothing in the direction the old man headed – only small caves explored on occasion by children.

Durian hated it but he couldn't stay here. Market Town awaited. A city within a city, Market Town was a burgeoning tent metropolis erected in the warmer summer and fall months. Though bustling now, another week would empty it, used thereafter for nothing more than the piling of excess snow. The Sea Games officially marked the end of autumn, but Market Town persevered until the weight of snow threatened the tents with perforation.

Durian hurried to retrieve his wares. Pulling his cart with no small effort down the cobblestone road from his home, he arrived on the scene breathless with still a hundred paces to go. The lanes of Market Town were narrow and grooved, and one of his wooden wheels quickly fixed itself in a rut. Struggling without success, Durian stopped a moment to catch his breath.

"That's a full load you've got there," said a nearby spectator.

It was Harper, one of the marketplace vultures. Not craftsmen themselves, these middlemen dealt exclusively in the selling of struggling merchant's wares who were forced to part with unsold goods at the end of each season.

"Some of us are more industrious than others," Durian replied.

One final effort freed his cart and Durian leaned forward on his handles for some moments.

"Perhaps I could lighten it for you," said Harper, with a slowly widening grin.

Durian looked at him blankly, then shoved off. Luckily, things hadn't gotten so bad that he'd yet consider an offer from Harper.

Arriving at his booth, he populated it with cookware, cabinetry, and wooden axe handles. The handles were once a mainstay for him, the woodsmen crippling their own in the course of their labors and requiring replacements. But the strange happenings in Thob Forest had brought a swift decline.

A log lay on its side in Durian's booth, untouched since the axe, bark still intact. He had in mind a large mantle for a fireplace, and would soon occupy dull hours with its construction. One of Durian's greatest thrills was peeling the bark from a freshly hewn timber.

Hidden beneath the bark of a log was a mystery – sometimes rot and worm, or spongy core, unfit for anything but the fire; other times a beautiful grain. The logs recorded a history. A year of drought or blight made a thin, discolored ring, while years of rain and plenty produced thick and creamy bands.

In the old world, more than a dozen centuries ago, it was said men existed who could manipulate trees with their hands, as if by magic. They could

22

rearrange a tree's grain, molding it like clay to render it strong as forged iron. They were called the Woodlanders. Others existed who had likewise abilities to manipulate stone. These were known as the Builders.

There was little known about the old world. All Durian knew of it he'd learned from a book given to him as a small boy by a traveling merchant. *Tales of the Prosperous Age* described a time when the world was clothed in abundance – not a harsh and inclement realm scattered sparsely with habitable regions. Unknown forces regulated the seasons and adorned the land in plenty.

There was almost nothing known of that age, at least in the history books of Suriya. Whether it existed at all or was just a myth – man's imagined paradise to cope with the harsh realities of the difficult present world – no one could say, for the Prosperous Age mysteriously ended over a dozen centuries ago after a Great War fractured the Houses of Men. Or so the story goes.

*Tales* contained accounts of a fabled type of wood called Candlewood that had always intrigued Durian. Candlewood was the pinnacle of the Woodlander's creations – feather light, tough as the strongest shield, and contained a magical property that caused it to glow from deep within. Durian often dreamed what it would be like to peel away the bark from a log of wood and see a glowing gleam like gold beneath.

*Tales* also contained his favorite poem, written by a king of the Prosperous Age, to his wife, Sheyla.

Seeing the log reminded him of the dream he had had this morning. He'd only had the dream once before. But he clearly remembered it. For it happened only days before the strange things in Thob Forest began.

Footsteps from behind drew Durian's attention. It was his father's old friend Joram – one of the woodsmen Durian bought timbers from. Durian's father, Doran, had formed relationships with the laborers who felled trees for firewood. For a fee, they had let Doran scour their log piles for anything worthy of a craftsman's knife amid the common timbers.

The woodsmen had honored the arrangement made with Doran after Durian took up his father's business. Joram had aided him greatly, showing him the kinds of logs his father had always hunted for.

*See the end from the beginning,* was what Joram always said. *Decide what the log will become before you ever buy it. That's how your father made a good living.*

"Hello Joram," Durian greeted.

"Hullo Durian." He paused. "I um. Well I..."

But then something caught his eye and he smiled warmly.

"Is that the maple you found last week?" referring to the mantle Durian was carving. Durian nodded. But Joram's solemn demeanor returned.

"Durian I um. I came here to tell you. We can't sell you any more timbers, at least not for awhile. I'm very sorry."

Durian was taken aback.

"It's the forest, Durian. No one knows what's happening. The smoke and the perfume... And there

24

hasn't been a day without the fog in three months. Something's in there. You've heard the rumors. We're all living on scraps waiting for it to pass. Ever since the lumber camp burned down, we've had to work twice as hard just to get by."

The woodsman's lumber camp at the edge of Thob Forest caught fire under dubious circumstances.

"It's alright, Joram. I'm very thankful for everything you've done. Don't worry about me. I'll be okay."

Durian gave him his best smile and Joram nodded slowly with a sigh.

"You're a good man, Durian. Your father would be proud."

Joram took a step forward and placed a hand on Durian's shoulder. He lingered only a moment and then departed.

Durian returned to his work, scarcely lifting his eyes from his log the whole of the day. He drew his knife mechanically against the large piece of wood, pondering this sudden turn of events. He couldn't afford the premium timbers sold to the craftsmen at auction. And he had already sold everything of value in his cottage, waiting, like the others, for something to change.

He might only have one choice – find Harper or one of the other vultures, and work out some kind of a deal. And he should get to it straightaway. The longer he waited, the worse his position would become. But he couldn't appear desperate.

"Are you alright?" said someone close by.

Durian looked up to find Baron standing there. Durian stared at him blankly until remembering the question.

"Oh. Yes. Just busy."

Baron didn't press him and perused the various articles laid out on the table.

"This is a nice piece," he said, maneuvering a large wooden spoon in his hand and gazing at it from different angles.

Durian snatched the spoon from him and returned it. Baron smirked. He was clearly bored and restless. The blacksmithing trade was always bustling in Suriya. Metal was scarce throughout the realm, and those who first settled Suriya had long ago fashioned their swords to plowshares to work at honest trade. Tools required constant repair. And though Baron pawned off much of the work on his brother, the two made a good living. It wasn't Baron's fault he had stumbled into a thriving business.

"The Sea Games aren't what they used to be," Baron commented, gazing at the slowing pace of the marketplace.

Durian nodded, glad for the distraction Baron provided.

"You know things have laxed when an ordinary blacksmith can win the Race for Skull Island."

Baron turned his head back to Durian and gave a wide grin.

"That's not exactly what I meant."

Baron scanned the crowd again. He picked a nearby piece of tall grass and began slowly shredding it.

"I've not seen even one outsider this year," Baron continued. "No herdsman from Echlin, pasturing cattle in the plains. No merchants from the Laborer's Guild up north. And I doubt folk up in Eulsiphion even know the Sea Games exist!"

Baron hurled what was left of the shaft of grass, punctuating his frustration. Durian chuckled. Baron's victory at Skull Island was meant to be admired by the whole kingdom. Instead of earning himself a name in the capital city of Eulsiphion, far to the north, he had gained only the applause of his neighbors. Baron continued his tirade.

"My old man once earned a full month's wages just from pounding out horseshoes for the mules and steeds of travelers at the Sea Games one year," Baron declared and glanced back emphatically. "Horseshoes!"

"I saw an outsider," Durian cut in.

Baron spun around.

"Really?"

"An old man," Durian continued. "He had the look of a wanderer. Thick coat and beard, lightly tanned skin. He witnessed your heroic conquest of Skull Island."

Durian expected a slew of questions, but Baron grew suddenly thoughtful.

"Blair took in a piece yesterday for repair. 'A decorated walking stick' he called it. I wonder if it belongs to your old wanderer?"

"Why would someone bring a walking stick to a blacksmith shop?"

"That's what I wondered," Baron continued. "Blair described it as being beautifully inlaid with silver at the handle, and having an iron cap on the bottom tip to protect it from wear. The iron tip had worn through. Blair was fascinated by it because it was so beautiful. And he said the wood looked different from anything he had seen in your shop."

The notion piqued Durian's curiosity.

"What did it look like?" he asked.

Baron shrugged his shoulders. "Wood."

"Fantastic," Durian responded. "Why do I bother knowing you?"

Baron let out a laugh.

"Come and see it for yourself if you want."

"You have it here?"

"*I* don't have it here," said Baron. "Blair's working on it. Going to bring it over as soon as it's finished."

"I can't just leave my booth."

Baron spun round with his arms held wide to the nearly soulless marketplace.

"Why not?"

The day truly was growing late, and most were heading to shore for the Race of Boreol Bay, culminating the Sea Games. But the thought of abandoning his work brought a wave of emotion. Durian didn't know what to do. He only knew what he could do – keep working.

"I have to finish this mantelpiece."

"Mantelpiece! You can do that anytime."

Durian's jaw clenched. Baron's distraction had worn out its welcome.

"There's only one more good week at market. I want to get this done and sold before the winter."

"You'll miss the whole race!"

"I don't care about some ridiculous race."

Baron seemed surprised, but more by the tone than the statement.

"I'll meet up with you and Blair at Walloway's after," Durian offered.

"Yeah," Baron responded. "Definitely."

Baron departed. Durian had half a mind to call him back and apologize, but he didn't. It didn't really matter that Durian sold the mantelpiece before winter. Without a flowing supply of new wood from Joram and the woodsmen, it would be for naught anyway.

Durian didn't know what to do. He couldn't just abandon the business his father had left him. But he couldn't save it either. The only thing he knew to do was keep working.

# The Race of Boreol Bay

Durian was left alone. Market Town had emptied. He picked up his knife and brought it toward the wood, but hesitated. This was the last day of the Sea Games and his problems would assuredly still be there in the morning.

Packing up, he returned home with his goods. Then he departed. He was among the last to reach Boreol Bay, but the race had yet to begin. There were over a dozen boats poised to challenge the shoals.

The villagers were everywhere. Durian pushed his way through the crowd in search of the twins. Beyond, the announcer's voice rose above the general clamor.

"Shiffendol!" he called out. "Outrigger from Banner's Bruck! The famed schooner that once hauled a catch of one hundred and thirteen fish!"

The crowd cheered. Durian couldn't help but chuckle that a fishing boat be spoken of with such renown and ceremony. Villagers seemed to blend together, moving slowly, bulky arms and legs warmly dressed for the event. Everyone looked the same. Scattered fires amongst the crowd jealously demanded their fuel but rewarded little heat.

But he caught sight of Baron standing amidst a group from the East End. Durian came up beside Baron who was arguing with one of them about the terms of a newly forming wager. The man took advantage of the arrival of Durian.

"You a betting man?" he asked Durian before Durian could utter a word.

Durian shook his head, no.

"Sure he is," said Baron, stepping forward to reassert himself, and slipped a few coins covertly into Durian's hand. "Now do we have a deal or not?"

The man scowled but nodded. Baron turned to Durian with a wide grin.

"I was worried you wouldn't come. I need you to guard my bet."

Baron still had a role to fulfill in this final race. The Race of Boreol Bay was just a simple race, but there were secondary goals also. The rescue of the castaway of Skull Island, in this case, Baron, for instance.

"What'll it be then?" the man asked Durian, his bet with Baron concluded.

"My money's on the Lord Gaffney," mentioned Baron. "Gaffney's a stout old fellow and he's due for another win."

Durian smiled, recalling the taunts of Gaffney this morning. Gaffney was a crowd favorite, often arriving dead last in the Race of Boreol Bay, and occasionally first, but rarely in between. His nautical practices were questionable at best. And though loved by the crowd, he was the bane of all other racers.

The Lord Gaffney, his boat, was equally baneful. Its namesake communicated nothing of its true form. Hardened to stone by years of wind and weather, its hull was a tapestry of scrapes and scars, and was fearless of gaining more, a point which the other sailors were fully aware.

As Durian pondered, Baron turned to leave. Durian caught him by the arm.

"I'm sorry for earlier," Durian said. "It's just this business with the forest is driving me mad."

Baron nodded.

"No problem. I had forgotten how much the things in Thob Forest were straining your trade. Does anybody know what's going on?"

Durian shook his head.

"All I know is what I've heard from Joram. The fog comes early every morning, covering the whole forest. And the smell of smoke and perfume is often in the air."

Baron gave Durian a dubious glance.

"Perfume? Sounds like the woodsmen are lonesome for home."

"Whatever it is, it's got them spooked," Durian replied. "No one knows who or what's causing it. Some are saying that one of the beasts of the deep forest has come down from the north. Others are talking about Night Wanderers. The woodsmen are too unsettled to delve deep into the forest anymore. Since the lumber camp caught fire and burned down, the flow of wood has slowed to a crawl."

"Night Wanderers!" Baron exclaimed. "I never took the woodsmen to frighten at ghost stories."

Durian nodded in agreement.

"Why haven't the Magistrates sent the Town Guard to investigate?" Baron questioned.

"The captain says the forest is outside their bounds."

Baron rolled his eyes and shook his head. Folk were just scared and their fears were made manifest into all the terrifying stories they'd heard as children. Though Thob Forest stretched north of Suriya nearly the whole length of the kingdom, it had never been *really* explored and was assumed to be uninhabited.

"What about the woodsmen in Echlin?" Baron wondered aloud. "What are they doing about the fog and *perfume*?"

"From what I've heard, the fog stops halfway between here and there," Durian answered. "Whatever's happening, it seems confined to our lucky corner of the kingdom."

Just then, the announcer called for Baron.

"I've got to go. We'll talk more after the race."

Baron, because of his victory at Skull Island, now had another role to play. Soon to be marooned on the black rock, he would await rescue by any boat daring enough. Durian turned his attentions back to the man who held Baron's bet.

"What are the terms?" Durian asked.

"Same as always," he said, foot tapping.

"And the castaway?" Durian questioned.

"You get ten-to-one on your choice of boat that picks up your friend. Two-to-one that anyone grabs him. And two-to-one they leave em stranded."

Nearly ever year the castaway of Skull Island was rescued. One of the trailing boats would give up the main race and veer off to pick him up. Although the rescue didn't count if that same boat finished dead last.

33

As he still considered, cheers and hollering erupted from all around. Durian craned his head and when he saw it, he burst out laughing. Baron was being carried on a wooden raft, dressed as a mermaid, with long flowing blonde hair and a scaled fishtail. But even with the noise, the laughter of Gaffney rose above, who would indeed get his chance to net himself a mermaid. Baron blew Gaffney a kiss and set sail for Skull Island. In garb like that, Baron was sure to get rescued.

"I'll take two-to-one that someone picks up the mermaid."

The man clenched his jaw.

"You west-enders. No sport in the lot of you."

Durian wasn't interested in sport. He needed a sure thing. He gave the man the coins and shook his head at Baron, who now sat waving from Skull Island. Just then, Blair arrived alongside Durian.

"This should be good," Durian commented.

"The man has no decency," Blair said, hand extended to the bay. "I just hope our father isn't here."

Durian laughed.

"I'm sure he's grown quite accustomed to Baron by now," he replied.

"I'm sure he has. So has all of Suriya. Two hundred years we've been building a good family name. Then along comes Baron. I'm moving to Echlin."

Durian slapped him on the back with another laugh.

"I just might join you!"

The bell rang out and the sails of each ship unfurled to the wind. Making slow headway at first, the sailors scrambled to tie down their rigging and avoid fatal collisions.

The courseway was laid out like a giant 'M'. The first leg of the journey led straight out from shore, coming to a turn and veering diagonally back toward shore and Skull Island, where Baron waited. The second half of the race shot back to sea and around a final turn, sending the boats to shore – the finish line.

Neck and neck, the boats had yet to fall into line but vied for an early lead. One of the edge boats swung inside around a jutting rock, striking the nearest boat with a crash of wood. The crowd came alive with hoots and hollering. Less than fatal, the two vessels sailed on, though now in the last positions.

The channel narrowed, scarcely wide enough for two boats to sail abreast. Forced to travel single-file, the twelve boats sailed for the first turn. As they approached, the bottleneck opened, spreading the ships across the lane.

The Lord Gaffney held the inside track, which would ordinarily be considered the worst position. But as the other boats swung out wide to make a broad turn around the first marker, Gaffney made straight for it. The spectators stood in delight at the first act of Gaffney to menace the sport of "highborn boating."

With the rest of the boats swinging wide around the turn to keep their speed, Gaffney sailed sharply round it, his vessel stalling briefly in the middle of the lane and rocking back and forth. He was well ahead of the other vessels, but they were already halfway through the turn at full speed.

The distance closing, Gaffney picked up speed and entered the narrows of the second lane. As the other vessels reached him, he began to sail erratically, consuming the bulk of the courseway. Though a slower vessel, the others were forced to oblige him or risk a collision, dropping the wind from their sails and pulling away.

Even at such a distance, the surly laughter of Gaffney sounded clear, the crowd joining in at the spectacle of frightened and angry sailors. The dozen boats made straight for Skull Island. Now compactly piled, Gaffney swung his tail end out, slowing his boat and likewise forcing frantic sailors to engage in similar maneuvers. All the while, surly laughter erupted from the lead vessel.

The ships were halfway down the second lane, soon to reach Skull Island, which marked the midway turn. Any ship hopeful of rescuing Baron would have to take the inside track and perform a similar maneuver to Gaffney's on the first turn.

As the waterway opened up, the three closest vessels to the Lord Gaffney made for the inside track. The other boats picked up the distance. On his feet, Baron was hollering and waving at the three vessels coming his way. He had taken off his ridiculous fishtail, but he still wore the long blonde hair. The racers wouldn't slow as they passed him by. If they got close enough, he could try jumping for it. But if he missed the first boat, the second or third could very well dash him against the rocks.

The first ship was nearly to him. It was Shiffendol, famed hauler of fish. It's captain, however, was clearly more interested in gaining the lead over Gaffney than rescuing Baron. Not nearly close enough for Baron to jump, one of the deckhands threw a rope in a vain attempt, which landed in the water far shy of Baron. Onshore, boos erupted at the weak attempt.

Shiffendol made his sharp turn and set off down the third waterway. He was in the lead, though the others would close fast. Two more boats had chosen the inside track toward Baron. Waving his hands, Baron readied himself for rescue. Too far to jump, Baron crouched low for a rope.

As the boat passed Skull Island, a bundle of rope sailed from the deck. But it tangled midway through the air, falling in a jumbled mass in the water. Even so, the rope almost made it and Baron overextended himself reaching for it, losing his balance with arms flapping wildly, trying not to fall. The crowd onshore gasped.

Baron still worked to right himself when the third boat reached him, another rope already inbound. He slipped and fell backward but pushed himself up just as the rope hit him, knocking him back on the slick rock.

The crowd roared and craned their necks, none discerning whether Baron took hold of the rope. Seconds ticked by as the slack shortened and shortened until the rope grew taut. Baron burst up from the rock and into the water, dragging behind but hanging on with all his might. The crowd cheered, and Durian and Blair let out a holler.

The crew worked frantically to stow him topside, making the turn while drawing Baron on board, then falling into line among the latter half of the vessels. It was rare for any ship to rescue the castaway and finish better than last place, a honor nearly equal with a win in the race itself.

Durian glanced to the main race. During Baron's rescue, Shiffendol, the Lord Gaffney, and two other vessels vied for first position down the third lane. But the Lord Gaffney maintained his lead and angled for the final turn.

Coming wide round it in single file, the three followups had yet to make their move. The Lord Gaffney took up position in the middle of the lane, occupying as much area as possible. Unable to stifle all of them, the two closest boats took a chance, veering to either side of the Lord Gaffney.

The boat on the inside track wasn't very fortunate. With no room to maneuver, Gaffney had only to adjust his course slightly to squeeze the inside vessel toward the shoals. The vessel tried to dart forward, but in the end dropped anchor to keep from dashing against the rocks. The crowd hollered. Shiffendol now was poised to take up the lead.

But Gaffney set his sights on him. Shiffendol's skipper had grown weary of being bullied, for he maneuvered toward Gaffney instead of out of the way. With a mighty crash the two boats met. Both withstood the impact, and for many long seconds, the hulls ground together as they moved forward as one, neither ship willing to give up the lane.

The race nearly over, neither boat had a clear advantage. But another sound filled the air, of wood scraping stone. Gaffney let out a roar and scrambled to turn frantically. After only a few more moments, Shiffendol arrived to shore victorious.

Baron's boat arrived in the middle of the pack. Durian smiled at the man who held his bet and extended his hand, the jubilant clanging of coins filling his pocket. Laughing and breathless, Baron got to shore with hoots and hollering. Through it all, the long flowing horse hair wig had remained atop his head. Durian and Blair came to greet him.

"Your hair, madame, is like a flock of goats descending from the mountains," Durian said.

Baron pulled off his blonde wig with a laugh.

"Here," Durian said and extended a handful of coins in Baron's direction.

"What's that?"

"You lost. I won. So you're back to square."

"Interesting conclusion," Baron smiled, not reaching out to retrieve the bounty. "You ever find your old wanderer?"

Durian blushed at the awkward exchange but turned to the dispersing crowd, returning the coins to his pocket and shaking his head. The old man could be among the spectators. Durian hadn't seen him.

"Ah well," Baron said, throwing his arm around Durian and pointing the three toward home. "I'll let you buy me a drink."

# At Walloway's Tavern

Darkness took hold of the land, driving the villagers from shore en masse. In minutes, the huddled group dispersed down the darkened lanes of Suriya, just as the glow of streetlamps sprang into life.

"I'll meet you both at Walloway's," Baron said and disappeared into the crowd.

"Where's he going?" Durian questioned.

"Home to change, I'd guess. Come on."

Time was of the essence. Pushing their way past the shuffling villagers, Blair and Durian arrived at a tavern already bursting at the seams.

"How in the world?" Blair marveled.

Durian shrugged his shoulders.

"Come on," Blair said, and made for the entrance.

Hovering at the door, Blair gazed inside to survey the scene. But the doorway was an unfortunate choke point for laughing patrons who slid past them into the open air, singing as they went and splattering drops of ale. Blair caught the worst of it and grabbed Durian's arm, pulling him inside.

But a large man occupying the lane stalled their progress. Tapping him on the shoulder to no avail, the man relayed a story with great animation to a handful of listeners.

Something caught Durian's attention. It was an ornate walking stick standing upright against a nearby wall. For long moments Durian studied it, discerning

40

little of the fine detail. The wood was very beautiful and exotic – more so at least than the varieties harvested in Thob Forest.

Durian felt eyes on him and glanced over, finding the old wanderer gazing at him intently. Durian tried to mask his surprise and turned his attentions to the lively banter of the tavern. But a hand grabbed his shoulder, startling him.

"Sorry," Blair said. "Didn't mean to scare you. There's a table open over there."

Durian flushed but nodded eagerly, knowing that a glance to see if the old man still watched him would only incriminate himself. The pair shoved off, and Blair slumped into the small booth and smiled with contentment. Sliding into a chair opposite him, Durian stared at the table, lost in thought.

"What is it?" Blair asked.

"Did you see the old man we passed by a minute ago?"

"Where?"

"Behind us at the table near the front door."

"Wow, he landed quite a spot. Good for him."

Durian was confused for the moment, but then it dawned on him. Blair had thought Durian was remarking on the fact that such a frail traveler could occupy one of the prime tables in the packed tavern while they had had such trouble. But that wasn't what Durian was saying.

"That's the same man you repaired the walking stick for, right?"

Blair nodded.

"Did he say why he was here or where he was going?" Durian asked.

"He didn't say much. Just needed a new iron cap for his walking stick...needed it by today."

"Then he must be heading north tomorrow. But why come all the way to Suriya?"

"For the Sea Games, I'm sure."

"That's what I thought, at first. But how could he have gotten here so quick before the rest of us?"

"You don't think he was at the races?"

Durian shook his head slowly. Blair's brow furrowed. Just then, Baron entered, still wearing his blonde wig. Skull Horn raised above his head, many turned and cheered. But he glanced slowly round the room until seeing Durian and Blair.

"Evening gents."

"Well aren't you a fetching Barbarian princess," Blair observed.

Baron ignored the insult and sat down.

"Why don't either of you have a drink?"

"We're trying to work something out," Durian responded. "That old man there...The first time I noticed him was during your race at Skull Island. He was apart from the crowd and then wandered off alone while the races still ran. And now we come here and somehow he's got the best table in the house. How could he have gotten from the races here before the rest of us? But if he wasn't there, why come all the way to Suriya during the Sea Games just to ignore them?"

Baron's eyes shot like a hawk toward the old man.

"It's probably nothing," Blair offered.

"There's something else," Durian said. "His walking stick isn't made from any wood I've ever seen."

The significance was lost to the two brothers.

"Thob Forest stretches the whole length of the kingdom. If the wood didn't come from there, then where could it have come from?"

Baron eyed the old man narrowly. The next closest kingdom was the barbarian kingdom to the north, currently at war with their own kingdom, Forthura.

"It's going to sound crazy, but I had a dream this morning."

"A dream?" Baron said, glancing to Blair.

"I had the exact same one three months ago, just before the strange things in Thob Forest started. It can't be a coincidence."

"Are you saying you think the old man is involved with what's happening in the forest?"

"I don't know what I'm saying, really."

Baron nodded slowly. But a slow smile grew on his face.

"I'll figure out what the old codger is up to."

And with that, Baron set off to the old man's table before either of his friends could stall him.

"I'm off to Echlin tomorrow on business," Baron announced as he arrived at the old man's table.

The old man only stared at him blankly.

"I need supplies for the shop," Baron explained, but the blank stare remained.

43

Close on his heels, Blair and Durian had also heard the announcement and Blair didn't keep his confusion to himself.

"Echlin?  What in the world..."

"Why don't we travel together!" Baron blurted out, cutting Blair short mid-sentence.

"No.  Thank you," said the old man.

"Oh, I'm sorry, I thought you were leaving tomorrow," Baron continued and seated himself in an unoccupied chair.  "Blair mentioned you needed your walking stick finished for an urgent journey somewhere.  I assumed you were leaving in the morning and would naturally be passing through Echlin."

The man was silent, a hard stare scrutinizing Baron.

"Neither my business, nor my travels are any of your concern."

"But surely you're passing through Echlin," Baron persisted.  "It's on the way to everywhere from here.  It's always safer to travel together in groups after all.  Everyone knows that."

Durian smiled at the exchange.  Baron made a convincing simpleton.

"My business takes me elsewhere," the man said with a courteous smile.

"Elsewhere?" Baron returned in feigned surprise.

"Yes," said the old man, now standing to his feet.  "This is a wide world my young Suriyan.  You will find in time that not every road you mean to travel passes through *Echlin*.  Now, if you'll excuse me."

He arose and left for the door. The three occupied the now vacant table, suddenly pensive amid the tavern roar.

"Where in the world could he be going?" Baron wondered aloud.

There was nothing south or east but the sea, and Thob Forest sprawled across the west.

"I'm sure he's going north through Echlin," Blair said. "Could you blame him for lying to avoid a two day journey with you?"

Baron smirked. The old man would probably set off early, hoping to leave before Baron stirred from bed.

"I say we travel to Thob Forest tomorrow," Baron declared.

Durian's eyes raised in intrigue, waiting for further explanation, which didn't follow.

"Are you mad?" responded Blair.

"If Durian's right and that old wanderer is somehow part of what's going on in the forest, somebody's got to check it out. We know what inn he's staying at. You brought the walking stick there this afternoon, didn't you?"

Blair reluctantly nodded.

"I'll wake up early and see if he's really heading north," Baron continued. "If not, we'll set out after him. If nothing else, we'll at least see for ourselves what all the fuss is about in the forest."

The notion struck Durian. He himself was more than a little anxious to find out what was going on.

"I'm not going to the forest," declared Blair, standing to his feet, as though to show by action how revolting the idea was.

"Why not?" demanded Baron. "What are you so afraid of? Old wive's tales of ghosts and monsters?"

"How about going out of business? Need I remind you that work has already been piling up in the shop?"

Baron extended his hand for Blair to resume his seat, which he did at length.

"Everything slows down after the Sea Games. The town takes a whole week to recover."

Durian smiled at Baron's persistence. Though he didn't fully understand Baron's interest, he suspected the Sea Games had produced in Baron a taste for adventure he couldn't quite shake – a restless need for something more than the humdrum of normal Suriyan life. Just then, an idea struck Durian.

"I'm willing to go," he said, to the utter shock of Blair.

Even Baron was surprised and gazed with intrigued pleasure at Durian, unsure but hopeful that an explanation was to follow. But Durian kept his thoughts to himself and merely smiled. If Baron wanted to drag them all out to Thob Forest, and if Durian happened to have a full sized axe with him brought for 'protection', he could get his own timber with the help of Baron and Blair. No more relying on the graciousness of the woodsmen.

Felling a full sized hardwood tree was arduous business, not to mention quartering it into manageable pieces for hauling. Durian couldn't accomplish it on his own. But if Baron and Blair just so happened to already be at the forest with nothing but time on their hands...

"This is complete nonsense," said Blair exploding to his feet once more. "What's wrong with the two of you?"

But Durian disregarded the question and turned to Baron.

"Once you make sure he's not headed north, we should leave just after him. Make sure we get there by evening of the second day."

"That's the spirit!" Baron exclaimed, slapping Durian on the back.

Blair hovered there speechless as the two continued to plan. After many moments, Durian and Baron looked up at him to see what he would decide. Blair shook his head and then nodded, and at length sighed in frustration.

"Alright," Blair resigned and resumed his seat. "It's not like it'll matter anyway. I'm sure the old man will head north. But if he doesn't," he added to Baron. "You get to explain to father."

Baron smiled, confident in his ability to concoct some clever story to assuage their father.

"And you get to fix Tobin's plow this year," Blair continued.

The smile turned to disgust. Baron opened his mouth in protest, but Blair intervened.

"I'm not staying behind to slave away while the two of you go out adventuring. And I'll be hanged before I explain to Tobin why his plow is *rusting in our shop* while you're off following some old man out to who knows where. If we're going to Thob Forest, then that's the price."

After a moment, Baron offered up a defeated nod. Durian wore an impressed smile. It was rare for Blair to universally rout his brother. In the end, Baron had wound up with the short end of the stick.

Durian and Blair stood and moved toward the door.

"Where do you think you're going?" Baron said, dropping a hand down on Durian's shoulder.

"Home to sleep," replied Durian, brushing Baron's hand free from his body.

"The night is young!" Baron complained.

Durian smirked and headed off nonetheless. Baron, unwilling to abandon his fellow celebrants, stayed on in the tavern while Durian and Blair exited. They reached the outside air. Blair turned to Durian.

"This had better be worth the trouble."

Durian only shrugged his shoulders. The idea seemed ludicrous – an old man making a two day walk to the forest just at the onset of winter. Durian was nearly convinced that nothing would come of it.

Arriving at his cottage in short order, he took the coins in hand he had won at the race, smiling again at his good fortune. It wasn't a lot, but it would help him get by. Tonight was a night for a warm fire. Grabbing a handful of kindling and hay, he struck his flint rock and blew gently on the growing glow.

Adding a few goodly logs, he reclined in his favorite chair, a contented smile on his face as he glanced around at the shifting shadows sporting about. The day had begun so poorly. He could scarcely believe it had ended so well. If he were lucky, he and his two friends would procure enough lumber to satisfy the whole of his winter endeavors.

After the fire had matured, Durian retreated to his bedroom, kneeling down by his bed and producing an item wrapped in cloth and twine that he hadn't examined in years. It was his father's axe. Durian unwrapped the item slowly. The blade was still sharp and slick with a thin coating of oil. In the first days of his adulthood, his father, Doran, had begun his business with nothing, bartering much of his worldly possessions for the axe which Durian now held. He had spent two whole weeks felling an oak in Thob Forest, quartering it and hauling it back to Suriya on his own.

Durian felt a swell of pride. Though life had taken a hard turn, Durian had met its course in stride. He would persevere onward in the fashion of his father. But what would he find in Thob Forest? An intense feeling of mystery and intrigue filled him. The townsfolk had spoken of much concerning Thob Forest these past few months – of beasts and ghosts, and old things long forgotten.

Durian returned to his main room, to his chair in front of the fire, laying the axe down beside him. As he sat, Durian took a moment to drink in the night. The firelight danced against the furnishings of his cottage, casting shadows into the recesses of his home. Simple things he had once taken for granted – a warm fire and hopeful future – now supplied to him idealistic notions rarely felt these past years: a longing to live his life to the full and find his true purpose.

He opened his favorite book: *Tales of the Prosperous Age* and began flipping slowly through. Many of the tales were deeds of men from the lost House of Cavanah, who according to legend disappeared at the end of the Great War, twelve centuries ago. Suriya belonged to one of the two remaining Houses, the House Forthura, which occupied the southern peninsula of the continent. To the north were the scattered tribes of the Horctura, the barbarians. And to the northwest, over a thousand leagues away was the House of Kester.

Durian continued to scan the book until at last landing upon his favorite portion, the story of the last great king of Cavanah, who reigned until the time of the Great War that ended the Prosperous Age. King Euthor was one of the Builders – men who could mold stone as though clay in their hands, and create new forms of stone with stronger properties, even magical ones. He had wrought great works in the latter days of the Prosperous Age, but had tragically lost his wife, Sheyla, just before the last battle that changed their world, over twelve centuries ago. After her death, he disappeared along with the rest of the House of Cavanah, never to be seen again.

Durian recalled the dream he had had this morning and slowly read the poem before him:

*Dismissing hours as they pass*
*Soft upon the windswept grass.*
*The hopes of men have come to naught.*
*Nothing fair for eyes or thought.*

*For Sheyla lies on golden plain,*
*Of Cavanah, the fairest slain;*
*Who met her last and final day*
*When all was brought to disarray.*

*Of gladful things now nevermore –*
*Now bitter wind, now salty shore.*
*The peaceful world bound to unrest*
*And darkness looming in the west.*

*The world and all its light shall fade.*
*I'll stay with her beneath the shade*
*And wait until the world's remade...*

# Thob Forest

Pounding on the door jolted Durian awake. He sat up in his favorite chair, the muffled voice of Baron calling out his name. Still dark out, Durian didn't know if it was night or morning. A sudden chill hit him and he glanced to the cold fireplace, where only a handful of stoutly embers lie amid the ash. He must have fallen asleep. He was still in his clothes from the night before and a book lay on his chest. Baron still pounded on the door.

"Just a minute," Durian called out and arose.

"Hurry up, it's freezing out here," Baron said.

Durian quickly changed and came to the door. Rubbing his hands furiously, Baron stood waiting in the dark.

"What do you want?" Durian asked.

"What do you mean what do I want?" Baron replied back and pushed his way indoors. "It's time to go."

Durian was surprised. But before he could say anything, Baron shoved a large woolen greatcoat in Durian's face.

"Here. Blair said you needed it."

Coming to the fireplace, Baron packed it with kindling and struck the flint rock furiously. Durian was about to complain, but hurried off to his room to pack.

"Did you see the old man?" Durian called out.

"Mostly," Baron responded.

"Mostly?" Durian asked and reappeared in the main room, on the verge of ripping the kindling from his fireplace.

"Keep packing," Baron demanded. "I'm sure it was him. I didn't see his face...it was too dark. But I heard the tap, tap, tap of his iron tipped walking stick."

"And he didn't head north?" Durian asked, still hovering.

"No. He ventured west along the main path. I lost him near the edge of town."

"And you're sure it was him?"

"Yes, now get going!" Baron shooed.

Durian assented reentered his bedroom, packing quickly to save what he could of his woodpile from the hands of Baron. Soon Durian emerged with a large pack and an axe in hand.

"What do you propose we do with that?" Baron asked.

"You're not bringing any weapons?"

Baron smiled and produced a small dagger from within his tunic, one he had undoubtedly fashioned himself. It was rough and unpolished, but would do in a pinch.

"Where's Blair?" Durian asked.

"Oh, I'm sorry," Baron responded in concern. "I forgot to mention. Blair decided not to come."

"What!" Durian exclaimed. "Why?"

But Baron only smiled, and Durian realized he was joking. Baron grabbed another log for the fire but Durian caught his hand and returned the log to its place. Baron smirked.

"I just need to pack some food," Durian said.

"There's no time! You can eat from our stores. I brought plenty."

Durian grabbed what little he could – boiled eggs and cured meats. Durian never kept more than a few day's store on hand. Dried fruits and nuts were more than he could afford. One last thing struck him, and he dashed to grab his book.

"Come on," Baron demanded.

A few minutes' walk brought them near the westward end of town, the last crossroad before emerging onto the golden plains. Escaping in puffs of vapor, their breath dissipated quickly against the fresh gleam of dawn.

Baron glanced about for signs of Blair. Maybe he decided not to come after all. But a faint whisper turned their heads.

"Baron!" came the hushed shout.

They searched in vain and the voice called out again. Blair was against one of the nearby buildings beckoning them.

"What are you doing hiding?" Baron questioned, hands extended.

Blair took him by the shirt and pulled him into the darkness.

"I think the old man's nearby," Blair responded.

"Where?"

"I don't know," said Blair. "I heard someone walking, so I hid and waited for him to pass by. I tried getting close, but never saw him."

"Did he see you?" asked Baron.

"Of course not," Blair said. "Don't be ridiculous."

"You got lucky this time, little brother."

Durian couldn't help but chuckle at the severity in Baron's voice. If Baron had seen the old man half an hour earlier, then whoever Blair heard must have been just a random passerby, which Baron knew full well.

"Let's get moving," Baron said.

"What if we overtake him? Shouldn't we wait a bit."

"We need to get clear of town. We'll slow down later."

Baron set off. Surprised by his eagerness, Durian and Blair were close on his heels. Farms dotted the sweeping countryside with livestock in fenced off pens and the occasional haystack, yet to be brought indoors from the harvest.

Baron set a very quick pace. If the old man had indeed come this way, they'd overtake him quickly. Entering a rocky field with quite a few mounds of hay, Baron's glance darted back and forth as he ran from haystack to haystack.

Durian was surprised to see so much hay still in the field, for winter was already knocking. Already the baleful southern wind had torn away shoots of hay from his fresh piles and strewn them roundabout. Baron was darting from pile to pile as though hiding from some mysterious foe. Durian made likewise maneuvers, though still unsure as to why. Just then, a far away voice called out.

"You there! Stand fast!"

Baron's whole body went stiff. His eyes shot about, searching for a safe haven to flee. But the farmer was already upon them. Durian recognized him as Tobin and couldn't help but smile.

"Why are you in my field and where is my plow?" Tobin demanded.

Baron searched for a response but only stood there mouth gaping.

"We're heading to Thob Forest for lumber," Durian said, which seemed reasonable, tapping the axe now resting at his side.

Tobin's face went red.

"This is little more than thievery. I won't have my tools rotting and rusting in your shop all winter. I'll send for the Magistrate."

"But you won't need your plow till springtime," Baron complained. "What could you possibly want it for this time of year? The rocks are already frozen fast in place. You'll ruin it completely!"

"What did you say about my land?" he exclaimed and took a step forward. "If I had proper tools to work with, I'd have the finest fields in all of Suriya. How dare you sneak onto my fields and insult my farm. If your father..."

"Tobin, we've got to go," said Baron. "Blair will have your plow for you straightaway."

And before another word could be uttered, Baron shot to the far end of the field, Durian and Blair just behind him.

"Not a chance," said Blair, catching up to Baron.

But Baron didn't respond until they were clear of Tobin's field. Once free, he paused and took in a breath of fresh air. The plains were a blanket of swaying golden yellow, and would soon wear another layer of white. Already patches of snow were clinging to the shadowed hollows of every hillside.

The three friends set off, this time at a slower pace, passing through farmlands until arriving at the edge of the Commonwealth Pasturelands. These were the broad plains surrounding the townships of Forthura where herdsmen were free to pasture their cattle at no expense. But the fields had emptied weeks ago, man and beast alike driven indoors till springtime.

They walked in silence, Thob Forest filling Durian's thoughts. Though the forest sustained his livelihood, Durian had been there only once as a child, to the Shelengol Glades, which were a favorite of Suriyans. A series of interconnected glades, Shelengol was beautiful in the summer and fall months, and was oft visited until the strange things in Thob Forest began.

An overcast gray filled the sky. Baron examined scattered piles of snow as they passed, looking for signs that someone had come before them. But the plains about them seemed untrodden. If the old man was traveling westward, he was taking a different course.

After an hour, they came to a weathered wooden post stuck fast in the ground, with two footpaths stretching diagonally away. The northerly route lead toward the Shelengol Glades, while the southerly path veered toward the coastline and then to the Estees Mountains, which lie not far within the southern edge of Thob Forest. Once well-frequented, the Estees Mountains were abandoned some years back when one of the expedition leaders wandered off strangely in the night and fell from a cliff.

The Estees contained a cleft that was the only known place with a clear view of the Frostlands – the frozen waste across the sea, beyond Boreol Bay. Upon this cleft sat a rock, a mysterious large stone with streaks of gold and silver spiraling upward along its face.

The solitary stone lay eerily at the edge of the cliff and was a great mystery throughout the years. Said to be a relic of the old world and Prosperous Age, none knew whether the stone was natural or man made – a work of the Builders of the last age. But a similar stone was said to exist in the palace hall of Eulsiphion, the capital city of Forthura.

Baron knelt down and ran his fingertips along the ground at the base of the wooden post. Though none of them were by any means trackers, it did appear that someone had come this way recently. Searching in a broader circle around the post, the group didn't find anything definitive.

"Which way?" Durian asked.

Baron tapped his foot as he pondered.

"It's possible, I guess, he's just visiting the Glades," Baron offered.

"It's also possible he's halfway to Echlin."

Baron smirked.

"He wouldn't take the southern route, would he?" Baron wondered aloud.

Dark thoughts stirred in Durian's mind at the possibility of a connection between what happened at the Estees Mountains years ago and the things happening now in Thob Forest. Had something been stirring all that time? It was clear Baron and Blair shared his concern.

"Isn't there a hill halfway between here and the forest that overlooks both the Glades and the mountains?" Baron asked.

Durian faintly recalled the same notion.

"If we make for it, maybe we'll get lucky and spot him," Baron said.

Durian shrugged his shoulders and Baron set off due west through the open plain. The gray haze of the sky mingled with the ominous thoughts swirling in his mind, producing a creeping fear that he and his friends had stumbled into something they weren't prepared for.

Near midday, they came upon a moderate boulder. Blair started a small fire against the northern side while the others gathered bits of straw and brush. A few eggs would cook quickly even with scant fuel.

As they ate, Durian thought back to the first time he had seen the old man. His demeanor was distant...absent...as though entrenched in something beyond the Sea Games and Boreol Bay. Perhaps a better view of the Frostlands was his true aim. But why?

The three friends finished and set off without a word. Durian hoped they were wrong about the old man, that he was indeed halfway to Echlin by now. Adventuring into the forest wasn't Durian's true aim and the closer they came, the more his trepidation grew.

After a few hours, the lively gray deepened toward evening. Hoping to find a boulder for shelter, they settled for a natural bowl in the plains and erected their shelters of canvas. Wrapped in their thick wool blankets, they ate a sparse dinner and then fell asleep.

Durian awoke before dawn, body stiff from cold and exertion. With the new day dawning, a fresh feeling of relief filled Durian's mind. How could an old man be a part of such a dark plot? Durian was confident that nothing would come of it, and soon he would have his pick of timbers to fell.

But the frost already on the ground made him reconsider the viability of his plan. If a hard rain fell, or worse, the first snowfall, his hopes of hauling timber to Suriya would come to ruin. Transporting chunks of hardwood was difficult enough. But plodding through a layer of thick snow or soggy ground was impossible, even with a pair of mules. If he didn't move quickly, his felled timber might be stuck in Thob Forest the whole winter.

Baron and Blair stirred from their tent. Too cold to handle metal cookware, they ate a meal of dried meats and nuts. If they walked swiftly today, they would arrive at Thob Forest by late afternoon.

They set off, exertion a better remedy than blankets for reclaiming the vital heat. By late morning, the dull gray above transformed to a light blue, the sun's mellow rays dissolving the frost and restoring Durian's hope. By midday, Durian's shoulders throbbed under the straps of his pack. Still no sign of the large hill, they stopped for lunch and rest.

"What happens if we get to the top of the hill and find no sign of the old man?" Blair questioned.

"It probably means he's already in the forest," Baron replied.

Blair gazed at him with incredulity. The three friends had set a quick pace, quicker than an old man could sustain.

"If we truly don't see anything, we can spend the night in Shelengol Glades and then come home."

Durian could only hope for such luck. But the day growing long, they set off west. After an hour, they saw a looming hillside in the nearby distance, stretching above any others they'd passed.

The three hiked the shallow incline, slowing as they crested its peak, almost apprehensive to reveal the distance beyond. A striking scene came into focus: the sparkling sea in the south and Thob Forest directly ahead. The forest was a league away, gray and vague in the airy distance, concealed by a blanket of clinging mist. Through the fog rose the peaks of the Estees Mountains. Here, now, gazing at the dark forest, Durian better understood the fear of the woodsmen. Then suddenly, Baron's arm extended, finger pointing.

"Look! I see him!"

Far to the south by the coast, a lone figure was wandering toward the misty forest. None could believe their eyes. The old man was here.

# Questions and Answers

The three friends lingered on the hilltop.

"What should we do?" one asked.

"I don't know," another answered.

"It's getting late."

"We need to get to the forest."

"Shouldn't we turn back?"

The final question hung in the air. Durian and Blair weren't nearly as keen as Baron to delve headfirst into the dark forest. Baron opened his mouth to downplay their fears, but hesitated and only clenched his jaw. The danger was very real and he couldn't just shrug it off.

The distant form began to blend with the dark treeline, his figure now vague against the backdrop. Durian felt suddenly vulnerable. What if the old man looked back and spotted them?

"Let's make camp at the Glades tonight," said Baron.

They descended the hill the way they had come. At the base they turned north, coming round the hill and then west toward the forest. The treeline was still an hour off and evening was falling fast. But fear of discovery drove them, and they drew near the forest edge quickly.

The haze obscured the inner forest. Wisps of jutted through the treeline in places and into the open plain before disappearing in the warm sunlight. Still a short distance to the north, the trio made for the Glades but kept their distance from the forest. Their packs jangled as they ran, each step signaling their arrival to Thob Forest.

Up ahead, another weathered post stood half buried just at the forest edge. Making for it, they entered the forest just as the sun set behind them on the plains.

The air was cold and damp beneath the trees, and the light of the waning sun powerless against the mist and foliage. And though the fog was ominous from the plains, now in the midst of it, Durian felt somehow safer.

The mist began to clear as they reached the first glade. A boulder stood at the entrance, and as they passed by, Durian was surprised to see that writing had been etched into its surface and lingered to read it in the failing sunlight.

*The weather-beaten trellis falls,*
*The autumn wind sweeps over all;*
*A blanket for the sleepy deep*
*Of forest things that dart and creep.*

*The windy whispers falling down,*
*Grayish echoes of a distant town,*
*Fall soft amid the scratching leaves,*
*As silently as one who grieves.*

*There is a distant passerby:*
*The summer fading from the sky,*
*Dancing devilish on the hill,*
*Out-driven by a stronger will.*

63

*Alas, is gone that cheerful friend*
*Whose company would daily lend;*
*Now warming regions far away,*
*A stranger till some distant day.*

The clanging packs trailed away as the mist consumed the two brothers. Durian ran to catch them, the imagery of the poem filling his mind. The once tranquil forest had been out-driven by a stronger will and he thought of the old man as the distant passerby dancing devilish on the hill.

Entering the glade, the fog diminished, revealing the first of the evening stars. Boulders scattered roundabout in piles were colorfully adorned with mosses, and the few leaves yet hanging from the trees still wore their mantle of orangy red. The Glades were more beautiful than Durian remembered, which struck him. For he wasn't otherwise in a frame of mind to appreciate it.

Baron stopped at one of the outcroppings of boulders that stood on reasonably flat ground. Dropping their packs, they raised their shelters for the night.

"I'll go for wood," Blair declared, the first to finish, but then hesitated and helped Durian instead.

Dusk fell on the forest. Needing kindling for a fire, they set off into the open woods, discovering quickly how damp and mossy the uninterrupted months of fog had left the forest. If only they'd brought some straw from the plains. But a dead pine not far away, whose bark was still intact, looked remarkably dry.

They stripped the bark and brought the driest of its limbs to camp.

With night, the mist receded, shrinking back to its hidden lair somewhere deep in the forest. The bark of the pine prevailed through the moisture, and a small but smoky fire grew in their midst. They circled it closely, cooking an evening meal, their shadows dancing on the boulders behind them.

Noises erupted from the darkness – the snapping of a twig or the rustling of leaves, or even the distant howl of a beast in the deeps. Now still and calm, Durian caught scent of something that startled him. Very faint and detecting it only for a moment, it was the distinct smell of a lovely perfume. Durian breathed in deep, but the fragrance had passed.

"What are we going to do about the old man?" Blair asked.

"I've been thinking about it and I just can't figure it," Baron responded. "Nothing's adding up. I don't know how the old man's connected, but he has to be involved somehow. How else could he march alone straight into a dark forest unless he knew there was nothing to fear?"

"If that's true, then it can't be some magical beast come down from the Westward Wilds," Blair said.

Baron's eyes narrowed as he thought, gazing deep into the fire crackling in front of them. He grabbed another small log to throw on the fire but stared at it for many moments.

"The woodsmen said they smelled perfume and smoke, right?" Baron asked.

Durian nodded.

"Well, where there's smoke, there's fire. And where there's fire, there's got to be people. What if the old man's not alone?"

Durian glanced to Blair who seemed equally in the dark as to what Baron was implying.

"What if he's a spy?"

"A spy?"

"He'd make the perfect spy – an unassuming old man. And it's convenient – he happens to show up just at the only time of year when he could go unnoticed."

"Spy for what? The only people we're at war with are the barbarians, and they're hundreds of leagues to the north."

"What if they've sent a force down?"

"How could they send a force to Thob Forest undetected?"

"What if they came through the deep woods, even skirting the Westward Wilds between here and Kester?"

The other kingdom of men, the House of Kester was on the far northwestern side of the continent, cut off from their own kingdom, Forthura. Between them to the west was a labyrinth of forest and mountain and swampland. And to the north, the barbarian kingdom cut off any roads that once existed between kingdoms.

Durian could well understand why the barbarians would want to sneak around the defenses of Eulsiphion and attack from far behind. Though the barbarians outnumbered them greatly, the capital of Forthura, Eulsiphion, was a massive walled city at the edge of the barbarian kingdom, near-impenetrable by ordinary means.

It was widely accepted that Eulsiphion was not built by the people of Forthura, but rather was found almost a thousand years ago. Whatever ended the Prosperous Age of Man also forced the people of that day to wander the world for a time, nomadic drifters making their way across the plains. There were more than a few centuries of unrecorded history. The people of that day slowly spread across the highlands of the north where the Horctura now dwell and came at last upon a deserted city, one terrifyingly beautiful in size and splendor.

Unsure at first about the city's strange state of abandonment, they set up camp nearby to watch for its rightful owners to return. But no one ever came and Forthura claimed it as its own. Small Forthurian villages spread out across the plains from there throughout the broad southern peninsula.

"They must be making the fog somehow," Baron decided. "To cover up their workings. And the smoke is obviously from their fires. The perfume... that's just strange. But what if everything happening in Thob Forest is all a ruse to keep us too scared to search the woods?"

Durian's thoughts drifted back to the old man. Though he was mysterious, the old man didn't act like a spy. The only times Durian had seen him, he was off wandering away by himself, or seated alone in a tavern. He wasn't out sneaking around the city, measuring its defenses or spying on its chief officials. Perhaps it was because he had already seen how defenseless a place Suriya was.

Baron had the only explanation that made any sense. And whatever the old man's intentions, they could hardly be innocuous. Durian felt suddenly exposed. If there really was a force of barbarian warriors in Thob Forest, they could be anywhere. They could be watching them now.

"Where do you think he was headed?" Blair asked.

The old man had been far south when they spotted him, near the old pathway to the Estees Mountain range.

"If I were building a secret fort, a mountain range like the Estees would be perfect," Baron contended. "It's defensible and out of the way and no one goes there anymore."

But as Baron continued his train of thought, something still felt wrong to Durian. His gut feeling told him the old man couldn't be a barbarian spy. But then who was he? Nothing made sense. Their discussion had led to more questions and yielded no answers. But everything felt connected somehow...the old man, the tragedy at the Estees years ago, and the fog now blanketing the forest.

Had dark things been stirring in Thob Forest for that long, building slowly, patiently, all this time? An uneasiness was growing in Durian's mind, one that told him to leave this place and never return. He felt convinced that something menacing and purposeful was carrying out a dark and devious plan. Durian thought of the stone that lay on the edge of a cleft on

68

the nearest mountain. Was it some ancient magic, long forgotten, now again being wielded?

His heart beat faster in his chest as the three gazed deep into the fire. Though everything within him wanted to flee, Durian knew they couldn't leave. No one would give gravity to a report of an old man spotted entering Thob Forest. No alarm would be raised on that account.

The three laid down for the evening. But every time Durian fell asleep, the cracking of a twig or the rustling of leaves snapped him back awake.

Thob Forest was now to him a living, malevolent thing. The thought of straying into its bounds in the morning brought a tinge of terror to Durian's heart. What if they disappeared, never to be found? They would be gone and no one would ever know why. Or for what.

# Whispers and Shadows

Baron was the first to stir, leaving his tent to check for coals. Stirring the sparsely glowing ash, he worked to revive the fire. Durian heard him and arose.

"I wouldn't," Durian said. "Someone might see the smoke."

Though a thick veil of fog once more encompassed them, above them a mere stone's throw beyond, was open air. Baron stomped out the fledgling fire. The mist was thicker than the day before, and carried with it the scent of perfume and smoke, though the latter could very well have been their own fire.

The three packed their things, concealing as best they could the evidence of their lodging. Then they departed, making for the plains. Drawing near the forest edge, the world was suddenly bathed in a blanket of light.

They ran a few paces into the plains and turned round to face the forest. The eerily undulating fog laid claim to the woods, but some intervening force kept it from seeping into the plains. There was something unnatural in it all. The fog was a solid wall but for thin wisps that broke off in regular intervals, escaping the indefinable mass and creeping forward, only to dissolve in the sunlight.

Standing here, now, at the edge of the dark forest, they each seemed to realize the foolishness of their misadventure. They should have taken precautions, should have told people where they were going and why. But none could have anticipated the events to unfold as they had.

"Come on," said Baron at length. "We better get moving."

Jogging along the treeline, they made for the forgotten trail to the Estees Mountains. None of them had ever taken an expedition to the mountains but they knew of an outcropping of boulders that marked the head of the trail. The expeditions always camped there and made for the mountains at first light.

There were five large stones against the treeline in the distance. The boulders were partially in the forest and partially in the plains. Reaching them, they scanned the treeline for evidence of a trail. But Durian noticed something odd about the boulders, or rather, the ground at the base of the largest boulder. It looked ruffled and soft.

He stood over it, moving the dirt with the toe of his boot. The dirt was loose. Bending down, he grabbed some with his hand but quickly drew his hand out with a gasp.

"What happened?" Baron said, running over to him.

Durian didn't answer them, but continued to disturb the ground with the toe of his boot. After a few moments, a thin band of smoke came up from the ground.

"I thought I was bitten by a snake."

"The old man must have stayed here," exclaimed Blair. "He tried to cover his tracks."

As Blair said the words, a feeling of unease hit the three Suriyans. Why would he hide his tracks? Or rather, from whom?

"He must be onto us," declared Baron.

"What? How?"

"He's probably just being cautious," commented Durian.

"What if he's not hiding from us?" Blair asked. "What if he's hiding from whatever's in the forest?"

"That doesn't make sense," said Baron.

"Of course it does. The old man can't know we're following him. So if he is hiding from someone, it can't be us."

Every new discovery ended in more mystery. But Blair's reasoning struck a chord with Durian. Durian didn't know why but something told him the old man wasn't an enemy.

"Let's find the trail," Baron said.

Though the pathway to the mountains hadn't been used in years, signs of it should still exist – a vague indentation in the earth accompanied by brushy new undergrowth but nothing mature.

Durian saw a small fern that looked as though lightly trampled. He scanned the forest slowly, waiting for his eyes to hit on something out of place. After a moment, Durian whistled for Baron and Blair, motioning to a barely perceptible footpath. Baron traveled down it slowly, running his hands through various bent ferns and trampled verdure.

"Come on," said Baron.

Just inside the forest, the curtain of fog drew thickly around them. Baron set a quick pace but it proved too quick. After only a minute he was forced to stop, the pathway no longer before him. Durian marveled that the trail could only be seen when one stared directly down it. If slightly off to one side, the path would disappear from sight. After backtracking a few paces, they were able to resume their course.

Sections of thick underbrush also hindered their sight, forcing them to trek whole sections without direction. But the brush was matted and trampled in places, proving a better guide than the path itself.

Hours melted away, all their focus on keeping to the trail. After midday, they happened upon a bubbling brook that paralleled their course for a time. There were very few sources of fresh water in Thob Forest, and coming upon one was no accident. Overjoyed to refill their water skins, they stopped for lunch.

"How long to the mountains?" Durian asked.

The sound of a voice seemed out of place in the misty woodlands.

"We won't make it today," Baron answered.

"Why don't we stop here then, where there's fresh water?" Blair asked. "There's always the danger that if we push too hard we'll overtake the old man."

Durian needed little encouragement to drop his pack, and rubbed his aching shoulders. After making camp, they came together and rested on a nearby fallen log.

"Do you think it's safe for a fire?"

That was a question none could answer.

"Let's do it," Baron said. "I don't want my eggs spoiling."

They set off in search of dry wood.  But finding wood that hadn't succumbed to months of damp was a difficult feat.  Durian ambled along the stream.  He was deep in thought as he mechanically scanned the forest for the driest of timbers.  But something brought him back to his senses.

The faint smell of smoke was on the mist. Durian froze and peered outward, breathing deeply. Though the smell was faint, he clearly detected the scent of burning wood.  And he almost thought he saw a glow through the trees.  Anxiety hit him as he realized he was alone.

Durian dropped what little wood he had and ran up the stream toward camp.  Finding it empty, his heart beat quickly as his eyes darted about the forest. Darkness descended through the trees.

Where were they?  Why had they gone so far from the campsite?  Had they been taken?  Durian heard the sound of a cracking twig behind him.  He spun round in fright and saw Blair walking up to him, a pile of wood in his arms.

"Why aren't you gathering any firewood?" Blair asked.

But Durian didn't answer him.  He held his finger up to his lips and came toward him.

"There's someone here, I think," Durian whispered.  "We need to find your brother."

Blair dropped his pile of wood.

"What!  Who's here?"

"I'm not sure.  I didn't see anyone.  But there was a glow in the distance and the smell of smoke."

Just then, Baron approached.

"What are you two doing?"

"Durian saw something downstream."

He motioned to the area and set off, followed by the twins. With the encroaching darkness, the mist began to recede. They came to a spot where the stream curved away and stopped, fearful of getting lost.

Breathing in deeply, the three detected the smoke. The smell was different than before. It was an oily smoke. Blair's hand shot up, finger pointing to a barely perceptible glow not far beyond them. Baron set off in its direction to the horror of Durian and Blair. Durian almost called out after him, but he dared not.

The three crept forward, ever so slowly. As they drew near, the sound of flowing water came back to their hearing. The stream must have curved around and doubled back. Durian took heart. The sound would mask their movements and keep them also from getting lost.

The glow was only a stone's throw beyond. Baron was coming dangerously close. The trees were obscuring anything definite from view, but they heard the sound of muffled voices. There were people in the distance ahead.

Baron held up his hand for the other two to wait while he alone advanced. They halted, concentrating with all their might to discern any of the words being said. But a thick treeline stood between them.

As Durian stood there, a realization dawned on him. There were very few sources of fresh water in Thob Forest. It wasn't an accident they had stumbled into someone here in the forest. Baron moved through the trees quietly. Now that darkness filled the forest,

Durian could see that the glow was actually an array of smaller lights. It had to be torches. Baron was almost out of sight.

Durian heard the unmistakable clang of metal from up ahead. It sounded like armor. Baron reached a large tree and peered his head around it. He lingered for many moments. But the glow was diminishing.

Baron returned to their side.

"What did you see?"

Baron shook his head slowly.

"They were leaving by the time I got close enough. They were soldiers of some kind."

"Soldiers?"

"They were having a meeting it looked like. They broke company just as I got there, moving off in different directions."

Silence filled the night air. Their worst suspicions had come true. Suriya was in grave danger.

"Let's get back to camp," said Durian.

The others nodded and set off toward the stream north of them. Drawing near their campsite, Durian scanned it closely for signs of tampering. But it looked undisturbed. They hadn't been discovered yet. When they arrived, Baron sat down on a fallen log, content to settle in for the night.

"I don't think we can stay here," said Durian.

"Why not?"

"It can't be an accident we stumbled into someone here. Whoever's in Thob Forest, they're using the stream for water, same as we. It's only blind luck they didn't discover us. We can't stay here. We've got to get back and warn Suriya."

76

Baron clenched his jaw. That left them in a bind. The pathway through the forest was difficult enough to follow by day. They had no hope of keeping to it by night. If they left tonight, it would be through the open woods without direction. Baron glanced to Blair, but Blair only shook his head.

Quietly, they dismantled their camp, camouflaging the evidence of their presence as best they could in the meager starlight. Then shouldering their packs, they came together in a circle.

"I hope you both are up for a long night," Baron said.

Then they set off through the open woodlands. The mist was all but faded from the forest and Durian felt strangely naked, having grown accustomed to the fog's haunting presence.

Weariness took hold, striking hard as the fright of their encounter passed. Every part of Durian's body ached. They walked till what must have been midnight and stopped at a downed log to rest. It was a well-sheltered, brushy patch of forest.

"We're not going to make it out of here tonight," Baron said. "This looks like as good a place as any."

Durian was overjoyed and plopped his pack down, erecting his shelter hastily and falling into it fast asleep without a bite of dinner. But he awoke to a ravenous hunger just at the glow of dawn and couldn't fall back asleep.

Leaving his tent, he found the mist just beginning to gather among the trees. Like a snake, wisps emerged from the deep forest, slithering among the timbers.

Now that it was certain that soldiers had occupied the forest, the mystery of the fog and perfume struck him more than ever. How in the world was it possible for the barbarians to cover an entire forest with fog day by day? Whatever was happening, it seemed bigger than a barbarian invasion. He couldn't help but wonder about the strange dream he had awoken to only days ago. What did it all mean?

Baron and Blair emerged, snapping Durian from his ruminations. Without a word they packed and ate, setting off into the forest, hoping to be clear by late morning. But there was no guarantee they were even going the right direction.

Midday passed and day descended to evening. They all knew what it meant. If they really were headed east, they'd have cleared the forest hours ago.

As they walked, a stiff chill entered the air. Up ahead, forest was even more dimly lit than usual. They paused. And then, like a torn blanket, the mist broke in scattered patches, revealing the ominous form of a mountain face. There was no mistaking what it was. The three adventurers stopped in their tracks, speechless.

"Well, at least now we know where we are," Baron encouraged. "Like my uncle always says:

*The road is only longest when,*
*When all you know is where you've been.*"

But the Estees Mountains were the last thing any of them wanted to see. Deep within Thob Forest, the three friends were now days from escape. Their

78

food was running out. Their water was running out. And once they set out from here, there was no guarantee they wouldn't get turned around again. A small portion of a haunting poem rang through Durian's mind as he faced the base of the mountain:

*The shadow falls upon the floor,*
*The forest shudders cold;*
*And even young men bear the weight*
*Of cares so very old;*
*Within the shadow of the mount*
*And on the cliffs of yore.*

*Upon the lonely mountainside*
*The roamer finds his way;*
*But soon his gold will lose its shine*
*And all his hopes decay;*
*Alas, for such a haggard road,*
*For such a wretched guide!*

# Encounters

The three friends lingered in the shadow of the mountain.

"Let's get out of here," said Blair.

"We're so close to the mountains," Baron argued. "Shouldn't we at least find the path and go the rest of the journey?"

"What for?" demanded Blair.

"If the old man was coming this way, there's got to be something worth seeing. We only need to climb a little to get above the mist."

"Let's be quick about it then," said Durian.

The three set off, reaching the base of the mountain in short order but failing to find a navigable pathway up. Baron searched along it for minutes to no avail.

"Baron, this is hopeless," said Durian.

"It's got to be around here somewhere."

"Nightfall is only a few hours off."

Baron slowed with a sigh and turned round. His look expressed the question they all shared. If they set off, how were they going to keep from getting lost again?

"I say we make south for the coast," said Blair. "It can't be far and we'll follow it west straight out."

That was a very good idea. Baron set off swiftly through the misty trees. If they moved quickly enough, they could reach the coast by nightfall. But after an hour, darkness crept into the forest of the world, reviving the animals that stalked the woods by starlight.

Baron slowed his pace and came to a stop at a fallen log. They couldn't keep going without rest. Removing their packs, they brought out what little food they had left – another day's rations at most. As they ate and recovered their strength, Durian thought he saw something in the imperceptible distance. He stood to his feet and took a step closer, gazing intently in front of him.

The others jumped up beside Durian. There was light in the distance, barely perceptible at first but growing brighter.

"Are those torches?"

The question hung in the air, the glow intensifying with each passing moment.

"We need to leave, now!"

Reaching for their packs, the clanging of pans filled the night air. Baron took his pack and shoved it into the nearby brush, leaving it behind. Motioning for the others to do the same, they reluctantly set off without supplies. They were decently hidden, but a soldier passing by would still see them. Having almost no food left, there was little need for packs. But sleeping outdoors without tents would be miserable business.

Durian glanced back as they ran. The glow behind them was growing brighter. But something even more appeared. Another glow was filling the forest in front of them.

The three dropped to the ground and scrambled for cover. Seconds passed. They only had low lying brush for cover. Durian squeezed his eyes shut. He couldn't bear to watch. The soldiers seemed to slow, the sound of their armor changing. Had they found the packs? Were they searching for them?

Scattered torches appeared, half a dozen lights spread out among the trees. Durian's heart beat quickly. The soldiers were searching for something and they were nearly to them. Durian opened his eyes and looked up. A warrior clad in armor was in the distance ahead. His armor was dark with a streak of red on his breastplate. Durian had never seen a barbarian warrior before, but he'd heard of them, and these in front of him weren't what he expected.

Some of the torches had moved beyond them. Durian glanced to where Baron and Blair were hiding. But as he did, he noticed something. A solitary torch was unmoving, its bearer standing still and faced in Durian's direction. Durian froze. Had he been seen? His heart beat wildly.

Just then, the torch sprang toward him. Durian stumbled backward as the soldier closed the distance, sword raised. Durian tried to stand and flee but the soldier kicked him back to the ground.

Standing over Durian, sword poised, Durian raised his hands over his face with a yell. Time seemed to freeze. But suddenly, the soldier fell onto Durian, arrow protruding from his back. Durian yelled again, pushing the man off him and scrambling backward into the nearest tree.

A battle erupted. Durian heard the clanging of sword on sword and the death cry of at least two persons. What in the world was going on? But Durian was too scared to find out. He couldn't open his eyes or stand to his feet. The battle continued. Durian could hear more armored men approaching from the other direction. He breathed in deep and found the resolve to stand up and see just what was happening.

Three soldiers were dead on the ground. Three more were holding their ground against two assailants, waiting for reinforcements to arrive. But the two attackers advanced on them fiercely. The battle disappeared behind a line of trees as the attackers pushed the soldiers back.

Durian was scarcely breathing. Why were these men fighting? But in only moments, the battle ended and the two attackers emerged. One set out straight for Durian, the other toward Baron and Blair. Durian scrambled away and let out a muffled yell as the man placed his hand over Durian's mouth.

"Be silent," the man commanded.

Nearby, more soldiers were approaching their position. The man holding Durian scanned about the forest.

"Sheabor, we must get them out of the open," cautioned the other man who held Baron and Blair by the collar.

"This way," said the lead man and pushed Durian along with resistance.

"Do not struggle," said the man. "Or we will leave you to them."

Durian glanced to his friends. Baron nodded to follow them. Durian assented and the group set off. The two men were well camouflaged to the forest, with brown leather armor and green cloaks. They were taller than average height for Suriyans, broad-shouldered and muscular. Each sported a short beard and long brown hair.

The two men led them stealthily away from the other group of soldiers not far from their position. Many times, the lead man would crouch low against a tree, pulling Durian down and placing a hand over his mouth. For nearly half an hour the men at arms were close around them. But soon the sounds faded, leaving them to the night.

Durian got the distinct sense the two men were leading them back in the way they had come. After walking for the better part of an hour, the forest grew even darker and more cold.

"Look! The Estees Mountains," exclaimed Blair.

"Yes," said the lead man. "There is a cave not far from here."

The group skirted the base of the mountain until it leveled off enough to ascend. Climbing the first few paces, they traversed the small distance until coming to the mouth of a cave. Entering, they found it remarkably shallow, and not even a real cave, for the top was exposed to the night sky, a thin patch of stars overhead.

There were red coals half buried in the sand at the far wall. The three Suriyans made for it and plopped down in the dirt, warming themselves.

"Thank the stars," said Blair.

The lead man watched them silently while his compatriot began adding kindling to the glowing

84

embers, unburying them from the sand with a stick..
After a few moments, the lead man spoke.

"I am Sheabor, and this is Straiah. Now tell me,
who are you, and why are you in this forest?"

"Believe me, if we could leave this forest we
would," said Blair.

The answer didn't seem to suffice the man for
his gaze grew stern.

"We're from Suriya," Durian answered, "just
east of here. We set out three days ago after an old
man. We thought he was a barbarian spy sent to gather
information about our town. Who were those warriors
you fought with?"

"The old man, what did he look like?" Sheabor
asked, disregarding Durian's question.

"A wanderer," said Baron. "Long beard, tanned
skin. Definitely not from around here."

"You didn't know him?"

"No," said Durian.

"Did he tell you where he was from or what he
was doing? What his name was? Anything?"

"No" replied Durian. "He was very secretive."

Sheabor looked gravely at Straiah.

"Malfur," muttered Straiah. "It must be."

"Who is Malfur?" Baron demanded, rising to
his feet. "Who are the soldiers who attacked us? What
in the world is happening?"

"Sit down," said Sheabor calmly and took a seat
himself by the fire.

Straiah unstrapped a nearby leather pouch and
returned with three rabbits in hand, skinning and
cooking them while the others spoke.

85

Sheabor gazed into the fire thoughtfully for a time. It was clear that he meant to offer an explanation, but seemed to be searching for the means to deliver it with brevity.

"What do you know of the old world?" he asked at length.

That was an odd question. The three Suriyans looked at one another in surprise. Baron and Blair nodded to Durian, who knew more of the lore and history of their world than either of them.

"Not much is known of the old world," said Durian. "Only that it was called the Prosperous Age of Man, and that it ended twelve centuries ago after a Great War that somehow changed everything. Legend says that during the Prosperous Age, there were three Houses of Men, each with a different ability. The House of Forthura were the Woodlanders who could manipulate wood with their hands as though clay, and breed new forms of trees with magical properties. The House of Kester were the Wise Men who could somehow breathe spirit temporarily into ordinary objects and call them to life. And the House of Cavanah were the Builders who could manipulate stone like clay, and create new forms with stronger properties, even magical ones. The House, Cavanah, disappeared at the end of the Prosperous Age, never to be seen again."

Sheabor seemed pleased at Durian's knowledge. Durian gained a measure of confidence and continued.

"It was said that the whole world was temperate and mild, that gentle rain often clothed the lands, and fruit and game were rich even in the harshest, wildest places. The world never knew famine or drought. There were forces at work which strictly governed the seasons."

"Not forces," interrupted Sheabor. "Men. They were called the Keepers of the Wind. They were wanderers of the lush world, each controlling his own wind and season. Aravas, Keeper of the East Wind and Spring. Faegean, Keeper of the West Wind and Summer. Pallin, Keeper of the South Wind and Fall. And Malfur, Keeper of the bitter North Wind and Winter, whom the three of you have been following."

The Suriyans gazed at Sheabor in disbelief. Could that really be possible? Durian had read stories about mythical beings called the Keepers of the Wind. But they were supposed to be spirits that dwelt in the furthest places of north, south, east, and west.

Straiah handed each of the Suriyans a cooked rabbit, which they ate ravenously.

"Who are the soldiers you fought with?" asked Baron, mouth full of meat.

"They're called the Dungeon Core, personal guard to Corcoran, who rules the Banished Lands."

The mention of the Banished Lands struck Durian. He had read about a mystical realm ruled by an ancient evil, but he didn't know anything about it.

"What are the Banished Lands?" Baron asked.

"The Banished Lands are nothing more than a second continent, much like this one with forests, deserts, mountains and valleys. At the end of the last Great War, the continent split in two, sending the Banished Lands off and away to the west, seemingly never to return. The House, Cavanah, is trapped there, hiding from the rule of Corcoran."

Durian's heart was racing and he stood to face the back wall, lost in thought. At length, he turned round and opened his mouth. But there so many questions, he didn't know where to begin.

"If the Keepers of the Wind are real, what happened to them?"

"We don't know. They might have perished at the end of the Great War. Before the Great War, the world was once one landmass. There were no salty seas or harsh deserts. Fresh water abounded in streams, pools, and rivers. No one knows how it happened, but at the end of the last Great War, the Keepers of the Wind unleashed something terrible, some primal force so potent that it ripped the world in two and covered most of the lands in flood waters which became the salty oceans.

Your continent, the Eastern Realm, is only half of a once vibrant world. Did you ever wonder why your continent was called the Eastern Realm if there were no Western Realm somewhere else?"

Durian was speechless. His mind exploded with questions. He thought of his dream and of the poem, written by the last king of Cavanah, King Euthor, which described the downfall of the Prosperous Age:

> *Of gladful things, now nevermore;*
> *Now bitter wind, now salty shore.*
> *The peaceful world bound to unrest*
> *And darkness looming in the west.*

Durian paced back and forth in the small cave. At many intervals, Durian turned to the group to speak, but the words wouldn't form.

"What is it?" asked Sheabor.

"I don't know. It just can't be a coincidence."

"What?"

"Three months ago when the strange things started in Thob Forest, I had a vivid dream of a woman lying slain in a field. A rider approaches and carries her away beyond the sunset. I didn't recognize either of them but the dream felt somehow familiar. I had the same dream again just days ago, right before we set off for Thob Forest. The dream seems to be linked to an old poem that was written by the last king of Cavanah. I didn't know it until tonight, but the poem describes the same events you've been telling us about."

Sheabor stared at Durian gravely, so much so that it made him uncomfortable. But Sheabor arose and unstrapped his leather pack, revealing a war hammer. The head of the hammer was made of a dark, translucent stone, and as he removed it, to their surprise, the ornately decorated wooden handle was glowing with a golden gleam. The glow emanated through the translucent stone, giving it a faint inner light. Durian's eyes grew wide with realization.

"That's Candlewood!" he exclaimed.

Sheabor nodded and handed him the hammer slowly. Durian took it and examined it. It was lighter than he expected. One end of the hammer head was flat, while the other came to a sharp point. It looked as though constructed yesterday, completely free of wear or damage. Flipping the hammer over, Durian was surprised to see writing inscribed onto the reverse side. The writing was gently illumined by the gleam from the hammer's inner core. It was absolutely beautiful. As he read, he could scarcely believe his eyes:

*Dismissing hours as they pass*
*Soft upon the windswept grass.*
*The hopes of men have come to naught.*
*Nothing fair for eyes or thought.*

*For Sheyla lies on golden plain,*
*Of Cavanah, the fairest slain;*
*Who met her last and final day*
*When all was brought to disarray.*

*Of gladful things now nevermore –*
*Now bitter wind, now salty shore.*
*The peaceful world bound to unrest*
*And darkness looming in the west.*

*The world and all its light shall fade.*
*I'll stay with her beneath the shade*
*And wait until the world's remade...*

Durian's heart beat wildly as he held the mystical weapon in his hand. He looked up to Sheabor whose troubled countenance showed that he also was mystified as to what it all could mean. Was the hammer somehow calling out to him? Was it responsible for Durian's dreams? Could such a thing be possible? At length, Durian handed the hammer to

Baron and Blair, whose eyes went equally wide as they read the poem and saw its obvious connection. Durian raised his eyes to Sheabor, mouth open but the words didn't flow.

"It is called the Hammer of Haladrin," Sheabor said. "It was made by the hand of King Euthor himself, over twelve centuries ago. It is the heirloom of his family. The head is formed of Shade Stone: harder than diamond and unyielding against anything it strikes – indestructible by ordinary means. Shade Stone was the invention of King Euthor himself, and he alone of the Builders was able to form it."

"Are you a descendant of King Euthor?"

Sheabor nodded. Durian opened his mouth to ask another question, but Sheabor held up his hand.

"There isn't time for more questions. For now, you must tell us exactly what Malfur was doing in your town and where he is now."

"We don't know really," said Blair, handing Sheabor back the hammer. "We think he was taking the abandoned trail to one of the southward peaks of the Estees Mountains. There's a cleft overlooking the Bay of Boreol and the Frostlands beyond."

Sheabor glanced at Straiah.

"That's close by. Are you sure that's where he was headed?"

"We think so," said Durian. "But we lost him more than a day ago."

"Where were you when you lost his trail?"

"Many miles east of here," replied Durian. "Our course mistakenly turned southwest. We meant to head east out of the forest but lost our way."

"Then it stands to reason that Malfur is still not far ahead."

Sheabor stared into the fire and pondered.

"What is it?" asked Durian.

"Malfur and the Dungeon Core are building a fort against the northern face of these mountains. They plan to lay siege to your realm. More than likely, Malfur was heading back there. But if there's a chance he's traveling elsewhere, alone and unguarded, we must take the opportunity. It's odd that he would travel to the southward side facing the coast. You're sure he was alone?"

"He was alone."

"If we could bring you close by, could you find your way to the mountain cleft?"

The three looked at one another and then nodded in affirmation.

"What about Suriya?" Blair demanded. "They must be warned."

"They will be," Sheabor assured. "Rest for the night."

"There's something else," said Durian. "Malfur may know we're here."

"Are you sure?"

"Not completely," said Durian. "He concealed his campsite at the edge of Thob Forest. He may have just been using caution. We're not sure."

Sheabor nodded slowly.

"We'll know soon enough. Rest now. We leave at first light."

Durian laid down to rest, but his mind was bursting. The poem of King Euthor and the mystical hammer claimed his attention. The stone of the hammer head was called Shade Stone, Sheabor had said. Durian had heard stories that in the palace hall of Eulsiphion, there stood a statue of King Euthor. And in his outstretched hand there lay an orb of darkened stone that was said to be unbreakable. Was it made of the same stone as Sheabor's hammer? Durian was desperate to question him further, but Sheabor had already exited the cave, keeping watch. At length, Durian succumbed to exhaustion and drifted slowly off to sleep.

# The Mountain Cleft

Durian awoke to a nudge on his shoulder, with Sheabor crouching beside him. The warm aroma of cooked meat filled the air.

"Make yourself ready. We leave immediately."

Durian sat up and rubbed his eyes, his head throbbing in protest with the meager amount of sleep he'd gotten. Straiah handed him a piece of rabbit meat and berries. There was little to pack, and the group set off into a forest still overshadowed by starlight.

"So much for first light," said Baron, yawning.

Straiah chuckled.

"We always leave before the mist gathers, to get our bearings," he said. "The fog comes down from the northwest at dawn."

"Why is that?" asked Blair.

"The Dungeon Core are using the Omri stones to blanket the forest with fog, obscuring their comings and goings. The mist spreads out like a thick blanket over the southern end of the forest."

"What's an Omri stone?" asked Baron.

"We make for the southern edge of the Estees Mountains," said Sheabor, disregarding Baron's question. "From there, you will be our guide."

Sheabor descended the mountainside. Baron smirked and followed behind with the rest in tow. Soon they reached the forest floor, Straiah disappearing ahead to scout. They walked at a swift pace in silence before Sheabor finally spoke.

"Long ago, the Omri stones were a gift to the Lords of Forthura from the Lords of Cavanah. When the Builders had grown in skill at creating different forms of stone, they crafted a special type of stone for the forests of Forthura. The Omri stones were very porous and contained a property that caused them to draw in large amounts of liquid. Being dark, they warmed rapidly in the light of the sun. Placing them in open spaces in the forest, those of Forthura would pour water and fragrant perfumes onto them. The waters would rise into the air of the forest, and then, in the cool of each morning, a fragrant mist would gather. The woodlands of Forthura were once filled with such stones. That is why you detect the faint aroma of perfume in the mist – a visage of faded beauty; a relic from a forgotten time."

Even as he spoke, the mist crept in around them. It was even more ominous now, knowing that an evil force was using the fog to conceal their workings. The rock of the Estees mountain range was blueish-gray of color, jagged and sharp. Shards of rock were strewn across the forest, fallen from some distant height and shattering on the forest floor. All of a sudden, an arrow struck the face of a tree just in front of them, startling the three Suriyans.

"Get down," Sheabor whispered.

"What is it?"

"Straiah is warning us that danger is close."

Sheabor peered round through the mist, watching and listening. He slowly withdrew his sword from his sheath. The three looked around them. There was nowhere to hide.

"Do not move an inch," said Sheabor.

The three huddled close in fright, hearts pounding in fear of the unknown. Sheabor crept forward and stood with his back against a nearby tree. The sound of clanging armor filled their hearing. Then they saw forms in the mist, about a dozen warriors. Sheabor's eyes were closed as he waited for the right moment.

As the warriors passed him by, Sheabor swung with his sword and hit the man closest to him in the chest, dropping him to the forest floor. Just then, an arrow pierced the chest of another of the warriors. By the time they stopped and drew their own swords, Sheabor had already killed another. And then came the second arrow. Sheabor advanced against a group of three men to his right. The group to his left came up behind him. Another arrow found its mark as Sheabor parried and then struck down a sixth warrior.

The warriors advanced against Sheabor, blows coming from multiple directions. He narrowly parried them, falling back. But as the warriors advanced against him, another two arrows found their targets, leaving only four facing off with Sheabor. But even with such odds, the remaining soldiers turned and fled. With Straiah somewhere out in the darkness, the warriors knew they couldn't win. Sheabor let them go.

The three Suriyans arose from their hiding spots and wandered the battlefield in a state of shock. None of them had ever been to war or seen its aftermath. Though they had witnessed a brief battle the night before, they had been so apprehensive of Sheabor and Straiah that they hadn't paid attention to anything else.

"Quickly, we must be moving," commanded Sheabor.

"What about Straiah?" asked Blair.

Sheabor smiled at Blair's concern. Straiah hadn't reappeared. But Sheabor set off at a faster pace than before. The fleeing warriors would soon be reporting in. The group raced along the forest floor, skirting the mountain looming overhead.

"How much farther?" Sheabor asked.

The three Suriyans looked at each other, not knowing how to respond.

"We don't know exactly where it is," said Durian. "None of us have traveled it. Suriyans stopped using it more than five years ago."

"How did you find it initially?" Sheabor asked.

"An outcropping of boulders at the edge of the forest marked the trail head. It was hard to follow. The forest has nearly grown over it."

"Straiah!" Sheabor called out muffled into the fog. In another few moments, Straiah arrived.

"We need to find a pathway not used for some years. Scan the forest south of here."

Straiah nodded and jogged off. Sheabor went in the opposite direction, crouching low and scanning the forest for signs of an abandoned pathway. The three stood silently waiting.

"Sheabor," they heard called out from the mist.

The three moved off toward the voice, and Sheabor came up behind them.

"Straiah," Sheabor called out.

Durian marveled how the two men could send a hushed whisper across a great distance and how they moved quickly and stealthily though the forest. When the group reached Straiah, he motioned to his left, where the faint groove of a trail snaked through the woods.

"That's it!" said Baron. "That's what it looked like on the other side of the forest."

Taking the trail toward the mountain, they found the route upward. The first bit of the journey was more climbing than walking, but after that the pathway leveled off. Sheabor drew his sword and led them with caution.

All of a sudden, the scene brightened and Durian felt the warmth of the sun on his back. Turning round with the others, they saw a sea of mist stretching out before them, with scattered treetops poking through. They watched it for only a moment and set off again.

Durian thought of his brief encounter with the old man. Something still wasn't adding up. Though he was mysterious and secretive, he didn't seem evil. Could he really be the leader of an impending invasion? And did they really hope to find him here?

They ascended over a hundred paces above the forest floor. At length, the pathway flattened and the deep blue of Boreol Bay appeared in view. They had found the mountain cleft.

The ledge was wide and broad, and remarkably level. At least fifty paces long and jutting out over the airy distance, it provided a beautiful view of the coastline and the vague form of the Frostlands beyond. Out on the very edge sat a large stone, roughly the same height as Durian, a mound of dark rock that seemed out of place. The rock was of a different color and texture to anything surrounding it, clashing starkly with the smooth grayish-blue of the mountain. The mysterious stone was streaked with silver and gold running diagonally up from its base to the tip. Sheabor and Straiah came to it immediately.

"This is an Athel stone!"

"What's an Athel stone?" asked Baron.

"If one has the skill, they can use it to see great distances. The golden streaks harness sunlight and the silver streaks, moonlight. These stones were built by one of the men of Cavanah in the last age. No man now knows how to use it. But a Keeper of the Wind would. This must have been what Malfur was after."

"There's one of these in the palace hall of Eulsiphion," Durian declared. "But no one's ever known it had magical powers."

"Eulsiphion," said Straiah, alarmed and dumbfounded, turning to Sheabor. "The city still stands?"

"Yes," said Durian. "It's the capital city of our kingdom."

Durian had forgotten that Eulsiphion was a city built in the First Age, that the kingdom which now inhabited it wasn't its architect. Just then, pebbles rolled down the face of the mountain in the corner behind them. The group spun round. There was a form, barely perceptible in the shadows.

"You there," said Sheabor. "Reveal yourself."

An old man emerged slowly. They had found him at last!

"That's him!" Baron announced.

Silence followed as Sheabor studied him. The faint howl of the wind slid through the lonely corridors of the mountain. The old man eyed them narrowly, no one yet voicing his thoughts.

"This is not Malfur," Sheabor said.

"What?" exclaimed Baron.

The old man's eyes grew wide at the mention of the name.

"What do you know of Malfur?" the old man inquired with a step forward.

"Who are you, old man?" Sheabor demanded. "And what are you doing in Thob Forest?"

"Please, if you know of the whereabouts of Malfur, you must tell me!"

"His whereabouts?" Sheabor said, taking a step forward himself. "His whereabouts are in Thob Forest, where he and the cursed Dungeon Core are building a fortress from whence to make war against this Eastern Realm."

"Dungeon Core?" asked the old man. "He is a prisoner then?"

"Prisoner?" Sheabor exclaimed. "He is their leader."

"No, I don't believe you," said the old man and turned around away from them, facing southward toward the distant coast and the Frostlands, far beyond.

"Who are you, old man?" demanded Straiah.

The old man remained motionless for many moments, a pained expression on his face, his chest heaving as he drew in long breaths of air. At length, he straightened his posture and took a final deep breath, turning round to face them.

100

"I am of the Four," he declared. "I am Pallin, Keeper of the South Wind. As for my presence here in this forest, I am searching for that same Malfur whom you now seek, one whom I have always known as friend and brother, whom you now declare is my enemy."

Sheabor gripped the hilt of his sword and clenched his jaw.

"You are in league with him then?"

The question seemed to strike the old man and he grew thoughtful.

"No," he responded gently. "No, I am not."

"Then why are you here?"

The old man sighed and looked pensively at them.

"I feared that Malfur was in distress," he said warmly. "I have not seen him in over twelve hundred years. We had thought him dead, Aravas, Faegean and I. For an age, I have wandered this world, watching it darken and diminish from its former splendor, the harsh chill of winter and scorching drought of summer driving men from all the lovely places they once treasured. But then, after centuries, I felt the presence of something I almost couldn't believe. I felt the subtle power of the north wind on the breeze; the power of Malfur.

I was in Eulsiphion at the time. I felt the north wind waft up with the nightly breeze from the southern peninsula of Forthura. I quickly traveled there, not knowing what to expect. I came as far south as Suriya, to the edge of the known world, only to find that the power of Malfur was coming from somewhere even

101

further south, from the Frostlands at the edge of the world. But then, as quickly as it had come, it was gone again. I felt nothing more.

I feared the worst, that he was in danger or lay helpless somewhere, captive to an evil will. So I set off from Suriya toward these Estees Mountains, where this Athel stone lay, showing a clear view of the Frostlands beyond. But I saw nothing more than ice and snow. I feared to leave this mountain cleft, not knowing what strange force was inhabiting the forest."

"You cannot be one of the Keepers," broke in Straiah. "The Three died at the end of the Great War. If Pallin, Aravas and Faegean still dwelt here, this Eastern Realm would be a lush and beautiful paradise."

The man looked pained as Straiah spoke the words.

"In a way we did die," he replied. "In a way I wish we had died."

His words and his tone carried a brokenness that struck the five listeners. But his expression darkened and he looked up at them angrily.

"Believe me," he said. "If we had known what darkness would creep into the world in these latter days, we would never have made our foolish choice. We had no concept of drought then, of famine or widespread deserts. We had thought the world would go on much as it had always done, once the Three were gone. We were very wrong."

"What are you talking about?" asked Sheabor.

"We only wanted to keep the forces of Corcoran at bay! Wanted to show them it was foolish to advance any further against the peoples of the peaceful lands!"

The man seemed almost frenzied as he spoke.

"At the end of the Great War, nearly twelve centuries ago, Corcoran was marching onward, conquering city and village and town. Nothing could stand in his way. Nothing! The world of men was nearing its final hour. The Four came together high atop a mountain to watch and to wait. The House of Cavanah had gathered its remaining forces to oppose the armies of Corcoran. But they were too few.

So the Four loosed their combined powers onto the plains between the two forces, and loosed a cyclone right into the midst of the battlefield. Man and beast fled in terror. For no power on the face of the world can withstand the strength of the four winds. As the two armies fled, we congratulated ourselves on a great victory and waited for the cyclone to dissipate. Our warning had shown the enemy that his conquest would not be permitted.

But as we watched on, the cyclone continued to swell. Once it had taken form, it seemed to take on life as well. It ripped through the plains, splitting tree, rock, and earth. It was all we could do just to hold it in place. If we hadn't, it would have torn the whole world apart.

No one knows how deep it dug. The Four summoned winds from every corner of the world in a vain attempt to contain it. But then it happened. With a snap, something broke within the deeps of the world. An earthquake followed. The world was rent in two. And as the earth shook, waters flowed out from the deeps – bitter, salty waters that now surround every land. What the earthquake did not destroy, the flood consumed. Almost nothing of that time now remains.

The mountain on which the Four stood was toppled from its place. We were separated. When we came together again, we found that we were only three. Malfur was gone. Fearing him dead, or else forever trapped beneath the rubble of a shattered mountain, and seeing the utter destruction we had loosed, we vowed to banish our powers forever.

With the aid of King Euthor, we gave up our powers, locking them into an orb of Shade Stone, never to be freed again. That is why this Eastern Realm has not felt the power of the Keepers of the Wind the whole of this last age. That is the choice that I have come to bitterly regret.

I had no concept then, how the long years would draw out before me – that I would wander this world as one cursed, useless and purposeless. The world I once clothed in plenty now lies waste, diminishing into dust and decay, and I left to wander it as a spectre, I too reduced to shadow and dust."

Pallin leaned against the nearby rock wall, unable to continue. Durian felt pity for him.

"Why have you not tried to reclaim your powers?" Sheabor asked.

Pallin shook his head.

"They are lost beyond recovery."

"I do not believe that," Sheabor said. "Nothing is ever lost beyond recovery."

Pallin clenched his jaw but didn't respond. Sheabor glanced to Straiah, wearing a very troubled look. Their own situation had grown far worse. Pallin and the other Keepers of the Wind had ended the Prosperous Age of Man. The Three had given up their powers, thinking their brother Malfur was dead. And now it seemed, only Malfur remained with the power of the wind at his command. Things had just become very dire for the Eastern Realm.

# The Swamplands

"Sheabor, we should leave this place," Straiah said. "We must not linger."

"And where will you go?" said Pallin, regaining his composure. "If it is as you say...if Malfur has a will of evil...if forces have returned from the Banished Lands and the three remaining Windbearers are now powerless to oppose them...then all is lost."

"We are going to Eulsiphion," Sheabor declared. "We will gather the strength of the Eastern Realm and stand against this coming darkness. Stay here if you wish. Or continue your aimless wandering. But if you choose to come with us, we will help you reclaim your powers."

Pallin clenched his jaw and gazed at Sheabor. Sheabor sheathed his sword as he met Pallin's gaze, and after another moment headed off without a word, leaving Pallin behind. The others reluctantly followed behind. Durian kept glancing back to see if Pallin would follow them, but he saw nothing.

"We can't just leave him!" Durian exclaimed.

Sheabor didn't answer. Durian stopped and spun round to Straiah.

"We have no choice," said Straiah. "Pallin must decide for himself. Come on."

Straiah grabbed Durian, pushing him onward down the pathway. How could they just leave Pallin behind? But there was nothing Durian could do. He was surprised by their harshness towards Pallin.

106

But then it dawned on him. Sheabor and Straiah must have been counting on Pallin and the other Windbearers as powerful allies in their fight against Malfur and Corcoran. To find the remaining Windbearers powerless was a crushing blow.

The group moved quickly along the pathway, descending the winding mountain face to the forest floor. Straiah headed up the rear and when they were assembled, Sheabor set off without a word.

"Wait," pleaded Durian. "What if he changed his mind?"

Even as he said the words, the form of Pallin came into view. He moved with remarkable speed down the mountain path and joined them on the ground.

"I am sorry for my behavior earlier," Pallin said in a strained tone. "I wish to aid you if I can. I will accompany you to Eulsiphion and guide you along safe pathways through Thob Forest."

"Very well," said Sheabor. "What do you advise?"

"If Malfur is as you say, on the eastern side of this mountain range, we ought to avoid him altogether. If we head north from here, we may yet pass him undetected. But this will take us deep into the heart of Thob Forest, into the marshlands where evils more sinister than Dungeon Core lurk."

"Lead the way," Sheabor commanded.

The group jogged along the base of the Estees Mountains, through the thin strip of forest between the mountains and the sea. But they quickly left the sea behind as the mountains turned inward.

Midday had come and gone before the group left the shadow of the mountains. But once free and on the other side, the air changed, drawing in thick and warm around them and the mist cleared. They were approaching the inner swamplands of Thob Forest.

"I think we are well away from danger," Pallin said, stopping at a fallen log for rest.

The three Suriyans were overjoyed.

"The thought of Tobin's plow doesn't seem so bad anymore, I bet," said Durian.

Baron let out a laugh, but Pallin shot a gaze of disapproval the disturbance. Sheabor smiled and turned to Pallin while Straiah produced dried meats from a pouch, handing them to all his companions.

"Pallin, you said initially that you felt the power of Malfur from Eulsiphion. But then when you arrived at Suriya, it was gone."

"Yes, I have pondered that notion myself. The only explanation is that Malfur must have been using his powers to travel from the Banished Lands to the Frostlands. Once arriving at the Eastern Realm, he must have stopped using his powers, hoping to avoid detection by the Three."

"Then he has no idea that you and the other Windbearers gave up your powers?"

"No, but he must suspect something," Pallin replied.

"Where are your powers exactly?" Sheabor questioned.

Pallin shook his head. He didn't know. But Durian spoke up.

"You said that King Euthor locked your powers up inside an orb of Shade Stone. There's an orb of Shade Stone in Eulsiphion, in the hand of the statue of King Euthor."

Sheabor shot an excited glance to Pallin.

"So when we reach Eulsiphion, we'll use the hammer to unlock your powers."

But Pallin's brow furrowed and he grew thoughtful.

"I do not believe that orb contains our powers," Pallin said. "King Euthor made the Three one promise only – that he would take our powers with him to his grave and that no one would ever find them. I do not believe he would put them on display for all to see, especially with the knowledge that the Hammer of Haladrin was somewhere out in the wide world."

"Then what's inside the orb?" Durian asked.

"None knows for certain. Legend says that the wedding rings of Euthor and Sheyla are in the orb, along with her Seer's necklace that she would use to find him when he was away from the castle. Tokens of the love they shared."

The Seer's necklace intrigued Durian but Sheabor spoke before he could inquire.

"Pallin, where are the other Windbearers?"

"Faegean is with the giants in the northwest, and Aravas is in Melanor."

"Melanor?"

"The lost city of Kester, the Wise Men," Pallin responded. "It lies due east of Eulsiphion in a sheltered cove, hidden from sight. There is a pathway through the Squall Highlands. But none can find it except they

109

who know the way. Melanor alone, of any, still possess their abilities from the Prosperous Age."

"They can still call objects to life?" exclaimed Durian.

Pallin smiled.

"Yes, though that is a rather brutish way of putting it. And not all of them possess the ability. It is a shadow only of what it once was."

At length, Pallin arose and the group set off, walking till late afternoon, when the ground grew spongy and soft. The air carried the tinge of murky water, and though the mist had long departed, in its place, a warm and foul haze hung about their feet.

"Pallin, we should stop for the night," Sheabor said. "Trudging through swampland is arduous work."

Pallin nodded and walked until a suitable spot was found. Straiah disappeared almost immediately, returning after dark with a string of fish on a pole. Durian marveled at his skill as a woodsman. More than a little exhausted, as soon as the three Suriyans had eaten, they fell fast asleep by the fire.

They were tapped awake and arose, rubbing their eyes into focus. The glow of dawn was just entering the forest.

"We will reach the dry side of Aridatha by midday," Pallin declared, "largest of the swampland lakes."

The ground was wet and marshy, turning to mud by late morning. They journeyed on with difficulty, all the while Pallin declaring the lake was only a short way off. But by midday, the mud gave way to higher ground. A large lake lay to their right, sparkling deep blue in the full light of day.

"That is Lake Aridatha," said Pallin. "We should rest here."

Durian had never been to a lake before. The cool and crisp waters looked so inviting. He looked to Pallin eagerly, who smiled and nodded, extending his hand toward the lake. Straiah set off again in search of food, and the rest ventured toward the lake, taking a dip in the cool blue and washing the filth from their clothes and skin. Durian couldn't remember ever having been so dirty. When they returned, Straiah was waiting with a string full of fish. But they set off without cooking them. At length, they came round the large lake, descending back to the marshes until evening, when they finally left the swamps behind.

"We should stop here," Pallin said. "We must not venture too near Lake Enlath today."

"Why not?" questioned Blair.

"For that is where Arathama lives," Pallin responded. "Beast of the murky waters of Thob Forest."

"A monster?" questioned Straiah.

Pallin nodded his head.

"Straiah and I have met the likes of many beasts in service to Corcoran," said Sheabor.

"I can lead us along reasonably shallow pathways," Pallin said. "Perhaps, with my guidance, we may yet avoid Arathama altogether."

Darkness descended on the forest. And though the evening came, a heat hung around them like a damp cloth. The moon was low in the west, its light filtering strongly through the trees. And the smell of cooked fish filled the air.

Straiah handed Durian a roasted fish on a stick, and he wandered over to Baron and Blair, who sat nearby on a log, each with their own fish. Durian wasn't partial to fish any more than the twins, but being the only meat he could afford, he had accustomed himself to the flavor.

"These freshwater fish aren't bad," Durian said.

Baron shrugged his shoulders and Durian chuckled.

"Blair's spoiled you rotten with venison stew! Now you get to see the lot we lesser folk get to live with."

Baron smirked, but the mention of home made the three Suriyans pensive. Durian arose, walking the edge of their campsite, staring into the darkness while slowly eating, wondering just how far this adventure would lead them and how long it would be till Suriya was warned. A distant howl sprang out of the deeps and the crack of a nearby twig. He was struck by how much bigger and mysterious the world felt.

A hand came down on Durian's shoulder, startling him.

"We're off to bed," said Blair.

Durian nodded. Coming near the fire, they laid down on some leafy bedding and fell to sleep. But Durian awoke before long to the crackle of the fire. Pallin and Sheabor were sitting on the other side and having a conversation.

Durian joined them and listened. Sheabor was asking Pallin questions about King Froamb, who ruled their kingdom from Eulsiphion. But a question arose in Durian's mind, and he waited for a good time to pose it.

"Pallin, I'm confused," said Durian. "I heard you say that Corcoran marched against the peaceful peoples of the land twelve hundred years ago. But Sheabor said they live in hiding from Corcoran on the Banished Lands. How can Corcoran still be alive?"

"I would not believe it possible myself but for the assurances of Sheabor that it is so."

"Pallin, first tell what you know of Corcoran," Sheabor said.

"He was not always called Corcoran. His real name was Madrigan, which means 'Path-Maker.' His father was of the House of Cavanah and his mother from the House, Forthura, a union seldom seen in those days. As a young man, Madrigan set off to explore the many beauties and treasures of the lush world.

But as he traveled the world, his strange ability began to grow. With his mixed heritage, he had abilities of both the Builders and the Woodlanders. Because of his Woodlander blood, his feet were drawn to all the world's fair places. But because of his Builder's blood, he brought order to the wild.

It was said that wherever he went abroad in the open world, the grasses and rocks receded and a path of simple dirt spread out before him. Many loved to wander the pathways created by Madrigan's travels, for they always led to fair and undiscovered places of the world. It seemed as though his feet were called to all the hidden wonders yet unseen by human eyes. It was he who discovered the majestic Caves of Clinthia that ran beneath the old city of Illdegron.

113

His ability grew in time, and sometimes, instead of a dirt pathway, his feet would leave behind something similar to a small cobblestone road. But as time went on, Madrigan began to speak of a mystical land, which he called Eskédrin:

*A vision I see often in my dreams, of a land in the west, fairer than any my waking eyes have perceived. How my feet long to forge a trail to this blessed realm. But must I go alone?*

It was then that many from the Three Houses began to follow Madrigan, that they too might share in the wonders of Eskédrin. There were many in those days without a place to call home. It was easy for Madrigan to gain a following. Then one day, suddenly, Madrigan and his followers left without a trace. There was no pathway left behind by the feet of Madrigan.

Long years passed, until the wanderers were all but forgotten. But then, one fateful day, they returned to the peaceful realm, though not as they had left. Before them Madrigan still walked, but in his wake was a pathway not of cobblestone and dirt, but one of molten stone and fire. His power had grown dark and terrible, as had those who had followed him into the wilds. It was then that he gained the name Corcoran, which in the ancient tongue means, 'World-Splitter.'"

Durian was awe struck by such a grand tale. But Pallin was gazing at Sheabor for his explanation.

"Corcoran is not alive as you and I are alive," Sheabor began. "Our people have seen him only a small handful of times through the centuries, an

114

elemental form of molten stone and fire. When the world first split in two, the Banished Lands was moving westward, the oceans between the two realms growing. Corcoran realized this. He disappeared not long after the Great War ended. Our forefathers were convinced he perished.

But Corcoran had delved deep underground. Some say to the very foundations of the Banished Lands. His body perished, but his spirit was tied to the continent. None knows how he did it, but slowly, he was able to alter the course of the Banished Land's drift from west, to southwest, to south, to southeast, and finally east."

Sheabor unsheathed his sword and drew on the ground.

"This is an approximation," he said, while drawing. "Undoubtedly the shapes are wrong, but you'll see the idea. The X is where we currently stand."

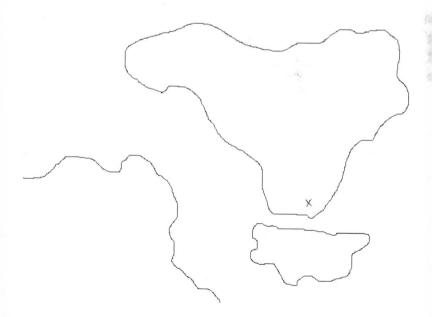

"He's moving the entire continent?" Durian asked. "How is that possible?"

"None knows," Sheabor replied. "But Corcoran's power has always been tied to the earth. From his earliest youth he had power to subdue and control the natural world around him. None knows how much his power has grown these past centuries."

"If he is a creature of molten stone, how do you kill something like that?" Durian asked.

The question hung in the air.

"Defeating Malfur first will surely weaken his plans," Sheabor encouraged.

"And how do you propose we do that?" questioned Pallin.

"We'll have to march against his fortress in Thob Forest."

Pallin clenched his jaw.

"Sheabor, that will not be an easy task. The king of Eulsiphion will not be quick to believe you. There is a reason those lands were called banished. If something had returned from there, it should not have happened in secret."

Sheabor eyed him inquisitively.

"At the end of the Great War, the Bearoc, the giants of the north made a vow that nothing would ever return from the Banished Lands. They built great watchtowers from which they vigilantly watch the west."

The giants were something Durian had only heard of in myth and legend. Their lands were fabled to exist far to the north, beyond the realm of the Horctura and Kester, locked away behind tall mountain ranges and walls of stone. They were referred to as the Bearoc in the ancient tongue.

"Sheabor, how did you and Straiah reach the Eastern Realm?" asked Pallin.

"The Banished Lands are now only a hundred leagues southwest of your shores. When the continent had come close enough, Malfur set off with a large detachment of Dungeon Core. He froze the waters before them, creating a narrow pathway. We set out a day behind them, Straiah, I and one other. The pathway was already beginning to fracture beneath our feet. We lost the other, and almost lost ourselves. After weeks of travel, we arrived at a bitter frozen land of wind, ice, and snow."

"The Frostlands," said Pallin. "That is why I felt his power there. You must have been southward enough to escape the Bearoc's detection. That is an unhappy accident."

Durian yawned as drowsiness again took hold.

"You only slept an hour," commented Sheabor. "Tomorrow will be a difficult journey. You ought to get your rest."

Durian nodded and arose, walking to the other side of the fire. He laid his head down to rest and was soon asleep.

He was the last to awaken. As he stood to his feet, Pallin was already laying out the day's course.

"The upper swamplands of Thob Forest consist of four large waterways," Pallin began. "In the middle is a small patch of dry ground, upon which we now sit. We have come by the southernmost lake, Aridatha. Three waterways still lay ahead, as does Arathama. His lair is in Lake Enlath, where a strange magic is at work. So be on your guard."

After a quick breakfast, they moved off, heading north. They moved quickly until midday, when Pallin cautioned that Lake Enlath was near. Straiah disappeared ahead, searching for any signs of the creature, Arathama.

After midday, a change came over the forest. It was darker here, and colder, the trees themselves stretching higher, as if malevolently blocking what little sunlight could reach the forest floor. Durian could see something gleaming in the distance. It made his heart beat faster.

They caught sight of a lake, smaller by far than Aridatha, but bordered entirely by boulders, making the water exceptionally clear. The gleam coming from the lake seemed elusive and other-worldly – one moment there, and the next moment gone.

They walked near the southern edge of the lake. A small outlet trickled into a disconnected pool of water, which they passed close by. But Durian noticed a quick flash of bright color to his left. Curious, he lagged behind and walked around the small pool. Another flash of golden blue erupted from the middle of the pool, quickly dissolving.

Standing there, Durian saw a fish gently flapping its tail as it wandered the confines of the shallow pool. Each motion of its fin erupted an array of color. Pallin and the others came up beside Durian.

"The magic of Arathama," Pallin declared. "He is near."

"It's incredible," said Durian.

"Yes it is," said Pallin. "Arathama is a creature from the old world. He and his kind once lived abroad amongst the lakes and pools of the forests, clothing them with vibrant beauty. But now that darkness has come to our world, Arathama uses his power to stalk his prey. He is the last of his kind. He sees every motion of every creature in Enlath. Even vibrations along the shore can send out waves of color into the waters. We must be very cautious now."

Durian walked very slowly, transfixed on the beautiful, clear lake. The blueish golden gleam was subtle and ever-changing, as though the lake itself were alive. Durian stepped closer, but felt a hand quickly come down upon his shoulder.

"Go no further," Pallin commanded.

Durian nodded and fell into line with the rest of the group. The landscape around the lake grew steep, forcing them nearer to shore. Pallin crept atop the bouldered edge.

There was a stream ahead, wide but gently flowing out of the lake. Pallin came to its edge and scanned their surroundings for a dry crossing. At length, Pallin stepped gently into the crystal stream. As his foot touched the water, streaks of azure and gold surrounded his foot and streaked out in all directions, even creeping against the current toward the lake. But the color weakened and faded before reaching the lake.

"Be very careful," cautioned Pallin and continued on.

Durian followed behind, wrapped up in fascination at the color around their feet. The color emanating from each person was slightly different, and every step he took mesmerized him and filled him with wonder. How could a creature that used such beauty seek to cause them harm, Durian wondered?

Durian's toe suddenly struck the back of Pallin's foot. Horrified, Durian stumbled forward, nearly knocking Pallin down. The rest froze. The violent crashing of his feet filled the stream with color.

Time seemed to halt as the color streaked against the current toward the lake. Bright wisps of color slithered forward, tendrils desperately reaching outward. Just before fading, one of the wisps of color made contact, and as it did, a roar erupted from Enlath's furthest side.

"Run!"

# The Edgewhic Isles

"Pallin! Take them out of here!" Sheabor
shouted, and then broke company, sprinting back in the
direction they had come.

"Sheabor!" Pallin called out. But he could not
stop him.

"Run!" Sheabor called back again.

Straiah came behind Baron and Blair and
pushed them forward. Then he ran to meet Sheabor.
Pallin grabbed Durian and pulled him to the other side
of the stream. Once clear of it, the four scrambled up a
nearby hillside as far as they could and then waited.

Sheabor unsheathed his hammer instead of his
sword. He moved to the edge of a boulder overhanging
the lake and swung powerfully down with the hammer.
The sharp tip of Shade Stone made contact with the
stone, shattering it and sending large chunks into the
lake below. Another roar erupted, closer and louder
than before.

Sheabor rushed to the nearest small tree.
Striking the base, it splintered and fell to the waters.
The tree floated for a moment before being suddenly
wrenched below the surface. Durian saw a form
disappear beneath the waters where the tree had been.
The lake was now full of vibrant swirls of color – reds,
greens, and golden yellows.

"We must continue on," commanded Pallin.

The four descended the hillside and sprinted
along the edge, Sheabor continuing to menace the lake

shore. Straiah followed him at a distance, bow in hand with arrow drawn, waiting for the creature to reveal itself. But Arathama was nowhere to be seen.

"Sheabor!" Straiah called out as he loosed an arrow toward a huge form soaring through the air. Sheabor turned and rolled away right as two powerful fists pounded the ground he had just occupied. The creature let out another roar.

Arathama's form was terrible, resembling what could only be described as a frog-like gorilla, with large amphibious legs, and a powerful, muscular upper torso, covered with armored scales. His arms were long and his hands looked large enough to clutch Durian's entire body. Straiah immediately shot another arrow, which struck between his shoulder blades.

The arrow didn't seem to pierce, but the creature turned with a hateful roar toward Straiah. Arathama lunged at Straiah striking the tree Straiah stood behind, uprooting it, but not knocking it down completely. Straiah darted for another tree.

Sheabor sprang forward with a yell. Arathama turned and swung across Sheabor's chest, keeping him at bay. Straiah drew his sword and the two men faced off with the creature. But then, Arathama turned to see the other group sprinting along the shoreline behind him. With a mighty leap, he disappeared into the lake, only to reappear on the other side, flying through the air and landing only paces from Pallin and the others. The group dispersed in fright and terror.

Durian fled, but a large, powerful hand caught hold of him. Durian couldn't breathe. He couldn't even scream. Arathama jerked him through the air as he moved toward another victim.

Durian still couldn't breathe. His lungs were on fire. The cry of Sheabor rang out through the air, and he felt the creature swing round to face it. Arathama roared and clenched Durian even more tightly. Darkness took hold and sounds grew dull.

Sheabor and Straiah charged forward, yelling out. Arathama stayed his ground. As they neared, Arathama swung his arm toward them, missing Sheabor but knocking Straiah backward with a crash. Sheabor dashed forward and swung his hammer down on the hardened scales of Arathama's head. The creature's eyes grew wide and he dropped Durian.

Arathama staggered backward toward the lake. Sheabor raised his hammer yet again, and Arathama scrambled anxiously away to the waters. Soon he had disappeared into the glimmering lake and was gone again. The group rushed to Durian, who lay still on the ground.

"Durian!" Baron yelled, shaking him.

Durian winced in pain and opened his eyes. He blinked his eyes a few times and saw five forms standing over him. They helped him to his feet. Durian struggled to take in breaths. He leaned over and nearly fell, but Sheabor caught him.

"That thing almost made a meal out of you," Blair said.

Just then, the distant roar of Arathama erupted from the far side of Lake Enlath. Baron slapped Durian on the back, but Durian only winced and shuddered at the thought.

"We must leave here, now!" Straiah commanded. "If any Dungeon Core are nearby, they will have heard the battle."

"Pallin, lead the way."

The group set off, away from Lake Enlath. Durian pitied the Dungeon Core who might come that way in search of them. Back in the open woodlands, they set a quick pace the rest of the day and the next morning.

But then, Sheabor and Straiah grew cautious, which surprised Durian. Surely the Dungeon Core weren't still tracking them. They had come many leagues north. But Straiah bent down on multiple occasions, examining tracks.

"A group of Dungeon Core passed this way, heading north," said Straiah. "These tracks are fresh."

"They are searching for us," Pallin declared. "We will reach the forest edge by nightfall."

"I thought Thob Forest stretched northward the whole length of the kingdom?" Sheabor questioned. "Why would we leave it so soon?"

"It does," Pallin replied. "But soon the forest will veer west, leading away from Eulsiphion. And a second mountain range lies to the north, which would take days to go around. Our best chance is to leave the forest through cover of night. With luck, the Dungeon Core won't expect it and will lose our trail."

Sheabor nodded slowly, glancing to Straiah for his thoughts. But he had nothing to offer. The group jogged on, afternoon passing into evening. They had covered many leagues through the open forest when darkness finally took hold. At times, they could see a glow in the distance.

"Why are they using torches?" asked Baron. "It makes them easy to avoid."

"It's merely a decoy," said Straiah. "Only one in ten carries a torch. They're hoping to herd us the direction they want us to go."

"Pallin, we should rest," advised Sheabor. "If we're discovered on the open plain, we'll be forced to run a great distance."

"We are very near the edge of Thob Forest now," Pallin replied. "We can rest here."

The three Suriyans were exhausted from the day's walk, and gathered some bedding around the small fire Straiah was building. Though they tried to stay awake for the evening meal, they fell fast asleep.

Durian awoke to a tap on his shoulder and arose. It was still dark and Durian felt as though he had only barely slept.

"Pallin, how far to Eulsiphion?" Sheabor questioned.

"A week's journey, at least," he said.

"Pallin, that isn't going to work. We aren't going to escape undetected. Straiah and I have seen forms moving through the plains. They're trying to conceal themselves, but there are many Dungeon Core there."

Pallin grew thoughtful for a moment.

"There is a place not far from here called the Edgewhic Isles. There are tall spires of stone and many ravines and cliffs. The Isles end at a sheer wall called

125

Ridgewall, a narrow pathway leading up. If you could destroy the pathway after us, we may yet escape them."

The group departed eastward bound. Half an hour's walk brought them to the edge of the forest, and Durian was surprised it had been so close. Beyond were the plains, brightly bathed in moonlight.

"Sheabor, we ought to wait until the moon sets," Straiah advised.

"It will be near morning by then," he replied.

Sheabor and Straiah scanned the darkness. All was silent and still but for the gently flowing breeze swaying the tips of the low-lying grasses.

"Pallin, lead them onward," Sheabor commanded. "Do not look for us. We will be near."

And with that, Sheabor and Straiah burst forward into the open plains. Pallin set out after them at a quick pace, but not too quick, in case the time came when they truly had to flee for their lives. Durian felt incredibly exposed out in the open. Though it was night, the moon was bright enough to cast their shadows down in front of them.

They jogged until reaching a small hill, upon which Pallin laid down, peering outward on the wide plains. The three Suriyans did likewise, heaving deep breaths of air as they watched the night. Durian's mind might have been playing tricks on him, but he saw things moving in the darkness, though never once did he make out their forms.

"They haven't seen us yet," Pallin declared.

"Where are Sheabor and Straiah?"

"Keeping the soldiers off our trail."

And with that, Pallin arose and descended the hill, his pace a bit slower than before. Each moment they escaped detection made it more difficult for the Dungeon Core to find them. Durian suddenly heard the sound of boots on the earth behind him. He turned round in fright and almost yelled out, before seeing the form of Sheabor.

"Pallin, you must move more swiftly," Sheabor declared. "There are too many. And some travel by horseback. We need to be well away from them by morning."

Pallin picked up the pace and Sheabor ran off to the north. They jogged for hours, taking breaks only briefly. Durian's muscles burned with exhaustion. If the enemy discovered them, it would be hopeless to try and outrun them. But the moon finally set, leaving a sprawling sky full of stars.

The landscape began to change and slope upward, the grasses of the plains giving way to rocky ground. Pallin was forced to slow the pace.

"How far to the Edgewhic Isles?" Durian asked.

"We will arrive by morning."

Durian thought he heard the sound of battle in the distance behind them. But it was brief. Steep, rocky hills lay in the distance ahead, and looming spires of rock reaching up a stone's throw into the heavens.

"Those are the Isles," said Pallin. "It will be difficult for them to find us here."

Durian saw quickly what he meant. The rocky hills and spires were a maze of narrow corridors and side routes that quickly curved out of sight. And because the ground was rocky and hard, they left no tracks to follow. Durian didn't even know how Sheabor and Straiah would find them.

But they continued on, the glow of morning just beginning to fill the horizon. Their course led them through into a narrow ravine barely navigable between two tall rocky hills.

Durian again heard the distant sound of battle wafting down the corridor and a not so distant crash of stone. The group turned round, but saw nothing more than a plume of dust rising in the air. What was happening?

"Quickly now," said Pallin and hurried down the corridor.

The sound of battle intensified. It was just behind them now. All of a sudden, a soldier flew into the corridor from around the corner, crashing to the ground. Sheabor ran through just behind him, followed by Straiah and more soldiers.

Durian saw nothing more, for they curved out of view. But the battle continued in the narrow passage, Sheabor yelling for them to hurry their pace. Their course opened up into a wider basin, but narrowing again after only a few dozen paces.

Pallin raced to the far side. Sheabor and Straiah were just behind them. But as Sheabor reached the broader section, he swung his hammer into the stone on either side of the opening, piling fresh rock into the gap. It wouldn't stop them completely, but it would slow them down.

He kept at it, filling it more and more until the soldiers finally caught up with him. Then Sheabor raced after Pallin and the others, catching them quickly. The Candlewood of the hammer glowed in the darkness of their passageway, and the head of the hammer held a deep seated gleam.

"Pallin, how far to the Ridgewall?"

"It is moments away."

The passage finally emptied into a broad and flat basin a few hundred paces wide. High walls surrounded them on all sides. It looked impassible. Had Pallin made a mistake? But he ran for the far side of Ridgewall.

Before they reached it the Dungeon Core began pouring into the basin. Pallin's eyes darted along the wall ahead, searching for the pathway up. If it was there, Durian didn't see it. But Pallin found a handhold and pulled himself up the Ridgewall. Baron and Blair went next, followed by Durian.

Sheabor and Straiah lingered at the bottom of the wall. Straiah loosed an arrow and quickly set another. The first arrow missed its target but the second found its mark. Then he unsheathed his sword.

Pallin and the three Suriyans were making slow headway. This pathway wasn't much better than the one they used on the Estees Mountains. It was more of a climb than a walk. The soldiers reached Straiah and Sheabor.

Sheabor ducked the first man's blow, throwing him over his shoulder and slamming him into the wall. He lashed out at a second and was blocked, but leaped up upon the Ridgewall. Straiah ducked and parried a flurry of blows, striking the nearest soldier to him dead and then leaping upward to catch the outstretched arm of Sheabor, who pulled him onto the Ridgewall just as swords slashed beneath his feet.

Sheabor took up the rear, smashing as much as he could of the pathway behind him. The soldiers climbed and inched their way forward. After the initial ascent, the pathway leveled off and the three Suriyans and Pallin ran along it, lungs burning. The path reached the end of the wall and then doubled back. Sheabor and Straiah were now just below them. Sheabor still swung his hammer but the lead soldier lunged for him.

"Look out!" yelled Durian.

Sheabor narrowly ducked a blow and struck the lead soldier with his hammer, knocking him from the ledge to the ground below.

"Sheabor, your hammer!" Straiah called out, hands extended.

Sheabor threw him the hammer, which he carried up ahead. Then Sheabor drew his sword. Straiah came to where the road doubled back and continued a few paces until he was directly above the Dungeon Core. Sheabor was engaged with the lead warrior, bringing the rest to a standstill.

Straiah smashed the ground and splintered it, sending large chunks of rock down, knocking one of the soldiers from the ledge and forcing the others back. Sheabor and the lead soldier fought until Sheabor ducked one final blow. He kicked the soldier into the others and then ran up the narrow path.

By the time he reached Straiah, he had demolished a large section of the pathway, so much so that Sheabor had to leap across the distance. Then,

130

taking back his hammer, he smashed the ground furiously. The soldiers were rounding the bend, approaching fast. Durian and the others halted, watching anxiously.

The lead soldier sprinted for the gap looking as if to try and clear the distance. But as he neared, he slowed and stood facing Sheabor with steely eyes. Sheabor rose, breathing deep and returning the soldier's gaze. Then, raising his hammer straight out in front of him, he spoke with a loud command.

"Go back to the dungeon. The schemes of Malfur and Corcoran have been outwitted. Soon all the Eastern Realm will know of your presence here."

The leader of the Dungeon Core stood his ground for many moments. But then, without a word, he and his band turned round and moved quickly down the passageway to the ground below. Sheabor ran up to where Pallin and the others waited and leaned against the wall for a few moments to rest.

"Will they be able to go around?" Sheabor asked.

"Doubtful," responded Pallin. "The way around is many miles, and through difficult terrain."

Sheabor nodded in relief and put his hands on his knees to rest. After a few more moments, he lifted his head and smiled.

"What other dangers does your perilous land have to offer?" Sheabor asked.

"None that I can name," responded Pallin. "At least between here and Eulsiphion. Still, we ought to travel as far as we can before resting, just to be safe. And the journey through the plains will be long."

The three Suriyans gazed in awe and wonder at the Hammer of Haladrin still held in Sheabor's hand. Pallin too, was enamored by its beautiful, yet destructive form.

"Candlewood and Shade Stone," Pallin remarked. "The hammer has the properties of both light and darkness. I have never seen anything formed by the hands of man quite so magnificent."

"Or as menacing," Straiah commented.

"Very true," responded Pallin. "And thankfully so for our sake."

"Are there any other weapons like this?" asked Baron.

"A few, perhaps," responded Pallin. "But they are lost or hidden. There is so little left from that age."

"Hidden?" Baron pressed him. "By whom?"

"Well, I don't know really," Pallin said.

Baron gave him a discontented look. Durian glanced to Blair with a smile. The group journeyed on, up the rest of Ridgewall and back onto the open plains.

"I know of a well nearby," said Pallin. "We can rest there till morning."

"We don't have much food left," mentioned Straiah. "And I used the last of my arrows, so hunting will be difficult."

"We'll make do," said Sheabor.

Though Eulsiphion lay still a far way off, they would reach it well enough. Durian for one, couldn't wait to see the capitol city of Forthura, a city from the old world, of which he had only heard fables and stories.

132

The morning sun had risen before they reached the top of the Ridgewall, warming their faces and the grasses of the plains. It felt like home to Durian, though warmer.

"Pallin, what is Eulsiphion like?" Durian questioned.

Pallin smiled at him warmly.

"Like nothing you've seen or imagined. Truly."

"Do you think they'll believe our story?"

"We have a saying," said Sheabor. "Anything that must happen, will happen. They will believe us because they must believe us."

"Is King Euthor buried somewhere in Eulsiphion?" Durian questioned.

Pallin seemed struck by the question.

"No, I don't believe so. I have pondered that question much in recent days. When you consider what we know, the outcome is quite startling. We know that the Hammer of Haladrin, which Sheabor carries, was constructed after the Great War. We know this because the love poem dedicated to his beloved wife, Sheyla, is inscribed on the hammer.

Her passing was at the end of the Great War. That would suggest that King Euthor was trapped on the Banished Lands with the House, Cavanah, at the end of the war. And yet, a statue of King Euthor exists in the Hall of Eulsiphion which carries a replica of the Hammer of Haladrin, that same poem inscribed on its side. So the riddle becomes: how did the farewell poem of King Euthor to his wife, Sheyla, end up on both continents?"

133

The question filled Durian with intrigue. Though he knew of the orb of Shade Stone in the hand of King Euthor's statue, he hadn't know that a carved replica of the Hammer of Haladrin was also a part of the statue.

"Sheabor, does your history say anything as to where he is buried?" asked Pallin. "You carry his hammer with you, after all."

"We have no record of it," he replied. "From our earliest days on the Banished Lands, we have had a burial chamber for our noble kings. But King Euthor's tomb is not among them."

"I'll need some time in the hall of records of Eulsiphion then," Pallin concluded. "There may be something in the writings of King Euthor that gives a hint to his life after the Great War."

With that, Pallin's gaze grew distant. Durian was eager for more questions to be answered, but he thought it best not to disturb him. Something was building in Durian, a feeling telling him that much more lay waiting for them to discover than any could guess. The dreams, the poem, the hammer...something was unfolding.

Durian's mind was bursting. He felt so close – on the verge of discovering the key to the mystery. But every time he got close to an answer, it faded again.

Dagron

Arnor

hob
forest

Izben

Squall Highlands

Ewsiphion

Jlich

Commonwealth Pasturelands

Geldon

Edgewhic Isles

# Eulsiphion

The trip to Eulsiphion was many days through the open plains. And though they traveled the Commonwealth Pasturelands where all were free to feed their livestock, they scarcely saw another soul. Those who pastured cattle had already been driven closer to home by the onset of winter.

There was little wood for fires, making sleep difficult, and food was scarce. Without arrows, Straiah had made a sling for throwing smooth stones, but his aim was less than proficient, and he rarely struck a rabbit. But the hunger drove them.

By morning of the fifth day, they came to a large and looming boulder, out of place in the middle of the wide plains.

"This is one of the ancient boundary stones," Pallin declared. "We may yet arrive in Eulsiphion by evening."

As evening approached, Pallin led them up a small hill. It struck Durian as odd, since they could have easily gone around it. But as they neared the top, the snowy peaks of distant mountains filled the airy vast. Cresting the top of the hill, a striking scene came into view.

At the base of the tall mountains lay a castle beside a lake, a waterfall pouring into it from the mountains and a lazy river flowing away. It was Eulsiphion.

"That is the River Shay," Pallin said, motioning to the river.

Durian looked up in surprise, as did Baron and Blair. Shay River flowed all the way down to Suriya, right through the heart of town. Durian had no idea that their quaint stream also flowed down a wondrous waterfall and past the capital city.

They set off. After an hour, they drew near enough to the city to discern some of its features. Durian's eyes grew wide with wonder at the sight before him. The city's outer wall was brilliant white like polished marble, gleaming in the light of the sun. But each stone had a narrow streak of the brightest red, like a trapped bolt of crimson lightning.

"I've never seen such stone," Durian commented.

"It's called Omnivar," Pallin responded. "Eulsiphion is one of only two cities ever constructed from it."

"It's exquisite," Durian exclaimed.

"Yes it is," Pallin replied. "The stone has a magical property that changes with the hearts of its citizens. Many centuries ago, when the house Forthura came and reclaimed the fortress of Eulsiphion, the stone was a pleasant lemony green. At that time, the barbarians of the north were spreading southward. They became warlike and often battled with the people of the city. After nearly two decades of battles, the Horctura invited Eulsiphion to peace talks. Forthura agreed and took the pass to the east where the mountains lay, through the Squall Highlands and into barbarian territory. But the delegation never arrived at

139

the barbarian lands.  They were ambushed in the highlands and killed.

The king's son was part of the delegation and when news of the ambush reached the king, the stone went white and streaks of vibrant red shot out from his hall and cut through all the white stone in the city.  The color has never changed, and Eulsiphion is still at war with the Horctura to this day.  They have a vendetta against them.  They say that the very walls of the city cry out for vengeance, and they will not rest their swords until justice is done for their murdered ones."

The barbarians were mad to attack this city, Durian thought.  It was the most defensible structure he could imagine. The walls were at least fifty feet tall and immensely thick.  Descending toward the city, the mountains loomed tall above them and the sound of the waterfall wafted on the breeze.  The gates were open.

"Quickly," said Pallin.  "It's nearly sunset and the gates will close."

They sped along, Durian's legs and lungs burning from overuse.  The group entered Eulsiphion just as the sun set over the distant west.  They were allowed access by the two guards posted at the main gate.  Durian was astonished at what he saw as he walked through the city.  Not only was every structure built with the same beautiful stonework he had seen on the outer walls, but even the ground beneath his feet.  Columns lined the elevated buildings, with broad stairways leading up to them.  The walkways were bordered with small grassy parks, each containing benches and fountains and many of the citizens had already begun to recline there.

140

The palace was up ahead, seated above the rest of the city and containing its own set of walls and towers – a castle within a castle. Lying at the top of a flight of wide stairs, the palace was ornately decorated with columns, each made of a single stone that contained streaks of red stretching diagonally upward. Several guards with shields and spears were patrolling on the upper platform, and two waited at the large entrance. The group ascended the steps and came to the large palace doors, which appeared to be solid silver. The guard on either side of the door held out his hand.

"Halt," one said.

"We bring news of a threat to this kingdom," Sheabor stated. "We must speak to the king at once."

"Wait here," the guard replied. Each guard took hold of one of the large metal rings on either door and pulled. The large doors opened slowly, creaking deeply. One of the guards disappeared inside and returned minutes later, escorting a man in fine dress. He looked them over for moments, judging what to do. But the haggard state of the group, that they had come a long distance, argued their case for them.

"You will leave your swords and wait in the great hall," said the man. "I will rouse the king."

The group assented and unsheathed the weapons they carried. The man motioned with his head at the handle protruding from Sheabor's tunic. Sheabor produced the hammer and the man's eyes grew wide with surprise. But he didn't say anything. The guard next to the man held out his hand for the weapon but Sheabor shook his head.

"The king will want to see this," he said.

"Leave the hammer with him. But summon a dozen warriors and rouse the commander. Come back quickly!"

Then the adviser led them into the great hall of the large palace. The large doors creaked to a close behind them. The great hall was very large and rectangular in shape. There were two guards at the other end of the hall, guarding the entrance to the inner court rooms. A large throne of stone sat against the far wall.

"Stay here," the adviser commanded.

Then he walked to the far side of the room and past the two guards. Durian ambled about the room. There were a dozen windows on either side of the hall and between each window hung a finely woven, colorful silk standard. Below each of the standards stood a life-sized statue.

Durian walked to the western wall to examine them. But as he did, he saw something even more intriguing. It was an arched doorway that led to a flat pavilion of stone overlooking the city and the plains beyond. On the edge of the pavilion was a dark stone streaked with gold and silver. It was the Athel stone!

Durian changed his course, glancing at the guards to see if they would stop him. But they held their ground and Durian opened the door to the outer pavilion. Moonlight rained down on the large circle of stone, and Durian came to the edge, running his hand along the jagged Athel.

The wind whipped against his body as he stood in the heights. Cradling his arms, he was driven back indoors. Reentering the palace hall, he saw that the statue directly on the opposite side of the hall held a dark orb of Shade Stone in its outstretched hand. The other hand grasped a hammer resting at the statue's side. Durian came quickly to it, bending down to read the pedestal at the base:

# King Euthor

His eyes wandered up to the hammer now just in front of him. In the stone was carved the words he knew only too well:

> *Dismissing hours as they pass*
> *Soft upon the windswept grass.*
> *The hopes of men have come to naught.*
> *Nothing fair for eyes or thought.*
>
> *For Sheyla lies on golden plain,*
> *Of Cavanah, the fairest slain;*
> *Who met her last and final day*
> *When all was brought to disarray.*
>
> *Of gladful things now nevermore –*
> *Now bitter wind, now salty shore.*
> *The peaceful world bound to unrest*
> *And darkness looming in the west.*
>
> *The world and all its light shall fade.*
> *I'll stay with her beneath the shade*
> *And wait until the world's remade...*

Durian's heart beat quickly, as again something inside him surged forward, searching for a voice. But he couldn't put the feeling into words. It wouldn't take shape into thought. Durian stood and gazed into the stone face of the ancient king. His expression touched Durian. His countenance was one of longing and sorrow as he gazed toward the Athel stone on the pavilion.

Durian's eyes wandered down to the darkened orb of stone, peering deeply into it for any clues to what it might contain. He hadn't gotten the chance to ask Pallin more about it. Turning round to find Pallin, he was surprised to see the whole group standing right behind him. Sheabor was at the head of the group, standing tall and reverently in front of the statue of the greatest of the kings of old.

"Pallin, you said there's something called a Seer's necklace inside the orb. What is that?"

"King Euthor made it with a special stone that, when combined with an Athel, would always bring Sheyla's gaze to him. She could see him, no matter where in the far world he happened to be."

The door behind them opened, revealing a dozen warriors, headed by a soldier in finer armor than the rest. Soon after, the door on the other end of the hall opened, revealing half a dozen men and the king of their lands.

Durian and his companions were summoned forward by the man who had initially led them into the room. As Durian approached, his heart began to beat quickly. He had never been in such a room before, nor had he ever expected to be standing in the presence of

144

the king of their lands. His name was Froamb, and Durian had only heard stories of him.

The king took his seat on the throne, and as he did, all in the room bowed. When they arose, the king was staring intently at them. He was younger than Durian had expected. The hall was silent; the torches flickering lightly, filling the room with a mellow glow.

"Archulus has told me that you bear news of the creeping darkness that has come to our realm, and that you carry something of great importance," the king said. Sheabor was the one to respond. He stepped forward from the group.

"Yes, sire. A force more than a thousand strong now dwells within Thob Forest in the places few venture – warriors that move under the cloak of fog and night. They are the Dungeon Core, servants of Corcoran, come from the Banished Lands to make war against this Eastern Realm."

With that, the hall was blanketed in quiet. Froamb didn't answer, but leaned forward as he scrutinized them. Then he held up his hand and the room grew silent. He leaned back in his chair and spoke.

"Forces from the Banished Lands have come to the Eastern Realm? What you say is folly and cannot be true."

"It is true," Sheabor insisted. "Please stay your judgment, until the whole tale is told. We have all been betrayed. You do not know the things that have transpired upon the Banished Lands these last centuries. Corcoran was not killed in the Great War, nor in the cataclysm that followed. Many centuries ago, when the world was still flooding, Corcoran realized that his entire realm was moving further and further west away from the continent to the east. He was filled with rage and refused to rest until he could find a way to change his fate.

Somehow beyond our understanding, many centuries ago, Corcoran gave up his physical body and bound himself instead to the Banished Lands. He delved deep underground, searching the lower realms for a means to control the motion of the Banished Lands. No one knows how, but he found a way. Ever so slowly, he began to change the direction of his continent's drift. Imperceptible to those who lived upon its surface, the Banished Lands began to angle south, then southeast, and at last east. His continent has been moving toward your lands for the greater part of this last age. They are coming, and they are close."

"Impossible!" declared the king.

The hall was filled with an eruption of hushed voices and worried whispers. King Froamb rose to his feet. The hall again filled with voices and Sheabor raised his hands to quiet them.

"I have not yet told you the whole of this evil. In recent years, Corcoran has gained a new ally, Malfur, Keeper of the North Wind. Three months ago, when the Banished Lands still lingered far off, Malfur left from there with a thousand Dungeon Core. Malfur summoned the bitter wind ahead of them, freezing a passage of ice for them to walk across the seas. They walked for weeks before finally stepping across, coming to the southern end of the Frostlands. Straiah and I set out after Malfur a day behind, using their

146

passage, which had already begun to rift and splinter. I am Sheabor, last of the Lords of the noble House of Cavanah, keeper of the Hammer of Haladrin, and leader of the free peoples of the Banished Lands."

With that, he took the Hammer of Haladrin from its sheath behind him and held it high above his head for all to see.

"Then it is true!" exclaimed Froamb. "The Hammer of Haladrin has been found."

"It was never lost," replied Sheabor. "It is the birthright to the Lords of Cavanah in hiding on the Banished Lands, of whom I am the last. We have forsaken the defense of our homes and cities to come and warn the Eastern Realm. Have we risked such a journey only to meet with deaf ears? Have we come through ice and death only to find a land of fools? The giants watch the west, and Forthura's eyes are fixed upon the barbarian hordes of the north. Who among you watches the south? Who among you knows what lingers behind the borderlands of Thob Forest? Who from any of your lands has set foot there in a hundred years?"

"You are an impostor! Where you found the Haladrin Hammer I do not know. But you have used its legend, along with a cleverly invented story to try and earn a birthright that is not rightly yours. You are stirring madness into the hearts of my people, and I will suffer it no longer. Guards, seize them!"

With that command, many men from the crowd stepped forward, swords drawn. Durian couldn't believe what was happening. But then, he heard a powerful voice call out.

"Stay your ground," Pallin commanded, looking up sternly at the king. "I knew your father, Froamb, and he was not nearly as stubborn a king, nor as senseless."

"Who are you, old man?"

"I am Pallin, Keeper of the South Wind."

"The Keepers of the Wind are a myth! You are this man's cohort."

"I am no myth. I will show you."

Pallin extended his hand for the king to come down and join him. The king descended slowly and walked toward Pallin. Pallin led him over toward the open doorway, to the Athel seated on the small pavilion. The whole group followed him, packing onto the small expanse of stone. The moon had just begun to rise in the west, and Pallin places his fingers on the silvery streaks of the Athel. His expression grew distant, and after many moments of maneuvering his fingers, he reached out and took hold of King Froamb's hand. The king's eyes opened wide with amazement as he gazed upon the places and lands surrounding his kingdom. Pallin had activated the Athel stone.

"I see the distant forest," said Froamb, looking west. He turned his head slowly to the south. "I see..."

But he didn't finish his sentence. Instead, a deeply troubled look appeared on his face. Pallin released his hand and Froamb gazed at him gravely. What had he seen in the south along the plains, Durian wondered?

"Sheabor has not deceived you," Pallin said softly. "The words he has spoken are a solemn truth."

Then Pallin detailed his own story, of himself and the Three Windbearers giving up their powers and his detection of Malfur's powers on the breeze from beyond the lands of Suriya. Froamb walked slowly through the crowd and into the great hall. He ambled up the small flight of stairs and seated himself on his throne, his head in his right hand. All were watching the king now, who had become torn.

"What would you have us do?" Froamb said at last. Sheabor stepped forward from the rest.

"Malfur is yet unprepared," he said. "He doesn't have support enough to wage war against this kingdom. Without Corcoran by his side, we may be able to defeat him."

"Do you really mean to march a detachment of warriors to the deeps of Thob Forest, leaving my own people exposed to the wrath of the barbarian hordes?" Froamb asked.

"Malfur will not remain hidden behind the trees of the forest forever. Now that he knows some have followed him from the Banished Lands and have warned the Eastern Realm, he will move against your defenseless southern towns."

"Leave us," Froamb commanded. "And we will discuss what we have heard."

Sheabor stared at the king for many moments, unwilling as yet to heed his demand and leave the chamber. But then he assented, and he and his companions bowed low and walked toward the large silver doors, which were opened for them. As they departed the hall, Durian heard many voices erupt in discord over what they had heard. But soon the doors were closed behind them and Durian and the others were outside beneath the stars in the cool night air. They descended the stairs toward the main road and Sheabor began to pace back and forth.

"Pallin, your lands are weak. When Straiah and I set off from the Banished Lands, our goal was to rouse the noble Houses of Men, both Kester and Forthura, and seek the three remaining Windbearers, imploring them to aid us in the fight against Malfur and Corcoran. But I have seen in Froamb's eyes that he does not intend to help us. And though you are willing, you no longer have the power to oppose Malfur. This realm cannot even stand against one of the foes who now march to challenge it; how could we possibly hope to defeat both? The Eastern Realm is ripe to fall."

# King Euthor

"What about Suriya?" Baron demanded. "They're defenseless."

Pallin clenched his jaw.

"Perhaps it's best the three of you return home. You can warn your town and convince them to flee north before the siege begins."

Baron was taken aback. Though his powers of persuasion were better than most, convincing an entire town to abandon their homes was an impossible task. It would never work. It felt like Pallin was brushing them off.

"Now you wait just a minute," Baron said. "You dragged us into this. What if Sheabor came with us? They would believe him."

The group glanced to Sheabor who paced back and forth at the base of the steps to the palace in great frustration, not even aware that the rest were speaking of him.

"Pallin, I need to see a map of your realm," Sheabor insisted suddenly.

"Yes," said Pallin. "The hall of records is in the center of town. I must go there as well. We have little time."

Then he turned to Baron.

"We will not abandon your town," Pallin assured. "Stay with us until a better plan presents itself."

Baron wasn't going to leave their sight until they guaranteed him that help would come to Suriya. Durian was glad for Baron's fervor, for his mind was on other things. He had become completely enchanted with the mystery of a world he had never really known.

The group set off, Pallin leading them through the busy streets toward the center of town. Durian was surprised to see how many people were walking the avenues by night. The city was amazingly well lit with torches all around. And there were little parks scattered about with grass where many reclined. The contrast of the green grass against the white stone marbled red was strikingly beautiful. He had never imagined that such a place existed. What a wonder the old world must have been.

But his thoughts kept returning to the legend of King Euthor. There was so much mystery surrounding him, so much done so long ago by his hand that now affected their present world. Not only had he created the Hammer of Haladrin, which was the birthright of every Lord of Cavanah to inherit, but he also created the orb which protected the powers of the three Windbearers, and another orb sitting in hall of Eulsiphion. What had he done with the Shade Stone that contained the powers of Pallin and the others?

Durian's mind was consumed with questions and he quietly pondered them as the group marched onward. They arrived at a large building that sat upon another small hillside. It was ornately decorated and was seated atop a flight of stone stairs. Pallin led them up to the building's large metal doors, which creaked opened. There in the entrance stood an elderly man.

"Who seeks records at this hour?" asked the man.

"We have come from the palace on an errand for the king," Pallin responded.

The man eyed them for a few moments and then motioned for them to enter. He led them indoors and grabbed one of two torches from the wall. The hall was one single room with a large, round wooden table in the middle. The table's edge was dark, cherry colored wood, but its center was inlaid with cream colored wood made to look like a large compass.

The room was smaller on the inside than Durian had expected. Everything was in disarray. The room contained only a few shelves which were filled to overflowing with books. Most of the books were scattered about the room, piled from floor to ceiling. But hanging against the far wall was a large map of the Eastern Realm. The map hung at eye level and was made of cloth. Durian thought it looked hand woven. He was taken aback at the skill it must have taken to construct. But more than that, Durian had never seen a map of the whole Eastern Realm before. Everything he had seen in Suriya only showed the southeastern corner of the continent. Suriyan maps ended abruptly in the north and the west, showing the outline of Thob Forest and the mountains surrounding Eulsiphion but nothing more.

Pallin set off, scouring the books and scrolls, clearly frustrated at the lack of organization roundabout him. Durian carefully studied the large map in front of him. Directly north of them now lay the barbarian lands with the scattered tribes of the Horctura. To the northwest on the far side of the continent was the Kingdom, Kester. North of them were the lands of Aeleos, the homelands of the Bearoc – the giants. The Kingdom of Forthura seemed tiny by comparison, occupying only the small southern peninsula of the continent.

"Pallin, whose lands are these by the far western coast?"

Pallin looked up briefly.

"Those are the lands of Kester, and their capital city, Delphirion," Pallin responded.

"Is there safe passage?" Sheabor asked.

Pallin shook his head and continued his quest.

"I'm afraid not," he said, unrolling a large scroll. "The only road is along the northern edge of Thob Forest, through barbarian territory. They patrol those regions heavily."

"All of this is their territory?" Sheabor said in great surprise. The region where the barbarian tribes dwelt was twice as large as the lands of Forthura.

"Yes," Pallin answered, while quickly scanning a document then tossing it aside.

"What of their allegiance?" he asked. "What side will they take?"

"More than likely, they will take neither side," Pallin replied.

"Are you sure of that?" Sheabor asked. "Malfur is more crafty than you know. The promises he could make them in return for their allegiance would be hard to resist."

"You may be right," Pallin responded, again thoughtful for the moment. "But do not fear. We have

154

friends ourselves. Melanor, for instance, is a powerful ally, as is Aravas, Keeper of the East Wind, who has been dwelling there since the last age."

"Where is Melanor?" Sheabor asked. "I don't see it on the map."

"And you never will," Pallin replied. "When they are told the news, they will have wise guidance and counsel."

"Pallin, we don't need guidance and counsel. We need soldiers and arms. I cannot believe that we have traveled through ocean and ice and swampland and forest, only to be trapped by the high walls of a city!"

"Do not fear. Froamb speaks rashly at times, but I am confident he will do what he knows is right."

"Let's hope so."

"We still have time on our side," Pallin labored to say while lifting a pile of books that looked especially weathered onto the nearby table. "Malfur knows we have come to Eulsiphion. He will not dare attack the city now. And I doubt he will show his hand by attacking the smaller settlements like Suriya. He will occupy Thob Forest until Corcoran arrives. That will give us time to form a plan."

The large doors creaked open before Sheabor could respond, and the man, Archulus, who had originally met them at the steps of the palace, came into the room.

"The king has ordered a banquet. It will be ready within the hour."

The group left the hall of records behind, following Archulus down the small hill and off toward the palace. They had been in the record hall for less than an hour, but the streets were now mostly empty. The few citizens still at large in the city gazed warily at the group of outsiders being led toward the palace, making Durian suspect that word of their evil tidings had spread throughout the city. After walking the short distance toward the steps of the palace, Archulus led them back inside hall whose center table was fast filling with food.

Various distinguished guests had already gathered. The king had obviously invited the most important men of the city to hear and discuss what should be done regarding the news. Archulus led them to the middle of the table and motioned for them to sit down. They took their seats and waited for the rest to arrive.

Durian couldn't keep his eyes off the food before him. The array of delicacies was finer than anything he had ever seen. The sight and smell of them made waiting to eat almost unbearable. More people continued to enter and when the table was full, the king stood and held out his hands for the group to begin the meal. The feast began, turning Durian's mind from the cares of a troubled world. The others ate slowly, and King Froamb watched them silently, analyzing them. After a few minutes he spoke.

"Something troubles me," Froamb began. "If what you say is true and Malfur alone still bears power to control the wind, how are we to counter him when he comes against us?"

Froamb's glance passed slowly from Pallin to Sheabor.

"I don't know," said Sheabor.

Froamb then turned to address Pallin. "And there is no way for you and the other two Keepers of the Wind to regain your powers?"

"I have not as yet discovered the whereabouts of the orb containing our powers," Pallin replied. "It could take many years to find, or it may never be found. It is buried with King Euthor in his hidden grave, somewhere out in the wide world."

Froamb nodded and glanced around at those of his table.

"It seems we have but one reasonable option. Malfur will not attack Eulsiphion as long as he knows another Keeper of the Wind is here. To leave would be folly. Our best hope is to hold our ground here and give the other kingdoms a chance to learn of the treachery of Malfur and Corcoran. Perhaps in time, even the barbarians will join our cause."

"And what if the Horctura join Corcoran?" Sheabor asked, standing to his feet.

Before Froamb could reply, the large metal doors began to creak open. Durian turned to see a pair of guards leading an older man and a young woman into the great hall. The two walked with grace and elegance, gliding softly across the hard stone floor. They came to the head of the table and stopped.

"I am Thalen," the man declared. "This is Estrien. We are from Melanor."

Many hushed whispers erupted from those seated at the table. The young woman bowed and then gazed around the table.

"Melanor," Froamb said in surprise. "None have ever called on us from Melanor."

"The time has never before been right," Thalen responded.

As the pair approached the table, Straiah suddenly arose, offering his seat to the new arrival, Estrien. The exchange was a bit awkward, since empty seats were available at the table. Straiah flushed red as he stood behind the chair, waiting to Estrien to occupy it and then pushing it in behind her.

"Thank you," she said with a smile.

Thalen was also offered a seat of higher honor, closer to the king. When seated, Thalen addressed them.

"If you will allow, good King, we will explain ourselves. Our people have always been adept at reading the stars for signs, signs of famine or war, or great change in the heavens. Over a decade ago, the sign of the ancient enemy appeared among the stars in the heavens. At first, we disbelieved. But another sign soon followed of war and death. Since that time, we have become ever watchful, scanning the world for signs of the ancient enemy. Only too soon did the creeping darkness appear in the south, concealing its presence with fog and shadow.

We have used the decade well. We created a school in the art of combat for the day when Corcoran might appear. Estrien is our finest disciple. She is here to aid the cause of the two who have come from the Banished Lands to warn us, and to be the guardian of Pallin the Wanderer."

Pallin rose to his feet.

"Does Aravas know of the treachery of Malfur?"

"No," responded Thalen. "We have just learned. We are grieved to hear that Malfur is in league with Corcoran. That news will prove most devastating to Aravas, and to all. Malfur has no challenger now to oppose him."

"Yes," replied King Froamb. "That is the plight before us."

Estrien's seat was next to Durian. Though he tried not to stare, she captivated him by her elegance. She had flowing blonde hair, accented with a white tiara, and wore a green silk gown which matched her eyes. Being from a small town, Durian had never met someone like her before.

Durian quickly glanced away when her eyes met his. Separate conversations had begun all over the table. Thalen now spoke with Sheabor and Pallin, and Estrien leaned over to Durian.

"You have the look of a Suriyan," she said.

Durian looked back at her in surprise.

"I have been to Suriya," she continued, "and to the Shelengol Glades."

"You have?"

"In Melanor, we are allowed once to leave and journey to a place our heart has longed to see," she replied. "I visited the 'Land of Sunshine,' and the glades in late autumn. They remain now in my heart. It is shameful that evil has found a place to dwell and prosper there."

"When did you come to Suriya?" Durian questioned. "I don't remember hearing about anyone coming from the hidden city!"

Estrien smiled.

"We do not announce our presence and heritage. We dress modestly, as wayfarers and lonely travelers."

"Have others from Melanor traveled to Suriya?" he inquired.

"Many," she replied. "But over a long course of time."

Durian thought long about any he might have seen in the past that stuck out and didn't belong. But try as he might, he couldn't remember anyone in particular, save for Pallin.

"Why do you only get to leave once?" Durian asked, not realizing the barrage of questions coming from his lips. Estrien smiled and answered him politely.

"The people of Melanor still possess their skills from the First Age. But our skill is weak now, and we cannot allow influences from the outside world to come and destroy the little we have managed to save."

"Pallin told us about the talents of the wise before the Great War," Durian replied. "He said that some had speech so fair and graceful that it contained the very words of life and could make things come alive."

"Quite true," Estrien responded. "Though I had to undergo many years of training, now every weapon I carry responds to the sound of my voice. They will come alive if I call, to aid me in battle."

Her words seemed out of place. Everything about her was graceful and fair. Durian couldn't imagine her as a warrior. She must have seen it in his expression.

"Do not be misled, my fine young Suriyan," she said. "Though we of Melanor are for peace, we understand that there are some who would rather die than live in peace. We have trained ourselves for battle in order to grant them that wish, if they will not be dissuaded from it."

Durian's mind was fascinated. To hear not only that Melanor was real, but that those from the hidden city had been among them all along. It was almost too much to consider. But before Durian could pose another question, she interjected.

"How did three Suriyans come to be involved in this adventure?"

"We have my brother here to thank for that," responded Blair. "We got lost in Thob Forest and were rescued by Sheabor and Straiah."

Estrien looked up to Straiah, who was already gazing in her direction.

"Thank you, sir, for your courage in risking your lives to warn our peoples."

Straiah bowed and then returned his eyes to her.

"Thank you for believing and trusting us," he replied.

Straiah held her gaze until Estrien blushed a bit and turned away. Baron's eyes raised in intrigue and he turned to Blair with a nudge, who didn't seem to notice the interaction.

"Where is Melanor?" Durian cut in again. "Pallin said it's somewhere to the east."

She turned to him with a smile.

"What Pallin says is true, but I will tell you nothing further. When the Great War first began, the people of Kester began constructing the hidden city, a place of refuge if the war turned dire. It was one of the few cities not destroyed in the earthquake or flooded by the roving waters. Many have tried to find the lost city, but very few have succeeded. Aravas, Keeper of the East Wind, found us just after the Great War, where he has dwelt the whole of this last age. King Euthor dwelt with us also in those days, but only for a short time."

"Why did King Euthor go to Melanor?" Pallin said suddenly and unexpectedly from the other side of the table. As he did, the other conversations in the room stilled.

"We're not sure entirely," Thalen answered. "According to our history, after the war ended, he used Sheyla's necklace to find her body. She had left just before the start of the Great War to try somehow and stop it. But she was cut off from escape and never returned. King Euthor buried her and then came to Melanor, where he made the Hammer of Haladrin and the orb of Shade Stone in the hand of the statue there."

Pallin's brow furrowed deeply, and all eyes in the room watched him. After a few moments more, Thalen continued.

"Near the end of the Great War, a falling star shot down from the heavens and was recovered by our people and brought to our last great king. King Euthor arrived at nearly the same time. Together with the king

162

of Melanor, they stayed a week behind concealed doors with the star. All we know is that the king of Melanor called the star to life, and that they learned from it many things – hidden things, and knowledge of what was to come. It was after that time that King Euthor made the hammer and the orb. Then the two kings disappeared suddenly, presumably each on some mission, but neither speaking of it."

As the silence filled the room, something again seemed to strike Durian's mind, a feeling at the edge of thought. Durian stood to his feet and walked to the statue of King Euthor, gazing down at the poem on the hammer.

"We never knew where King Euthor went after leaving Melanor," Thalen continued. "We always thought he had been trapped here on the Eastern Realm, while the rest of the House of Cavanah was trapped on the Banished Lands. We had no idea the hammer was on the Banished Lands until this evening. According to our history, King Euthor came to Melanor just a week before Aravas arrived. He brought with him an orb of Shade Stone that he had already constructed, made the Hammer of Haladrin and another orb of Shade Stone, and then departed with all three items.

He must have traveled to Eulsiphion to deliver the second orb, and then left from there, presumably to the Banished Lands. But why he did what he did in those days, none can say. He was a man stricken with grief. After King Euthor left our city, our own king set sail to the east, and was never seen or heard from again.

163

We don't know what they discussed, or where each set out on their own."

As Thalen spoke, the words of the poem seemed to leap up from the hammer at Durian. He considered Thalen's message. What had King Euthor learned from the fallen star? Why had both kings just disappeared? A phrase flashed through Durian's mind, something Joram had always told him: *See the end from the beginning.* Durian could feel the significance of the phrase, but didn't understand exactly why. He muttered the line softly to himself. "See the end from the beginning." And as he said the words a wave of revelation washed over him.

"That's it!" cried Durian.

His mind was racing with new thoughts coming into focus. The room was deathly silent as all eyes turned to him.

"What is it, Durian?" asked Pallin.

Durian whipped round, his excitement fading against the scrutiny of watchful eyes. He closed his eyes and gathered his thoughts.

*"I'll stay with her beneath the shade,* he wrote. *And wait until the world's remade."*

Pallin's gaze grew distant. Durian turned to the rest at the table, who didn't seem to follow him.

"Don't you see?" Durian continued. "It's a message. King Euthor hid Sheyla's necklace and their wedding rings inside this orb of Shade Stone. Those are symbols of the love they shared, are they not? He said that he would wait with Sheyla beneath the shade, and wait until the world's remade. In a very real sense, the world is being remade, and the symbol of the love

164

of King Euthor and Sheyla waits beneath the Shade Stone."

He paused for a moment and gazed back down again at the poem.

"Somehow, King Euthor and the last king of Melanor must have learned from the fallen star that evil would again come to this realm. He placed this orb on the Eastern Realm and brought the only weapon that had a chance of breaking it upon the Banished Lands. That way, the orb could only be broken if the worst happened and the two continents came together again. There must be something inside this orb, some tool or map or something that will lead us to the second orb with Pallin's powers."

The room fell silent as all considered the gravity of what Durian had just spoken. After a long pause, Pallin finally broke the silence.

"Sheabor, if you would be so kind," Pallin said, standing to his feet and motioning to the orb of Shade Stone.

Sheabor nodded and rose to his feet, taking his hammer from his tunic and holding it firmly in his hands. King Froamb stood to his feet as well, in shock, but said nothing. Sheabor walked over to the statue, bowing before taking the orb slowly from its outstretched hand. Then he laid it on the floor against the steps before the throne and took a few paces back. Raising the hammer above his head, he came down upon the orb with all his might, landing firmly against its surface with the flat end of his hammer.

The hall reverberated with the sound of the mighty crash, and the floor trembled. Sheabor lifted his hammer from the orb. As he raised it, the orb split apart and sat within the newly formed indent. Each half fell backward, revealing a hollow section in the middle, containing three golden items. Sheabor bent down and clasped them in his hand, raising them up and holding them out for all to see.

"It is indeed the necklace of Sheyla and their wedding rings," Sheabor declared. He brought them to the table and laid them before the group. Everyone at the table crowded round, gazing at the items intently. The three items were beautiful, made of gold and ornately carved. The necklace was inlaid with a large, brightly colored blue jewel.

Durian looked at them in confusion. He had been positive that something else would be inside the orb with the other three items, something that would lead them to the hidden orb with Pallin's powers.

"I don't understand," said Durian.

But as Pallin stared down at the three golden items, a thought was taking shape in his own mind as well.

"King Euthor made the Three one promise only," Pallin said. "He promised to protect our powers and take them to his grave. That is where the orb with our powers lies, I am sure. Until now, we have had no hope of finding it."

"Until now?" Durian questioned.

Pallin said nothing more but took the three golden articles in his hand and walked to the open archway and out onto the pavilion where the Athel loomed in the darkness. Clasping the necklace in one hand and touching the Athel with the other, he was

166

propelled westward in his mind's eye at great speed. Flying over the darkened treetops and past the coast, he found himself high above a very large body of water.

After an indeterminable amount of time, he was again over land, moving swiftly past a forest and over a mountain range. He began to slow as he arrived at the base of a large mountain in the range. And as he slowed, he floated through the solid walls and found himself in a dark room inside the mountain. Though it was pitch black, the sight of the Athel made the room glow with a mellow, silvery light. He could make out only one thing in the room: a stone sarcophagus. For many moments he gazed in silence until he was sure he would glean nothing more. Then he released his hand from the Athel. Instantly, he was back in the palace hall, now surrounded by everyone from the table.

"Pallin, what did you see?" demanded the king.

"Through the necklace of Sheyla, I was taken in spirit to the final resting place of King Euthor," Pallin declared. "Our fate has grown both better and worse. His tomb lies inside a cavern deep beneath a tall mountain range. King Euthor is buried on the Banished Lands."

"Then that is where your powers lay," said Sheabor.

Pallin nodded slowly. Somehow, King Euthor had left them everything they would need to reclaim their powers and stand against the coming darkness. He had hidden his plan in his farewell poem; hidden it from the wise and the learned, and instead revealed it to a simple Suriyan. It was almost too much to ponder. But had they discovered it all in time to act?

# The Beginning

The low-lit pavilion was silent as the group crowded against Pallin and the Athel stone. The moon shone brightly down upon the plains in the distance.

"King Euthor's tomb is on the Banished Lands!" someone exclaimed.

"I am afraid so," Pallin responded.

"And the orb?" King Froamb asked. "Did you see it?"

"Yes," Pallin responded. "It is there, by his design."

"Why in the world would he take that kind of power to such a perilous land?" King Froamb inquired.

"Only on the Banished Lands would it be safe," Pallin responded. "As long as the orb with Sheyla's necklace rested in Eulsiphion, the means for finding King Euthor's grave could only come about if the Banished Lands returned."

"But if his tomb is on the Banished Lands, then all is still lost," said Estrien. "We have no way to retrieve the orb."

The pavilion grew silent. Pallin extended his hands to usher the group back indoors. Once seated again at the table, Pallin spoke.

"There may yet be hope. Sheabor and Straiah are here, after all. They have come between worlds undetected. There may be other pathways we can take."

"Pallin speaks wisely," said Thalen. "I cannot believe that King Euthor constructed such an elaborate plan only to disregard the final means of completing it. Though we have not yet perceived the means, I am sure they exist. King Euthor must have left a way behind to travel to the Banished Lands. He found a way himself after all, so many centuries ago."

Durian marveled. Such an intricate plan, formed by the one man who had foreseen the days of the return of the ancient enemy.

"There is much to consider," Thalen concluded. "Sheabor, to the best of your knowledge, how far away are the Banished Lands from our shores?"

"Not more than a hundred leagues west of the Frostlands," he replied.

The statement hung in the air.

"Let us rest for the night," the king declared. "Your rooms have already been prepared. You will stay in the palace and the attendants will see to your needs."

It wasn't until King Froamb said the words that Durian realized how tired he was. The thought of a warm bed cast every other desire to the side.

Each person was given their own room and Durian was greeted by a steaming tub. Overjoyed, he reveled in the first warm bath he'd had in weeks.

When Durian awoke, he could tell that a considerable amount of time had passed. He dressed in a clean set of clothes and was met by an attendant in the hall outside his room.

"You are free to move about the city, sir."

"Do you know where the others are?" Durian asked.

"Most have gone from the palace, though they did not say where."

Durian nodded and thanked him. Perhaps it was time for a walk. Coming through the main hall and out the other side, he descended the stairs and was surprised to find the evening sun hanging low in the sky. He must have slept all night and most of the next day.

Torches were springing to life all around the city. Durian ambled to a nearby grassy park and watched the sky change from a deep blue to an orangy red. After awhile, Baron and Blair plopped down and joined him. Pallin also joined them.

"The sleeper awakens at last."

Durian smiled with a nod and Pallin sat beside him, placing his walking stick down beside him. Durian saw that the iron tip of his walking stick was already coming loose. But Baron snatched the walking stick and turned to Blair with a stern countenance.

"You see this," Baron said, shaking the stick in Blair's face. "This is what I'm talking about."

"Oh please," replied Blair.

The others chuckled.

"I think the run through the Edgewhic Isles was more than a simple walking stick could manage."

Durian turned back to the sunset with a sigh.

"How are you faring in all this?" Pallin asked.

Durian was surprised by the question and found Pallin gazing at him warmly.

"I feel like a grain of sand on the seashore. The world is a much bigger, darker place than I had ever imagined. I feel helpless."

Pallin gave him a thoughtful nod.

"I also was in despair last evening," Pallin said. "But my hope renewed this morning, as I felt the cool, crisp air wash over the plains. Though Corcoran's purpose is dark and vast, there is a greater purpose above his that drives the fate of our world. For consider the irony of our present circumstance. Corcoran, after all, is the only force in our world with the power to reunite the continents the lost House of Cavanah to its brothers. In that sense, he has unwittingly become a servant for good. For though he intends much evil, much good may also result."

Durian nodded pensively. He hadn't thought of that. He wondered if King Euthor had also considered it as he looked ahead to the future. Just then, they saw Estrien walking by.

"Estrien!" Baron called out. "Won't you come join us?"

Durian was surprised by Baron's boldness. But then, Baron had never had trouble talking to a beautiful woman.

Estrien walked to them but didn't take a seat.

"How does this lovely evening find you?" she asked.

"Very well," Baron replied. "Just reminiscing about life."

Baron sighed dramatically and Durian couldn't help but smile and shake his head. Baron the philosopher. He was up to his old tricks. Did he really think a woman like Estrien would be interested in a simple Suriyan?

"Is that so?" she said with an intrigued smile.

"Almost dying will do that to a person."

Durian glanced to Blair who only rolled his eyes.

"I don't think we would have made it if Straiah hadn't found us in the forest. We owe him and Sheabor our lives. You should have seen the way he took care of us all. Always showing up with rabbits or a string full of fish. He might be the most selfless man I've ever met."

Estrien's eyes narrowed as a slow smile grew on her face, seeming to sense that Baron was up to something. What was he up to? Praising another man wasn't the best way to win a woman's affections.

"I appreciate your insights," she said.

Baron glanced to Durian and Blair with a mischievous smile but Durian returned it with confusion. But before anything else could be said, the loud ring of a bell sounded out in the darkening sky. The group stood.

"The alarm has been raised," Pallin said. "The city is under attack! Quickly, we must return to the palace."

They made haste, finding the doors wide open and soldiers speaking with the king.

"Where have they attacked?" Durian heard the king ask.

"The western wall."

"Have any breached?"

"No," the soldier replied. "But the men are asking for reinforcements. They fear being overrun. The attack came without warning."

"Summon the fighting men!" the king commanded.

The soldier bowed and departed. Just then, Thalen arrived, Sheabor and Straiah not far behind.

"King Froamb, I take my leave from you now," Thalen said. "I must return to Melanor and disclose what we have discovered. Estrien will stay behind to guard Pallin."

"Go in peace, friend," the king responded.

"Who is attacking the city?" Sheabor asked.

"The Horctura."

Just then another soldier ran up the stairs.

"The commander is in position," he said. "The enemy is being met by our forces."

"Guard!" yelled the king. "Get the Suriyans some weapons. Pallin, you and the Suriyans stay inside the palace. Sheabor, Straiah, and Estrien may accompany me if they wish."

"We would be honored," Sheabor replied.

"I must stay with Pallin," Estrien said.

The king bowed and headed quickly off. Sheabor, Straiah, and a personal guard accompanied him, running hastily through the streets, swords drawn. Durian and the others watched them disappear. They could hear shouting and the distant sounds of battle.

"Be cautious!" King Froamb yelled to Sheabor and Straiah as they ran. "The barbarians have

173

developed a longbow that can fire over our walls. Be wary of running or standing in open spaces."

The streets were empty as the group ran through them, the sounds of battle intensifying. Before they reached the base of the western wall, a volley of arrows came over.

"Take cover!" the king cried.

Arrows struck the ground around them, one piercing Sheabor's tunic as he stood with his back pressed against a nearby building. Straiah saw it and smiled. That was close.

They reached the stairs to the western wall as another volley sailed overhead.

"Return fire!" boomed the voice of the commander.

The group hurried forward and when they had reached the top of the wall, the king grabbed Sheabor's arm.

"Tell the commander I am in the southern tower!" Froamb shouted.

Then he broke company. The Horctura had erected ladders all across the wall with many hundreds of torches in the valley below, waiting to ascend. The soldiers of Forthura engaged them on the wall while others in the northern and southern towers fired from above. Sheabor and Straiah unsheathed their swords and sprinted into battle.


Meanwhile, the three Suriyans, having each been given a weapon, retreated back inside the palace, along with Pallin and Estrien. The table had been cleared of food and drink, and the five hovered around it, listening to the sounds floating in through the open window. They said little, anxiously awaiting the conclusion of the battle. Estrien took out her three weapons and laid them on the table. Durian gazed at them intently; he had never seen such beautifully decorated weaponry.

She carried a bow of pure white color, ornately carved from a wood unfamiliar to Durian. Her dagger and a sword proved equally fine, and perhaps more so. For jewels of deep purple had been set into each. Estrien, seeing his interest, extended the handle of her sword to him.

Durian took the sword in hand. The handle was of wood and metal, and was inlaid with four beautiful purple jewels. The pommel of the sword was also made of a matchless purple gem, quite large, to balance the blade. The blade itself was of finely folded steel, perfectly balanced. He swung it lightly through the air as though a stick. He had never held such an amazing weapon.

"This is Drune," she said. "Swiftest blade in all of Melanor."

Though it seemed fragile, Durian could tell that the blade contained a hidden strength. He handed the sword back to her. Then she offered him her bow.

"This is Illiock," she said, "made from Thay wood of the old world. He is twice as strong as oak, and unbendable against his will, which is a stubborn one. Convincing him that I would be his master was quite a feat. Now however, he is a very powerful ally."

"May I?" he asked.

She smiled and nodded. Durian gripped the bow tightly in his hand. He pulled on the string with all his might, but the bow bent very little, or perhaps not even at all. He couldn't imagine even the strongest warrior being able to bend it, much less someone as graceful as Estrien. He looked up at her in astonishment. But she had said that the bow would only bend under its own will. She must only be able to use it when it was called to life. That was something else that mystified him. Though he had had enough of battle and danger, still he hoped for the chance to see what would happen when Estrien called her weapons to life. He handed the bow back to her. Then she gave him the dagger, which was of similar design to her larger sword, Drune.

"This is Drune as well," she said. Durian looked at her curiously. "The sword and the dagger were forged as a single piece, years ago – a long blade with a handle on each end. When Drune was first formed and was still a single piece, I called it to life for the first time. After that, the sword and dagger were split and each one sharpened. And though they were separated physically, the bond still remains. Now, when called to life, each piece can feel the presence of the other. The dagger is made for throwing, and it will always return to the one who bears his other half."

Durian and the others marveled at the thought. Pallin himself began to shake his head slowly in wonder.

"It is such a pity, now looking back, that I have spent countless years wandering the world, and have never made my way to the hidden city," Pallin said.

"Their work and creativity are marvelous. I can see why Aravas chose to dwell there all these long years."

Estrien nodded.

"I have a question for you though," Pallin said. "Thalen mentioned that the astrologers in Melanor perceived a sign in the heavens some years ago that told them great peril was coming to the Eastern Realm. What did Aravas make of it?"

"None knew what to make of it," she replied. "The sign was indistinct. It could have meant that war was coming, or perhaps that some disaster or famine would soon arrive. Though all feared the worst, that Corcoran had somehow found a way to return, none knew anything for certain."

"Were the Bearoc warned?" he asked.

"No," she replied. "We always assumed that if Corcoran returned, it would be the giants to warn us, not the other way around."

"I see," he replied. "Then the giants still have no knowledge of Corcoran's plans."

Durian began to wander the confines of the great hall. The embroidered rugs and carved statues were absolutely marvelous. King Euthor was but one of a dozen or so statues, each carved with great detail. They had been great kings and the details of their reigns were recorded on their pedestals. Durian stooped down to take it all in. He was still beside himself that he was standing here in Eulsiphion, involved in such incredible events. As he stood to his feet, he noticed that the torch beside him began to flicker. He turned round to see Estrien gazing intently at the far wall.

"Estrien what is it?" Baron asked. But she did not reply.

"Illiock, Drune, awaken!" Estrien commanded.

The rest were taken aback. Before any could say a word, Estrien began speaking softly in the ancient tongue. It sounded like a flowing melody; Durian couldn't make out the individual words from the whole. Durian and the others gazed at her weapons but perceived little change. They still looked lifeless in her hands, but Durian could almost sense an energy of vitality emanating from them. Estrien was gazing intently at the back of the room. The rest were now standing beside her, their hearts beating quickly in confusion. But then, a form stepped out from the darkness. When they saw it, Pallin gasped and the eyes of the rest went wide. The first form was followed by another and then another. The Dungeon Core were here!

Meanwhile, the battle raged at the western wall. Sheabor and Straiah fought with the warriors pouring in. Arrows from the north and south towers were raining down on the multitude of barbarians below and those climbing the ladders, which held to the wall by thick metal claws. The soldiers of Forthura were holding their own, but the armies of the Horctura were better suited for this style of fighting.

Being larger and armed with large broadswords and war hammers, blocking a blow could often prove as fatal as taking it. For the force of the sword could send a soldier clear of the wall and to his death. The barbarians that managed to ascend the ladders swung wildly, pushing the soldiers back until the crowded wall became their doom.

"Straiah! We need to get to the ladders!"

But the nearest barbarian warrior, hearing him, charged his broadsword, swinging across his chest and forcing them back. The barbarian stepped forward and swung downward at Sheabor. But Sheabor stepped to one side, narrowly dodging the blow and struck the barbarian in the jaw with the hilt of his sword. Stunned, Straiah lunged forward and pierced him with the tip of his blade.

The pair sprinted forward toward the ladder but a warrior emerged before they arrived. Swinging his war hammer, Sheabor ducked the blow and rolled past him while Straiah blocked it with his sword, sending him nearly off the wall and to the ground. The barbarian reared up for another strike, but Sheabor lunged forward with his sword and the barbarian dropped to his knees.

Sheabor unsheathed his hammer. Another barbarian was nearly to the top of of the wall. But Sheabor struck the armored ladder with the hammer, reducing one side of it to splinters of wood and metal. The ladder buckled but held in place. Sheabor raised the hammer for another blow, but heard the yell of Straiah as a hand pulled powerfully on the collar of his shirt, sending him to the ground as a spear sailed past his face.

Sheabor glanced to Straiah, who wore a smile. The two sprang to their feet. The lead barbarian was just to the top of the ladder. Straiah engaged him while Sheabor struck two more blows with the hammer. The ladder gave way and slid down the wall, striking another nearby ladder, shattering it.

A shout erupted from the soldiers of Forthura. The battle was now in their favor. Sheabor scanned the scene. Though the barbarians were fierce, they couldn't hope to take a city like Eulsiphion. The towers on either side were raining down arrows right into the midst of them and weren't likely to be overrun. What were the barbarians doing?

Elsewhere, another battle was about to begin. The Dungeon Core were fast filling the palace hall. How had they gotten in? Durian's heart was pounding as his trembling hand gripped the hilt of a sword newly his own. Estrien was standing in front of Pallin, squared off with over a dozen warriors.

"Step aside," commanded the leader of the Dungeon Core.

They were here for Pallin. Estrien only pulled back her bow, aiming at his chest. The lead warrior halted, but those on the fringes continued to advance.

One of the warriors at her flank suddenly sprang forward. Estrien turned and loosed her arrow. It hit him with such force that he flew backward into two others, knocking them also to the ground. Then she grabbed her sword.

The warriors advanced against her, a dozen of the Dungeon Core. Durian froze. He was paralyzed with fear. But Estrien met the lead man, parrying his blow and dodging one from a second. A third warrior assaulted, pushing her back. But as she stepped away from the strike, she threw her knife at another advancing warrior, striking him dead and then blocking a fourth blow.

"Drune!" she called out, and the knife, now red with blood, flew to meet her hand.

The eyes of the Dungeon Core filled with surprise and rage. Durian and the others couldn't believe it, that the weapon responded to her call. But Estrien was greatly outnumbered. The surprise lasted only a moment and the group of warriors sprang at her again. Though she blocked and parried their blows, they were pushing her back toward the far wall. She had no choice but to give up ground to keep from being surrounded.

Without warning, Baron yelled and sprang forward. Some from the Dungeon Core split off and made for them, blocking Baron's attack with an aggressive parry that knocked Baron to the ground. Coming to Blair and Durian, two soldiers raised up their swords and swung at them. Durian held up his sword and caught the blow, but the force of it knocked him into a chair and tumbled him to the ground.

The two Dungeon Core grabbed Pallin's arms and began carrying him away. Durian looked desperately to Estrien. She had struck down another, but was still losing ground. What were they going to do? Pallin struggled in vain as the two soldiers dragged him away.

Just then, Durian saw Estrien's white bow and quiver lying idle on the palace floor. Durian rushed to them, taking the bow in hand and clumsily setting an arrow. He pulled, but the bow was somehow even more resistant than it had been the first time, as though it were now actively resisting him. Baron and Blair ran up to him, the three Suriyans huddling around the bow, each vainly taking it in hand to try and bend it. But Durian snatched it back from Baron.

"Your master is in danger!" Durian yelled, but the bow remained firm. "She'll die if you don't let me help her!"

Suddenly the bow softened, almost bending under its own power. It was unbelievable. There was an energy coming from it, making Durian's hands almost numb. Durian turned to Pallin, but the soldiers had already taken him beyond the palace hall and into the chambers.

Swinging round toward Estrien, he pointed, closing his eyes and letting the arrow go. The bow snapped with immense force, knocking him to the ground. The arrow sped along, striking one of the Dungeon Core in the back and propelling him into the other warriors. Estrien took the advantage of the surprise and struck a fifth soldier dead.

"Here!" said Blair, giving him another arrow.

Durian set the arrow, but two of the Dungeon Core were now sprinting at them.

"Hurry, hurry!" yelled Baron.

Durian fumbled about, the arrow nearly dropping from the string. He raised the bow just before the warriors reached them. The arrow sprang out, again knocking Durian back to the ground. But it met its mark. The second warrior swung at Baron and Blair, whipping the sword out of Blair's hands and knocking Baron into a chair. Then he stood over Durian, sword poised.

Durian looked around wildly for something to defend himself with. As the warrior brought the sword down, Durian raised his hands to his face. But the blow didn't come, and after another moment, the warrior crashed down beside him, Estrien's blade, Drune, protruding from his back. He heard the sound of her call and instantly the knife shot away.

Durian quickly jumped to his feet. There were only two now facing off with Estrien. They were crouched low, no longer on the offensive. Estrien came at them. Just then, Durian noticed the pavilion on the other side of the room. Running to it, he swung the door open wide and ran to the edge. Placing his hand against the stone, he breathed in deep.

"Sheabor!"

The sounds of battle from the western wall wafted through the great expanse. But Durian breathed in deep and called out again. Then he ran back to the main hall, just as Estrien felled the last warrior. Running up to her, but for a cut on her arm, they found her unharmed.

"Thank you," she said, placing a hand on Durian's shoulder. "Where is Pallin?"

"They took him!"

"Come on," she said, and made for the back of the room.

Running to the far side, they entered the empty hall. Rooms lined either side, and at the end of the corridor, the hallway split in a T, leading to more rooms. There was no sign of Pallin. They could be hiding in one of the rooms.

But just as they began to move off again, they heard large metal doors swing open from the far side of the palace hall. Sheabor was the first to rush in, followed by Straiah, the king and many warriors. Seeing the dead Dungeon Core warriors on the floor, Froamb slowed and gazed gravely around the room. Estrien and the Suriyans ran to meet them.

"Who are these soldiers?" he demanded.

"They are the Dungeon Core," replied Sheabor. "Warriors of Corcoran and Malfur."

As the group approached, Straiah looked around and smiled at Estrien.

"You did all this?" he asked.

"Mostly," she replied with a nod to Durian.

"They've taken Pallin!" cut in Durian. "But we don't know where."

"Impossible," said Froamb. "This fortress isn't some rabble of brick and mud, guarded by dogs. How could they have slipped out undetected?"

"Because they entered undetected," Estrien replied. "They must have used a hidden passageway. Are there any tunnels leading out of the city from the palace?"

The thought seemed to strike him, as though raising some buried memory of something he had heard long ago, perhaps as a child. But he shook his head no.

"Come on," she urged. "We need to search."

But King Froamb and his soldiers stayed behind, more concerned with the slain warriors in the palace hall than in the kidnapping of Pallin. Straiah and Sheabor ran down the hallway, pounding open each closed door. Reaching the end of the hall, they did likewise down the other two corridors. There were nothing but empty rooms. Running back to the rest of the group, Straiah suddenly stopped in his tracks.

"Wait. Look, blood."

The blood was in the doorway of a large room, undoubtedly King Froamb's. They ran their eyes and fingers over the smooth walls, looking for any clue. Estrien went to the far wall and bent down, touching her finger to a tiny drop of blood.

She closed her eyes and pressed her palms against the cool stone, speaking quietly in her melodious language. The rest stopped their futile pursuit and watched her. Then, without warning, the wall began to slide open, revealing a darkened corridor. Grabbing torches from the hallway, the group rushed into the darkness, Sheabor in the lead, followed by Straiah and Estrien. The pathway was small, dark, and musty, carved in the bedrock of the mountains Eulsiphion was built against.

"Good King Froamb is going to get quite a shock when he walks into his bedroom tonight and finds a wide open door," Straiah said to Estrien. She laughed.

"Hopefully that will be enough to free him from his stubbornness," she commented.

"I would think that meeting you would be enough to give any man the courage to fight," he replied. Estrien blushed, though none could see it.

"I think our worst fears are confirmed," Straiah said. "The Dungeon Core are in league with the Horctura of the north. The attack on the wall tonight was merely a distraction to allow the Dungeon Core to find Pallin and escape undetected."

Sheabor didn't answer, but his silence was an affirmation.

"When the two forces join to attack Eulsiphion, the city will not stand," Straiah continued.

"That is why we must be swift in Pallin's rescue," Sheabor replied.

Time was running out. The tunnel was long and remarkably straight and level. After some while, a kind of rumbling came from ahead and a distant glow of light. Nearing it, they saw that the corridor ended at a glistening pool of water. The rumbling from beyond had grown loud around them. Without a word, Sheabor dropped into the pool with a splash and disappeared beneath the waters. Straiah and Estrien did the same and Durian stood there for a moment, mouth gaping at Baron and Blair.

But Baron only smiled and hopped into the glowing pool. Blair extended his hand, giving Durian the lead and he took a deep breath and closed his eyes. Then he was engulfed in a frigid blue. The roar somehow intensified underwater. Durian opened his eyes to see bubbles and frothing water all around him. Swimming away from it and upward, he broke the surface just to the side of a large waterfall. The others had already climbed ashore on the rocky lake shore.

"It's taken us to Siphion Falls," marveled Estrien. "Do you see the Dungeon Core?"

"Not yet," said Sheabor. "But we know they'll head south along the plains toward Thob Forest. We

186

can overtake them if we hurry. I'm sure they're unaware we are following them."

Durian climbed ashore and turned round. Nearly a league away, Eulsiphion sat like a glowing gem amid the dark mountains. But Sheabor departed without a word, and the rest followed. Durian gazed ahead to the places they would soon travel. He almost thought he could make out forms in the distance, faintly glimmering in the pale moonlight. Maybe they were on the right track after all. Only time would tell.

# The Squall Highlands

Moonlight filtered brightly through the clouds and down on the plains the six companions sped through. Even by night, Straiah and Sheabor had little difficulty following the group of Dungeon Core. Their pathway was keeping along the face of the mountain range, on the small strip of land that lay between Shay River and the mountains of the Squall Highlands. They ran for quite some distance, until Sheabor suddenly stalled and held up his hand. The rest came to a halt. Sheabor's eyes were closed and his hand was raised for silence as though listening for something. Then he lowered his hand and studied the ground intently.

"They have taken a pathway into the Squall Highlands," he said, motioning with his hand to a somewhat steep grassy trail.

"That doesn't make sense," said Straiah.

Sheabor nodded in agreement. Surely the Dungeon Core were taking Pallin to Malfur in Thob Forest.

"What lies in this direction?" Straiah asked Estrien.

"Nothing," she responded. "Unless one intends to find Melanor. This is one of the old pathways."

"Then it's got to be a diversion," Straiah concluded.

"I don't think so," replied Sheabor. "I heard the sound of many footsteps on the mountain. And there aren't any tracks leading away from here, not even concealed ones."

"Didn't Pallin say that the people of Eulsiphion once used the Squall Highlands as a road to the barbarian lands?" Durian broke in. All eyes turned to him. "He said they sent an envoy and that they were ambushed in the highlands."

"Perhaps the questions should be kept for later," Estrien spoke up. "For now, we know they have taken Pallin this way."

The group set off, the ascent steep and winding. Durian's muscles burned as the three Suriyans struggled to keep pace. The mountains overhead stretched far into the night sky, illuminated by the moon and lightly sprinkling starlight. All was silence from Eulsiphion. The city was seated afar off now, glowing faintly against the flowing waterfall. The battle with the barbarians seemed over. It was all just a diversion to capture Pallin.

As time went on, the grass of the trail gave way to the bare rock of the mountain. The pathway wound around many bends, one of which offered their first glimpse of the north – the vast, sweeping realm of the Horctura. Though difficult to discern its features in the darkness, Durian thought he detected tiny dots of light. It could have been the torches of the barbarians who fled the battle. Durian couldn't say.

That was the last glimpse of the outside world, for their pathway made a sharp turn into the interior of the mountains. High walls of rock rose up around them, and in the lonely corridors of the mountain, a thick fog spread out overhead, obscuring the light of the moon.

"Just what we need," Baron declared. "More fog."

"Be silent, Baron," said Sheabor.

The mist was strange, hovering like a low-lying cloud just above them.

"Be very cautious now," said Estrien. "There is a strange magic at work in the Squall Highlands. Do not trust the ground and do not become separated."

"What is it?" whispered Straiah. "What's out there?"

"Long ago, some from Melanor sought the highlands as a place of solitude and contemplation. Those who came here never returned. Something happened. We're not sure what. We sent others to search for them, and these also disappeared. None from Melanor come here now."

The narrow passageway finally opened into a wide and level arena of stone. Solitary boulders and spires of stone were peppered about, some stretching upward into the mist. The ground was strangely dusty here, and each step brought a small eruption of very fine dust into the air, which swirled about their feet and settled again around them. Sheabor walked a few paces and came to a halt.

"Something's wrong. The tracks have disappeared."

"Did they take another route?"

"No," Sheabor replied. "Something in the dust is covering them. Even our own tracks are hidden."

"What should we do?" asked Baron.

"We'll have to quicken our pace."

"Sheabor, that is not wise," said Estrien.

"We'll stay close. Come on."

And with that, Sheabor set off. The three Suriyans were quick to follow, then Straiah and Estrien. Sheabor zig-zagged his way around the boulders and spires, attempting to keep a relatively straight course. But despite his efforts, it felt to Durian as though they were being shuffled in a particular direction.

They ran this way for many long minutes, the arena of stone yet to end. Durian passed a boulder he thought he recognized. Or was it his mind playing tricks on him?

Sheabor halted and surveyed the scene. Unsheathing his hammer, he brought the tip into the side of the boulder nearest him, leaving a fractured hole in its face. Then he set off again, periodically leaving his mark.

After a short while, the group ran past a boulder that Sheabor had struck. He halted again momentarily, then set off in a new direction. Durian felt dizzy and completely lost. What a horror it would be to be trapped here alone. But at length, the group cleared the arena and came to a high mountain face stretching upward into the mist. In the wall of stone were four corridors.

Sheabor and Straiah searched the ground for any clue. But the dust still worked against them.

"We need to split up," Sheabor declared.

"No, we must not separate," Estrien replied.

"If we stay as one and choose the wrong passage, Pallin is lost forever. I will take the Suriyans with me. You and Straiah search the right hand side."

Before Estrien could protest, Sheabor burst down one of the left hand passages, followed by the three Suriyans. The passageway was narrow and winding, and the mist still clung overhead. Durian's unease was growing and his feet ached from darting back and forth around sharp corners. Everything told him they were walking into a trap.

Sheabor darted around a corner and suddenly yelled out in fright. Before he could react, Durian came around the same corner to find Sheabor at the edge of a cliff, wavering, trying desperately not to fall. Durian's knees locked and he slid forward, ducking to his left to avoid a fatal collision. His left shoulder hit the wall but his right shoulder knocked into Sheabor. Sheabor began to fall and Durian lunged to grab the back of his collar, his left hand holding onto the wall. But Sheabor was too heavy.

Durian yelled, his fingers scraping ineffectually against the stony wall, about to lose hold. His fingers were inches from the edge of the wall. But a hand grabbed the back of his shirt, holding Durian in place for the moment. But Durian's fingertips were cramping and about to give way. The weight of Sheabor was too much. Baron, who held Durian's shirt, was sliding toward the edge.

"Blair! Grab onto something!"

"Hurry!" Durian yelled.

"I'm trying!" Blair called out.

Durian could feel his fingertips failing from fatigue. They were the only thing stabilizing them.

"Blair, pull!" Baron yelled. "On three!"

Baron yelled a quick count and Durian felt a strong tug on his shirt. Durian threw his weight back in tandem and fell to the ground in a tangled thud with Baron and Blair. Sheabor staggered back a few paces and likewise fell into the group. He laughed as he sat up in the dirt, but the rest were less than amused.

Durian's face was covered in beads of sweat. He lay in the dirt, eyes closed, waiting for his heart to slow. Only paces away from them was nothing more than a thousand foot drop. After a few moments, the group stood to their feet. As they did, something below in the vast distance caught Durian's attention.

"What is that?" asked Durian, finger pointing.

Meanwhile, Estrien and Straiah moved along another passageway, silent as they listened for sounds of the Dungeon Core. But only the shuffling of their own feet was heard. It was strange that the Dungeon Core was able to keep ahead of them.

As Straiah pondered, the ground gave way beneath Estrien's feet, and she yelled in fright as she fell into a hidden hole. But she didn't go far, for her feet hit solid ground after a short drop, as though she had stepped into a barrel of quicksand. Straiah stopped and bent down to help her up. Grasping her by the hands, he pulled to no avail. The ground had somehow solidified around her. She was trapped up to her waist in the middle of the pathway.

"What happened?" he said.

193

"I don't know," she said. "I can't move."

Straiah unsheathed his sword and thrust the tip into the ground just beside her. But it bounced from the surface, leaving hardly a scratch.

"Can you use your ability to free yourself?" Straiah asked.

Estrien placed the palms of her hands on the ground around her and began speaking in the ancient tongue. But as she did, she suddenly winced in pain, as though the ground itself resisted her call and tightened in response.

"Go," she pleaded, at length. "Rescue Pallin."

Straiah's heart beat quickly.

"Sheabor and the others might come this way," she said. "He can free me with the hammer. Go. Now!"

Straiah hesitated. If he left her, he might never find her again. He bent down, taking one of her hands in his, and gently kissed it. He looked at her intently, but she didn't meet his gaze, and after a few moments, he turned and ran into darkness.

Straiah's mind raced as he moved down the winding corridor. The pathway opened up a bit into a small arena. But abruptly, the passageway ended at a sheer wall. Straiah, unwilling to backtrack, began climbing. But the dust all over the ground seemed to cover everything, like a slick film of oil. He made only a few paces headway before slipping down. He had no choice but to turn back.

Meanwhile, Sheabor, Durian and the twins stood high atop the cliff they had nearly fallen from.

Before them were the lands of Forthura. Above Eulsiphion in the barbarian highlands, small points of light were converging into a line, a glowing serpent slithering toward the city.

"I thought the barbarians fled," said Durian.

Sheabor watched silently for many minutes. As the glow of lights continued toward the city, from the east, a thick fog formed atop the plains, just outside the city. Within minutes, the fog had completely enveloped Eulsiphion.

"Come on," said Sheabor.

What was happening? But the group set off down the winding corridor, coming back to the place where the four pathways met. Sheabor chose another and set off before Durian could stall him. Everything seemed wrong. How were the Dungeon Core navigating this maze with such success? And what was happening to Eulsiphion?

As they came around a bend in the road, there, stuck in the middle of the trail was a soldier half buried. The group halted and came round to the front of him. The soldier was one of the Dungeon Core and he was still alive. The three Suriyans marveled in fear over what had happened to him, while Sheabor locked eyes with the soldier.

"Tell us where your people are taking Pallin," he demanded.

He was met with silence.

"Is Malfur with the Horctura?"

At that question the soldier lifted his head back and laughed. The landscape seemed to react to the laugh, as though the desolation itself was pained at the

195

sound. The wind began to suddenly howl down the corridors. Durian thought he saw a slight tinge of fear in the man's eyes.

"Answer our questions and we will set you free."

The soldier's eyes narrowed and he clenched his jaw, summoning his resolve.

"Perhaps a night alone, helpless, will loosen your tongue," Sheabor said.

He sheathed his sword and moved off. Durian ran behind him, fearful of being left behind, but equally fearful now of the ground all around him. What had happened to the soldier? Durian followed closely in Sheabor's footsteps.

The group snaked their way through the mountain. Time seemed to stretch on. Everything looked the same and the fog hung above their heads, obscuring their view of anything beyond.

At length they came to an open arena of stone, not unlike the one before. Sheabor slowed as he analyzed the places ahead. But he tensed and held up his hand behind him, signaling the Suriyans to remain still. Then, silently drawing his sword from its sheath, he waited. Durian thought he heard the sound of boots on the stony floor.

The Suriyans crouched low against one of the boulders. Sheabor crept forward to the nearest boulder and raised his sword. As the sound neared, Sheabor stepped forward and swung his sword. But he suddenly dropped it mid-swing and stumbled toward the ground. Durian's heart beat quickly.

Just then, Straiah slid into view and came to an abrupt halt. Sheabor had nearly killed him. But Straiah was alone.

"Where's Estrien?" Durian asked.

"She's trapped. I couldn't free her. We need the hammer."

"We'll go back for her once we've rescued Pallin," Sheabor said.

Straiah clenched his jaw. But at length he nodded. Sheabor stepped forward and scanned the landscape. Judging from the direction Straiah had come, he set a new course. And though it seemed the wrong way to Durian, that was probably a good sign.

They ran through the arena until a change slowly came over the landscape, one which Durian didn't notice until after the fact. But the fog slowly lifted, an open sky of stars lay overhead, and grasses sprang up where only stony earth lay before. Then suddenly, a broad landscape of grassy hills and distant woods came into view. They had made it through the Squall Highlands at last! Turning round, Durian gazed at the looming mountains shrouded in obscuring haze.

"Thob Forest was a picnic next to this place," Baron exclaimed. "Remind me never to leave home again without a compass."

Blair and Durian chuckled.

"I see tracks!" Straiah exclaimed.

The group huddled around him to look. Then, staring off in the places before them, they looked for signs of the Dungeon Core. But the hills shrouded the nearby places. How had the Dungeon Core kept so far

197

ahead of them? Without a word, Sheabor sprang forward into the night.

"Try to keep up as best you can," Straiah said, jogging a few paces away. "If you lose sight of us, run directly toward the moon. If you run for longer than half an hour and do not see us, turn back to the mountains and wait for our return."

Then Straiah sprinted to catch up with Sheabor. The three Suriyans met one another's uneasy glances at being left alone in the barbarian kingdom, but set off at a jog to the north. It didn't take long to lose sight of Sheabor and Straiah. The fear drove them for a time, but exhaustion soon took hold and they slowed.

"Why don't we just go back to the mountain?" asked Blair. "What sense does it make to wear ourselves out when we're just going to turn around and run the other way?"

Durian nodded, his hands on his knees. He arose and opened his mouth to speak, but something caught his attention. It sounded like swords clashing. Baron's eyes darted over his shoulders and then back to the group.

"Come on," Baron said.

A shallow hill lay ahead, and the sound seemed to carry around it. Quickly climbing, Sheabor and Straiah were engaged with nearly a dozen Dungeon Core warriors just ahead of them. In the distance, over the next few hillsides, were dots of light. The barbarians were coming.

"Look!" said Blair..."I see Pallin!"

Lying motionless on the battlefield was the form of Pallin. Sheabor and Straiah fought with the

Dungeon Core in the small hollow between two hillsides, bordered to the west by a small copse of trees.

"Let's get him!" said Baron.

"He's in the middle of the battle," protested Durian.

But Baron paid no heed and ran down the hillside, sword drawn. Durian and Blair likewise followed him into battle.

"Baron!" Sheabor yelled. "Take Pallin to cover!"

Pallin was only a stone's throw away. Sheabor and Straiah were each locked with a separate handful of Dungeon Core soldiers. When Baron neared Pallin, two warriors broke to cut him off.

Baron, instead of engaging the warriors, darted left and continued towards Sheabor. Blair, just behind, darted to the right around them toward Straiah. The warriors chased after for a short while, leaving Durian alone to go for Pallin. But the soldiers weren't quick to fall for the ruse and left the twins.

Durian reached Pallin and bent down to shake him awake, calling out his name. But Pallin didn't stir. The soldiers were nearly back to him. Durian arose and retreated away, followed by one of the soldiers. Baron attacked the group of warriors who fought with Sheabor. The soldier blocked Baron's blow, but Sheabor was quick to take the advantage and strike him dead. But the other soldier guarding Pallin had come up from behind and now flanked Baron.

"Baron!" Sheabor yelled as the swing came in, reaching to block it and save Baron's life.

Sheabor parried the blow, but the other warriors advanced on him. He turned to meet their blows, but the force of them knocked him to the ground. The other soldier, still flanking Baron, struck him with the back of his armored hand, sending Baron down in a wave of dizziness.

Straiah was engaged nearby with two warriors, having already dispatched one. Three soldiers were now standing over Baron and Sheabor. Blair was left alone between Pallin and Straiah. He sprinted for Sheabor and his brother, throwing his whole body into the middle soldier and tackling the group to the ground. Then he rolled and scrambled away right as a sword struck the ground he had just occupied.

The soldier pursuing Durian saw what was happening and turned round to help his comrades. Durian turned and moved carefully back toward Pallin. Sheabor and Baron wrestled with the three soldiers on the ground and Blair sprang to his feet. But one of the soldiers on the ground also arose and came after Blair, who quickly retreated toward the copse of trees.

Sheabor struck one of the warriors on the jaw with the hilt of his sword, dazing him. Baron was locked on the ground with the other warrior, who had the upper hand against Baron, pushing his sword down dangerously close to Baron's throat. But Sheabor arose and struck him dead. Baron pushed him off and rose to his feet.

The other soldier arrived and engaged Sheabor, leaving Durian free to make his move. He sprinted toward Pallin trying in vain to pull him onto his shoulders. But dragging him to the copse of trees, he maneuvered Pallin away from battle. Durian's legs and lungs burned with exertion. If any of the Dungeon Core came at him, he'd be too tired to flee. But he was almost to the treeline.

With exhausting effort, Durian pulled Pallin to a large tree and sat him up against it. Then he collapsed into the forest to catch his breath. After a moment's rest, he used the tree's support to sling Pallin over his shoulder and began moving through treeline. Durian heaved deeps breaths of air, beads of sweat falling down his face. The sound of battle trailed away, now only intermittent death cries piercing the darkness.

Suddenly, a hand clamped down on Durian's shoulder. His body tensed and his legs gave way to exhaustion, tumbling him and Pallin to the ground. He turned to find a solitary Dungeon Core warrior standing over him, sword poised. Durian tried to call out, but couldn't stop from heaving in breaths of air.

The Dungeon Core must have overcome Sheabor and Straiah. Durian closed his eyes. But he heard the sound of a rock striking against metal and the yell of Sheabor nearby. Durian looked up to see the warrior turn and block a blow from Sheabor. But Straiah was close behind and struck the warrior dead.

"Are the two of you okay?" Sheabor asked, kneeling down to him and Pallin.

Durian nodded his head, but still lay unmoving on the ground.

"What do you think you're doing?" demanded Baron, and reached down with the help of Blair to pull Durian to his feet. Sheabor was gazing intently into the unconscious face of Pallin.

201

"They've drugged him," Durian said.

But Sheabor suddenly glanced over his shoulder to the west. The copse of trees seemed to end at a large cliff overlooking the lands of Forthura. Durian could hear something faintly coming from the direction. Sheabor stood and moved toward it, followed by the rest.

As they drew near, the sounds of battle traveled through the leagues of open air from the lands of Forthura. A vast fog blanketed the plains, covering the place Eulsiphion had stood. Muffled lights and distant yells were all that came to them. The group watched on in silence. Eulsiphion was completely besieged, not just by barbarians, but by Malfur, Keeper of the North Wind.

Just then, a form came and stood behind them. They turned round in surprise to see Pallin.

"It's just as I feared," said Pallin. "The words of King Froamb have come to pass. Malfur wouldn't dare attack the city with another Windbearer dwelling there. It was all a ploy to get us out from the city."

Pallin's words hung in the air. What were they going to do now? If Malfur took Eulsiphion, the entire Kingdom of Forthura would fall, including Suriya. Durian's heart beat quickly. He turned to Pallin, who seemed lost in thought.

"Pallin, what are you thinking?" asked Sheabor.

"There may yet be hope," he replied. "Not for Eulsiphion, but for us. We have only moments to spare. If most of the barbarian forces are down in the lowlands besieging the city, they have likely left not more than a handful back to patrol their borders. If we

202

leave now, fleeing north, we may be able to slip past their sentries and continue westward toward the lands of Kester and the Bearoc."

"We can't do that!" said Durian. "What about Suriya and the other townships?"

Sheabor glanced to Pallin, who warmly placed a hand on Durian's shoulder.

"Suriya will be safe for now. Now that they've taken Eulsiphion, the barbarians and Malfur will work to fortify their position against Kester and the Bearoc. In a way, Suriya is safer now that Malfur has left Thob Forest."

But Straiah unexpectedly raised his voice.

"We must go back through the highlands."

All eyes turned to him in confusion. Sheabor took a step toward Straiah and looked at him solemnly.

"I am sorry, my friend," he said. "North is our only chance of escape."

"I will not leave her behind to die alone in that wretched place," Straiah replied.

Durian had forgotten that Estrien was trapped in the highlands. Straiah was right, they couldn't just leave her there. But Durian could see in Sheabor and Pallin's eyes that they weren't going to turn back for her. Straiah saw it too. Though none of them wanted to leave Estrien behind, Straiah was unyielding. He seemed to be completely taken with her. None spoke a word as they waited for Straiah to realize what had to be done. For the sake of everyone, she had to be left behind.

"Sheabor, we have been friends for many years," Straiah said. "We have fought side by side from the day our hands could lift a sword. I'm asking you to give me your hammer and let me stay behind."

His plea rendered the others speechless. All eyes turned to Sheabor.

"Sheabor, if Malfur captures your hammer, this continent will fall," said Pallin. "Its fate is more important than any one of us."

Sheabor gazed into the eyes of his long-time friend.

"Straiah knows what he is asking," said Sheabor to Pallin. "If we cannot trust our friends and put our lives in their hands, what is left worth fighting for?"

Sheabor slowly unsheathed the Hammer of Haladrin and handed it to Straiah. The gleam of the Candlewood filled the darkened trees will a mellow glow.

"Friend," he said, "you hold the fate of our world in your hands."

With that, the two embraced. Straiah stood tall in front of his companions and bowed low, knowing he would probably never see them again. Then he departed swiftly toward the ominous mountains. The rest watched him go until he disappeared into the darkness.

"Come on," said Sheabor at length. "We have a long road ahead of us."

# Part 2

Thay Iphilus Forest

Ruhkan Mountains

The Maelstrom

Trakhendor

Thob Forest

Hadrach
Shay River
Schadelmar
Seven Secrets
Mt Skultira
Duriac
Squall

# The Descent From the Highlands

Durian and the others watched as Straiah disappeared into the rolling hillside. The battle for Eulsiphion was still being waged. And though they wanted to stay, they couldn't linger here. Time was no longer on their side. No one knew what to expect in this vast realm of the Horctura. None of them had traveled here before, except perhaps Pallin.

Durian took comfort in the words of Pallin. Now that Malfur and the barbarians had captured Eulsiphion, they would care little for conquering distant townships at the edge of the world.

"Pallin, have you traveled these lands?" questioned Sheabor.

"I have traveled every land there is to travel. Though these my eyes have not seen since the days before the barbarian kingdom took dominion of it. They are not kindly toward outsiders and wanderers."

"How will we avoid detection?" he continued.

"We will travel in disguise if we can manage," responded Pallin. "My former captors have given us an advantage."

They wouldn't get far in Dungeon Core armor. It would get them past the first fort perhaps. But Durian was skeptical that Dungeon Core soldiers traveled at large through the barbarian kingdom.

"What are the settlements like?"

209

"Most are wooden forts, built solidly for war."

"With Forthura?"

"With each another, more often as not," Pallin replied. "Many of the tribes are nomads. They are accustomed to taking what they wish and being on their way."

"Will we reach any of the settlements by morning?"

"I don't know," Pallin replied. "But we had best get moving."

"They can't be far," said Sheabor. "The Dungeon Core were on foot."

"We saw torches in the distance earlier," said Blair.

"We saw them too," said Sheabor. "The barbarians must have been rendezvousing with the Dungeon Core."

Sheabor set off through the trees, back to where the slain Dungeon Core soldiers lay in the field. Each found a suitable disguise, but none of the Suriyans had ever worn armor and the pieces flopped about as they moved. Sheabor and Pallin helped tighten them as much as possible, and in the end, Pallin, with his long beard was the most conspicuous of all. This wasn't likely to work. But it was their best chance.

The group left the battlefield behind and made north, careful to watch for the barbarian party sent to meet the Dungeon Core. But after a short while, it seemed as though the barbarians had already gone. Sheabor angled to the east as they jogged. After a short while, Shay River came into view.

"Where are you taking us?" Pallin questioned.

"Any barbarian settlements will undoubtedly be along the river. We'll never escape without horses. We have no choice but to enter one of the forts."

Durian's heart raced. How could they ever hope to accomplish such a feat? But Sheabor wasn't a fool. He'd form a plan.

The moon hung low in the north, turning orange as it dipped toward the far horizon. Durian's muscles burned from the extra weight of the armor. It had to have been past midnight by now.

There was a hillside ahead. Sheabor made for it. By the time they ascended, the moon had disappeared below the horizon, the sky now awash with stars. Standing on the crest, the landscape was a sea of black in all directions. Sheabor's hand extended, finger pointing to the north.

"There, do you see it?"

Barely perceptible was a glow emanating from somewhere below the hilly landscape to the north.

"You four will rest here," Sheabor continued. "I will enter the fort alone and bring back horses."

Durian was taken aback. How in the world did he hope to manage that? Then he turned to Pallin.

"If I don't return, your best hope might be to try and find Melanor to the east."

"You will return," Pallin replied.

"Get some rest."

Then Sheabor descended the hill and blended at length with the pervading dark. The group laid down to rest at the base of the hill and quickly fell to sleep. The mellow glow of dawn awoke them. It was quite cold and Durian's body ached as he arose. He made his way slowly up the hillside.

A sweeping view came into focus. Surprisingly, far to the east, he saw a sliver of coastline through the mountains. North was a mixture of grassy and rocky hillsides. And to the west were a pair of ominous mountains that looked once to have been a single massive boulder shaped almost like an armored loaf of bread cleaved through the center as if by some earthquake long ago.

"That is not a natural mountain," said a voice just behind Durian.

It was Pallin.

"Not a natural mountain?"

"That is Mount Skultira," said Pallin, "Through the Gap of Skultira is where we make our westward turn toward Kester and the Bearoc. It was once a single mountain. But the earthquake at the end of the Great War undoubtedly split it in two. This whole region was once the land of Cavanah. The Builders went through a phase in their creativity in which they sought to mimic the natural world. They created piles of boulders, river rapids, and even small mountains. This whole region is rife with their work. Mount Skultira, as it is named by the Horctura, was one of their constructions."

Durian couldn't believe it. The thought was almost beyond comprehension.

"Why did they do that?" Durian asked.

Pallin smiled.

"Why do painters paint, or poets compose lays of epic deeds? It is in man's nature to explore the depths of his creativity."

What a wondrous place the old world must have been, Durian thought. But then his mind drifted back to Sheabor.

"What do you think Sheabor will tell them?"

"What they want to hear," Pallin responded. "I'm sure the barbarians have been instructed to give the Dungeon Core full cooperation."

Then the pair were silent. The breeze from the west came warm as the sun broke the far horizon behind it. It made Durian think of Suriya and the baneful wind from the south that arose from the Frostlands each morning in winter.

"Suriyans are a hearty people," said Pallin suddenly. "They will flee and survive the rule of Malfur – perhaps to Thob Forest, or beyond Boreol Bay to the Frostlands for a time to wait out the darkness."

Durian nodded and smiled. Then he resolved to put his worries behind him for good.

Meanwhile, Sheabor jogged toward the wall of the large fort. Though the sky was just beginning to lighten, the stars overhead still held sway. Wooden spikes jutting from the walls and ground were all that greeted him. Archers patrolled the low wall, paying him no mind as he came to the main gate and pounded hard. A small window was opened in the gate and the face of a guard appeared.

"What news do you bring?"

213

"We have captured Pallin the Windbearer," Sheabor said. "We require fresh horses."

"A squadron came to meet you," declared the guard. "They reported you never arrived. Where is the rest of your detachment?"

"They've hidden in the Squall Highlands," Sheabor continued. "We were tracked by a group from Eulsiphion – the two from the Banished Lands and many others. I was sent ahead to acquire horses for our escape. The group tracking us is on foot."

"Where are they now?"

"Just north of the Squall Highlands, waiting for us to emerge."

"We'll send a detachment."

"Do you have men to spare? I was told that all the fighting men had gone to Eulsiphion."

"We can give you half a dozen men. That should be more than a match for whoever followed from Eulsiphion."

Sheabor bowed but said nothing. To refuse would look suspicious. A half dozen barbarians was more than he could handle on his own. If Straiah were here, that would be one thing. But three Suriyans and an old man...

At length, the large gate opened and four men on horseback emerged, dressed in leather armor for battle. Sheabor sighed in relief. They must have been more shorthanded than the guard had let on. The four barbarians carried six additional horses in tow.

The barbarians were large men, muscular and mostly golden of hair. They wore boots of leather and fur, and fur vests beneath their leather armor. Their

214

arms were unclad and their legs wore only thin leather pants. They descended away from the fort and down toward the river. Sheabor could only hope the others would see them from a long way off.

Pallin and Durian stood atop the shallow hillside, the morning sun creeping above the western horizon. Their thoughts were turned to Sheabor, wondering when he might return, if at all.

But something caught their attention. In the distance, a barely perceptible plume of dust was rising. Moments passed and the plume dissolved. But Durian thought he heard the whinnying of a horse.

Another plume of dust closer to them. Then the unmistakable galloping of horses. Pallin darted down the hill, followed by Durian.

"Quickly!" he said. "Arm yourselves. Sheabor is not alone."

"What? How do you know?"

But Pallin crept toward a nearby boulder at the base of the hill, sword drawn. The Suriyans glanced about for cover. The galloping grew louder. Durian and Blair darted to another boulder on the opposite hillside, while Pallin picked up a stone and handed it to Baron, now behind him.

"When I tell you, throw it with all your might."

Pallin leaned against the large boulder, eyes closed. The pounding was loud all around them. Baron tensed and took a step forward. But Pallin grabbed him by the arm and stalled him. The riders would be past them any moment!

Just then, Pallin released his grip from Baron's arm. He sprang round the boulder and leaned back, throwing the rock squarely at a barbarian warrior not more than five paces away. Hitting him in the chest, the barbarian fell backward off his horse, landing with a thud.

The other warriors were just to Baron, about to ride over him. But Pallin pulled him to safety by the collar of his shirt. Sheabor struck another of the barbarians from behind, just as they halted and turned round.

The Horctura unsheathed their weapons. They each carried a large broadsword, and turned on Sheabor. Sheabor parried their blows but weakly, the barbarians clearly more proficient at horse-borne warfare. The three Suriyans picked up more stones and hurled them at the pair of barbarians. One of them broke and rode for Durian and Blair.

Coming fast he swung across their chests, sending both their swords flying and each of them to the ground. Turning for another pass, Blair and Durian ran behind a nearby boulder to keep from being trampled. Sheabor was still locked in combat. He ducked and parried his blows, but couldn't get close enough for his own strike.

The barbarian reared up for another strike, but Sheabor kicked his horse, closing the distance between them and met the barbarian's blow mid-strike, locking their two swords. The barbarian was powerful, pushing against Sheabor with all of his might.

Sheabor, losing the battle of strength, ducked back hard, watching the slash pass just over his head, then rolled from the back of his horse, hitting the ground on his feet but subsequently falling down. The barbarian also lost balance and nearly fell from his horse. But he began to right himself as Sheabor stood. He lunged for him, grappling with the barbarian and pulled him from his horse. Each stood to his feet. Sheabor advanced, making swift strikes. The broadsword was very effective on horseback, but not as much on foot. Frustrated, the warrior struck back at Sheabor who ducked his blow and then buried his sword in the man's torso.

Meanwhile, Blair and Durian, having been disarmed, retreated up the hillside. The barbarian still on horseback made for Pallin and Baron. They were no match for him and retreated up their own hillside. He dismounted and pursued them.

He caught up with Pallin quickly and hooked his arm round his neck, pulling off his helmet to the realization that this was the man whom Malfur wanted captured. Pallin struggled in vain as the barbarian drug him down the hillside. Once more on the valley floor, the barbarian now squared off with Sheabor.

"Halt, or I will kill this man."

Sheabor was only a few paces from him. Blair and Durian now joined him. Sheabor advanced quickly toward the warrior. What was he doing?

"I said halt!"

Sheabor reared up and swung down at the barbarian. Throwing Pallin to one side, he blocked Sheabor's blow and another. But being caught by surprise, Sheabor made quick work of him.

Sheabor came over to Pallin and helped him to his feet. Rubbing his throat in a bit of shock, Pallin offered his thanks. The others ran up to join them.

"How did you know he wouldn't kill Pallin?" Blair asked.

"He knew I was the one that Malfur was after," Pallin responded.

Sheabor surveyed the scene for the horses. Most had fled, but three were in sight. The barbarian whom Baron had struck with a rock still lay unconscious on the valley floor, and they were content to leave him as such. Mounting the three horses, they soon found a fourth and fifth and were riding away speedily north.

Soon they would curve west, when the landscape leveled enough to traverse it. For now, the high cliffs overlooking the Kingdom, Forthura, pervaded.

"We must make for the Gap of Skultira!" Pallin shouted and pointed at the ominous mountain rock, cleaved in two. The group veered directly into the heart of the barbarian kingdom.

# The Return to the Highlands

Straiah ran toward the looming mountains of the Squall Highlands, the Hammer of Haladrin gleaming in the darkness. He clenched it tightly, knowing Pallin had been right about its fate. Sheabor's hammer was more important than anyone or anything. Without it, the Windbearers would never regain their powers and the Eastern Realm would fall to the rule of Malfur and Corcoran.

His mind raced to form a plan. What was he going to do after finding Estrien? Would they still have time to catch up to Sheabor and Pallin? How could he put the welfare of Estrien above the fate of the kingdom? But every time he thought about her gentle elegance, it brought a rush of feeling he had seldom experienced.

Soon the sparse grasses gave way to the stony highlands. The fog hung thickly overhead as he entered the scattered arena. It was the same as before, yet somehow different, as though the pieces of the board had somehow rearranged themselves. A malevolent presence seemed just out of sight, hovering in the mist and watching him carefully.

Straiah didn't have time for this. Coming to a nearby spire of stone, he smashed the base with a handful of blows, sending it to the earth with a mighty crash.

Straiah continued on, striking stones as he went until finding his way at length to the other end of the arena, where a handful of corridors lay. But it was different than he remembered. Coming to one of the corridors, he peered down it.

"Estrien!" he called down it.

The wind seemed to float back through the passageway, playing off the walls like a gleeful laugh. Straiah set off down the winding corridor. It snaked along this way and that, and coming round a corner, suddenly, in the pathway was a skeleton, half buried in the middle of the path. The wind swept past him, again carrying the faint laughter of some malevolent force.

His heart beat quickly. It couldn't be Estrien. The world seemed to suddenly spin and he leaned against the stony wall for support. The mist undulated thickly above him. Time seemed like a foreign thing in this place, locked in an eternal, dismal now of some shadow plane of existence.

He closed his eyes and took a deep breath, gripping the hammer ever more tightly and setting off again. The wind whistled down the pathway and halted him in his tracks. It seemed to carry the familiar voice of Estrien. He stopped and listened. Again with the whistle of the breeze came her voice calling his name.

"Estrien!"

But nothing more. Straiah sprinted forward darting around the endless bends. Then, coming round a corner, the pathway ended abruptly at a sheer cliff. Straiah tried to stop, but it was too late. His legs locked and he fell to the ground, his shoulder impacting hard as his body slid forward over the edge. He reached desperately with his free hand for anything to grab hold of, but there was nothing. The dust was too slick.

In a final effort, he dragged the tip of the hammer along the ground at the base of the wall. It wasn't enough to stop him. But the hammer caught hold of the edge of the wall and stuck fast. Dangling by one arm above a massive precipice, his shoulder burned and tore. He reached upward to grab hold of something with his free hand, but felt the hammer slipping, and stopped. Straiah closed his eyes and took a deep breath.

When he opened them again, he analyzed his surroundings. There was a foothold against the cliff near him. Reaching his foot to make contact, his toe slipped from the edge and he grimaced in pain at the jarring which threatened to dislocate his shoulder. Taking a deep breath, he extended his foot slowly until reaching the foothold. Putting pressure down and relieving his shoulder, he found a handhold.

Climbing the short distance back onto the ledge, he laid down on his back for many moments, watching his breath dissolve in the cold mountain heights. He couldn't believe that such a place as this existed.

When he arose, he looked out over the distant expanse. Eulsiphion was far below, shining like a star in the darkened plains, the enveloping cloud gone. It looked at peace. Departing once more, he came to the junction of passages. Straiah chose another and darted down it.

But this one quickly dead ended. Frustrated, Straiah yelled and smashed a hole into the smooth wall.

Hitting it again just above, Straiah realized suddenly that he could make his own handholds. Though the wall stretched upward and out of sight into the mist, it might be only a low wall.

Smashing small holes as he went, Straiah ascended upward in the left side corner of the wall, using both sides to scale the wall with ease. After a short ways, the mist enveloped him. But the wall soon ended and he climbed down the other side into a different corridor.

Running down this one, he suddenly stumbled into the beautiful form of Estrien. He almost couldn't believe it.

"Straiah!" she exclaimed.

"Estrien! I thought I'd never find you."

He bent down and embraced her tightly.

"Did you rescue Pallin?"

"Yes, he's with the others," Straiah responded.

"Where are they?"

Straiah straightened his posture and took a deep breath.

"I had to leave them," he replied. "They went north, through the lands of the Horctura, toward Kester and the Bearoc."

"What's happened?" she asked. "I don't understand."

"Let me free you, and I'll explain everything."

With that, Straiah raised his hammer. He swung down with all his might, driving the point of the hammer into the solid ground near her waist. The ground didn't shatter, and the tip sank downward, as though he had struck soft clay. Straiah tugged on the handle to free it, but the hammer was stuck fast in place. He pulled with all his might, but the hammer didn't budge. Panic hit him.

"It's stuck," he said.

"What? You have to free it!"

Straiah glanced round. There was a mid sized stone nearby. He took it in his hands. It was almost too much to bear. Straiah stood over the hammer with the stone. Summoning all his strength, he raised the stone above his head with a roar. Then he threw the stone down onto the handle. The stone's heavy weight jarred the hammer free, flipping it through the air, narrowly missing both him and Estrien. Straiah sighed in great relief and took the hammer in his hands.

Raising it once more above his head, he hit the hardened ground, this time with the flat end of the hammer. The ground cracked a bit. Estrien grimaced in pain. Straiah struck the ground again, and this time Estrien let out a yell. The impact of the hammer was sending jarring waves of force through the hardened rock. He would break all her bones before he ever freed her. He looked at her in desperation, the image of the skeleton half sunk in the ground frozen in his mind.

"You need to leave me behind," she said, her face stern but her eyes betraying fear. "You can't risk losing the hammer."

Straiah hesitated, drawing heavy breaths of cool night air as the moments slid by. His mind was racing.

"Go!"

Straiah turned round and called out into the night.

"I'll smash this whole place to the ground!" he yelled. "Do you hear me!"

And with that, Straiah smashed the hammer into the wall beside him, sending a crack upward and away into the mist. Then he set his sights toward the end of the corridor where the arena of stone lay with its many spires and boulders.

"It's loosening!" Estrien exclaimed.

He spun round and ran to her as she pushed herself free. Whatever dark forces were at work in this place, they were more content to lose a prisoner than see Straiah on the loose with the Hammer of Haladrin.

Straiah pulled Estrien up from the ground and into his arms. They hugged tightly for many moments, and then she stared into his eyes, stroking his cheek with her fingertips.

"You reckless man," she said, shaking her head.

He smiled. But then her gaze turned serious.

"Why didn't the rest come back this way?" she asked.

Straiah took a step away.

"Things are worse than we had imagined," he said. "I'm afraid we've underestimated Malfur. Kidnapping Pallin was just a ploy to get him and us away from the city, while he and the Horctura attacked it. As far as we can tell, Eulsiphion has fallen. Sheabor and the others went northward while they could, with the barbarian horde down in the valley. They're hoping to keep ahead of them."

"But the hammer..." she said. "We can't let it fall into Malfur's hands."

224

"And we won't," he encouraged. "Even now, Sheabor and the others are heading northward through the barbarian kingdom. They're sure to have encounters with them. When word reaches Malfur that some have passed that way, he'll never suspect that two have stayed behind in the highlands. He won't search for us here."

Estrien clenched her jaw and looked down at the dusty ground.

"You shouldn't have come back for me."

Straiah searched for words as he gazed at her defeated countenance.

"I had to," was all he could say.

She raised her eyes to meet his and nodded amid misty eyes. He closed the distance between them and took hold of her hands. Then he kissed her. And for a brief moment in the desolate, stony highlands, everything was perfect.

"We need to keep moving," Estrien said at length.

"We'll find a quiet place to hide for awhile."

"I don't want to just hide," she said pushing away from him and turning round. "My duty is to protect Pallin. You can't know what an honor it was to be given that responsibility. We can't just wander the highlands while Pallin and the others face danger and death."

Straiah said nothing, but stepped behind her and placed his hand on her shoulder. She pulled away from him and walked forward. But she didn't get very far. Estrien heard it only a moment before Straiah and drew her sword quietly from its sheath. At first they couldn't tell what it was – a faint sound echoing down the corridor. Straiah came forward and stood next to Estrien, hammer poised to strike. It sounded like footsteps and muffled voices, but Straiah had been tricked more than once in this cursed place.

Straiah motioned to head a ways down the passage to find a more concealed location. If it was barbarians or Dungeon Core, avoiding them would be better than a confrontation. Coming to the crossroads, the arena of scattered boulders and spires came into view. Straiah darted to one of the boulders. They could lose themselves easily here. But as they darted from boulder to boulder, a familiar voice called out.

"Stay together men, and stay close," said the voice. "There's something foul amiss."

Straiah looked to Estrien in wonderment. It was King Froamb. Straiah stepped out from hiding, startling those who stood nearby.

"Sire, look!" said one of them. "It's one of the men from the Banished Lands."

King Froamb came forward.

"Straiah!" he exclaimed. "What are you doing here?"

"We tracked Pallin's kidnappers here. Sheabor and the others have gone on ahead. We saw the attack on Eulsiphion from afar. What happened?"

"Eulsiphion has been overrun," the king responded. "We are the few who have escaped."

"Who attacked the city?" Estrien asked.

Froamb shook his head slowly. It seemed he didn't fully know.

"It came just before midnight, moving east across the open plain, against the wind. At first, it seemed nothing more than a bank of fog, a mass of darkness clinging low to the ground. But as it crept closer, an icy stillness settled over us, chilling each man to the bone, as though an angel of death was drawing near. We shot volleys of arrows into the mist to rout out whatever lay hidden within its form. But never did we hear a sound. So we waited.

Then the fog reached the outer wall. It enveloped us, a mist so thick that soldier lost sight of soldier, though they stood but paces apart. And as the fog poured over our walls, the very city began to change. The stone darkened wherever the mist touched it, as though a presence stronger than ours was in the fog. Spikes of ice and snow fell from the heavens. The soldiers shot wildly into the mist, even as the barbarians were already climbing onto the wall. They swept over our wall as one, barely losing a man. We fought them, but it was too late. I ordered the retreat to the palace.

We would have perished there, the rest of us, but for a stroke of fate. When the few survivors were sealed inside the palace, one of the soldiers found something we couldn't believe; an open passageway in the inner chambers. It was our only hope. It brought us out behind the falls of Siphion, between the lake and Squall Highlands. We knew we would never make an open trek through the plains undetected. And so I led us here, into the highlands, to hide until the time becomes right to reclaim Eulsiphion."

Straiah glanced in surprise at Estrien.

"Does Malfur know of your escape?" Estrien asked.

"He must," King Froamb replied. "We sealed the passage behind us, but we need to keep moving all the same."

"Where?" asked Straiah.

But King Froamb didn't answer him. There were too many of them to hide, and to the north lay the barbarian kingdom. It looked as though several hundred people were with him, many of them women and children. Straiah turned to Estrien.

"I think we only have one choice," Straiah said. "You need to take us to Melanor."

Estrien was shocked.

"Melanor? No. I can't."

"You said earlier that the Squall Highlands was one of the old roads to your city. North is the realm of the Horctura. South is now in the hands of Malfur. East is their only chance."

"The law of my people forbids it. To bring this many...I'd be outcast, or worse. You don't understand. If this many from the outside were to come to Melanor, our way of life – everything we've fought for centuries to protect would be over."

Straiah stepped forward and placed a hand on her shoulder, truly sorry for the position she was in. She stared down at the ground, her eyes filling with tears.

"Why did you come back for me? Why couldn't you just leave and go with the others?"

But before he could answer, she stole away, disappearing into the arena of stone. King Froamb stepped forward after her, but Straiah forestalled him with an arm across his chest. King Froamb turned with a smirk, not accustomed to being roughly handled.

"Just let her alone for awhile."

King Froamb joined the bulk of his forces, encouraging them in the good fortune of finding Estrien and Straiah. Straiah, meanwhile, followed slowly in Estrien's direction. Hearing him approach, she turned.

"Estrien, what are we going to do?"

"We don't have a choice. I won't condemn these people to their deaths."

"I'm sorry," was all he could say.

There was much he wanted to tell her in that moment, that he knew exactly what she was feeling – what it meant to be separated from everyone she loved because of duty. He had made that sacrifice to follow Sheabor across the icy strait after Malfur to warn the Eastern Realm. But he didn't really have anyone back on the Banished Lands. His parents and sister had been killed in a raid by the Dungeon Core, long ago. Sheabor had looked after him like a brother. Sheabor was his only family now.

Estrien said nothing more but brushed past him to rejoin King Froamb and the others.

"There is a narrow pass that begins at Mount Kongol, south of here. Our journey will not be an easy one. There are many dangers along the way. Keep close to each other and take plenty of rest. Straiah will keep watch at the rear."

Her last declaration stung. She was leading them south. If they were to encounter danger, it would most likely come from head on, not behind. But she didn't want to be near him.

Estrien set off without another word. Straiah hung back, away from the group, the weight of his choices falling hard on him. When he had asked Sheabor for the hammer, he had done so knowing that he was placing the world in jeopardy. Now, all his visions of a grand rescue were shattered. Estrien would have rather died honorably and there was nothing Straiah could do to bring the hammer back to Sheabor. What had he done? At least the hammer would be safe in Melanor.

But even that brought a streak of fear. If Malfur somehow deduced that the hammer was in Melanor, Straiah had just placed Estrien's home in great peril. Straiah was lost in thought, scarcely noticing his surroundings as the group passed from the foggy maze and traveled down to where the narrow road came up from Siphion Falls.

They traveled with great care, knowing the barbarians and Dungeon Core could spot them. But their course soon led again to the range's interior, and away from prying eyes.

By morning, their pathway seemed to end at a sheer mountain face. From a distance, Straiah saw Estrien pass her hand slowly along the mountain face, walking along with eyes closed until something caused her to stop. Then, placing both hands upon the wall, she began to speak in the ancient tongue.

After a few moments, the loud sound of stone grinding on stone emanated from deep within the mountain face. The wall in front of Estrien began to part, and a narrow pathway was revealed. Estrien gazed slowly around until her eyes landed on Straiah.

"Straiah, lead them on," Estrien said. "I must close the pass behind us and erase any tracks that might lead Malfur here."

Straiah pushed his way through the crowd and found King Froamb near Estrien. Motioning for him to enter first, he glanced up to Estrien, who wouldn't meet his gaze. King Froamb stepped into the narrow passageway.

After less than fifty paces, the corridor opened up into a green and spacious valley, a stark contrast to the stony mountains. The road leading into the valley cut along the mountain face. It was narrow and the drop steep.

A warm breeze arose with the sun, and after an hour of walking, they had left the mountains behind and had found a broad and lush meadow.

"We will rest here for a time," the king declared.

The people were overjoyed. They were overtired and hungry. Straiah had in mind to try his luck at hunting, but to try and feed this many people...Estrien appeared through the crowd.

"Your lands are beautiful," Straiah commented. "I can see why you fight so hard to protect them."

Estrien glanced with a nod and then addressed the king.

"We can rest here a short while. But we still have many leagues to travel before we reach the walls of Melanor."

Then she departed again. King Froamb invited Straiah to sit with him in the shade of a large tree. Straiah did, but failed to give the king his attention, as his gaze wandered the pleasant valley, himself lost in thought. A slow smile grew on the king's face.

"You are a noble fellow," he said.

Straiah turned to him.

"Both you and your companion, Sheabor. I'm sorry I was not cordial to you in the palace. I can see now that Eulsiphion needs men like you if she ever hopes to rid herself of the scourge of Malfur."

"Thank you," Straiah replied. "Once we reach Melanor, we'll form a plan. Perhaps with their help, we can outwit the schemes of Malfur."

The king nodded pensively, then laid down to rest. Straiah could sense what the king was wondering. Would the Melanorians help them? And how would they react to a large group of refugees arriving at their walls? The people of Eulsiphion were spread all over the grass of the meadow, basking in the warm sunlight. The mountains behind them did a remarkable job of blocking the roving wind of the plains. It nearly felt like spring here. Straiah likewise laid his head down, but sleep was slow to find him.

Near midday, Estrien came and awoke the king. He likewise, roused his people and they made the slow descent down the valley toward the coastline. Estrien and King Froamb traveled together, but Straiah hung back amid the crowd. There was much talk and much excitement over seeing the hidden city.

The sun began to sink behind the mountains of the Squall Highlands and to the places far west. He thought of Sheabor and the others, streaking through the barbarian kingdom. Were they still alive?

They reached the coastline and headed north, turning inland again into a different wooded vale. Just as sunset took hold of the land, someone shouted, "I see a city!"

Lights gleamed through the trees, and after a few moments, the group entered a broad meadow upon which a large, walled city lay. A trumpet blast filled the air from the walls of the city. It was Melanor. They had arrived.

# The Seven Secrets

The group trotted at a brisk pace toward Mt Skultira. They would reach it within the hour. So far, the nearby fort hadn't spotted them. Once they did, they would wonder why the group of Dungeon Core were turning west instead of heading back to the fort with their barbarian escort and the Windbearer, Pallin.

But for now, the rolling hillside kept them from prying eyes. Within the hour, the hillside gave way to a flat and rocky basin of bare earth. Sheabor paused, glancing to the north to gauge the distance to the fort.

"What are our options?" he asked.

"We need to buy as much time as possible," Pallin replied. "The gap is perhaps five hundred paces wide. The barbarians have towers on either side to rain down arrows on intruders. But they're largely prepared for a large force, not a few fleeing trespassers. If we get inside the gap before they begin firing, we may yet escape them."

"How do you propose we manage that?"

"The barbarians will not be quick to fire on the Dungeon Core," Pallin replied. "If we can cast enough doubt into their minds as to our true identities and purposes, they'll hesitate."

With that, Pallin dismounted his horse and removed his Dungeon Core armor. Then, climbing atop Sheabor's horse, he sat back to back with him, as though a prisoner.

"This should buy us some time."

"They'll send a party from the fort to question us."

"That is a risk we must take," Pallin said. "Baron, take the reigns of my horse and tow it behind you."

Then Sheabor set off, keeping a quick pace but not enough to tire the horses. Less than a league from Mt Skultira, its form rose above them into the heavens. Its walls were sheer and smooth, and the gap was wider than Durian had imagined, showing the intensity of the earthquake that had rent it asunder eons ago.

Pallin's gaze was fixed on the barbarian fort to the west. So far, they had yet to stir. The group was halfway to the mountain.

"Sheabor," said Pallin. "The gates are opening."

Sheabor glanced back. At least half a dozen barbarians on horseback were making for them at full gallop, though still a few leagues away. Sheabor picked up the pace, not enough to raise the alarm, but enough to reach the gap first.

Durian noticed objects in the distance, objects scattered by the barbarians no doubt – spikes of wood and boulders to push trespassers toward the arrow towers on either side.

Minutes passed. The group was nearly in range of the towers. Mt Skultira loomed hundreds of feet overhead. Durian glanced behind him. The barbarians were halfway to them, closing fast. They were close enough to the towers now to see movement. The soldiers there were getting into position to rain down death if the order was given. But nothing so far.

The group entered the arena obstacles. Sheabor maneuvered around them, keeping close to the center, but not so close as to arouse further suspicion. Durian could hear the galloping riders behind them. His heart was racing.

They entered the gap on the right hand side. The towers were poised to strike and watched them silently go. Another minute passed. Durian kept himself from looking behind. But the pounding of horses hooves was growing.

"Baron," Pallin said with a nod. "Come ride alongside us."

Baron slowly changed direction, veering just beside Sheabor. Pallin sprang onto it and took the reigns, a horn erupting from the near tower. Sheabor didn't react but remained calm. What was he doing? Durian's heart beat wildly. But just after the volley of arrows sailed into the heavens, Sheabor burst forward with a yell.

"Come on!"

After a few moments, the arrows struck the field behind them, about a dozen shafts protruding from the ground they had just occupied. The towers were sparsely manned, just as the fort was, and the array of obstacles pushed them in and out of the range of the tower.

Sheabor and Pallin pulled their horses with skill around the clusters of spikes. Durian and the twins followed as best they could, inexperience drawing them further and further behind. The barbarians knew where the choke points were and covered them with arrows.

236

The trio lingered just outside the range of the tower, waiting for a chance to make their dash around a cluster of spikes. But there was scarcely a second gone by without an arrow landing somewhere in front of them. Baron grabbed his reigns tightly, springing forward with a yell, two arrows narrowly missing him. Blair went next, darting around the corner, just in front of an arrow.

Durian glanced back. Three barbarians were only seconds behind. He sprang forward. But two arrows landed just to his right and pushed him toward the spikes. As he made his turn, one of the spikes scraped into the side of the horse and it reared up, throwing Durian to the ground with a yell. Sheabor heard him and swung round, a stone's throw ahead.

"Get back against the spikes!" Sheabor yelled.

Durian scrambled backward as two more arrows hit the spikes just above him. The barbarians came round the corner, the trampling of hooves kicking dirt into Durian's face as a broadsword cleaved the tip from the spike nearest his head. The barbarian's horse kicked at him as the warrior raised his broadsword for another strike. But Sheabor rode into the midst of them and attacked them before the stroke fell.

Pallin and the twins rode free of the obstacles. They turned round and hesitated, unsure what to do.

"Pallin! Keep moving," yelled Sheabor.

One of the three barbarians broke to pursue the others. Durian was pressed tight against the spikes, the two barbarians attacking Sheabor and pushing him back, giving Durian some space. He pushed against the spikes and stood, but felt one of the spikes move under

237

his weight. It had gotten knocked loose in the commotion.

Pulling with all his might, Durian yanked it free. It was heavy and awkward in his hands, but he ran up beside one of the barbarians and thrust it toward him. The barbarian turned in anger and pain, grabbing the spike and ripping it free from Durian's grip. Sheabor took the opportunity and struck him dead.

"Durian, your horse!" Sheabor yelled.

Durian sprinted to his horse a short ways down the gap. Sheabor was still engaged with the second barbarian and more were riding in.

But just as Durian climbed atop his horse, an arrow struck it in the hind quarter. The horse reared up in pain and threw Durian backward. He hit the ground hard, knocking the wind from his lungs. Sounds grew dull and his vision narrowed. He faintly heard someone calling his name.

Fighting the growing dark, he felt a pair of hands grab his shirt and lay him over the end of a horse. His lungs burned and his head swam in nausea. The next set of warriors were nearly to them, and archers were setting out from the tower in pursuit also.

Durian and Sheabor were nearly clear of the gap. Durian finally sat up just as the dazzling light of the sun hit them, while Sheabor glanced round for signs of Pallin and the twins. But they had already disappeared into the sweeping hillside.

The region was tightly clustered with bare hills and stony mountains, growing lightly forested in the outlying areas. Sheabor set off along the base of the hills, scanning the ground for tracks. The sound of their pursuers faded.

"There's still a barbarian warrior following the others," Durian said.

Sheabor was well aware.

"Pallin is clever. He will find a way to elude him."

But just as he said the words, they heard a muffled yell and a thud from up ahead. Sheabor quickened their pace and came around the bend to find a barbarian warrior on the ground, Pallin hovering over him on horseback, a large club of wood in his hand.

The barbarian was stunned and slowly pushed himself up. But Sheabor quickly dismounted and struck the warrior with the hilt of his sword, knocking him unconscious. Mounting the warrior's horse, Sheabor headed away. Pallin abandoned his makeshift weapon and set out after Sheabor. Durian rode up to his two friends.

"That old codger has a trick or two up his sleeves," said Baron.

Then they set off. They spent the morning snaking the winding hillsides until midday brought little copses of trees to view. Durian could hear a flowing stream somewhere nearby. The horses seemed to hear it too, for they glanced to their left on more than one occasion with a longing grunt.

Sheabor veered toward it. None of them knew how far behind the Horctura were, but they wouldn't get far without water. It was a risk they'd have to take. Finding the stream, they dismounted and filled their water skins. The horses drank ravenously, grunting in delight.

Flowing at the bottom of a short but steep slope inside the treeline, the ankle deep stream was crisp and cold. Pallin walked it slowly, lost in thought.

"Pallin where do we go from here?" Sheabor asked.

"If I'm not mistaken, this stream flows down out of the highlands and into a series of mountain valleys called the Seven Secrets. It was once a refuge for raiders before the Horctura wiped them out. There are many hidden pathways in and out and tracking us will be difficult."

"Staying down here is too vulnerable," Sheabor replied. "If the Horctura discover us, we won't stand a chance."

"Much of the barbarian kingdom is barren and desert. We should keep to water as long as we're able. And in the places ahead the walls grow too steep for horses to descend. Though they might find us, they'll not be able to pursue."

Sheabor gave a whistle to the others to make ready. Before long, Pallin's prediction had come true. It grew cold as the ravine slope rose up around them. The stream, though small, had cut a deep channel through the rich, loose dirt of the region. No horse could now descend it. But archers from the towers had also set off after them and could rain death down from above.

They quickly realized that the severity of the slope was a double edged sword. For every fallen tree of the past decade had tumbled down the ravine and now lay strewn across the river. Some were easily navigable, but most took minutes of pulling and prying to get around.

Durian could hear the sound of hooves pounding above and distant shouts. Sheabor held up his hand for them to halt.

"Pallin, how much farther?"

Pallin looked to the sky, but the sun was obscured through the trees. It must have been late afternoon.

"Not far," he replied.

Sheabor set off on a slow trot through the shallow stream. The horses were on edge, sensing the anxiety of their masters, their eyes darting about in search of danger. Just then, a loud call erupted from the ridge line above. Sheabor burst forward, followed by the others.

More shouts and more barbarians appeared, though none dared venture into the steep ravine. An arrow struck the dirt just beside Durian. Startled, he whipped his head in the direction only to find another arrow loosed his way. Durian hunched forward, hooking his arms around his horse's neck. But the barbarians disappeared from the ridge line.

"Pallin! They're trying to head us off," Sheabor called out.

"Keep to the path!"

They had the good fortune of meeting with few additional obstacles. At length, the stream emptied over a twenty foot waterfall and into a broad valley. They had arrived. Searching in vain for a way down, Sheabor finally dismounted his horse.

241

"Come on."

Pallin was hesitant, knowing they'd never traverse the whole of the barbarian kingdom without horses. But the group wouldn't survive the next hour if they tried to keep them. Climbing down the slippery rock of the waterfall, the group made it at length into the valley.

Coming away from the crashing waters, shouts and pounding of hooves could be heard from the other side of the steep incline beside them. The barbarians were searching for a way in. Their footpath ran along a narrow strip of land, the stream continuing down the valley along a steep decline, now hundreds of paces below them.

The landscape grew rocky, scraggly trees groping outward through the crevices of boulders. Coming around a corner, the narrow trail led directly into a large, steep boulder. Sheabor stopped in his tracks and turned round, seeing where best to traverse it.

"Come on!" he shouted, and ran for the boulder, using his hands as a step and beckoning Pallin and the others to ascend.

The rock was smooth and slippery, with little to use for handholds. But the three Suriyans supported Pallin's other leg and pushed him near enough to the top to pull himself the rest of the way.

"After you, little brother," Baron said.

Soon, Blair was with Pallin at the top of the boulder. Baron joined them, and as Durian began, the barbarians appeared on the path a hundred paces out. Durian's heart raced.

"Go!" Sheabor commanded, lifting Durian's foot with all his might.

Durian's outstretched fingers barely met with the twins' but their tight grip pulled him to safety.

"Sheabor!" they called out, and he turned to make a leap.

"Watch out!" said Pallin and pulled Baron away forcefully just as an arrow shot past him.

"Pallin!" Sheabor yelled. "Take them out of here!"

Sheabor ran for the cover of a large tree, unsheathing his sword just as two arrows struck the tree. Another arrow sailed just over the heads of those on the boulder. Pallin laid down and stretched his feet over the opposite side, Baron and Blair lowering him down by his hands. Letting go, he fell a few paces and landed firmly on the other side. Blair followed.

There were at least a dozen warriors on the trail only a stone's throw from Sheabor. Durian's heart raced. Sheabor didn't stand a chance. But the pathway was narrow, so he couldn't be surrounded. The lead barbarian rushed Sheabor with a shout, swinging a large axe across Sheabor's torso. He ducked and the axe fastened itself firmly in the tree.

Sheabor stabbed the warrior in the gut, sending him tumbling down the ravine. Baron and Blair were descending the other side of the boulder. The second warrior came in, broadsword raised high. But Sheabor lunged forward foot first, grabbing the axe handle and swinging under it, striking the barbarian squarely in his chest and into his comrades. He and one of the archers sailed down the ravine, tumbling amid grunts and shouts. But more barbarians were on the trail.

"Durian!" his friends called from below.

But he couldn't leave Sheabor. He might try to make a jump for Durian's hand. The next barbarian also carried a broadsword and made powerful swings across Sheabor's torso. He parried and ducked them, but was being pushed back. His movements were limited by the barbarian only a few paces back ready to loose an arrow at the first opening.

But Sheabor dodged a blow and then struck him dead, slamming his back against a nearby tree just as an arrow flew past. The next warrior came in while Sheabor was still off balance. The archer notched another arrow. Sheabor dodged and parried but he never regained his balance. One final blow sent him tottering toward the edge. The archer aimed squarely at his chest. Sheabor dove toward the ravine.

The archer turned his sights on Durian. Before Durian could react, the arrow was loosed. Durian threw himself out of the way, falling from the boulder. He heard Baron call out his name and fell clumsily into the arms of the twins. But he hit the ground hard and the world went black.

# Sheyla

Durian stood atop the moonlit plains, a gentle breeze flowing through his hair and swaying the golden grasses. A woman stood in front of him, facing away and gazing at the moon, her white silken gown fluttering in the breeze. Durian took a step toward her but something gave him pause. She was crying and despondent. Time seemed to stretch on. The breeze continued to blow and the woman turned, clenching her arms for warmth. She didn't notice Durian, only a stone's throw away. She was beautiful. At length, she lay down atop the grasses, becoming motionless.

Another form appeared in the night, riding up on a large white steed. He dismounted and ran to the woman, taking her head in his arms and turning his weeping eyes to the night sky, swaying gently back and forth. He arose and took her body in his arms, riding away into the night.

Durian awoke to the sound of a crackling fire. It was night and the stars shone brightly down from above. His head was throbbing and he raised his hand to rub his temples. But a sharp pain entered his left wrist and he winced and put his arm back down.

Closing his eyes again, he took deep breaths, trying to remember what had happened. He had fallen from the large boulder and must have been knocked unconscious. As he lay there, images of the dream coursed through his mind. It was the same dream as before, though slightly different this time. What could it mean? The lines of the poem replayed through his mind. He felt as though something was still missing...but what? Durian blinked his eyes open and tried to sit up.

"He's awake!" Blair said, standing to his feet.

"Easy now," Pallin said. "Rest."

"What happened?" Durian asked. "Where are we?"

"You fell from the boulder. Your arm is hurt but I do not believe the bone is broken. We made it to a hidden fork in the road before the barbarians spotted us. They would have found our tracks, but night fell and allowed our escape."

Durian felt a sudden and extreme thirst. Glancing around, Pallin guessed what he was after and handed him a water skin. Durian drained it and felt reinvigorated.

"What about Sheabor?" Durian asked, wiping his mouth. "Has he come back yet?"

The three shook their heads slowly.

"Just rest," Pallin said. "Have some food. You need to recover your strength."

Durian gazed at his surroundings as he slowly ate. They were in a large hollowed section at the base of a mountain, almost a cave but not deep enough. The trees were thick around them and at times he could feel the light spray of water on his face.

But as he stared into the fire, the visions of his dream kept coming to mind. What was he still missing? He kept seeing visions of the woman standing in the field, waiting for the rider who was too late to save her:

*For Sheyla lies on golden plain,*
*Of Cavanah, the fairest slain;*
*Who met her last and final day*
*When all was brought to disarray.*

Durian stared pensively into the fire. In his dream, the sweeping landscape was similar to the highland plains of the lands of the Horctura. And he remembered Pallin saying that the barbarian kingdom occupied what was once the lands of Cavanah.

"Pallin, do you know where King Euthor buried his wife, Sheyla?" Durian asked suddenly.

"No, I don't. Why do you ask?"

"Don't you think that's strange? We know he found her after she died. He had her Seer's necklace and her wedding ring, which he put into the orb at Eulsiphion. So he must have buried her somewhere. But why hide her tomb?"

Pallin's gaze grew distant and Durian hesitated a few moments before continuing.

"I was just thinking, we know that King Euthor wrote his poem to help us find his own tomb and the orb containing your powers. But only the last stanza of the poem talked about him. The first part of the poem is all about Sheyla and what happened to her. It talks about the two of them upon the plains after her death:

*For Sheyla lies on golden plain,*
*Of Cavanah, the fairest slain;*

King Euthor must have buried her somewhere on the Eastern Realm before going to Melanor and creating the hammer and the second orb. Since the second half of the poem is about his final resting place, what if the first half of the poem is meant to lead us to her tomb? Maybe he left us a way to get back to the Banished Lands."

Pallin stood to his feet and turned away. He paced for many moments as he thought. Then he turned back to the group.

"I can't believe it!" he exclaimed. "You're absolutely correct."

"You mentioned earlier that the lands of the Horctura were once a part of the kingdom of Cavanah. Her tomb could be somewhere close by."

His statement hung in the air. It had been twelve hundred years since Cavanah had owned these lands. Finding a hidden tomb was like looking for a needle in a haystack. Unless it was meant to be found. In that case, King Euthor would have left them clues.

As Durian pondered, he was struck in amazement at the fact that he, a barely grown man from a backwater town, was helping to uncover a mystery over twelve hundred years in the making. Why had he been given the dreams? Were there others having similar dreams? Or had Durian alone been chosen? Durian thought of the hammer that Straiah now carried. He didn't know why but he felt as though the hammer itself was somehow responsible for his dreams. Was it really King Euthor and Sheyla he saw? Or was it the imagination of his mind?

Visions of the woman in the silken white dress and the despair of the rider who carried her away filled his mind. How difficult it must have been to bury her in some hidden, lonely place on the wide open plains – no honors, no burial monument to celebrate her life.

Even more difficult still to depart from her and entomb himself on the other side of the broad world, himself too, forgotten for centuries. What a sacrifice it must have been. The poem struck him now as it had never done before.

*I'll stay with her beneath the shade*
*And wait until the world's remade...*

For the first time, the poem struck him as a plea...a plea from King Euthor for someone, someday to reunite him with his beautiful Sheyla. Durian felt in that moment as though the poem were speaking directly to him, he being the one who had deciphered its hidden message. He felt charged by the great king to find their graves and bury them side by side. Durian vowed silently in that moment that if it was the last thing he did, he would find a way to reunite King Euthor with the woman he loved – that they would be together again, if only in death.

Durian's mind was put at ease. Pallin still stared intently into the fire, wondering, of all places in the barbarian kingdom, which one King Euthor might have chosen to lay his beloved wife to rest.

"Do you think the barbarians are still searching for us?" Durian asked at length.

"I'm sure they are," Pallin replied. "And by now they're growing impatient. I doubt they set out well provisioned. Though they have water, their archers may shoot a rabbit or two – hardly enough to feed them all."

"Then we'll hide here until they leave?"

"No," Pallin replied. "We'll keep moving. But not until you're better rested."

Durian nodded slowly. He had lost a lot of blood and was undoubtedly very weak. And at length, he fell asleep. But it felt like only a few hours had passed when Pallin tapped him awake. Durian rubbed his eyes open and was greeted once more by starlight.

"I'm sorry, but we must be going."

Baron and Blair helped Durian to his feet. The pain in his forearm was the same as before, but his head at last felt normal.

The group moved off, Pallin stepping cautiously in the lead. Coming down from the shallow cave, they descended a stony embankment to a level, sheltered alcove that split the rocky hills. Pallin crept toward the exit, peering outward. Then he turned to the group.

"This is a parallel valley to the one from yesterday. So far, it looks as though the barbarians haven't discovered it. But be cautious. Do not speak unless you must."

The glow of dawn appeared beyond the mountain rim. After a time, Pallin found a relatively shallow descent down into the ravine, where they would be more out of sight. Though they stepped lightly, small pebbles and clods of dirt heralded their descent, making slight commotions that weren't likely to be heard.

Sounds of flowing water came to their hearing while they were yet a few hundred paces from the valley floor. As they came closer, whitewash and large stones filled their sight.

"Do your best to walk atop the boulders," Pallin said. "It will make tracking us more difficult."

"Why won't they just wait for us at the far side of the valley?" Blair questioned.

"They may well be," Pallin answered. "But as I said before, the barbarians aren't known for their patience. When their provisions run out, they'll likely return to their fort."

The four ambled from boulder to boulder. Each time they arrived at a narrow spot in the river, Pallin would jump across to the over side of the stream and continue forward. That was clever; it made tracking them even more difficult, perhaps impossible.

But near sunset, Pallin left the river for a sheltered alcove where the hillside recessed a bit, and thick trees grew up round, keeping them safe from prying eyes above. The valley was still quite steep, but the area was forested enough to gather wood for a fire and leaves for bedding. But they waited till well past sunset to risk a fire. Though the scent of the fire would undoubtedly carry, the dark obscured the ribbon of smoke rising up to the heavens.

They sat in silence, eating what little they had left of their stores. Was Sheabor really gone? Would the rest escape this place alive? With little food and nothing to hunt with, their options were slim. Even so,

Durian felt hope and excitement for the future. He didn't understand how, but King Euthor was in some way looking after and guiding them. Would they really find the tomb of Sheyla? Had King Euthor planned it this way so many centuries ago? Durian knew they would. They would find her and reunite her with her beloved husband. If it was the last thing Durian did, he would see it done. He had found his destiny.

# Melanor

The sun was setting behind the mountains of the Squall Highlands. Straiah and Estrien, with the group of refugees from Eulsiphion, approached Melanor with caution, for the gates had yet to open. Estrien went in front of the group, hands raised in submission and stood before the walls.

The city was silent for some time, the light of the setting sun giving way to darkness. King Froamb waited beside Straiah, growing agitated at the long delay. The people began to murmur. Surely Melanor wouldn't turn them away. After the better part of an hour had passed, King Froamb departed Straiah's company and marched the short distance to Estrien.

"Would it help if I knocked?"

"No, good king. They are in deliberations."

"Do they understand that while we're lingering here idle, the Horctura are ravaging my kingdom?"

"Just give them some more time."

"That is unacceptable! I'm the king of these lands. I will not be denied entrance to any city within my bounds."

King Froamb broke toward the city gate before she could stall him. Estrien turned round to Straiah with eyes pleading for help to stop him. Straiah dashed ahead, but just as he did, the deep creaking of wood sounded out in the night as the gates of Melanor swung open.

A great sigh went up from the people, all hungry and exhausted. Straiah and Estrien caught up with King Froamb and the three entered the city, followed at a distance by the rest. Immediately, they were met by Thalen.

"The elders require your presence," Thalen said to Estrien.

She bowed and departed. Thalen gazed at King Froamb for a long while as though trying to work something out in his mind, but at length, he extended his hand toward the interior of the city.

Made of a whitish stone, the city was large and beautiful. Low-lying metal bowls on stone pedestals contained burning oils and lit the walkways.

"I'm sorry for the loss of your city, good king," said Thalen.

"At the rate we're going, soon you'll be sorry for the loss of my whole kingdom. Where are you taking us?"

"To see Aravas."

"What's going to happen to Estrien?" Straiah questioned.

"I don't know."

"Speculate."

Thalen stopped and turned to the pair with a sigh.

"She will be imprisoned for abandoning her mission and for leading you here. Her actions may have spelled doom for this city."

"There's a war raging around you," Froamb roared. "And you would imprison one of your finest soldiers just to save your pride?"

254

"A war, which less than one week ago, you yourself refused to believe in, nearly arresting Sheabor for bringing you tidings of Malfur in Thob Forest. Be careful who you accuse of pride, good King."

The two men held one another's gaze for long moments.

"Please, this arguing is pointless," Straiah declared.

"Agreed," said Thalen, once more extending his hand.

The roads of Melanor were curved, with grassy hillsides and overhanging trees and buildings. Its layout led one's mind to imagine the city was larger than it could have been. At the end of the road was a building ornately decorated with columns, seated atop a flight of broad stairs. Ascending, an attendant opened the door at their approach and they entered to find a handful of persons seated around a large circular table.

"May I present King Froamb, of Forthura, and Straiah of the House, Cavanah."

The pair gave a bow and those seated at the table arose to show their respects. They invited the two to be seated but King Froamb elected to stay standing.

"So Pallin has left in search of the orb containing our powers," one of the men said.

It was Aravas. An elderly man, something in his countenance made it seem as though he was an older brother to Pallin. Straiah nodded.

"Has he forgotten that it was because of our role in this very situation that we chose to banish our powers?" Aravas continued. "Why is he so presumptuous as to assume that Faegean and I will willingly take up our powers again, if he discovers the orb?"

Straiah was somewhat taken aback by his line of questioning. It wasn't what he had expected.

"Pallin assumes that you and Faegean will do what is right," Straiah responded.

Aravas looked at him and smiled.

"Indeed we will," he said. "Though in your eyes it may seem like folly."

"Will it seem like folly in Pallin's eyes as well?"

Aravas didn't respond but gazed at Straiah thoughtfully for a few long moments.

"Enough of this," King Froamb said. "We have more pressing matters. What is going to be done about Malfur? We need to form a strategy against him."

"Strategy?" said another of the men. "The strategy you refer to may not exist. Malfur's stroke was powerful and swift. Now that the Horctura occupy Eulsiphion, it may be years before the city is retaken, if at all."

Froamb clenched his teeth and fists but didn't respond.

"The barbarians have already begun to spread into the outlying areas," Thalen said. "The northern townships have begun fleeing south. You must have a mind of escape, good King, not of vengeance. The barbarians will grow quickly weary of a long campaign southward at the onset of winter."

"What are you saying?" roared the king. "Run away south to Suriya and hope the barbarians just lose interest? No. My people will come here to Melanor. From here we can mount an offensive against the barbarians and Malfur. From here we can stem the tide."

The room was silent.

"I'm afraid that isn't possible," said Aravas. "Melanor cannot become a way station for the kingdom of Forthura."

"You refuse to stand with us?" King Froamb said, shaking with fury.

"I am truly sorry," Aravas replied. "But you do not have the larger picture in mind. Patience is our only chance of survival."

King Froamb stormed from the building. Straiah remained behind, his mind racing. What in the world was he going to do? If King Froamb left for the southern townships, would Straiah stay behind in Melanor? Maybe he could leave the hammer with them and aid King Froamb. But Sheabor needed it returned to him.

"Do not lose hope," said Aravas, gazing warmly at Straiah and breaking his ruminations.

"What are our options?" Straiah asked.

"For the moment," began Thalen, "to survive. At least until word can be sent to the other kingdoms. Kester would be a powerful ally and the giants will surely rally once news reaches them that the ancient enemy has returned."

But the thought didn't give Straiah hope. He remembered back to just days ago, the welcome they received from King Froamb when they brought tidings of Malfur and Corcoran. Why would the rest react any different?

"What about the hammer?" Straiah asked. "It's imperative I get it back to Sheabor. If he's going to travel with Pallin to the tomb of King Euthor, the mission will be in vain without the hammer. I never should have brought it here."

Thalen glanced to Aravas.

"There is one path you could take," said Aravas. "But it is fraught with dangers. The Kingdom, Forthura, occupies the whole of the southern peninsula of this continent. To the north are the Horctura, and west of them are Kester and the Bearoc. Today, the only route connecting Kester and Forthura is through the barbarian kingdom. But there was once a pathway through the Westward Wilds, starting in the south, through Thob Forest and beyond, in the places none now travel. With luck, you could meet the others in the lands of Kester."

"But how would I get back to Thob Forest?" Straiah asked.

"We are preparing ships for King Froamb and his men to set sail for Suriya, the southernmost township of his kingdom. If you accompany him, you can set off from there along the coast toward the Westward Wilds. But be warned. A normal man wouldn't last a week there in fair weather. And winter is upon us now. You may well be going to your death."

Straiah nodded slowly.

"If that's my best hope of getting the hammer back to Sheabor, then it's a risk I'll have to take."

"Yours will be a lonely road," Aravas said. "But as the old saying goes: Heroes have the whole world for a tomb."

That was a new one. If Aravas was trying to encourage him, he hadn't succeeded.

"Heroes don't foolishly risk the fate of the world in reckless rescues," Straiah commented.

"Yes they do."

Straiah smirked.

"Come take a walk with me," Aravas said, hooking his arm around Straiah's shoulder, leading him into the cool night. After they had descended the stairs, Aravas spoke.

"I must also foolishly risk the fate of our world on a reckless rescue of sorts."

Straiah glanced to him, unsure of his meaning. But Aravas only sighed as he gazed into the starry sky.

"I'm glad you're bound for Suriya with King Froamb. He may need you. Make for the Westward Wilds, but don't close your eyes to other paths that lay before you."

Why was Aravas speaking in riddles? And what was he talking about, him recklessly risking the fate of the world? Straiah opened his mouth to question him but Aravas spoke first.

"You should go. Your ship departs within the hour."

Straiah bowed and turned to leave, but stopped.

"Where is Estrien being held?"

"Why?"

Straiah clenched his jaw, uninterested in explaining his motives.

"This pathway here will lead you to her. Look for the building under guard at the end of the road."

"Thank you."

Straiah set off swiftly down the road. But before he had gone far, King Froamb and his people were assembled in a large grassy park off to one side of the road. The king saw him and motioned him into their midst.

"As you all may have heard," the king began, "our hosts are anxious to see us on our way. So much for the fabled city of the wise."

The men around them began to chuckle.

"And yet, wisdom is not always a brother to courage," he continued. "I do not begrudge them. No. Wise and fool alike, we all follow the same code: Protect your own. They are safe here, and they wish to remain safe for as long as they may. Our path is along a different road. Make yourselves ready. We leave for Suriya within the hour."

The people began to disperse. Straiah was surprised by the change in demeanor in the king. Only minutes ago, he had been wroth at the decision of Melanor. But now, he seemed in high spirits, making light of the grave peril his people faced.

"Then Suriya is where you'll make your stand," Straiah said.

King Froamb nodded.

"What about Kester?" Straiah questioned. "If you buy some time, won't they come to your aid?"

"They would perhaps, but the time you speak of isn't enough. "Malfur has been both cunning and cautious. To anyone watching from the outside, it will look as though the Horctura have finally won the war. The truth is, the war with the Horctura has been going badly for some time. Kester has been withdrawing its support over the years, and has instead been fortifying its northeastern cities. They've recently erected a massive military fortress named K'venneh near their border to warn the Horctura not to set their sights on the west."

Straiah nodded and stared ahead, not willing to meet the king's gaze. Froamb was confident and resolved, a man left with one path and striking out boldly upon it, no matter where it may lead. Straiah knew his eyes would betray his hopelessness.

"Will you join us?" King Froamb asked.

Straiah didn't know what to say. Yes he would accompany them to Suriya. But how could he tell King Froamb of his plan to swiftly leave them and flee toward the Westward Wilds? The king would count him a coward, and perhaps rightly so. Straiah, at length turned and met his gaze.

"I will accompany you to Suriya and I will fight for you as long as I am able. But understand, my first duty is to protect the Hammer of Haladrin and return it safely to Sheabor and Pallin."

Straiah opened his mouth to say more, but the words wouldn't form.

"Then I'll see you on the boat."

King Froamb slapped Straiah on the shoulder with a smile and headed off. Straiah couldn't help but chuckle to himself. The king was a very interesting personality, definitely given to extremes. What it must be like to be a noble in his court.

But the weight of what he had to do next hit him powerfully. He had precious little time and he knew he had to visit Estrien. What would he say to her? How could he face her knowing he'd put the city she loved and the whole world in grave peril? But he couldn't leave without seeing her.

And so he departed, following the instructions of Aravas and arriving to a guarded building at the end of the road. The guards permitted him to enter and he walked slowly into the low-lit room. It was small, harboring only a handful of cells – yet another testament to why Estrien was right to fight so hard to protect the way of life here in Melanor.

Estrien was in the corner, against the far wall. He lingered there for a moment, until seeing him, she arose and came to greet him. He was surprised by how, even here and now, he was struck by her elegance and beauty. Her blonde hair fell loosely past her shoulders, and her green eyes watched him approach. She reached out to take his hand in hers, catching him off guard. He took her hand, but seeing the gentleness in her eyes made him pull away, face downcast to the ground.

"I'm so sorry, Estrien. I've made such a mess. Everything is spinning out of control."

She reached out again for his hands, which he gave and she waited for him to meet her gaze before responding.

"You did what you had to," she said. "I don't blame you. I was just afraid of what would happen. And now that it's done, it wasn't as bad as I thought. I'm at peace. I was unfair to you and I'm sorry."

Straiah found himself unprepared for her words and turned his eyes down to their interwoven hands. Stroking her fingers softly in his, he knew he had only moments left. At length he turned his eyes back to hers.

"I'm going to Suriya with King Froamb and his men."

A hint of fear entered Estrien's eyes.

"They won't survive the battle. Suriya is defenseless. And with all the refugees fleeing southward. It'll be a bloodbath."

"I know."

"But the hammer..."

"If things turn ill, I'll take the path through the Westward Wilds and reunite with Sheabor and Pallin in the lands of Kester."

Estrien shook her head, her eyes filling with tears.

"You'd never survive."

"I'll find a way through. This will not be the last time we see each other. I promise you."

Estrien gave him a teary smile and nodded. Then he kissed her. And again, even in the face of such a bleak future, he felt peace, and held fast to the moments slowly slipping away.

"What's going to happen to you?" he asked at length.

"I don't know," she responded.

He could tell she was keeping something from him but he didn't press her.

"I risked the fate of our entire world to free you from that place. I didn't do it so some bureaucrat could lock you away in another prison."

Estrien nodded slowly.

"I know."

He clenched the hammer angrily in his hand, and suddenly an idea flashed through his mind, one that made his heart race with guilt and excitement for even thinking of it. She seemed to sense what he was thinking and preemptively shook her head gravely before the words even escaped his lips.

"Come with me," he said.

"No. Please, you mustn't talk like that."

"I could free you right now. I could smuggle you onto one of the ships. You could come with me to Kester and resume your mission to guard Pallin."

He could tell by her gaze that her resolve was firm, though her eyes showed a gladness at his fervor for her.

"I believe your promise," she said with a smile. "We will see each other again. But not here and not now."

Straiah looked to the floor, nodding slowly and feeling guilty now for wanting to make her a fugitive from her own people. She pulled his chin up to meet her gaze.

"I'm very glad to know you, Straiah of the House, Cavanah. One of the Suriyans told me you were the most selfless man he'd ever met."

Straiah lifted his head back with a laugh.

"And which one was that? Baron I bet."

Estrien nodded with a laugh, recalling Baron's gushing declarations on the streets of Eulsiphion.

"I can see why you visited Suriya on your leave from Melanor," Straiah said. "They have a subtle beauty and the people there surprise you. I very much hope King Froamb and I can see them safely protected."

Estrien opened her mouth to respond, but before she did, the door to the prison opened, revealing the person of Thalen walking in to meet them.

"I thought I would find you here. The boats are ready. It's time you were on your way."

Something in his voice seemed troubled.

"What is it?" Estrien asked.

"I've just been informed that Aravas has left the city. We don't know where he has gone."

Straiah thought back to the last conversation he'd had with him and his cryptic statements about a reckless rescue. What could it all mean?

"He left a note with a single instruction," Thalen continued. "Be ready."

# The Shady Marshes

Durian awoke to a nudge on his shoulder, Pallin standing over him. Durian sat up, rubbing his eyes and glancing around for the others. The light of dawn was just filling the sky. He pushed himself up onto a nearby fallen log, rubbing his left wrist.

"Let's have a look," Pallin said.

Removing the bandages, he examined Durian backwards and forwards, at times a look of concern appearing on his face.

"You're healing slower than I'd prefer. But you're on the mend. That's what matters. I'm going to go and clean these bandages. Your friends are cooking breakfast."

"Breakfast?" Durian asked.

Just then, he noticed the aroma of roasted meat on the air. Durian walked over to find Blair cooking a rabbit on a stick in a small, roughly domed oven made from smooth river rock. Inside the oven were flat smooth stones as a base, and Durian could see hints of red coals glowing beneath. The oven was giving off quite a lot of heat and very little smoke.

"Where in the world did you get that?" Durian asked.

"Pallin trapped it," Blair replied. "He was already skinning it when we woke up and he had this pit of coals going."

"Trapped it? With what?"

266

Blair only shrugged his shoulders. Durian glanced down to the river, where Pallin was washing his bandages. He suspected Pallin had gone to such trouble on account of his injury. Durian went down to meet him by the river.

"Are you sure we have time for all this?" Durian asked.

"The fact the barbarians haven't yet found us is a good indication that Sheabor is still alive and making a menace of himself. In some ways, it was good we were parted from him. A woodsman of his stealth and skill could drive the barbarians mad with false tracks and hit and run attacks. Giving him time to run riot will only ease our escape."

"Escape to where?"

"I think I have worked out where King Euthor may have buried his beloved wife. Since he didn't seem to leave any specific clue in his farewell poem, I can only guess that he would have buried her in a place special to her heart. Now go and have something to eat."

Pallin began fashioning a small piece of metal into a hook, attaching some thread to one end and a worm to the other. Pallin certainly was full of surprises.

"Where's Baron?" Durian asked, arriving back at Blair.

"Pallin sent him after bait."

Durian chuckled, watching Blair methodically turn the rabbit in the domed oven.

"You look like you've done this before," Durian commented.

267

"Not often. I usually cook rabbit in stew. The coals don't give a consistent heat base, so it's hard to cook evenly."

Though warm food had been an untasted luxury these past days, Durian was growing more and more anxious to be on with their quest to find the tomb of Sheyla, more so now that Pallin claimed to have worked out its location. What would they discover there? Durian still couldn't believe that he had become a part of a mystery twelve centuries in the making.

"Make sure mine's extra well done," said Baron to Blair, walking up from behind.

"It's all going to be the same," Blair responded in annoyance.

"That's what I'm afraid of. You should've seen our poor mother the last time Blair tried to roast rabbit. Sick for days..."

"She was already coming down with something and you know it," Blair said.

Durian laughed.

"Find any worms?" he questioned.

Baron opened his fingers to reveal a handful of bait and wandered down to deliver them to Pallin, who had already hooked his first fish. Pallin came with Baron back to the group.

"We'll depart at sunset. Under cover of night we'll flee these valleys and make again for the open plains. With luck, Sheabor will be waiting for us somewhere on the fringes."

Durian took the fish from Pallin and prepared it for Blair. By late morning, all had had their fill. But the coals were nearly spent and the oven had all but grown cold. New wood meant smoke, which they couldn't afford.

"I'm going up ahead to scout," said Pallin. "Don't leave the area unless you must."

The three friends watched the morning progress to afternoon. The sun moved overhead and then was quickly gone again on the other side of the valley. With winter, the days were shorter and Pallin returned quickly.

"The way seems clear," he announced.

He set a quick pace down the river, atop the boulders. The valley was broad and shallow here, and the hillsides on either side were more verdant and less rocky as the landscape transitioned back within the purview of the plains. But before night had fallen, they saw a thin band of smoke rising from somewhere ahead along their side of the river. If the barbarians were still here, they weren't taking pains to conceal themselves.

Pallin found a narrow spot where a tree had fallen over the stream. Crossing, they set off across the field for the far hillside, leaving the stream behind. Durian thought he head the sound of a horse whinnying.

The moon had yet to ascend from below the horizon, but the first of the evening stars was poking through the failing light. The treeline ended just ahead as the group crept along the edge of the shallow hillside. Soon, they'd be back in the open spaces. How far did they expect to get without horses?

Pallin came to the edge of the treeline and hesitated, scanning the scene. But soon he sprang forward into the plains. This was crazy. They hadn't

269

even looked for Sheabor.  But the three friends followed, jogging north for a short while and then veering west.

Then Durian started to hear the rumble of horses from behind.  He glanced back as they ran, seeing nothing, but the sound grew louder.  Pallin, if he heard it, was paying it no mind.  They kept moving.  Durian's head began to throb and his wrist ached from overexertion.  Glancing back, Durian saw indistinct movement against the dark and the sound of galloping clearly growing.

"Pallin!" Durian called out, as softly as he could manage.

"Keep moving!" Pallin commanded.

The barbarians were nearly on top of them.  If they didn't do something now, they'd be discovered.  But it was too late.  Glancing back, Durian saw a pack of horses galloping straight for them.  They were going to trample them!  The three Suriyans veered out of the way.

"Pallin!" Durian called out.

Just then, the horses passed them by.  To his surprise, it looked as though only one rider accompanied the horses, riding the lead horse and towing three others behind.  Coming past Pallin, the horseman reared up and halted.  It was Sheabor!  The group ran to greet him, overjoyed.

"Sheabor!" Baron exclaimed.  "You're alive! Where did you get these?"

"I've been slowly stealing them from the barbarians," Sheabor said with a smile.  "We shouldn't have much trouble escaping now. I managed to steal four, so one of us will have to share."

The group climbed atop the horses and Pallin handed Sheabor a water skin and something wrapped up in a piece of leather. Sheabor drained the water and then unwrapped the leather skin to reveal a cooked fish. Laughing, he devoured it, taking little time to free the meat from the bones.

It was then that Durian realized Pallin's eagerness to eat food might not have been only for Durian's benefit, but more for Sheabor, who had industriously been stifling the plans of the Horctura. The group smiled as they watched, for he ate like a man starving. His clothes were tattered from his tumble down the ravine, but he looked otherwise unscathed.

"Where do we go from here?" Sheabor asked at length.

"A place called Schadelmar," Pallin replied, "which in the ancient tongue means Shady Marshes. That is where I believe the final resting place of Sheyla lies."

"Sheyla?" Sheabor said in great surprise.

"Yes," Pallin responded. "While you were away, Durian discovered that King Euthor must have buried her somewhere in the old plains of Cavanah just after the Great War. I've thought long, and Schadelmar seems the most likely spot."

"Where is Schadelmar?" he asked.

"Northwest," Pallin responded. "Near the forest of Thay Iphilus."

271

The group set off at a modest pace, knowing the journey was far. Durian trotted up next to Pallin with a question he'd been meaning to ask.

"It was the place she loved most," Pallin said.

Durian was surprised by his declaration. For what he had been wondering about was what was so special about the Shady Marshes.

"King Euthor constructed a large mound of stone there, not unlike Mt Skultira, but much smaller. She loved the sunset view along the plains and they would often wander there near evening. He wrote a poem for her in the early days of their union, of the two of them wandering to the Shady Marshes. When I recalled the poem to mind, I could think of no other place he would have entombed her."

The group followed the river throughout the night, mostly north until it veered to the east. They filled their water skins and rested. Then, after morning had dawned, they set off to the west.

"We will arrive at the Shady Marshes by evening," Pallin declared.

Durian's mind was consumed in thought, with visions of the dreams flashing through his mind and lines of the poem inscribed into the Hammer of Haladrin popping in and out of the foreground of thought. What other mysteries lay hidden, waiting for them to find?

By midday, the ground grew spongy around them. The grass changed to tufted bundles of swamp grass the horses wouldn't eat. And in the distance slowly rose the only feature in the landscape, a large mound of stone, shaped like a gray loaf of bread.

272

It was leagues away and took the rest of the afternoon to reach. But by the time they arrived, Durian could see why the place had been named the Shady Marshes. For the thirty foot tall stone cast a long shadow over the marshes in the light of the setting sun.

As they approached, they saw that the rock itself lay within a small pool of crystal blue water and seemed largely featureless. Pallin dismounted his horse and waded through the chest high water to the stone's edge. Running his hand along the smooth surface, he traversed along the stone, searching for a clue to its entrance.

Durian glanced to the west. Already the sun was waning low atop the far horizon. Durian longed to climb atop the rock, to stand in the place where the great king and his beloved wife would share in the joy of living.

"Pallin, what if we need the hammer to get inside?" Sheabor asked.

"I do not believe so," Pallin replied. "He would not have wanted us to damage or destroy this place."

Sheabor dismounted as well and entered the pool.

"There's an opening!" Pallin exclaimed. "At the base of the stone. A small tunnel."

The three Suriyans dismounted and came to the edge of the pool. Though they were in a swamp, the pool of water around the stone was a deep blue. Entering the icy water, they waded toward Sheabor, who waited at the stone where Pallin had disappeared. Baron went first, taking a deep breath and disappearing into the waters. Blair followed. Sheabor helped Durian, pushing on his legs when he had submerged beneath.

Durian felt around and kicked with his feet. The tunnel was dark and circular, ascending upward into the stone's interior. After a few moments, he popped up inside a dark cavern with a single shaft of sunlight coming down brightly from above. The light fell upon a large, rectangular stone sarcophagus, over which Pallin already stood.

Just then, Sheabor popped up beside him. The sarcophagus lay on a small mound. Durian and the others approached it with reverence, Durian's heart beating quickly, not knowing what he was going to find. But even his wildest imagination couldn't have prepared him for what he was about to see.

For coming the short distance, he found that the stone sarcophagus contained no lid. Inside the lidless tomb was a pool of solid and perfectly clear crystal. Lying motionless within the crystal was the undecayed form of a beautiful woman in a white silken dress. She looked so peaceful and fair, as though merely asleep beneath tranquil waters. But her face carried a hint of sorrow, barely perceptible.

Durian's heart beat wildly. For the woman before him was the same woman he had seen in his dreams. But how could that be? His mind raced for an answer that never formed. But he noticed that at the base of the sarcophagus was a stone tablet that seemed to have writing etched into it. Durian came over to read it:

*Our footsteps amble down the dusty lane.*
*Daylight sinks to twilight once again.*
*And her, her tender, far-off looking eyes*
*Watch amending colors fill the skies.*
*And I, my thoughts are drawn to distant lands,*
*Where we could flee beyond the world's demands,*
*And live, disburdened from the many pains,*
*That ever keep the race of men in chains...*

*The final beams of sunlight warm her face.*
*I feel pervading goodness in this place.*
*A breeze picks up and stirs her silken hair.*
*She brings a warmth of goodness everywhere.*

The poem brought a mist to Durian's eyes. It was beautiful and overwhelming to read in the presence of the woman to whom it had been written. Durian came back to the head of the tomb, gazing once more at the form of Sheyla. His mind was a jumble. Had King Euthor done this for him, to show him that the dreams were real?

But he sensed there was something deeper at work, some other purpose to which he wasn't privy. Baron and Blair began to wander the confines of the small cavern. Sheabor turned to Pallin for his thoughts. Baron came to the far side of the room and bent down.

"This looks like Shade Stone," Baron said. "And I see a keyhole."

The rest came to see. It indeed was a square floor of Shade Stone with a keyhole in the direct center.

"There must be a key around somewhere," Baron continued and arose to look about the room.

Pallin's gaze grew distant, as did Sheabor's. Where would King Euthor have left a key, and what was inside the compartment? But Baron saw something on the far wall and hurried over to it. It was a shaft of metal sticking out from the wall. Just beside it on both sides were indents that seemed to be made by fingertips. There were ten of them in total surrounding the key, like fingertips sunk slowly into wet sand and then pulled free again. Baron placed his fingers into one side of them and pulled on the metal shaft. Though it seemed to move, it didn't come loose.

"I think I found what we need the hammer for," Baron said. "I think he buried the key inside the wall."

The rest came to examine his findings.

"It felt like it moved," Baron said. "Sheabor, you try it."

Sheabor grasped the metal and pulled with all his might for a few long moments.

"It didn't budge."

Baron took it again, placing his fingers again in the indents on the right side.

"I could've sworn it moved when I pulled on it. Don't just stand there, little brother. Help me."

Blair took up the other side, placing one hand on Baron's and the other in the finger indents surrounding the key. Then, pushing against the wall and pulling on the shaft, somehow, the key began to move. Sheabor joined in, helping to pull on the hands of the twins. And at length, the key was freed from the wall.

"How did you do that?" marveled Durian.

"I don't know," said Baron. "The wall just seemed to soften a bit. Did you feel it?"

"I'm not sure," Blair responded.

Pallin gazed gravely at the wall and also at the two twins from Suriya standing before him. But Sheabor wasted little time. Taking the key to the other side of the room, he plunged it into the keyhole with a half turn. A loud click emanated from within.

He pulled the door open. The compartment seemed to glisten with a golden glow. Sheabor knelt town and took an item in hand. Raising it up, he produced a large dual-bladed axe whose head was formed of Shade Stone and handle was made of gleaming Candlewood. Nearly identical in type to the Hammer of Haladrin, this weapon was both larger and more menacing, clearly unique in the world.

Kneeling back down, he produced a large shield. The shield was of a different wood than Candlewood. It was white, not unlike Estrien's bow. But the front of the shield seemed recessed, and within the recess was a layer of pure Shade Stone. It was large, able to shield the whole person when kneeling. And a spike of Shade Stone protruded from the bottom tip of the shield, which would allow the shield to be fastened to the ground against attack.

Sheabor admired the two objects now in his hand, swinging each slowly through the air to get a feel for their weight and balance. But Baron bent down and thrust his hand into the compartment. After a moments digging, he pulled up another weapon. It was a spiked mace, whose head was of Shade Stone and whose handle was of Candlewood.

Laying the weapon at Sheabor's feet, he reached in again, this time pulling out a chest-piece of armor. More complex than any piece of armor they'd ever seen, this chest-piece was a combination of hardened leather, metal, and stone. The leather was woven throughout the metal breastplate, binding plates of Shade Stone to the metal base.

Baron laid the chest-piece down at Sheabor's feet and produced three identical others before declaring the chamber empty. Sheabor stood chuckling to himself, holding a large shield, mace and battle-axe, with four suits of armor piled at his feet.

"I suppose you'd like me to fight this war by myself."

Durian didn't know why, but he was wary to take hold of any of the weapons or armor. He wasn't a warrior, and it felt out of place for him to carry such ancient and powerful items. It was clear that the others felt the same way. These weapons and pieces of armor clearly hadn't been constructed for such as them. But Pallin smiled and stepped forward. He took one of the chest-pieces of armor and held his hand out for one of the weapons. Sheabor handed him the mace. Baron and Blair also took a chest-piece, leaving Durian the odd man out. But Durian, glancing down at the compartment, seemed to notice a very faint blue glow.

"I think there's something more."

Stepping down into the compartment, he took hold of a crystal, glowing faintly blue in the darkness. Durian climbed free of the compartment and held the crystal up to Pallin and Sheabor. As he turned it toward

278

them, the glow intensified a brighter blue. Pallin took it in hand and gazed intently into it.

"What is it?"

"It seems to be some sort of compass," Pallin replied. "It glows brightest when pointed to the west. Perhaps this is the key to finding our way to the tomb of King Euthor."

The group returned to the side of Sheyla, paying their respects one last time, and then left the tomb of Sheyla behind. The light was dazzling as the sun hung low over the horizon in front of them. Already, a beautiful orangy red was filling the sky, a testament to the verse inscribed just inside.

Durian came out of the water more quickly than the others, skirting the base of the rock on the other side and searching for a way up. Finding small handholds gouged in the stone, he ascended with ease and stood atop the broad stone. The others soon joined him.

The view was beautiful – the distant dark treeline silhouetted in the bright orb of the sun; the golden plains beyond the marshland swaying in the gentle breeze. And above, the crimson orange of the sky darkening to deep purple. Durian tried to recall the poem inscribed at the foot of the sarcophagus.

*And her, her tender, far-off looking eyes*
*Watch amending colors fill the skies.*
*And I, my thoughts are drawn to distant lands,*
*Where we could flee beyond the world's demands...*

If only they had gotten their wish. But dark times had befallen and had changed the face of their world. The group lingered until the sun had set and then descended. Sheabor patted his horse's head and spoke to it, as though an old friend.

"I had a horse just like this – white with tan spots," Sheabor said. "My first horse. He was smaller in stature than most, but bigger in heart. I got him on my fourteenth birthday."

Durian himself had scarcely ever ridden a horse. Suriyans rarely traveled and mules were better beasts of burden. The group mounted and then huddled together round Pallin to see where their course would take them.

"Thay Iphilus Forest is near and there are no barbarian settlements between us and its bounds. If we can enter the forest unnoticed, we'll travel north through cover of trees and at last come to the edge of the barbarian kingdom."

"Why not just travel west and come out the other side of the forest?" Blair asked.

"Because the Ruhkan Mountain splits the forest in two. It runs roughly north and south nearly the whole length of the continent."

Durian had heard of Thay Iphilus Forest before, but never in a fond context. It was said to be haunted with disembodied spirits known as the Night Wanderers.

"There are many leagues of open plains between here and there, so be on your guard."

The group departed just as darkness took hold of the land. Durian gazed back at the large stone until it faded into the pervading dark. One day, he would come back to this place. Sheyla and Euthor would finally get the burial worthy of the greatest of heroes.

# A Reunion of Old Friends

The night was cold as a lone, cloaked wanderer descended from the highlands toward the newly conquered city, Eulsiphion. Skirting the base of the mountains along the river, he came to a deep blue lake, standing there a moment, watching the waterfall shatter the orb of the full moon held within the waters. But then, he dove into the lake and disappeared.

Within the castle, Eulsiphion, the barbarians reveled in the palace hall, over which a thick cloud had formed, lightly dropping snow. And on the throne silently watching, Malfur, Keeper of the Winter Wind, purveyed.

The cloaked wanderer ascended the pitch black tunnel, groping about in the darkness. At length, he reached the end, finding the secret latch and pushing the door slowly open. The sound of laughter and feasting came to ear. He hesitated. Would he reach Malfur before they struck him dead?

He crept into the king's bed chamber, coming to the near wall next to the door. Then he listened and waited. Finding the chamber rooms unguarded, he moved in silence toward the main hall, sliding his footsteps along the smooth stone floor.

He arrived to the entrance of the main hall. He stood there for many moments in silence, listening and waiting. There was still time to turn back, to abandon his plan. But at length, he breathed in deep and stepped into the hall.

For the moment, he went unnoticed by the dozens of barbarians at the banquet table. But two of them sprang to their feet, grabbing the axes beside them. Malfur, only paces from him, shot his head round, his eyes widening in great surprise as they met the new arrival.

"I don't believe it!" said Malfur, standing to his feet. "My brother, Aravas."

Aravas took another step into the hall.

"Hello, brother."

The barbarians rushed forward, axes poised, but hesitated to strike him dead. Still, they moved to detain the new arrival and bind his hands. But Malfur held up his hand to stay their ground.

"Thank you," said Aravas.

The two were silent, each gazing firmly into the eyes of the other. All commotion in the hall ceased as Malfur sought to read the intentions of the new arrival. Aravas wore an entertained expression, trying to fathom what Malfur could be making of his unannounced appearance.

"Why are you here?" Malfur asked at length.

"I came to see for myself if the rumors were true – that my brother, Malfur, Keeper of the North Wind was alive and well."

Malfur's eyes narrowed.

"And now that you've seen? What do you intend now? Go back on your merry way to your friends, the Melanorians?"

Aravas let a slow smile grow on his face.

"I came for your help, actually."

"My help?"

Malfur lifted his head back in laughter, the barbarians joining in at the bold declaration. But Aravas began walking away toward the other side of the hall. The barbarians quickly cut him off, crossing their axes in front of him.

"I want to show you something," Aravas said.

"Let him pass."

The barbarians raised their axes, allowing Aravas to arrive at his destination, the statue of King Euthor. He gazed at it for long moments and the hammer resting at the statue's side.

"Do you know why the Hammer of Haladrin was formed?" Aravas asked, turning his eyes back to Malfur.

"I'm not interested in a history lesson, Aravas."

"You will find it less historical, and more imminently pressing than you suppose."

Then Aravas walked back toward Malfur.

"The Hammer of Haladrin was formed because of a choice...a choice made by three brothers fearing the fourth was dead."

Again Malfur's eyes narrowed. He sat slowly down in the throne, leaning back, his brow furrowed.

"I don't know what kind of deal you've made with Corcoran," Aravas continued. "But I'm going to tell you a secret. I hope that the years haven't dulled your wits, that you have sense enough to side with your brothers over Corcoran's heedless malice."

Aravas paused, letting the suspense grow thick in the room.

"But first, tell me. When you first arrived at our lands, did you find them strange?"

Malfur didn't speak for many moments, but Aravas could see his question had struck some kind of a chord with Malfur.

"In what way?" Malfur responded.

Aravas only smiled.

"Did you wonder why you never felt the powers of any of your brothers on the wind? Or were you too busy planning the slaughter of innocent townspeople to notice?"

Malfur stood to his feet.

"Enough of your games, Aravas."

"Very well. I will tell you. At the end of the Great War, after we loosed our powers onto the world, forming the cyclone that split the world in two, Pallin, Faegean and I found one another as the world fell to chaos. But we did not find our brother, Malfur. Fearing him dead and seeing what havoc we had loosed, we made a vow to never again use our powers.

With the help of King Euthor, we imprisoned our powers into an orb of Shade Stone, which he took with him to his grave, never to be found. And now you know why the Hammer of Haladrin was formed. It was made by King Euthor, inscribed with the farewell poem to his wife, Sheyla, so that if the fateful day ever came for Corcoran's return, the Windbearers could once more take up their powers."

With that, Malfur paced back and forth before the throne, lost in thought. Aravas watched him carefully. At length, Malfur descended the throne and took Aravas by the collar.

"Tell me where he's hidden your powers!"

Aravas smiled.

"I will not tell you anything more until you swear to me that you will help your brothers to reclaim what it rightfully theirs and not allow our powers to fall into the hands of that madman, Corcoran. If he found the orb first, his dominion over this world would never end."

"I swear it. I will not allow your powers to fall to the hands of Corcoran."

"Pallin alone knows the location of the tomb of King Euthor. I assume you've been watching him?"

Aravas motioned with his head toward the Athel stone on the pavilion.

"Only once, as he and his party fled from Mt Skultira. But I've had many reports concerning him. We will retrieve him in short order."

"I would move quickly," Aravas replied. "If he makes it to Thay Iphilus Forest, you'll lose him for good."

"Leave that to me," Malfur replied. "Now tell me where you've hidden the hammer."

"In plain sight. It's heading toward the last village of Forthura, a town called Suriya. Its bearer plans to flee toward the Westward Wilds and reunite the hammer with Pallin and his companions in the lands of Kester."

Malfur turned to one of the barbarians.

"Summon your commander, Belagur. And rouse Bolgrin of the Dungeon Core. Bring them to me immediately.

"And what of him?" another barbarian asked.

286

"He will accompany us on our quest for Pallin. You will keep watch over him and see that he doesn't flee."

"There's no need for that, brother."

Malfur turned to Aravas with a look of contempt.

"Brother? What bond can there be between a mere man and a Keeper of the Wind? But I will keep my promise to you. I will not allow your powers to fall into the hands of Corcoran. Now take him away."

The barbarian grabbed Aravas and began to drag him away.

"Malfur! Do not forget who you are! You are of the Four. No one man can have that kind of power."

But soon, Aravas and his captor had reached the palace doors. Malfur sat back on the throne of Eulsiphion, a surprised but contented smile on his face.

"Aravas the wise," he chuckled to himself.

But something seemed to strike him then, some sudden thought. His brow furrowed and his gaze grew distant. He glanced to the door through which Aravas had just passed and his eyes narrowed.

But just then, the doors opened once more. Two men in different garb approached the throne. One was a tall barbarian with long blonde hair and thick furs. He wielded a large axe and a heavy broadsword. The other was, Bolgrin, leader of the Dungeon Core. As they approached the foot of the throne, both men bowed and awaited their address.

"I have just received word that my brothers, the three Windbearers, are no longer a threat," Malfur began. "But it is imperative we capture Pallin the

Wanderer before he leaves the bounds of the Horctura. He has information that will be vital to us. If he enters Thay Iphilus Forest, we will tear the forest down. The Ruhkan Mountain range will block him from escape.

Belagur, you will send a detachment of five hundred warriors to Suriya, along with your second in command, to reclaim the Hammer of Haladrin and destroy what remains of the House Forthura. You and the rest of your forces will accompany Bolgrin and the Dungeon Core in search of Pallin. We leave within the hour."

"As you command," said Belagur.

The two warriors bowed and departed, leaving Malfur alone to his thoughts. Aravas had changed everything. Only one question remained: was Aravas really such a fool to blindly trust Malfur? Or was he playing at something deeper?

At length, Malfur arose from his throne and strolled to the statue of King Euthor, bending down to read the poem inscribed on the hammer. Was it really as Aravas claimed? Was the hammer made to break the orb containing the powers of the three Windbearers? Malfur had seen the hammer on occasion before, most recently in the hands of the new lord of Cavanah, Sheabor. Sheabor, like his fathers before him, had proved an effective nuisance.

Malfur looked to the open and empty hand of the statue then glanced to the circular divot in the floor where an object had been pounded there only recently. But at length, he returned to his throne and waited. After nearly an hour, Belagur and Bolgrin returned and bowed.

"Everything is ready, my Lord."

"You know your orders," Malfur replied. "Carry them out precisely and mercilessly."

"As you command."

Then the three walked to the end of the palace hall. Hundreds of soldiers were assembled and waiting. Emerging from the palace, Malfur stopped and addressed them.

"Our victory is at hand. Tonight will see the end of the House, Forthura, and the end of the Lord of Cavanah. In one swift stroke we will put an end to all resistance."

Shouts and roars went up from the two armies. Aravas was brought under guard to the side of Malfur.

"Aravas, good you've come."

"I hope you've had time to reconsider your thinking. Pallin will die before telling you where our powers are hidden if he knows you have a will of evil."

"Then perhaps Pallin should die. If the riddle to King Euthor's tomb is something you've so readily deciphered, then perhaps it isn't as well hidden as you think."

Just then, a very large brass weapon of some kind was rolled into the streets on large wheels. It resembled a very large horn used to call for battle, though more ornately decorated. Malfur glanced to Aravas, a smile forming on his face at Aravas' obvious concern.

"It is my own design," Malfur said. "It has proven most effective against the rabble of the House of Cavanah."

The group walked en masse to the edge of the city. The gates were opened and the battalion broke in two, the bulk of the barbarians headed south, with Malfur and the rest set to tear the whole of Thay Iphilus Forest down in search of Pallin.

# Onward to Suriya

Straiah leaned on the rail of the large boat, gazing at the dark woods that obscured the city Melanor, nestled against the mountains. The three ships weighed anchor near midnight, making east toward the open ocean before turning southward.

The ship moved with remarkable speed, more than what Straiah would have expected. The Melanorians told them of a swift current that ran just at the edge of the divide where the waters deepened into unfathomable depths. As the men made the last sounding at sixty fathoms, they felt a subtle but definite tug southward. The current would bring them to Suriya swifter than any horses.

That was good. They needed as much time as they could if they had any hope of combating the barbarian forces. The women and children had been allowed to stay behind in Melanor, and what remained was a force fewer than a hundred strong. What resistance would that pose to the entire barbarian horde?

Straiah knew it was hopeless. But worse than hopeless was the thought of fleeing away just before the battle. They would have women and children in Suriya, even the families of the three who had become their companions. What would Straiah tell Durian, Baron and Blair when he saw them next? Would he have the heart to tell them that he had abandoned the defense of their families, all for the frail hope of finding the powers of the Windbearers?

Straiah clenched the hammer tightly in his hands, gazing into the deep translucent Shade Stone. He felt trapped by it, shackled to a duty that prevented him from doing what was right and noble. But he had made Sheabor a promise.

"I meant to ask you back in Melanor," came a sudden voice from behind.

Straiah turned to find King Froamb standing close by.

"How did you come to possess the Hammer of Haladrin?" the king continued.

"I asked Sheabor to give it to me back in the Squall Highlands."

The king was intrigued.

"That's quite a request," said the king. "I'm surprised it was granted."

"So am I," said Straiah, chuckling.

But then he sighed. It truly was remarkable that Sheabor agreed, in the light of what Sheabor himself had sacrificed. It was clear the king awaited the rest of the story.

"I needed it to rescue someone."

"Would that be the fair Estrien?"

Straiah nodded with a smile.

"I still can't believe he gave it to me, especially since..."

"Since what?"

Straiah opened his mouth to continue, but halted, not being one to openly discuss other person's concerns. But the king was looking at him expectantly.

"Since he had to leave the princess, Cora, behind...imprisoned in the fortress of Malfur."

"Sheabor is married?" King Froamb said in great surprise.

Straiah nodded and his countenance turned dark, recalling the events leading up to their departure from the Banished Lands.

"Things have grown dark for us in recent years," Straiah said. "Malfur and Corcoran hit us hard, knowing they'd soon be setting their sights on your Eastern Realm and wanting little resistance from us once Malfur left. We think they must have persuaded a traitor for information, for their raids were precise and severe.

One of their last raids captured the princess, Cora. She was taken to the fortress of Malfur. We think that's what they had been waiting for, for only days later, Malfur set off with a contingent of Dungeon Core for your shores. They undoubtedly thought that Sheabor would be so consumed with rescuing Cora that Malfur could slip away.

But some of us saw the bigger picture. We knew we had such little time. If we didn't set out after Malfur immediately, all opportunity would be lost. It took every man we had to restrain Sheabor from taking the Hammer of Haladrin and smashing Malfur's fortress to the ground. But the captain of our resistance forces swore an oath not to rest until he had set Cora and the others free."

"I'm sorry," said the king.

Straiah nodded slowly.

"Do you think they'll find a way to free her?"

293

"I don't know. It's all we've been able to do just to survive."

King Froamb gazed into the darkness of the vast sea. The wind blew against their faces as the gentle swells heaved the boat and dropped it.

"I confess," the king said. "I still know very little of you and your companion, Sheabor. I'm sorry for that. Truly."

"Thank you," Straiah replied. "But it's your kingdom we should be talking about. This town, Suriya, have you ever been there?"

Froamb shot him an offended glance.

"It's part of my own kingdom," the king replied.

"Well I've never actually set foot in the town," he continued. "But I've seen it from a distance while visiting the Shelengol Glades.

Straiah lifted his head back in laughter. The king smiled, glad for his amusement.

"What kind of town is it?" Straiah asked. "Is it fortified?"

King Froamb shook his head.

"There has never been a battle there. And only a handful of Suriyans have ever seen open combat. They live on the edge of the world. We leave them largely alone. They pay their taxes and nothing more is required of them."

"How many do you think have fled there from the northern townships?"

"It's impossible to say," King Froamb said, shaking his head. "You have largely the same information as I do."

Straiah was surprised by the king's demeanor. He seemed genuinely hopeful and optimistic, even in the face of such odds. From what little Straiah knew of him, he had rather expected to find a brooding man, lamenting the loss of his throne and privilege. But even on the cusp of the fall of his kingdom and perhaps his own death in battle, he was a humble and thoughtful man. King Froamb saw Straiah analyzing him and gave him a slow smile.

"You seem in very high spirits." Straiah observed.

"I've never been one to fret. We will do our duty and what will happen will happen. Every king should be tested. Those who aren't become tyrants. A kingdom should be reborn with every king."

"Not a very friendly proposition for the peoples of the kingdom," Straiah said with a chuckle.

"No," Froamb replied with a sidelong smile. "I suppose not. But as the saying goes:

*Each man's life is but a breath.*
*Man is a mere phantom as he goes to and fro;*
*He bustles about, but only in vain;*
*He heaps up wealth, not knowing who will get it.*

What better way to spend one's life than to forge a kingdom?"

Straiah nodded.

"I've never been one for philosophy," Straiah said.

"Nor I," Froamb replied with a smile. "This is my father talking."

Straiah was again struck by the transparency and even vulnerability of the king of Forthura. He was grateful for it. For only a level headed man had any hope of surviving the coming battle. A brooding king, out for vengeance, would waste the lives of his men in a vain attempt at glory. In light of that, Straiah thought best to speak on other matters.

"We should use what little time we have to form a strategy for fortifying Suriya."

"Agreed," said the king.

"If only we had one of the Suriyans with us," Straiah declared.

"No," said the king in excitement. "We may have one better. Suriyans aren't warriors. They know their town but not how best to defend it."

Then King Froamb turned round.

"Has anyone here been to Suriya?" he called out.

The men on deck glanced about, their eyes falling on a young man in his early twenties.

"I've been there twice, my lord," the young man said, stepping forward.

"What is your name?"

"Deneck, sire."

"What can you tell us about the town?" Straiah asked.

"Nothing you'll want to hear, I'm afraid. Suriya is little more than a large village. Many of the homesteads are spread throughout the plains, and the village itself has no walls. Its only redeeming quality perhaps, is that the cottages are mostly made of stone. We can harvest them for walls if time permits. But when the barbarians come, they'll be able to attack from any direction."

King Froamb nodded slowly, gazing at the deck and pacing in a tight circle.

"What are you thinking?" Straiah asked him.

"By now, the barbarians will have sent scouts to Suriya," Froamb responded. "Without walls, they know they'll be able to ride horsemen into the city from any direction at any time. If it were my force attacking, I would send footmen to engage the front line and send the horsemen up from the back to flank them."

Straiah nodded slowly.

"That's what I would do as well," he replied. "But how can we stop it?"

"Shay River runs through the center of the village," Deneck spoke up. "It splits the town in two. If we burn the bridges, we can use it as an eastern border. One less direction to defend from."

"That still leaves three exposed sides," Straiah said.

"We'll have to use pikemen on the south and west," said the king.

"I would not recommend splitting your forces. The barbarian foot soldiers are fearsome. We'll need every last man to meet them on the front line."

"What do you suggest?"

"We have the hammer, don't we?" Straiah responded. "Why not cave in some of the buildings to block the southern and western roads."

"The barbarians will come with ropes and grapples. They'll pull the walls down."

"If we do a good enough job, we'll be able to fend off the horsemen with only a small force of pikemen."

King Froamb nodded slowly. That was a good plan.

"What are we going to do with the women and children?" Straiah asked.

"We'll put them on ships and send them into Boreol Bay. If the battle goes ill, perhaps they can make for Melanor."

"There will be hundreds of them," Straiah continued.

"I know."

Straiah opened his mouth to say more, but he knew it would only dishearten the listeners around them. Even with all the fishing boats of Suriya, they'd barely manage to fit even half the refugees. And the Suriyan boats were made for fishing, without the sails and rigging to make a long voyage up the coast. No. Suriya is where they would make their stand. But one more question tugged on Straiah's mind. He leaned in close to the king's ear and spoke softly.

"What do we do if Malfur is with them?" he asked.

The king turned to him gravely. Malfur. Even if somehow beyond reason they managed to defeat the barbarians tonight, the Dungeon Core would return with Malfur at their head. They would make quick work of their tattered band of soldiers.

But just then, the cryptic message of Aravas flashed through Straiah's mind. Straiah didn't know where he had gone or what he had done, but he chose

298

to hope and breathed in deeply the salty night air. And almost as if the world itself responded, the first glow of dawn appeared on the far horizon.

They were now somewhere off the coast of the lands of Forthura, skirting the shoreline at a gallop's pace to the town at the edge of the civilized world. As dawn lightened into day, the crew congregated along the western rail of the boat.

Few features were discernible beyond the rolling hillsides of the plains. But very thin bands of smoke seemed to rise in the far distant places. The barbarians were undoubtedly raiding the open countryside. King Froamb and his men took heart. It meant they stood a chance of getting to Suriya before the barbarians did.

Afternoon darkened into evening with scarcely a word uttered between the men. But with the failing light, a glow seemed to rise in the west. Too bright for torches and too far away, it could only be one thing. One of the villages.

"Captain, bring us in closer!" yelled the king.
"That will take us outside the current, sire."
"I don't care!"
The boat veered toward the coastline."
"It's Emri!" said one of the men.

Emri was only two towns north of Suriya, roughly four day's walk. As they neared, tips of flame poked above the scattered hillside. But nothing else was seen or heard. If there had been a battle there, it had already ended.

"Take us back to the current," the king ordered.

The rest of the night was spent in silence. Would they pass the barbarians by? Or would they arrive in Suriya to find it likewise destroyed? How had it all happened so fast, Straiah wondered?

"You ought to take some rest," Straiah advised, but King Froamb's countenance remained stoic.

"You've barely slept an hour in three days."

"I'll be along soon," said the king.

Straiah bowed and departed for the lower decks. He fell into a cot and asleep nearly that same instant.

# The Night Wanderers

Night was upon the plains as the moon rose up from the south. Though now in decline, it still cast enough light for Durian to see his shadow trotting next to him on the ground. The familiar pangs of hunger had once more found him, as the last of their stores had dried up, and days or even weeks of journeying still separated them from the lands of Kester. But that didn't concern him now. Thay Iphilus Forest filled his thoughts and he rode up alongside Pallin and Sheabor, whom he could hear speaking about the forest.

"How long will our journey be through the forest?" Sheabor asked.

"Less than a week, I would venture."

"Good. That will give us plenty of time to lose the barbarians for good."

"I wouldn't worry too much about that," Pallin replied. "Even though the barbarians are seemingly fearless, they rarely stray into the forest on account of the Night Wanderers."

"Wait a minute," Baron broke in, surging forward on his horse. "Are you saying that the Night Wanderers are real?"

Baron held a tight grip on his reigns, seemingly ready to bolt. Pallin smiled.

"It's not what you think."

"It better not be."

"And I suppose you'd rather face the barbarian horde?" Pallin snapped.

The others chuckled.

"I never took you as one to frighten at ghost stories," Durian said, recalling Baron's remarks about the woodsmen of Suriya.

"Funny," Baron replied.

When the fog and perfume first blankted Thob Forest, one of the first speculations was that the Night Wanderers had come down from the old forests to the southern regions.

"The forest is perfectly harmless, I assure you," Pallin said. "It may even harbor friends."

"What do you mean?" Sheabor questioned.

"Some may dwell there who will be sympathetic to our cause. I'm not certain."

Pallin didn't seem interested in explaining further. After a short while, Sheabor suddenly halted, his gaze fixed on the south, where tiny dots of light had appeared on the hills.

"Are those torches?" Blair asked. "Is that a barbarian patrol?"

"They wouldn't ride with torches," Pallin said. "It would give away their position."

"Whoever it is," said Sheabor, "I'd rather not make their acquaintance. Let's pick up the pace."

The group rode on heightened alert, Sheabor dropping back to keep watch. Who in the world besides a barbarian patrol would be trekking through the open countryside by night, Durian wondered?

They spoke little until morning and stopped to rest by a reedy brook, where they remained for the bulk of the day. Sheabor found a spot where the brook widened into a pool, and managed to pull a handful of small fish. Eating a few meager bites of food was almost worse than going hungry, but Durian knew it would help keep their strength up.

At evening, they departed westward. The moon rose up a glowing sliver in the south, casting its light over the dark silhouettes of distant trees. By midnight, they had reached the line of trees.

Even from the onset, the trees of Thay Iphilus Forest were larger in height and breadth than those of Thob Forest. Moss covered everything, emanating a damp sourness to the air. It was dark, almost inky black amid the trees, the glow of Sheabor's battle-axe the only light penetrating the darkness. But it did little to aid them. Rather, it kept their eyes from fully adjusting to the world around them. The horses grunted and shot their heads about at the many noises of the deep woods.

"Thay Iphilus is the oldest forest of the continent," Pallin began as they rode through the black.

The sureness in his voice calmed the horses and even themselves.

"Like Eulsiphion, Thay Iphilus survived the earthquakes and flooding. Some of the trees may have even been planted by the Woodlanders of that age. And it has relics besides from the First Age, if one knows where to look."

"What kinds of relics?" Sheabor asked.

"That's difficult to explain unless you know your history."

Then Pallin turned to the three Suriyans.

"Tell me what you know of the legend of the Night Wanderers."

"They say that there's a haunted place in the old forest that traps the souls of those who get lost there," Blair replied. "You feel drowsier and drowsier until at last you can't help but lie down a moment. When you wake up, you're a spirit chained to the deeps of the forest, never to be freed."

"Some of that is partially true, I suppose," Pallin chuckled. "Just before the start of the Great War, the different houses of men began working together on creative ventures. The Omri stones of Thob Forest are one example. The Builders were the first to start it. They noticed that some of their creations had almost magical effects, just like the stones Eulsiphion is made from.

A type of stone was discovered that seemed to hypnotize the bearer of it. A project began between the three Houses. A large mound of the stone was constructed in one of the forests of Forthura. When the forest was filled with the aromatic fragrances of the Woodlanders, the stone was called to life by those of the Wise Men.

Immediately, all who were there fell into a deep sleep. Their spirits were actually lifted from their bodies for a time, and were able to wander the forest free of physical restraints and boundaries. Those present called it the most extraordinary experience of their lives, and the stone of Thay Iphilus Forest was thereafter called the Soul Stone.

That was just before the Great War started. Once the war had progressed, the Woodlanders of Thay Iphilus Forest were cut off from the rest of their house. Rather than fight a hopeless battle, they sought the Soul

Stone. They knew that Corcoran had no knowledge of its existence and that if his forces came upon their bodies, they would appear dead and would most likely leave them be.

They may have succeeded. But the cyclone sent the land into chaos. Now, their spirits are cursed to wander the forest near the Soul Stone. Some have caught glimpses of them from time to time. And from those encounters have sprung the tales which now terrify your minds."

"What happened to the city the Night Wanderers lived in?" Sheabor asked. "Was it destroyed by the forces of Corcoran?"

"I don't know," Pallin responded. "Which is why I mentioned earlier that the forest may harbor friends we scarcely knew we had."

"Or more enemies," said a voice suddenly from the dark.

Durian nearly sprang from his horse in fright. The voice seemed to come from just behind him. The group froze. Sheabor's hand moved to the hilt of his sword, but he dared not draw it.

"Show yourself," said Pallin.

A torch suddenly blazed into life in front of them, its bearer, a cloaked figure armed with a bow. The light of the torch illumined the nearby forest, and other cloaked figures could be seen, moving about the trees.

"That was an impressive story," said the cloaked figure. "I wonder where you learned it."

But Pallin remained silent.

"Who are you and why are you in Thay Iphilus Forest?"

"The barbarians have overrun the Kingdom, Forthura. We are fleeing north toward Kester."

"Fleeing refugees don't carry such weapons and armor."

"You don't know what things have transpired these past weeks. The ancient enemy is returning. We are on a quest of the highest importance."

"Ancient enemy? Corcoran is long dead."

"He is alive. Not unlike your ancestors who still roam the bounds of this forest."

Pallin's words struck a chord in Durian. Sheabor had said earlier that Corcoran had given up his physical form and had somehow tied himself to the earth. Perhaps something similar to the Soul Stone was on the Banished Lands.

The cloaked warrior was still silent, considering what Pallin had said. But he was looking straight at them now, and Durian could finally discern some of his features. He had long brown hair and piercing green eyes. His chin was sharp and his frame broad and muscular.

"You cannot escape to the north," he said at length. "Only this evening, a pack of barbarian horsemen rode that way with all speed. They are searching for something...or someone. If you come out of the forest north of the Ruhkan Mountains, they will find you."

Sheabor gave a troubled glance to Pallin. Malfur was certainly going well out of his way to try and capture them, or at least keep them from leaving the bounds of the Horctura. It was surprising.

"If any of what you say is true, the Council will want to hear of it," the man concluded. "You will be granted entrance to Ogrindal. Come, the journey is long."

With that, nearly a dozen more torches sprang to life, revealing an array of forest warriors scattered about the trees and forest floor. The torches lit the nearby woods, bringing the outer places into an even blacker darkness. Durian had the sense that the torches weren't for the cloaked warriors, but for him and his friends. Warriors like these had been trained to move about a thick forest in darkness.

They went not far before stopping for the night. The cloaked warriors made a small fire and gave Durian and the others some food, which they gratefully accepted. As they sat around the small fire, Durian's mind was fixed on the idea of the Soul Stone.

What if King Euthor had used it twelve centuries ago to trap his own spirit inside the Hammer of Haladrin? Durian didn't know how he knew, but he knew the hammer was responsible for his dreams. And Thalen had told them that the last king of Melanor had disappeared with King Euthor at the end of the Great War. Perhaps he had helped him.

Durian was seated next to one of the forest warriors. Baron and Blair were making ready for sleep and Sheabor and Pallin were standing and having a quiet conversation a stone's throw away.

"If Ogrindal is a city from the First Age, do your people still possess their abilities like the people of Melanor do?"

The warrior turned to him with a stern countenance and glanced up to their commander, who gave him a slight nod.

"Some," the warrior responded. "But the ability is weak...nothing compared to our ancestors."

The mention of his ancestors brought more questions to mind.

"Is there nothing your people can do to free the Night Wanderers?"

"Free them?" the warrior asked. "Your friend was wrong about them. During the Great War, King Behlyn knew that Corcoran's forces would come and end the way of life in Ogrindal. Rather than be taken from the forest as slaves, they chose to become the Wineckdin, whom your people call the Night Wanderers. They are not trapped. They became spirits of their own will, so that no one could ever take them from the forest they loved. We are their guardians."

That certainly was different than the rendition Pallin had told.

"Pallin said this is the oldest forest on the continent – that some of the trees here were actually here before the Great War."

"Yes, that's true. And in the center of Ogrindal is the last of our Lorimor trees. It was planted just after the war and King Behlyn is buried beneath it. The Lorimor tree has a special fruit with which our people make elixirs, which impart strength and vitality for a short while."

"Rest now," said the forest commander from across the fire. "Save the questions for morning."

Durian assented and curled up next to the warm fire, falling fast asleep. He awoke to a nudge on his shoulder, Pallin standing over him and a faint light overhead. He arose and readied himself, surprised to find the horses were absent.

"The tracks are too easy to follow," said Pallin, seeing Durian's surprise. "Gwaren assured us we will reach Ogrindal by nightfall."

"Gwaren?"

"The commander of the Forest Guard."

In the light of the morning, Durian gazed at the forest around him. The trees were all massive and spaced far apart, having long ago claimed their places, stomping out competition for soil below and sunlight above. In Thob Forest, the trees still grew close together, each one vying for dominance over its fellows in the millenia long struggle.

The group departed, led by the man Pallin had called Gwaren. Durian followed not far behind, and Baron and Blair soon came up to him.

"I wonder if we'll get to see one of the Night Wanderers," Baron said.

"No," said Gwaren without turning around to address Baron directly.

"I didn't say we'd go looking for them," Baron defended. "I just thought we might happen across one is all."

"No," said Gwaren.

Durian glanced to Blair with a smile. By midday, they came to an open meadow in the forest.

The warming sunlight fell brightly down, banishing for a time, the cold damp of the sheltered forest floor. In the far distance, the snowy peaks of the Ruhkan Mountains came into view. Seeing them made him think of the Estees Mountains and Suriya. Had the barbarians already marched to conquer it? Or were they staying put in Eulsiphion?

It made Durian's heart beat faster. The one comfort he took was in Gwaren's words that the barbarians had sent a party of horsemen ahead of them to the north. The more Malfur focused on capturing them, the less he would care about a little fishing village at the bottom of the world.

Durian was eager to see Ogrindal – a city of the old world. They could become a powerful ally in the fight against Corcoran. He would soon get his wish. As they journeyed on, Durian found the man he had been speaking with the night before.

"Do your people still use the Soul Stone?" Durian asked.

The warrior shook his head.

"The knowledge has been lost to us. And we don't even know if it still functions."

"Why is that?"

"It has been damaged," the warrior replied. "Perhaps by King Behlyn himself to keep others from bringing them back to their bodies. And some of it seems to have been taken."

"Taken?" said Pallin from nearby. "By whom?"

"We don't know. It happened long ago."

Durian's heart raced. He glanced up to Pallin but Pallin's gaze had grown distant. Had King Euthor taken part of the Soul Stone? Had Corcoran? Durian was lost in thought. He scarcely noticed the sunlight wane and turn to evening, nor the lights of Ogrindal gleaming through the trees.

But soon, Durian found himself in an open grassland between the forest edge and the city, Ogrindal. Nestled against the towering mountains, its fifty foot wall seemed to be made of a single piece of wood. Durian was taken aback by the sight of it, for only a moment ago, he had been consumed with his own thoughts.

The group approached just as the evening stars began to appear in the sky. As they neared, a gate in the center of the wall opened. But as they entered, Durian studied what he could of the outer wall. Its grain flowed in long horizontal swirling lines, like the polished bowls he used to sell in Market Town. He marveled at how such a thing could ever be done.

But soon the group was in the city. The people were beginning to gather around them, descending from the many buildings, all made of wood. They seemed in awe of the weapons and armor the group carried, so much so that Baron and Blair grew embarrassed. They wore armor of the First Age, and the people were gazing at them as though they must have been the finest of warriors. It made Durian smile, for he rarely got to see Baron mousy and shy.

In the distance ahead, a massive treetop spread broadly over the city. Approaching, Durian surprised to see the tree still bore its fruit, though sparsely, even in winter. They passed beneath it, Durian reaching his hand out to touch one of the many round, orangy-red fruits.

"No," said Gwaren, powerfully enough to startle Durian.

He shot his hand back to his side, Baron and Blair chuckling beside him. They came to a building built against the mountain face. It was larger than the rest, ornately carved and well-lit. The building doors were under guard.

"This is the Council chamber," said Gwaren. "They are waiting for us."

The doors were opened and a large room revealed. Inside, four men and two women, all clad in the same flowing green robes, stood waiting for them. The lead man joined them to sit at the large circular table. Sheabor and Pallin sat, while the three Suriyans elected to stand at the fringes.

"I am Whinden," the man began. "This is the ruling Council of Ogrindal. We have been told that the lands of Forthura have been conquered by the barbarians. It has also been said that you believe that somehow, the ancient enemy has aided the barbarians in their conquest."

"Yes," said Pallin. "But we do not expect you to believe our words alone. The weapons and armor we bear are from the last great king of Cavanah, King Euthor, hidden until the days when the ancient enemy would again threaten our peoples."

The Council members seemed surprisingly stoic at the tidings of Pallin, and Durian couldn't get a read on whether or not they believed them.

"It is imperative that we reach the lands of Kester safely," Pallin continued. "Is there safe passage over the Ruhkan Mountains?"

"The passage is nearly closed," Whinden replied. "The snows grow thick atop the mountains."

Pallin considered his words. With the barbarians now patrolling north of the forest, taking the pass over the mountains was their best option. But they could just as easily freeze to death in the heights.

"You may stay and await the spring," Whinden continued. "You will be our welcomed guests."

"That is very gracious," said Sheabor. "But I'm afraid our mission is too vital. If the pass over the mountains is blocked, we'll have no choice but to venture north."

"If that is your choice, know that we will not accompany you."

His words hung in the air. Just then, the doors of the chamber opened and a young girl entered. She was young, in her early twenties, with long brown hair and wearing a flowing olive gown. She was beautiful. Durian saw Baron stir in his peripheral vision and glanced over to see him standing tall and proud, trying his best to belong in the armor he wore.

Durian stifled a chuckle. The girl also glanced over, seeing Baron and offering a slight smile. But she walked to the Council members on the other side of the room. One of them, a man, smiled warmly at her as though she were his daughter, and the girl came and whispered something in Whinden's ear.

Then the girl departed, glancing again at the three Suriyans and smiling at Baron, who nodded to her dutifully. Durian couldn't help but smile. It didn't do Baron any favors that his own twin brother standing next to him was giving the opposite air that Baron was trying to project. And the smile the girl wore seemed to be one of amusement, as though she had worked out just what Baron was up to.

"The evening meal has been prepared," Whinden announced. "You will join us."

The group began to disperse from the chamber. Durian was surprised at the response from the Council. They didn't seem overly concerned that the barbarians were hovering now just outside Thay Iphilus Forest, eagerly seeking to capture those who had now taken up residence in Ogrindal. Pallin had said earlier that the barbarians rarely entered the forest on account of the Night Wanderers, but Durian could only assume that Malfur had similar information to Pallin. He wouldn't easily frighten at ghost stories.

The group left the chamber. Outside, darkness had taken hold, and in the distance, the large Lorimor tree was lit up by mellow points of light. As they made their way closer, Durian couldn't believe his eyes when he realized that the glows were actually the pieces of fruit scattered through its limbs.

After passing the tree, the group turned right toward a sheltered, grassy park, where two large rectangular tables housed many guests. Baron was gazing intently around the tables, craning his neck as he walked for a better view. Durian opened his mouth to question him but realized with a laugh that Baron was searching for the whereabouts of the girl from just before.

"Even at a time like this?" Durian asked.

Baron only smiled wide. Sheabor, Pallin and the three Suriyans were given seats and the meal began. It smelled like venison stew and was delicious, made more so by the fact that it was the first home cooked meal they'd had since the banquet at Eulsiphion. The three Suriyans devoured it and were served another helping.

"Make sure you get the recipe for this stew, little brother," Baron said between slurps.

"Get it yourself," Blair shot back.

But just then, a commotion seemed to break out at the other end of the table. A group of the Forest Guard were running up to them, out of breath. Durian and the others were near enough the Council members to hear the report from the warrior.

"A force of thousands from the barbarian kingdom is approaching the forest. Their intent in unmistakable."

Whinden's gaze shot to Pallin.

"You have doomed us all!"

# War Preparations

The boats reached Suriya at first light, weighing anchor in Boreol Bay. The breeze from the south menaced their skin, making it difficult to move from the deck onto the smaller craft. By the time they arrived on shore, King Froamb and his men were already chilled to the bone.

But they were met by some from town who had seen the ships from afar. It was mostly a band of villagers armed with pitchforks, but a few soldiers between them. They came to meet the new arrivals, unsure of what to expect.

"Who are you?" demanded one of them.

"King Froamb. We are here to see to the defense of Suriya."

The townspeople glanced at one another gravely, clearly not ready to believe his claim.

"Take us to the town Magistrate," the king said with a step forward.

But the group remained on guard. King Froamb flushed red.

"Step aside, or be removed!"

Enough of King Froamb's forces had landed now to clearly outnumber the townspeople who had come to shore. They assented and led them from shore back to bounds of Suriya. It was a quick hike through the open plains.

On arrival, most who had gathered were near the center of town, in a bare spot that seemed recently vacated. Scattered fires provided little heat from the cold. Straiah was surprised to see so many out of doors in the early morning. But with all the refugees from the northern townships, there was nowhere to house them.

Though some took an interest in them, most huddled together with loved ones against mounds of snow, which provided little shielding from the wind.

"It's the king of Eulsiphion!" someone shouted.

The call rang out and they who had paid them little heed arose and drew near, crowding heavily around them.

"Someone find the magistrate and bring him here," King Froamb commanded. "Please, make way. We have much work to do."

Just then someone shouted: "When does the rest of your army arrive, good King?"

King Froamb paused and looked the man straight in the face.

"You are the rest of my army."

An eruption of murmuring ensued, as the reality of the situation sunk in. King Froamb had brought less than a hundred warriors. That, combined with however many were already here was all that stood between them and the barbarian horde.

"Someone find the magistrate!" King Froamb shouted. "And have everyone else gather in the middle of town. We will assign you tasks according to your skill."

The people began to disperse. The king turned to Straiah.

"Our highest priority will be the wall on our three borders," the king said. "If the barbarians get here before we've sealed the town, all hope is lost."

Straiah didn't know how to respond. As the bearer of the hammer, he was the logical choice to put in charge of the wall project. But Straiah still had his sights set on the Westward Wilds. He thought to slip away unnoticed. But that hope was slowing fading.

"Whatever it is, we have no time to waste!" he continued. "I need you to take a survey of the entry points and form a plan to barricade them. Take as many men as you need."

Straiah clenched his jaw and bowed.

"I need a dozen able bodied men," Straiah called out. "Some preferably from Suriya."

Some men stepped forward from the crowd.

"We'll need access to stone," Straiah continued. "Is there a quarry nearby?"

The men shook their heads.

"Where do you get the stone for the cottages?"

"It's field stone mostly," one of them responded.

That wouldn't work. Unless the fields were incredibly rocky, collecting scattered stone would be far too slow. They could cave in some of the buildings onto the roads, but with so many refugees already homeless, destroying what few dwelling places remained should be a last resort.

"Go to Tobin's field," one said and motioned to a nearby man whose fists were clenched and whose face had turned bright red. "He's got rocks for fifty walls."

Straiah gave the man, presumably Tobin, his attention. After a few more moments, the man's fists unclenched and he sighed.

"We'll need a plow," the man resigned. "Mine's stuck in that confounded blacksmith's shop, Baron. The rocks will be frozen fast in place."

"Baron?" Straiah questioned. "Twin brother to Blair?"

Tobin nodded, but somewhere in the crowd, someone called out.

"You've seen my sons?" A moment later, a man pushed his way forward to stand before Straiah.

"Yes," Straiah responded. "Both them and their companion Durian. We found them in Thob Forest weeks ago."

The man sighed in great relief. It was clear he had thought them dead.

"Where are they now?" the man asked.

"Traveling to the lands of Kester with Sheabor, Lord of the House, Cavanah."

The man was taken aback, his mouth opened as though to inquire further. But answers would have to wait.

"I'll show you the way," Tobin said, motioning to the far side of town.

"No, take some men with you," Straiah said. "I must make other preparations. Which way is your field?"

"Not far."

"Good. Then bring whatever stone you can harvest to the north wall."

319

King Froamb was still delegating responsibilities as Straiah turned to leave.

"When the barbarians come, we'll need to get as many women and children out of the city as possible. How many boats do we have?"

One man in the crowd answered him.

"One and a half dozen," he said, "but none so fine as mine, the Lord Gaffney. Send the wee ones with me. If the barbarians set sail after us, I'll dash them to pieces against the rocks."

"You will command the exodus then," Froamb said.

That was the last thing Straiah heard before he and his men moved out of earshot. They ran through the streets of Suriya, Straiah taking note of all the points through which the barbarians could gain access and flank them.

After a minute, they came to the town square, which was far too open a space to hope to block. Wherever they hoped to make their southern wall, it would have to be north of this place. Straiah was wary of boxing themselves in too tight. If they did, the barbarians could just surround them and wait them out.

But perhaps it wasn't such a bad idea after all. The barbarians wouldn't likely have the patience for a drawn out battle. And what army would be willing to make camp outside a place like Suriya in the dead of winter? Perhaps a tightly boxed encampment was just what they needed.

Straiah stopped and surveyed the scene. Many of the buildings here looked official. Though they could be used to house refugees, these would be the logical choice to demolish first. Straiah needed to survey the rest of the town, but nearly a dozen men now stood waiting for a task to perform.

Straiah went to one of the nearby buildings. Swinging the Hammer of Haladrin, he tore a chunk clean out of the building's corner. Making other careful strikes, he brought the building down in short order, crashing in a plume of dust.

"Fill in all the roads north of the town square. Start at the river and work your way west. I'll return shortly."

Straiah set off alone to the northwest. Coming to the edge of town, he lingered there a moment, eyes peering out onto the open plains. Only the swaying of golden grasses in the mid-morning breeze. The barbarians could arrive at any time. But they weren't here yet.

Straiah turned his attentions back toward town. He thought to demolish the corner building to save the workers the energy of hauling stones to the far reaching corners of town. But he stopped short. With a little careful planning, he could create something of a maze on the streets of town – keep the horsemen frustrated for as long as possible.

Straiah set off through town, running and making mental notes of where streets connected and ended. If he blocked only a handful of choke points, he could keep the horsemen riding largely in circles through town. But that would only work if the barbarians launched a full attack without even taking time to scout the town. Would they really be so foolish?

Straiah hesitated many long moments, knowing that his decisions here, now, could determine the outcome of the battle. Tactics were never his strong suit. That was Sheabor's arena.

He had to make a decision. But his heart raced as he stared down at the hammer in his hands. He hated being responsible for the fate of so many. How did Sheabor do it? How did he make decisions that would cost lives? It was so much easier being a soldier and following orders.

But clenching the hammer tightly in his hands, he turned with a yell and swung into the side of a nearby cottage. Stone exploded upon impact and the thatch roof sunk toward him. Swinging again in key places, he turned the structure to rubble.

Then he set off again. For better or worse, he was choosing misdirection and confusion over a solid wall. If luck went their way, the barbarian horsemen would be so busy riding through the city looking for entrance that the bulk of the men could engage the forward line. That was their only chance.

Straiah spent the next few hours smashing key structures and moving on, marking the places for the men to block the road. By midday, exhaustion and hunger drove him back to the center of town, where a meal, though meager, was being prepared for the masses. He was quickly spotted.

"Sir, the northern wall is well underway," said one of the workmen.

"Good," Straiah continued. "I've begun blocking off choke points on the west and southern ends of town. When the northern wall is complete, take the men and block off the roads completely. It's imperative that no weakness be found there. If any of the blockades fail, the barbarians will ride down on our forces and destroy us."

"Sir," he responded with a bow.

Straiah went for a bowl of soup, gazing around the crowded masses. King Froamb was nowhere to be seen. Straiah set off for the north of town. King Froamb was with the men there, supervising the construction of the northern wall, since there the brunt of the attack would fall. The construction was coming along nicely, just enough of a barrier to keep horsemen from riding them down.

"Straiah, good," the king began. "How are the other fortifications coming?"

"Good. We hope to be done by nightfall."

The king nodded pensively.

"Have we sent out any scouts?" Straiah asked.

"We have," the king replied. "They haven't returned, which is good. The barbarians are still some way off. Once they do, we'll know the strength of their position."

That was good news. Straiah could finish the wall and then slip away under cover of nightfall toward the Westward Wilds. It would be the hardest thing he'd ever do, run away from a losing battle, leaving brave men and women to their fate. But he had no other choice. If the hammer fell into the hands of Malfur, the war would be lost in an instant.

He still hadn't told King Froamb. Perhaps it was better that he just slip away. He glanced up to find the king gazing intently at him. Straiah was visibly conflicted and the king seemed to sense what he was thinking. Straiah opened his mouth to tell him, but the king turned his gaze north and spoke first.

"It's foolish, I suppose, for us to make such a stand here in this place. This battle, after all, will hardly determine the outcome of the larger war."

Straiah nodded slowly.

"If we can't fight for our homes and families, what is there left worth fighting for," Straiah replied.

Just then, they saw a rider appear on a distant hillside to the north.

"Is that one of the scouts?" Straiah asked.

But the king didn't respond. The rider made for town with all speed, others congregating around the king at his approach. The rider reached them and dismounted.

"Sire, the barbarians are sweeping in from the northwest, cutting off access to Thob Forest. They will be here by nightfall."

Straiah's heart raced. Why were the barbarians cutting off escape to the forest?

"How many are they?" King Froamb asked.

"It's difficult to say," the scout replied. "The barbarians are spread throughout the plains. There could be as many as five hundred."

"Five hundred?" replied Froamb. "That's hardly the bulk of their forces. Are you certain?"

The scout hesitated.

"We'll know more when the others return," he replied.

King Froamb shot an excited glance to Straiah, which he scarcely noticed. For he was confounded as to what the barbarians were doing. Why were they cutting off access to Thob Forest, for one? And why did they send so few warriors? Perhaps they knew they would meet with little resistance. But even with five hundred warriors, they would still outnumber their own fighting force two to one.

"What do you think?" the king asked.

Straiah glanced up in surprise to see King Froamb gazing at him.

"I don't know," Straiah replied. "If they've only sent five hundred warriors, they're clearly overconfident."

"That will be to our advantage."

"I was thinking," Straiah continued. "I haven't yet destroyed the bridges across the river. Those who can't fit onto the boats we could send to the other East End of Suriya during the battle. It won't save them for long, but will at least keep them out of danger while we face the invasion."

"Very well," the king replied.

Straiah bowed, then departed. His mind was still a jumble. What was he going to do now? He could try and fight his way through the barbarian line. If they really were spread throughout the plains, he might only have to face a handful between him and Thob Forest. But if the barbarians had really only brought five hundred warriors, King Froamb just might stand a chance.

Straiah ran throughout the town, finding the scattered piles of stone now blocking the various lanes. Testing them, he found them all secure. The horsemen would eventually break through with their ropes and grapples, but if they could just hold them for a little while, it might make all the difference.

Coming to the center of town, many of the villagers and refugees were busy turning planks of wood into long spikes. There were dozens of them piled in the center of the group. Straiah took one in hand and swung it through the air.

"Make these more narrow," Straiah said. "At least at the hand holds."

"Yes, sir."

Straiah set off for the East End. Two bridges ran across the river, connecting the two towns. Straiah stood there for many moments, gazing at the easy flowing river, trying to determine if horses could cross it, even if the bridge was destroyed. That was a risk they'd have to take.

The main bridge was worn and weathered, with short and fat chunks of wood that would do little for making pikes. With the hammer in hand, Straiah struck the near end, splintering its support and sending it into the river. But it remained a single unit and quickly lodged against the riverbank.

Striking it in a few key places, he was able to send the larger pieces floating down the stream, now flotsam for the crisp waters of Boreol Bay, erelong washing ashore on some forgotten beach. Straiah smiled as he imagined some small boy in the lands of Kester coming upon a spar of wood half sunk in the sand, and all the places his imagination would take him.

Straiah wandered south toward the other bridge. It was smaller, clearly for foot traffic, and would shatter easily under the might of the hammer. It connected what the Suriyans had called Market Town. Leaving it undamaged, he returned to the center of town. Day was already descending into evening. If the scout was right, the barbarians would be here soon. But would Malfur be among them? That was the real question.

Straiah arrived to find King Froamb among the villagers, he too examining the pikes piled in front of him. Seeing Straiah, he dropped the spear and addressed him.

"What is the state of our fortifications?"

"Everything that can be done has been done. The main bridge connecting the East and West Ends has been destroyed. The smaller will remain until we can evacuate anyone not able to fight."

"As you know," King Froamb addressed the crowd in a loud voice. "The barbarians will be here in short order. They think they can overrun us with a mere few hundred men. We will show them they are wrong. All who cannot fight will leave the city. Those who cannot fit aboard the ships will make across the river until the battle is over. The rest will stay and fight. The Horctura will soon learn that the price of Suriya is dear."

A shout went up from all gathered. Just then, Straiah had an idea.

"Have the barbarians sent any scouts on horseback?" Straiah asked the king.

"No. They're more concerned with drawing a broad net around us to keep any from escaping."

Straiah thought quickly. The people were beginning to disperse. It would be night soon, and the barbarians wouldn't be able to see much.

"Anyone going to the East End," Straiah called out. "Enter whatever home you find and get a fire going in the hearth. Light every lamp and make your presence clearly known. Do not fear. We will destroy the bridge behind you. The barbarians won't reach you."

The villagers weren't sure exactly what to make of the order. But King Froamb was nodding eagerly. If the barbarians didn't have a fix on their exact position, they could use what few archers they had to fire into the barbarian line while they searched about in darkness.

"Do as Straiah commands!"

It was only an hour till nightfall. If they could make it till them before the barbarians got here, they just might stand a chance. Straiah knew he was set now. There was no chance of escape before the battle. His fate was now tied to Suriya.

# The End of the Road

Whinden was standing, eyes blazing and finger pointing at Pallin.

"Commander," Whinden called out. Gwaren stood to attention. "You will take these men into custody to await the decision of the Council."

Gwaren bowed and came to where Pallin and the others were seated. Pallin and Sheabor stood to their feet slowly, their hands raised.

"I am truly sorry," said Pallin. "I had no idea Malfur would go to such lengths to capture us."

"Malfur?" Whinden said in great surprise. "Keeper of the North Wind?"

Pallin nodded.

"He was once my brother. But now, he has sided with Corcoran and chosen a will of evil."

"Your brother? Who are you?"

"I am Pallin, Keeper of the South Wind.

There were murmurs among the crowd, Gwaren making his way to Pallin and Sheabor.

"Please surrender your weapons and armor," Gwaren said.

Sheabor and Pallin both unsheathed their mystical weapons and handed them to Gwaren.

"Don't bring them far," Sheabor said. "We'll need them soon."

Gwaren extended his hand. As long as they came peacefully, it didn't seem as though the commander meant to bind and arrest them. As the group departed, an eruption of voices ensued, many of the townspeople leaving the park for their homes.

Durian still couldn't believe it. Thousands of barbarians and Dungeon Core on their way to Ogrindal? Was Malfur trying to conquer the whole continent single-handedly?

The group was brought to a building not far from the Council chamber they had just occupied. Inside were many cells, all empty and waiting for them. They were swiftly imprisoned and guards posted outside.

"Pallin, this isn't good," said Sheabor.

"No, it is not."

"Does Malfur know of the existence of Ogrindal?"

"Doubtful," replied Pallin. "But with thousands of warriors at his command, they will scour the forest until they find us."

"And when they find us, you know as well as I what decision Ogrindal will come to."

Pallin sighed and nodded slowly.

"What decision?" Baron asked.

"Rather than face the wrath of the barbarian horde," Sheabor began. "They will hand over Pallin and myself to Malfur."

"What! They can't do that."

"I don't begrudge them," Sheabor continued. "They've been apart from the rest of the world for a millenia. Now, without warning, they're asked to risk their lives to save it."

"It may turn out for the best," Pallin said. "I don't know what kind of alliance Malfur has with

Corcoran, but with the success he's having in laying siege to this realm, he may grow resentful in the day Corcoran comes to claim what he has already conquered."

"You think Malfur may turn on Corcoran?" Durian asked.

"I don't know," Pallin replied. "But he is a Keeper of the Wind, after all."

The group talked on, speculating of things to come. But after nearly an hour, the door opened to reveal Gwaren.

"What news?" asked Sheabor.

"Much talk but few decisions," Gwaren replied. "There's talk of turning the five of you over to Malfur's forces when they arrive. We'll do better if we use stealth to fight them from the trees. But if we kill a portion of them, the rest will be thirsty for blood and vengeance.

The simple fact is they are too many to stop. Do we attack them from a long way off, hoping to kill enough to give us the advantage? Or do we wait and offer the five of you up as a peace offering to Malfur?"

"I think you know what our vote is," said Baron.

"I've also heard whispers of something even more troubling," Gwaren continued. "Some are arguing that even if we give them what they want, it won't satisfy them for long. The barbarians aren't likely to let us live in peace once they learn the way to the city. That is why some are arguing that we use Pallin's knowledge to activate the Soul Stone and join our ancestors, the Wineckdin, in the forest."

331

"What!" Baron exclaimed. "You can't!"

"It wouldn't work," said Pallin. "We need one of Estrien's people to call the stone to life."

Gwaren breathed in deeply and sighed.

"I do not think anything will come of it. Fear is motivating vain imaginings. But while we sit here discussing, the forces of Malfur fast approach the forest."

"Gwaren, you know our only chance is to attack Malfur early – hit them from the cover of trees."

"And I trust that that will be the decision of the Council also."

Gwaren bowed and turned to depart. The group was left alone again. Durian couldn't believe that some in the city actually wanted to live as spirits, tied to the deeps of Thay Iphilus Forest. But as they waited, Durian thought he heard something like the distant call to battle. Sheabor heard it too, for he went to the barred window and gazed outward.

"What is it?" Pallin asked.

"Malfur has reconstructed his war horn."

"War horn?" asked Baron skeptically.

"A large horn made of brass, into which he funnels the wind, creating a blast that nothing can withstand. He'll carve out a pathway through Thay Iphilus Forest and nothing will stand in his way."

His words hung in the air. Little more was said. The group sat against the bars of the prison, awaiting the decision of the Council. A few times an hour, the blast of a distant trumped wafted in on the breeze. It was still a long way off.

Sometime in the middle of the night, Gwaren again arrived in their midst. He was visibly troubled and paced a time in front of their cells.

"Our scouts have reported in from the edge of the forest," Gwaren said. "It seems that Malfur has taken away our only advantage. The Forest Guard can't get close enough to his siege weapon to make any difference. I've ordered their retreat back to the city."

"What are you going to do?" Sheabor asked.

"The only thing we can. The Council has reached a decision. We will march out to Malfur and his forces and surrender the five of you over to them."

"How long do you think that will satisfy him? He's already begun carving a pathway to your city. Even if Malfur leaves you alone, the barbarians will surely be back. Now that they've conquered Forthura, who next do you think they'll turn their sights to?"

"That is a problem for another time – a time we may have years to prepare for."

Sheabor opened his mouth to protest, but Pallin grabbed him by the arm.

"We cannot rightly ask an entire city to risk their lives on our behalf," Pallin said.

Sheabor clenched his jaw but nodded. He had known from the beginning that this would be the ultimate decision of the Council of Ogrindal. Gwaren produced a key with which he unlocked their cell. Once outside, one of the guards accompanied them at the rear.

Gwaren led the off toward the Council chamber. Coming to the steps Durian could hear loud arguing,

333

even from behind the closed doors. Gwaren hesitated, and set off to the north instead of going directly inside.

"Where are you taking them?" the guard in the rear questioned.

"The Council members don't seem ready for our prisoners yet. I don't want to disturb them."

When they had come well away from the Council chamber and were near the empty corner of the town, Gwaren stopped and came to the guard.

"This should be far enough," Gwaren said, and extended his hand for the guard to lead the way back in the other direction.

The guard set off, but immediately, Gwaren drew his sword and in one quick motion hit the guard on the back of his head, rendering him unconscious.

"Quickly," Gwaren said, pulling the guard into the shadows of the nearby buildings. "I've hidden your weapons and armor nearby. We're very close to the pathway up the Ruhkan Mountains."

Sheabor went with Gwaren into one of the buildings, returning with their weapons and suits of armor.

"I always knew the day would come when the outside world would come to threaten everything we've fought to preserve. We cannot run from our fate."

Gwaren handed Pallin one of the chest-pieces from the tomb of Sheyla.

"Armor like this belongs on a true warrior," Pallin replied. "It would be wasted on one such as me. Please keep it, with my sincere thanks for what you are doing."

Gwaren seemed taken aback at the gesture.

"Follow me," said Gwaren. "We don't have much time."

Gwaren set off at a swift pace toward the northwest corner of town. In minutes, they arrived at the sheer face of the Ruhkan Mountains. The pathway looked more of a climb than a hike, but even so, it appeared navigable for the moment.

"I cannot guarantee the pass through the mountains is open. The snows may have already blocked it."

Pallin gazed up the mountain wall for many long moments. Then, turning back to the group with a warm smile, prepared to make his departure. Sheabor, seeing his intent spoke first.

"What are you doing? We're all going with you."

"You must stand and fight with the people of Ogrindal. I will go to the Banished Lands and the tomb of King Euthor."

Sheabor was visibly troubled by the idea of Pallin traveling alone without protection.

"But how will you enter the tomb?" Sheabor questioned. "We don't have the hammer back yet from Straiah."

"I'll use this," Pallin declared and held up the mace with the Shade Stone head. "Though this certainly won't break the orb with our powers, it should be enough to smash our way into his tomb."

Sheabor nodded slowly, still seemingly unconvinced. Though none of them wanted to leave Ogrindal to its fate, finding the orb with Pallin's powers was the most important mission.

"This may be our only opportunity to stop Malfur," Pallin continued. "He has spread himself thin to seek our capture – too thin perhaps."

Pallin placed both hands on his shoulders and looked him in the eyes.

"You are a brave and noble warrior. Men like you give me hope for this world."

"Thank you," Sheabor said with a low bow.

Then Pallin turned to the three Suriyans.

"You may accompany me if you wish," he said. "Or you can stay and fight."

Baron and Blair glanced to one another and Blair gave Baron a nod that signaled Baron to make the decision.

"Personally, I'm tired of running," said Baron. "If we can stop the barbarians here, it might keep them from invading Suriya. Fighting for Ogrindal is like fighting for home."

Pallin nodded with a smile. All seemed settled. But Durian's heart was still racing. He thought of his dreams and of his vow to one day reunite King Euthor with the woman he loved.

"I'll go with you," Durian said.

Pallin looked at him in surprise and intrigue.

"The road will be long. Full of danger."

"I'm ready for it," Durian replied.

"Are you able to climb?" asked Sheabor.

Durian rotated his wrist a few times.

"I'll make it to the lands of Kester."

It was settled them. Durian gave Baron and Blair a warm embrace, none knowing when they would see each other again. Then Pallin produced a glowing blue stone from the folds of his garments, the stone they had found in the tomb of Sheyla.

"Once in the lands of Kester, this stone will be our guide."

It was time to depart. Durian grabbed the stone of the Ruhkan Mountain range and pulled himself upward. It was freezing to the touch but manageable. Pallin came after. The group watched for many minutes, but soon the pair had ascended into the mountain's interior places. Durian did his best not to look down.

Back in Ogrindal, Gwaren led the group to the nearby Council chamber. They ascended the stairs and were stopped momentarily by the two guards outside the door who held their spears across the doorway.

"The Council is in session. They haven't sent for anyone."

"I have important tidings that will change the outcome of their decision," Gwaren returned.

The two guards lifted their spears and opened the door for Gwaren. Upon seeing him, Whinden and the others stood to their feet. Whinden opened his mouth to ask why Gwaren would come, but something gave him pause. Instead, he seemed surprised to see Gwaren wearing one of the chest-pieces of armor brought by Sheabor and the others.

But his surprise heightened by Sheabor now standing beside Gwaren, once more armed with his Shade Stone axe and shield.

"Gwaren, what is this?"

"Pallin is gone," Gwaren replied. "He is taking the pathway over the mountains."

"What have you done!" Whinden yelled.

"What you could not.  It is not the way of our people to live by fear.  We must stand and fight."

"You have condemned us all to death!"

"No," Gwaren roared.

Baron turned to Blair with a smile.

"We will not die.  We will stand.  We will fight. And we will prevail!"

# The Battle for Suriya

Night fell upon the plains as one by one, lights sprang to life in the windows of Suriya's East End. Straiah and the other soldiers watched in silence from the other side of the river behind the low wall they had built just in front of the northern row of cottages. Everything was set. Those fighting for Suriya were less than two hundred, many of them untrained in combat.

The barbarians were close – the distant whinnying of a horse, or faint glow of a torch heralding their coming. Straiah had a bow in hand, along with twenty others. He commanded the archers. The rest held swords or pikes and were under the command of their king.

Once the barbarians crested the final hill, they would see the gleaming lights of the East End across the river. They would have a choice – find a place to cross the river upstream, or enter the West End and use debris from town to make a crossing. Straiah could only hope the barbarian footmen would loathe the idea of wading through an icy river. The horsemen would be more likely, but they wouldn't want to separate from the main force.

Minutes passed, and with each one, the glow from the north grew faintly brighter. The barbarians were using torches, clearly more interested in capturing fleeing townspeople than fighting a strategic battle. It was surprising. This time it would cost them.

More minutes passed. And then, scattered along the horizon at first, small dots of light appeared across the hillsides. Straiah's heart beat quickly. If the barbarians were so concerned with capturing any who sought to flee, they might cross the river immediately to keep the East End from escaping north. The villagers on that side had been given a handful of pikes but only enough to defend against a small party of riders.

Straiah watched carefully for movements along the barbarian line. They had had enough time to see the lit cottages from the far side of Suriya. The dark forms of faster moving horsemen seemed to be patrolling without torches in front of the foot-soldiers.

Some of the horsemen broke from the main group and rode forward along the riverbank, searching for a place to cross. They paused a moment, a thousand paces out. Straiah couldn't make out what was happening. But the displeased grunting of horses told him the barbarians had plunged into the icy water and were crossing to the other side.

Straiah craned his head forward, trying to see how many were with them. It couldn't have been much more than a dozen. He could scarcely believe the barbarians seemed so little concerned with conquering Suriya, and so much concerned with making sure none escaped.

Something struck him in that moment that the barbarians must have been looking for the Hammer of Haladrin now strapped to his back. They wouldn't take such trouble just to keep villagers from escaping. But how could they know the hammer was here? What if he had already captured Sheabor and had learned from one of them the location of the hammer? That was the only explanation that made sense. A sinking feeling of despair hit his stomach.

They watched the small party of horsemen bear down on Suriya's East End. There were hundreds of unarmed refugees there. The rest of the barbarian force were still closing in on the West End.

The horsemen were only a stone's throw from the first building. They rode cautiously and slowly. Time seemed to still. Had the villagers seen them? Nothing but the riders stirred against the backdrop of the glowing windows.

But just as the riders reached the first of the buildings, the sound of battle cries rang out and the startled rearing of horses. A quick clash of sword and wood led to the horsemen fleeing back toward the open plains. The villagers let out a victorious roar. The horsemen made due west, searching for the bridges that connected the two ends of Suriya.

Finding nothing, they began a wide patrol around the East End, waiting for the rest to arrive. The tightly boxed encampment Straiah and the others had built seemed to go unnoticed by the riders. Their sights were now fully concentrated on the other side of town. Straiah sighed in great relief.

The main force was less than a thousand paces off, the marching of boots sounding through the dark. There were hundreds of torches and many dozens of horsemen besides. Even with the luck of going unnoticed by the initial scouts, Straiah didn't know how they hoped to defeat such a force.

341

Straiah raised his bow and bent back an arrow. The dozen or so archers on either side of him did likewise. They had only a handful of arrows each and the barbarians were fast coming into range. Straiah had a choice to make. Should he let the barbarians in close, maximizing the few arrows and potentially giving away their position? Or should he keep them at at a distance, while they wildly searched the dark for them?

The barbarian force was less than a few hundred paces away. The horsemen were keeping close to the foot-soldiers and those at the fringes were coming in to join the main group. The West End of Suriya lay in darkness.

Moments passed. Straiah and the other archers held their arrows tight against the strings. No signal would be given. Once Straiah loosed his arrow, the others would follow suit. More moments passed. The barbarians were within range.

Straiah took a deep breath and then exhaled slowly, loosing an arrow into the night. Just a moment later, the quiet snap of dozens of bows followed. The archers grabbed for more arrows. As they set them into the bows, an eruption of death cries and call to battle came from the barbarian line.

But their confusion lasted only a moment. For just after Straiah and the other archers loosed a second volley, the sky before them filled with the flaming arrows of the barbarian's own archers. In tandem, the barbarian horsemen and foot-soldiers burst forward. Straiah and the others ducked beneath the low wall. Most of the barbarian arrows sailed overhead, striking buildings or the plains just before them. But many of their own arrows met their mark amid the barbarian forces, taking down rider and footmen and archer.

But a glow, subtle at first, began to glow around Straiah and the others. For many of the flaming arrows lit the thatch roofs of the buildings all around them. The flames grew quickly, and within moments, the town was illumined all around them. Their position had just been revealed.

"Raise another volley!" Straiah called out. "Aim for the foot-soldiers!"

The archers loosed their arrows into the night. The horsemen galloped for them at full speed.

"Pikes!" called out King Froamb to his own group.

Dozens of pikes were thrust over the low wall waiting to meet the stampeding force of the barbarian horde. But just before they reached the wall, the horsemen veered off, skirting the northern wall and coming round it into the eastern part of the city. Just then, barbarian arrows began to fall on their position.

"Take cover!" yelled the king, but it was too late for many.

By the time they arose, the barbarian foot-soldiers were bearing down.

"Archers, make ready!" Straiah yelled.

Straiah stretched his bow and pointed straight ahead. This would be their last volley.

"Hold the line!" King Froamb yelled.

"Fire!" Straiah yelled only moments before the barbarians reached them.

A handful dropped just in front of the wall, stalling the rush of the others. Straiah and the archers dropped their bows and unsheathed their swords while King Froamb and his men held their pikes firm. The barbarians swung to get past the spikes, but in the fray, many of the barbarians met their end against the freshly hewn wooden tips.

Straiah barely managed to draw his blade when a barbarian climbed atop the wall and leaped over the men, coming round behind Straiah and swinging a broadsword across his chest. Straiah pulled his sword upward from his sheath, catching the blow and pushing it barely overhead. Then he pierced the barbarian in the torso. The pikemen and swordsmen were holding the barbarians at bay, but some were making it over the wall.

"Hold the line!" Straiah yelled.

The soldiers kept the majority of their assailants outside the wall, but some were crossing and causing havoc. Straiah darted toward a barbarian with a large hammer, who swung it toward the line. Straiah caught the blow with his sword, but the power of it knocked him back and nearly off his feet. The barbarian advanced against him, swinging upward.

Straiah barely moved to one side, feeling the hammer graze his cheek as it went by. The barbarian swung downward, but Straiah managed to sidestep the blow. Then he went on the offensive. The hammer was a menacing weapon, but poor for defense. Blocking two of Straiah's blows, he fell to the third.

The line was holding, but more barbarians were leaping through behind them. Straiah rushed to help a nearby soldier being pushed back by the blows of a broadsword. The barbarian swung and knocked the soldier into a nearby building, stunning him. But before he could deliver another strike, Straiah came at him with a loud yell.

The barbarian caught his blow with his own sword and the two swords locked. The barbarian thrust Straiah's sword away with a powerful heave and swung again. Off balance, Straiah narrowly ducked the blow, scrambling off to one side. The barbarian swung again. Straiah caught his blow, again locking the swords, but the barbarian shoved him into the wall of the nearby cottage.

Straiah hit the wall with a thud, nearly knocking the wind from his lungs and dislodging a handful of burning straw from above. The blades of the two swords inched toward his throat as the burning rooftop lit flames in the barbarian's eyes.

Straiah was pinned. The barbarian was too powerful. He glanced round for anything that could aid him. The cold metal of both blades now dug into his throat. But more of the burning straw fell from above, a large chunk landing on the barbarian's head.

He jumped back with a yell, brushing the embers from his face. Straiah stepped forward and blocked a wild swing across his chest. The barbarian reared up for another blow, but Straiah sidestepped it and struck him dead.

Nearby, the king was locked sword to sword with a barbarian, being pushed back into the line of men along the wall. Straiah darted forward with a yell. The barbarian backed away and blocked Straiah's blow.

345

The barbarian struck back, but Straiah narrowly ducked the blow and then stabbed the barbarian in the gut. Turning, he found the king leaning forward on his knees and catching his breath.

"Straiah...The horsemen...You must keep them from flanking us!"

"We can't leave you. The line is barely holding!"

"Go!" commanded the king, shoving Straiah backward.

He hesitated a moment.

"Half a dozen pikemen, with me!" Straiah yelled.

But just as he turned to leave, another barbarian sprang across the wall, landing just beside him. Straiah ducked the swing of his large battle-axe and came round behind him, but the barbarian followed through with the axe head's momentum, spinning around and rearing up for a downward blow.

Straiah barely hopped backward, the axe head burying in the dirt. Straiah raised his sword for a blow but the barbarian abandoned his axe and sprang forward, hooking Straiah around the waist. Straiah brought the hilt of his sword down and struck him in the head. But soon the two went tumbling down to the dirt.

The barbarian pulled a knife from his boot and plunged it down toward Straiah's chest. He caught him with both hands and plunged the knife into the dirt. Then he punched the barbarian squarely in the jaw. Straiah stood to his feet, grabbing his sword. The barbarian likewise found his axe but Straiah was on the offensive and made quick work of him.

A small group of pikemen had gathered round him waiting for orders. Straiah glanced down the line. It was holding but casualties on both sides were mounting up. The fires blazing on the rooftops were scorching the back of his neck. He unsheathed the Hammer of Haladrin from his back and departed.

The sounds of battle trailed away behind him as he and his small band sprinted through the streets of Suriya. The buildings all around were aflame and the sound of horse hooves on cobbled stone traveled down the lonely lanes. The crossroads were piled in with stone up to head level, just enough to keep the horses from hurdling them.

"Watch for grapples!" Straiah yelled.

Then he saw the streaking forms of horses galloping east through the town square with all speed. They were searching for a weakness.

"To the east!" he yelled and set off after them.

The fortifications were strong, but horses were powerful. With enough grapples, even the largest boulder could be moved. But Straiah had positioned the blockades in tight spots, to keep the horsemen from easily pulling them down. Still, if left uncontested, the barricades would crumble.

The sound of horses trailed away ahead of them. Most of the men with him carried pikes. If the riders broke through, they would use the narrow streets to their advantage and hold the horsemen back. Straiah heard the sound of metal striking stone in the distance. Hastening his pace, he came round the corner of a

347

cottage seeing a metal grapple held tight against the top stone of one of the barricades.

He sprang forward but just as he got near, the top stone exploded away. Just then, two more grapples fell. The pikemen darted forward, jumping onto the rock pile and lunging at the unsuspecting riders and startling their horses nearly enough to send them to the ground. But the horsemen rode away, the tension on the heavy rope keeping the grapples from being dislodged.

"Move!" yelled Straiah, who rushed forward with the hammer and swung down one of the grapples, maiming it beyond use and cracking the rock it was affixed to.

He reared up to destroy the other, but caught it just as the horse reached the end of the rope. The blockade was now only chest level, low enough perhaps for a horse to attempt a leap. The horsemen galloped forward.

"Pikes!" yelled Straiah.

The pikemen thrust their weapons over the top of the blockade, the horses at full gallop, bearing down. But just as the horses reached them, they reared up, the riders swinging at the pikes with their broadswords, trying to break them. Some of the other horsemen dashed to the west.

"One of you, defend this blockade! The rest with me!"

The riders were much swifter and would spread them thin along the edges of their boxed fortification. But they only needed to stall them awhile. The battle for the northern line wouldn't last much longer.

They sprinted as quickly as their feet could carry them. But far before they arrived at the western end of town, they heard the sound of smashing rocks. They came around a corner just in time to see two grapples tearing the top section off the stone blockade. The pikemen ran forward. But a barbarian on horseback appeared, bow in hand.

"Take cover!" Straiah yelled and darted for a nearby cottage.

But the barbarian loosed an arrow, striking one of the pikemen. Two more grapples clanked down on the rock. Straiah peered round the corner to see the barbarian archer holding fast, bow pointed in their direction. Straiah gripped the hammer tightly in his hand.

Then, with a yell, he sprang from cover, diving forward with a roll. He heard the snap of the bow, and felt a whizzing just over his head. Rolling forward onto his feet, he crouched and sprinted toward the wall, disappearing below the archer's line of sight.

Rearing up, he smashed the two grapples with the hammer. But the blows not only destroyed the grapples, they also shattered more of the barricade. Straiah ducked behind a nearby cottage. The blockade was still chest high, tall enough to keep horses out. But the barbarian archer still held his aim down the street sheltering Straiah and his small band of pikemen.

He heard another horsemen gallop forward. But instead of the familiar sound of a grapple, more stone exploded from the top of the barricade. Straiah peeked around the corner to see a large barbarian with a war hammer smashing the barricade down.

There was nothing they could do. The archer had them pinned. They would just have to wait. Some of the stone of the wall rolled down and fell near Straiah's feet. Crouching down, he picked up a smooth round stone and held it in his hands. The barbarian warrior continued to rip down the wall.

Then, between blows, Straiah came round the corner and hurled the rock at the unsuspecting archer. He turned and loosed his arrow at Straiah, but the shot went wide and the rock hit him in the chin, knocking him from his horse.

"Pikemen!" Straiah yelled and sprang forward.

The barbarian with the war hammer turned and rode off. The pikemen came out of hiding and rushed forward. But Straiah heard galloping quickly coming their direction. The wall had been smashed in half, barely hip high. Two horsemen were nearly upon him.

Straiah had no choice but to duck out of the way as two horses leaped the low barricade, one after the other and entered their boxed fortification. The pikemen were upon them in an instant, but both barbarians wielded broadswords and were striking out against the pikes and holding their own.

Straiah couldn't help them. The hammer was useless against horsemen with broadswords. Glancing around, he darted for the fallen pikeman struck by an arrow and took his weapon. Then he came against the barbarian horsemen.

They were still pinned against the barricade, but the archer had gotten back on his horse and was circling round just behind the wall, looking for a clear shot against the pikemen who ducked and darted to keep the two horsemen in the way.

Straiah ran forward, lunging with a yell toward one of the horsemen. The rider narrowly ducked the blow, swinging down wide at Straiah, who in turn dodged, and then struck out again, piercing the rider in the gut.

But the other barbarian cleaved his pike in two and swung the butt of his horse round, knocking into Straiah and sending him tumbling into two other pikemen. Then he swung out at the last pikemen still standing, chopping the tip of his pike with a powerful swing.

The rider came forward, rearing up on his horse and stomping down where the three soldiers had fallen. Straiah and the two men rolled out of the way, but the horse pursued them fiercely with its hooves, trying to crush them. By the time Straiah rolled to his feet, two more horsemen had leaped the wall.

Straiah was now disarmed, his pike and another lay on the ground behind the horseman. They had but one pike left between them. They had no choice but to retreat back to the forward line. Straiah could only hope they had bought King Froamb enough time.

"Back to the line!" Straiah yelled.

# The Battle for Ogrindal

Whinden was almost shaking in fury.

"Someone arrest them!" Whinden yelled. "And go and find Pallin!"

"It's too late" Gwaren responded. "Pallin is already gone. I am the commander of our Forest Guard. We will fulfill our duty to stop whatever comes to threaten the people of Ogrindal."

"You have violated the will of this Council, Gwaren," said another of the leaders.

"Tohrnan is right," said Whinden. "Why should we allow you the honor of captaining our forces any longer?"

"There is a war coming," Sheabor said, taking a step forward. "I'm sorry it's come so soon to your doorstep, but it was coming nonetheless. Gwaren has done you a service. The army you now face is but a fraction of what Corcoran will unleash on this realm."

"We must prepare for battle," said Gwaren. "If it is the decision of Ogrindal that I step down from command, I will fight alongside the men under a new captain. But whatever your decision, we need it now."

Just then, as a testament to Gwaren's words, the distant sound of a horn filled the air, drawing ever near.

"Go," said Whinden.

Gwaren bowed and departed, followed by Sheabor, Baron and Blair.

"How long until Malfur reaches us?" Sheabor asked.

"Tomorrow evening."

Gwaren descended the steps of the building and stopped at the base, turning to Sheabor.

"Tell me everything about Malfur. What are his weaknesses and how can he be killed?"

Sheabor shook his head. He didn't know.

"Ogrindal lies at the base of the Ruhkan Mountains," Sheabor replied. "That should shield us from the brunt of Malfur's power. And the wall surrounding the city is made of a solid piece of wood from the old world. If they're intent on taking this place, it will cost them many men."

"We have another advantage," said Gwaren.

Then he pulled from his pouch a vial of red liquid.

"This is an elixir made from fruit of the Lorimor tree," he continued. "For a time, it will give you strength and stamina. But they are in short supply."

"How long?" Sheabor asked.

"Not long," Gwaren replied. "Come on."

The group set off toward the wall.

"Shouldn't we give our armor to one of the other warriors?" Baron asked from behind.

Sheabor stopped and turned.

"You can use a bow, can't you?"

Baron glanced to his brother.

"Barely," Baron replied

Sheabor smiled and dropped a hand on each of their shoulders.

"We can live with barely. Come on."

Sheabor gazed at the bright red vial as they ran, wondering at its effects. They passed the large tree at

353

the center of town and came round toward the main wall, where the bulk of Ogrindal's forces had gathered. Seeing Gwaren, their captain, the warriors came in close.

"Malfur and his forces outnumber us four to one," Gwaren began. "He commands the power of the wind and countless centuries of knowledge."

Baron smirked. Hardly a way to motivate the troops.

"But we fight for our homes...our families."

A shout went up from the Forest Guard.

"Malfur will arrive by tomorrow evening. Make Ogrindal as secure as you know how."

The soldiers dispersed, preparing Ogrindal for battle. They worked all night without stopping. The glow of morning found them still hard at work, the trumpet blast growing ever near. But as midday arrived, Ogrindal was ready for war.

Bundles of arrows lined the top of the wall. Buckets of water were scattered near every building, ready to quench flames of fire. And every soldier knew his place in the defense of the city.

The group broke for a hurried lunch in the center of town. As they arrived, Baron noticed that nearly all the fruit which had hung on the tree the night before had been picked, undoubtedly to make as much of the elixir as possible.

Baron had never even considered what it would be like to be in a battle. Now, the soldiers looked at him with deference, him wearing the armor of the First Age as though some great warrior. It was almost too much for him to handle. He felt like such a fraud.

The meal ended with barely a word spoken. The soldiers embraced their loved ones, some for the last time, and slowly made for the forward wall. Each took their place. Then they waited.

The afternoon sun began to fall behind the mountain. A chill entered the air as the shadow of the mountain stretched across the treetops. The blast of the horn was nearly deafening now, and they could feel the rumble of its deep vibrations against the solid wooden wall.

Sheabor and Gwaren stood in the middle of the forward wall. Sheabor's thoughts drifted toward Cora, his wife, the princess of Cavanah, whom Malfur had imprisoned on the Banished Lands. Had he made the right choice to come here and warn these peoples? Had the resistance on the Banished Lands rescued her?

Night fell upon the forest, a glow now emanating from the deep woods. But just as the evening stars poked through the darkening sky, a thick haze drew in about the forest. The fog was so thick, the soldiers could scarcely see their own hands in front of them.

Sheabor clenched his jaw. If that's the way Malfur wanted to play it, his own soldiers would be just as blind. The fog was like a wet and icy blanket pulled around them, with stinging flakes of icy snow materializing out of the fog.

The war horn hadn't sounded for the better part of an hour. Sheabor could hear things moving in the places below. Sheabor glanced to Gwaren for his thoughts. Were the barbarians erecting ladders against the wall?

Sheabor set off to the south along the wall, pointing for Gwaren to patrol the other direction. They ran behind the archers crouched along the wall, searching for signs of ladders or any incursion. There was nothing. What was Malfur doing?

"Just what we need," said Baron, nearby. "More fog."

Sheabor smiled, coming up to him and placing his hand on Baron's shoulder.

"Have you seen or heard anything?"

"Just a couple of thuds, like they were dropping rocks at the base of the wall."

"Thuds?"

Baron shrugged his shoulders.

"I don't know what to tell you. There's definitely someone down there."

Sheabor nodded slowly.

"Keep your eyes open," he said and departed to find Gwaren.

"Did you see anything?" Sheabor asked.

Gwaren shook his head.

"I don't like it," said Sheabor. "Malfur is crafty. Whatever he's doing, we can't just wait and let him do it."

"Let's bring some men by rope over the wall," Gwaren said.

Sheabor nodded and the two set off, Gwaren tapping men on the shoulder and motioning for them to join in behind them, both archers and swordsmen. Attaching ropes to the wall, a dozen warriors repelled down in silence into the field between Ogrindal and the line of trees.

Once they were assembled in the clearing, Gwaren sent the dozen archers to the north. He was flanking them. The Forest Guard could enter the trees undetected and rain down death from behind. The other dozen ran with Sheabor and Gwaren toward the commotion near the base of the wall. Sheabor could hear what sounded like logs of wood being stacked. What was going on?

A faint glow was up ahead. Forms were moving in single file with chunks of wood atop their shoulders. In unison, the dozen warriors sprang forward, each striking a warrior dead before the rest could react.

The soldiers, a mix of barbarians and Dungeon Core, dropped the logs of wood they carried, unsheathing their weapons to engage the new aggressors. But Sheabor and Gwaren had caught them off guard, felling a few dozen, the others running back toward the treeline.

Sheabor turned round to find a large pile of logs stacked against the wall of Ogrindal. Malfur meant to burn the wall down. Sheabor grabbed for them, his hand slipping off the first one he pulled. The log was covered in oil.

"Quickly!" said Sheabor. "Pull these down!"

The others joined in, pulling the logs away from the wall and throwing them back into the field. But the pounding of many feet emanated from behind.

"Archers!" Sheabor yelled. "Fire into the clearing!"

The sound of dozens of bowstrings snapped from above. The arrows pierced the thick fog, striking all around in the grassy clearing. Death cries from dozens of warriors sprang through the fog. Malfur was launching a full attack.

"Archers! Fire at will!"

"Come on," said Gwaren, sprinting north along the wall.

But a sudden wind filled the air. The floating crystals of icy stung their skin as the fog was forcibly lifted away. Gwaren and the others didn't stop to look. They made toward the treeline with all speed.

The barbarians were at the front of the wall, stacking large chunks of wood as high as they could reach. The archers of Ogrindal were raining down arrows upon them, with some of the warriors down below firing back.

A handful of barbarians with torches ran forward toward the pile. The archers shot at them, striking all but two of them dead. The two reached the pile and plunged their torches into the heart of it. Instantly, fire sprang up.

Some on the wall poured buckets of water down from above, quenching part of the fire, but also spreading it along the pile of logs. And then the wind came, pulling through the trees and striking the front of Ogrindal's forward wall, spiraling up from the pyre like a cyclone and pulling the flames and embers upward.

Another pair of warriors set a bucket atop the wall, meaning to pour it on the fire. But the updraft of heat scorched them and they fell backward, the bucket falling from the wall and striking the side of the woodpile, splashing about to little effect. There was nothing they could do.

Sheabor, Gwaren and a dozen warriors were now hidden in the treeline just north of the forces of Malfur. The flames at the wall licked the top, embers flying hundreds of paces upward in the twisting cyclone of flame.

The barbarians and Dungeon Core had likewise retreated back to the treeline, waiting for the fire to do its work. But some were rolling the war horn slowly forward toward the flames. The fire lit up the entire clearing, blazing off the eyes of the warriors lined in the trees, waiting to invade.

Sheabor caught sight of Malfur in the midst of them. But another man stood beside him, nearly identical in appearance. At first, Sheabor's heart sank, thinking it was Pallin. But he could just make out enough differences to tell it was another. Even so, was this another Keeper of the Wind?

The war horn inched forward through the clearing. The archers along the wall were cramming away from the flames, though some shot down at the men pushing the war horn forward. But soon, they were within twenty paces of the wall.

The warriors stopped pushing and ran from the horn back to their own line. And then, the cyclone of wind stretching upward against the wall suddenly funneled backward and down, swirling into the war horn and coming out the other end in a fiery, deafening blast.

The blast struck the burning wall, shattering it clean through in an explosion of embers, extinguishing nearly all the fire, sending a wave of darkness again over the forest.

Gwaren tapped Sheabor on the shoulder before uncapping a bottle of elixir and drinking it. Sheabor quickly did the same, feeling a rush of vitality. Then they waited.

A hush of silence seemed to blanket the forest, the smoke rising from the charred wall, the heat visibly emanating from its surface. Much of Ogrindal was now catching fire but Malfur's forces held their ground.

But then, another rush of wind filled the air, this one icy cold. It blew across the clearing toward the wall, pulling upward through the newly formed gap and chilling the smoldering wall, extinguishing it.

A battle cry rang out from the forest as the warriors of Malfur's army ran forward in unison. The archers still on the wall began firing into the midst of them. Sheabor and Gwaren sprang forward with their men, engaging some of the unsuspecting warriors from behind. And scattered about in the trees, the Forest Guard were picking off warriors as they ran. The battle for Ogrindal had begun.

Hearing the battle erupt from the north, dozens of barbarians turned and engaged Sheabor and Gwaren. But Sheabor, armed with his battle-axe and shield, swung into the midst of them. The elixir flowed through his veins, his attacks too powerful to block. Those who didn't back away were struck dead by the mystical weapon.

The army of Malfur was pouring like a flood toward the city. Sheabor, Gwaren and their dozen men ran in the midst of them, engaging as many as they could. A line of soldiers had formed just within the gap to meet the invaders, and with a loud clash of metal, the two groups met.

The soldiers of Ogrindal held them, with dozens of archers firing down from above. The flood of warriors came to a halt in the clearing, Sheabor and his warriors dove into the midst of them. The forces of Malfur turned and engaged them, quickly surrounding them until Sheabor lost sight of Gwaren and the others.

But the closer they crowded, the more havoc Sheabor wreaked. His swing was too powerful to block, and too difficult to dodge in the tight quarters. The elixir made him an unstoppable force, but he was quickly tiring.

One barbarian ducked his blow, bursting forward and grabbing his shield with both hands as though to wrench it from Sheabor's grip. But Sheabor pulled with a roar, picking the warrior off the ground and sending him over his shoulder into the nearby warriors.

The other warriors near him hesitated with eyes wide. Sheabor could see that the forward line into Ogrindal had broken, the army of Malfur now pouring into the city. But the archers on the wall rained arrows into the midst of the gap, bodies piling up and stalling their advance.

Sheabor rushed forward with a swing of his axe, ending the lives of three. His shoulders burned with exertion, the elixir already beginning to fade. Two other advanced from opposite sides. Sheabor managed to duck one blow and block the other with his shield.

But the blow to his shield knocked him to the ground. He rolled back to his feet, swinging as he arose and striking two more warriors dead. But then, suddenly from behind, a voice sprang out into the night.

"Sheabor, last son of the tattered clan of Cavanah."

Sheabor straightened and clenched his axe tightly in hand. The warriors surrounding him halted at the sudden and bellowing voice of their leader.

"For over a decade, you have been a thorn in my side. Tonight it ends."

# Redemption

"Return to the line!" Straiah yelled, as the four men darted round a corner.

But Straiah himself rushed into one of the nearby homes. Hearing over a dozen barbarian horsemen gallop down the streets after them he emerged and sprinted back to the low barricade, where the now riderless horse of the slain barbarian warrior stood.

Straiah mounted it and quickly set off. The other horsemen were not far ahead. The last of them disappeared north at the end of the road a hundred paces ahead. But they would reach King Froamb before he did. Straiah had failed.

Galloping with fury, the sounds of battle and glow of fires grew around him. The battle for the wall was still being waged. Straiah came to the end of the road and turned north. A few hundred paces ahead, the barbarian horsemen were just arriving at the northern wall.

Straiah burst forward, unsheathing both his sword and hammer. Coming to the end at a full gallop, he struck two horsemen squarely in the backs and trampled a third barbarian before the horse leaped the low wall and was out in the open plains.

He quickly sheathed his hammer and turned round. The wall had been overrun. The barbarians were all over the city, fighting against the retreating force of King Froamb. Two barbarian warriors rushed at him, each bearing a broadsword. Straiah engaged them, blocking a blow, then striking one dead. The other barbarian came round to flank him, but Straiah parried his blow and darted forward a short way on his horse.

Then he turned round and with a quick gallop, bore down on the barbarian. Swinging powerfully, he hit the barbarian squarely in the sword, but the force of the strike was too much for his block and Straiah's blow slashed the warrior's shoulder, sending his sword flying out into the field.

Straiah turned his sights back to the town. Galloping the short distance, he leaped the wall toward an unsuspecting barbarian and sent him flying into the wall of a burning cottage with a thud. Two others quickly engaged him.

The tight quarters took away his advantage and it was all he could do just to defend himself against the blows on either side. Straiah looked for King Froamb. The forces of Forthura were retreating into the city, the barbarians plunging in after them. But no sign of the king.

A third barbarian came at Straiah, grabbing for the reigns of his horse while Straiah fought with the others. The horse reared up, kicking at the new assailant and throwing Straiah off balance in his defense. He began to fall.

But while he still had control, he sprang from the saddle and tackled the nearest barbarian, tumbling down. The other two were quickly upon him. Straiah rolled from a sword tip that sliced the ground just beside him. But he noticed then that the hammer had come free of its sheath.

Blocking another blow from above, he glanced around wildly for the hammer. Then he saw a barbarian standing still, holding it before his eyes and marveling at the mystical weapon. Another strike came in. Straiah blocked it but the blow was powerful and knocked his sword from his hands.

The other barbarian brought his foot down hard on Straiah's chest, raising his sword. Straiah was too exhausted to continue. He prepared for the end. But the foot holding him down grew suddenly limp. Straiah looked up in astonishment to see an arrow protruding from the warrior's chest.

The other barbarian turned round only to be struck by another arrow. Straiah felt the world spinning. The exhaustion and rush of adrenaline made him feel faint. But he closed his eyes and pushed himself slowly up.

Opening them, he thought as though he must have been dreaming. For standing before him was the beautiful form of Estrien. And she was not alone. Dozens of Melanorians were pouring into the city behind the barbarians. They struck dozens dead before the barbarians even turned round to face them.

Straiah rushed to Estrien and embraced her tightly, picking her up and spinning her round in blissful joy. Then he kissed her. But the world began to spin and he felt faint, nearly falling. Estrien steadied him, surprised at how ragged the battle had worn him. But Straiah regained his composure and glanced around the town.

"Come on," he said. "We have to find King Froamb."

"You're not going anywhere," she said, hand pressed firmly against his chest.

Straiah smiled, taking her hand from his chest and holding it gently in his own. Then he sighed and looked deeply into her green eyes.

"I can't believe you're here," he said, stroking the golden locks of her hair. Estrien beamed with a radiant smile. Barbarian warriors began to flee the lanes of Suriya out into the open plains northward but the pair paid them no mind.

"You're the one that's not supposed to be here, remember? You said you'd be fleeing toward the Westward Wilds, bringing the hammer safely away from danger."

Straiah's face went white as his eyes darted frantically about. But a sigh of great relief came from his mouth as he found the hammer lying nearby in the dirt. Estrien only smiled and shook her head.

"I'll try not to mention anything to Sheabor," she said.

Straiah laughed loudly. He had turned out quite a poor custodian. Estrien had saved more than just their lives. She had restored their hopes of winning this war.

"Imagine my shock," Estrien continued, "when the first thing I see is a madman on horseback, glowing hammer strapped to his back, dashing about a burning city and trying to get himself killed."

"Madman!" he said, in feigned surprise.

Then he scooped her up and twirled her about, laughing in the joy of the moment. Gazing into her smiling face, Straiah was struck with a feeling deeper and stronger than anything he had felt for another. He had never dared dream that a woman could be as beautiful, selfless and joyous as the one now in his arms, much less that one such as her could be interested in a man like him.

But just then, King Froamb emerged with what soldiers were left. Straiah set Estrien down just as the king clasped both her hands tightly in his own in gratitude.

"Words cannot begin to express our thanks. You've saved us in our most desperate hour."

Estrien gave a low bow.

"Call in the ships!" King Froamb yelled. "And send word to the East End that Suriya is safe!"

A cheer went up from the crowd and King Froamb shot both arms into the air with a roar of laughter, bringing his hands down on Straiah and Estrien's shoulders. Villagers began bringing water to quench the burning buildings, and the distant sound of music erupted from the center of town.

"You've given us time to regroup and form a plan," King Froamb said as they walked slowly along. "But the barbarians will return in greater numbers."

Estrien stopped and grew pensive.

"What is it?" Straiah asked.

"Malfur has left Eulsiphion," she said.

"What!" Straiah exclaimed. "Where is he?"

"He entered Thay Iphilus Forest a day ago with the bulk of his army. He's nearly emptied Eulsiphion.

He's obsessed with capturing Pallin before he reaches the lands of Kester."

"Then we can reclaim the city before he returns," King Froamb declared.

Estrien nodded slowly, but her gaze was distant. Why would Malfur be so desperate to capture Pallin? It didn't make sense. But the cryptic conversation Straiah had had with Aravas came suddenly to mind. He must have somehow been responsible for the strange turn of events.

"We may be able to retake the city without so much as a battle," Estrien began. "We'll use the tunnel behind Siphion Falls. But I fear, when Malfur returns with his army, we'll scarcely be able to mount a defense."

"We'll worry about that when the time comes," the king said.

"They may have blocked the tunnel by now," Straiah observed.

"We have the hammer, don't we?" said the king.

"I'm sure it's around here somewhere," Estrien said, glancing at Straiah with a smile.

"Come on," said King Froamb. "We have much planning to do."

King Froamb set off but the other two lingered behind.

"The planning can wait for one night, can't it?" Straiah said just as the king turned round to find out why he walked alone. King Froamb gave a wide smile.

"Take your ease tonight," he said. "But tomorrow, your time is mine!"

Then the king departed. Straiah shook his head with a laugh and squeezed Estrien tightly. They set off through town, arm in arm, as fires were lit in many homes. Town square was alive with music and dancers, and from somewhere, the warm aroma of stew filled the air. It didn't matter that it was the middle of the night. They had gone from certain death to victory.

The distant call of a trumpet rang out from shore and the wind came up from the south, whipping across their bodies and chilling them each to the bone. Estrien cradled her arms and Straiah turned to shield her from the wind.

"My goodness, it's freezing here!" she exclaimed.

"It's a good thing too," Straiah responded.

The gusting passed and the two continued on, Estrien gazing at him incredulously, waiting to hear how such an icy blast could be counted a blessing.

"The barbarians were in such a rush to conquer this place and return north, it gave us the upper hand."

"Upper hand?" Estrien said, eyebrows raised in a sidelong glance.

"Well," he retracted. "At least initially."

"I'll take your word for it," she said, smiling.

Straiah laughed and brought her back closely to him. The two wandered slowly through the streets of town, bustling villagers scooting past them in all directions. At length, they reached the edge of town, facing southward. Walking another few minutes, they came to a small hill and ascended it.

The moon had risen sometime during the battle and now lit up the dark Bay of Boreol. From somewhere beyond the Frostlands, Corcoran's forces would eventually flood this continent. When that fateful day came, the free peoples of the Eastern Realm might fall to his dominion.

But for now, everything was as it should be. Straiah had never imagined he would find a woman like Estrien. And now that he'd found her, he was going to do things right. They lingered there many moments, seated on the grassy hillside until the cold drove them back to town. They drew near the large fire and reveled with the rest in the music and dancing.

As the boats returned to shore and more piled into town square from the East End, there was scarcely room. The bulk of the kingdom, Forthura, now resided in Suriya. King Froamb stood on a nearby rock, gazing out over the sea of faces.

"Many of you have sacrificed your homes," he said in a loud voice. "Sacrificed your loved ones. We have defended this kingdom at the cost of many lives. Your sacrifice will not be forgotten, nor will the debt of gratitude we owe to those who came to our rescue."

Straiah glanced at Estrien warmly. The king opened his mouth to say more but at length, he only breathed in deeply and stepped down from the large stone.

"I remember Durian telling me of a beautiful stretch of shoreline by the bay," Straiah said with a smile.

"I see," she responded, eyes narrowing. "Well, do you remember Durian telling you where they keep the winter coats?"

Straiah laughed loudly.

"I'll keep you warm," he said. "Come on. I want to watch the sunrise."

Straiah set off, leading Estrien by the hand through the thick crowd. Though their victory here might prove meaningless in coming days, tonight, everything was perfect. They would watch a new day dawn and let hope fill their hearts for a better tomorrow.

# Vendettas

Sheabor stood alone in the middle of a ring of soldiers, his battle axe clenched tightly in his hand. Malfur was fifteen feet in front of him. He was clad in battle armor of the old world, and carried a dual bladed staff, as tall as Malfur from tip to tip. The shaft was white and ornately carved, as though a weapon from Melanor, resembling the craftsmanship of Estrien's bow.

Another man was behind him, hands bound and under guard. His appearance was similar to Malfur's and Pallin's, though Sheabor had never seen him before. The Horctura and Dungeon Core parted to allow Malfur through, but guarded their leader closely. Malfur took a step toward Sheabor, a slow smile growing on his face.

"If you surrender Pallin and the city, I'll let you live to see your wife one last time."

"Pallin is beyond your reach."

Malfur's jaw clenched.

"Then he is a fool. With my help, you could have opposed Corcoran. Now what hope do you have? Corcoran will find Pallin. And when he does, his dominion over this world will never end."

Sheabor was struck by his declaration. How did Malfur know where Pallin was going? Something told him that the other man now bound in irons behind Malfur was somehow involved. Sheabor dashed forward and swung his axe. Malfur ducked the blow and brought his staff down onto Sheabor's shield. A nearby barbarian took the opportunity and came at Sheabor from the side. Sheabor swung his shield toward him with all his might, knocking the assailant back into the crowd.

Malfur sidestepped Sheabor and hooked his staff under Sheabor's leg, pulling him from his feet. Sheabor hit the ground with a thud, the world spinning. But he swung his axe in a wide circle as he arose, pushing back the advancers. Malfur stood just outside the range of his menacing weapon.

"How tragic it must be for you," Malfur said. "Having abandoned your poor wife to come to a land of deaf ears. Conquering this realm was easier than I ever dreamed."

"We are far from conquered."

Sheabor lunged again, swinging down. Malfur narrowly dodged as the axe head buried deeply in the ground. Malfur swung his staff across Sheabor's chest. But he met the blow with the face of his shield. Some commotion came from the wall of the city. Malfur glanced toward it and Sheabor could see a hint of anger in his eyes. Ogrindal's forces were holding them at bay.

Malfur pushed free of Sheabor's shield and began to retreat. Sheabor thought quickly.

"Your self-importance is staggering," Sheabor said, axe held pointing at Malfur. "Your three brothers gave up their powers in grief over your death. And here you stand, betraying them and the whole world in simple lust for power."

Malfur turned and swung across Sheabor's chest. Sheabor ducked and rushed toward him. Malfur caught his blow, with the shaft of his staff, and the two locked for many moments. But Malfur glanced again to the city, and warriors from all around rushed to aid their leader.

Sheabor pulled away and engaged the new assailants. Malfur disappeared into the crowd. The elixir was rapidly wearing off and his muscles burning from exertion. But he advanced into the midst of them, trying to keep Malfur in his sights. A barbarian warrior swung at him with a large war hammer. Sheabor raised his shield and blocked the blow.

But the force of it halted him in his tracks and two Dungeon Core warriors sprang forward and slammed their shoulders into the shield, sending Sheabor flying. The elixir was gone. Sheabor lay on the ground, eyes closed, breathless and exhausted.

Warriors quickly overshadowed him. He didn't open his eyes, but waited for the end. He thought of his wife Cora, and felt his heart sink that he would die on this continent, never having rescued her. If only he had done things differently...

Meanwhile, Baron and Blair shot their arrows into the armies of Malfur. The Forest Guard stood in the gap of the wall, trying desperately to keep the warriors from pushing through the bottleneck. Smoke from charred wood rose all around, choking them and burning their eyes. But one thing they saw clearly through the haze.

"Ladders!" Baron yelled, finger pointing.

The archers concentrated their fire on the half dozen ladders popping up on either side of the wall. But they came nonetheless, digging their iron claws into the age old wood. Swordsmen from below ran up the stairs of the wall, ready to meet the attackers. The skilled archers of the wall picked off the climbers one by one. But they were too many.

The first of the climbers reached the top of the wall. A swordsman rushed to engage him while the barbarian was still at the edge of the wall. They sparred for some moments, but the barbarian, having little room to maneuver, fell to the skill of the Forest Guard.

A Dungeon Core warrior appeared to the right of Blair, though Blair was unaware, still firing arrows down into the crowd. The warrior darted for Blair, sword raised. Baron's eyes went wide. He called out in horror, but it was too late.

As the sword stroke fell, Baron felt an arrow whiz just past his cheek. It struck the Dungeon Core warrior and sent him over the wall, plunging to the ground below. Baron snapped his head round to see one of the other archers of the wall pointing his bow straight at them. Blair looked at Baron, face white.

"That was a close one, little brother."

Baron and Blair were nearly out of arrows, as were most of the other archers. The swordsmen were holding the climbers mostly at bay, but in time, the wall would be overrun.

Baron loosed an arrow, striking a nearby climber. He only had two arrows left. Taking careful aim, he found his mark and sent two others down to the ground below. Baron glanced round for another weapon. He hadn't been given a sword.

Another climber reached the top of the wall to his left. Baron darted to a slain barbarian, grasping his idle broadsword in hand. He lifted it clumsily, rushing at the Dungeon Core warrior who had turned away from him toward one of the archers still firing.

With a yell, Baron pointed the sword out in front of him. The Dungeon Core warrior turned and swung to parry Baron's strike, but the tip of the sword still caught him in the side. With a yell of pain, the warrior swung out with the back of his armored hand, striking Baron in the cheek. The world spun and he fell backward. He faintly heard the sound of Blair calling his name.

Meanwhile, Sheabor still lay breathless and eyes closed on the ground. A Dungeon Core warrior hovered over him, waiting to deliver the final blow. But the trampling of feet and loud clash of metal erupted just above him. He opened his eyes to see Gwaren standing locked sword to sword with the Dungeon Core warrior. And Gwaren wasn't alone. Two others fought with him.

Sheabor arose only to find a barbarian warrior advancing toward him. Sheabor was still exhausted, his muscles burning from overuse. The barbarian raised his broadsword. Just before he swung, Sheabor dashed toward him shield first, throwing the whole weight of his body into the warrior and striking him in the chest. They tumbled to the ground but the barbarian warrior was slow to get up.

Gwaren stepped in and kicked him in the jaw, rending him unconscious. Sheabor and Gwaren stood back to back, the other two warriors with them doing likewise. They were still surrounded by a circle of Dungeon Core and barbarian warriors. Sheabor gripped the axe and shield tightly in his hands.

But then, the sound of a horn filled the air...the signal for retreat. The slowly advancing circle around them suddenly tensed, jarred by the unexpected sound in their ears. But again, the horn blew. The world seemed to freeze. And then, all at once, the tide turned. Barbarian and Dungeon Core warriors began to flee toward the trees. A roar erupted from the wall of Ogrindal.

"They're retreating?" Gwaren asked.

"Malfur knows Pallin has fled the city. He's losing too many warriors trying to conquer it. He's going to destroy it."

"Then we must stop him! Quickly! To the trees!"

The four warriors set off north, perpendicular to the retreating forces, exchanging blows with them as they cut through their path. But before long, they came through them into the open clearing and turned west toward the treeline. Their only chance now was to flank them and somehow come around behind Malfur, catching him by surprise. But would they have the time?

A biting chill suddenly gripped the atmosphere. Dark and inky clouds swirled into life above the tattered city, a deep rumble echoing off the face of the mountain. Flashes of lighting lit up the sky for brief moments, and gusts of biting wind struck their faces.

But soon the four warriors were safe beneath the trees. The gusting wind chilled them to the bone, nearly forcing them to seek shelter behind the trees. But the growing storm also gave them cover to move closer to Malfur undetected.

A bright streak of lightning struck the face of the mountain, sending a chunk of rock downward to the city below. The four warriors moved forward, the wind roaring all around them. They advanced largely undisturbed, the armies of Malfur also in disarray as both sides huddled against the raw power of the north wind. A few warriors noticed and engaged them, but Sheabor and his band made quick work of them. The wind intensified all the more, and still no sign of Malfur.

"Where is he?" Gwaren yelled.

"What?" Sheabor called back, hand to his ear.

The wind was deafening in the trees, and they could barely keep their eyes open in front of them. Gwaren set off again. Another flash of lightning hit the face of the mountain, sending rubble down in chunks onto the city.

A hand dropped forcefully down on Sheabor's shoulder. He turned to find Gwaren pointing off to their left. There stood Malfur, just inside the clearing at the edge of the treeline.

The group sprang forward, but just as they set off, a large tree in front of them uprooted and fell toward them. They jumped back, but the tree limbs struck them, burying them in leafy foliage. Sheabor dragged himself free and searched about for Gwaren, who hadn't yet emerged. Sheabor groped through the leaves until his foot kicked a motionless form.

Pulling the leaves aside, he found Gwaren nearly unconscious below, a piece of tree limb protruding from his shoulder. He was alive, though could be badly injured. Sheabor had no choice but to leave him.

Trees all over the forest were starting to fall. Sheabor ran toward Malfur, but the biting wind gusted into him, keeping him at bay. He raised his hands in front of him and forced himself forward. Malfur was only fifty paces from him now.

But the closer he got, the harder the gusting vortex surrounding Malfur hit him. Sheabor trudged forward, battling for every step. He reached the back of a large tree and huddled behind it, exhausted. Glancing around, he scanned the forest for a bow or spear or anything to strike at Malfur. But he saw nothing.

Sheabor peered around the tree, hand in front of his face. Malfur stood alone in the clearing, the trees surrounding him felled and strewn about. Even his own guards had deserted, none able to contend with the ferocity of the north wind.

But what he saw next he almost couldn't believe. Someone was approaching Malfur from the forest. He was an old man, and he seemed little affected by the power of the wind. He was holding a sword.

At his approach, Malfur turned, as though he sensed his coming. For many moments, the two men stood there motionless. But the second man rushed at Malfur, striking out with his blade. Malfur blocked him with his staff and swung across his attacker's chest, which he ducked.

The two men fought for long moments, all the while, the storm raging around them. Malfur struck with both ends of his staff, the other man parrying narrowly. He continued his advance, striking low with the tip of his blade, then hitting the man in the forehead with the middle of his staff, knocking him backward to the ground.

Malfur stood above his now motionless assailant. He raised his staff for a deathblow. But before he could deliver it, the other man sprang upward, piercing Malfur through the chest with his sword.

Malfur fell to his knees, the wind suddenly subsiding. Sheabor ran forward, reaching the two men in moments. Malfur held the handle of the blade in both hands, gazing at it in disbelief. But he turned his eyes upward to the other man's.

"Aravas, my brother. Why?"

"I'm sorry, brother," he replied. "If only there had been another way."

Malfur closed his eyes and clenched his jaw. He fell over onto one side and breathed his last breath. Sheabor couldn't believe his eyes. He turned to the battered forest, where Dungeon Core and barbarian warriors were just beginning to emerge. They gazed dumbfounded at the slain form of their leader, lying in the field.

Sheabor readied himself for their charge, but the charge never came. They had taken heavy losses attacking Ogrindal the first time. Now, without their leader, they seemed to have no stomach for battle. They began to disappear between the trees.

Sheabor turned his eyes back to the other man, Aravas. He was staring down at the lifeless form of Malfur, his countenance deeply troubled.

"I'm sorry for what you had to do," Sheabor said. "Thank you for helping us."

Aravas nodded slowly but said nothing, not turning his gaze to meet Sheabor's. Sheabor departed from him back to where he had left Gwaren. Ruffling through the fallen trees, he found a form trying to arise. Sheabor grabbed him by the arm and helped him to his feet. His leather armor was soaked in blood from the sharp deadwood.

"Come on," Sheabor said. "Let's get you to the city."

Gwaren nodded, and with his arm around Sheabor's shoulder, the two hobbled toward Ogrindal.

"How did you defeat Malfur?" Gwaren questioned.

"I didn't," Sheabor replied. "Aravas, Keeper of the East Wind did."

As the two reached the open breach in the wall, they were met by the warriors of the Forest Guard, and also two others, Baron and Blair.

"Sheabor! You're alive!"

Sheabor gave Gwaren over to the care of his men and turned to the twins.

"How did the two of you fare?"

"I tell you what," Baron said. "After tonight, it'll be a long time before I complain about the weather in Suriya again."

Sheabor laughed loudly, plopping a hand down on each of the twin's shoulders. But as they stood there, Sheabor saw Aravas approaching through the clearing toward the city. Some of the Forest Guard tensed, not knowing who he was or if he was in league with Malfur.

"He's a friend," Sheabor said and went to meet him.

Sheabor was still lost for explanation as to how in the world Aravas had come to be here.

"Earlier I saw you bound in irons as Malfur's prisoner," Sheabor said. "I thought you were supposed to be in Melanor. How did he capture you?"

"I came to him at Eulsiphion," Aravas replied. "I knew something drastic would have to be done to save the peoples of this realm. So I told Malfur everything. I knew that if Malfur truly had abandoned himself to a will of evil, then he would risk everything for the chance to claim our powers before Corcoran found them. But if, somewhere inside him goodness remained, he would have chosen to aid his brothers against the coming darkness. Either choice could mean our salvation."

Sheabor was struck by his explanation.

"You told Malfur that Pallin was on a quest to reclaim the power of the Windbearers?"

"Yes. And that the weapon built to free those powers lay hidden in Suriya. Malfur split his forces to capture both."

A streak of anxiety flashed through Sheabor's heart.

"How could you do that?" he demanded. "You've signed them over to their deaths."

"I have faith that the people of Melanor won't long lay idle while the rest fight and die."

Aravas, Sheabor and the twins set off into the city. The fires had scorched many of the buildings. And even from this distance, they could see large piles of rock from the mountain laying atop the places buildings had once stood. Ogrindal had won the battle at a great cost.

But they hadn't yet seen the worst of it. The last Lorimor tree had caught fire sometime during the battle. Its branches had given way to the embers and the tree was now reduced to a smoldering stump.

Sheabor and Aravas halted when they saw it. Homes could be rebuilt, walls remade. But the tree which housed the final resting place of King Behlyn was the last of its kind. Sheabor felt truly sorry that the people of Ogrindal had been dragged forcefully into war without a choice. He resolved in his mind to repay them somehow. But for tonight, they would take a pause from war. They would assess what had been lost, would strengthen what was weakened, and would come against the darkness with new resolve and new courage.